LEONORA ROSS

A Life in Frames

First published by Leonora Ross 2025

Copyright © 2025 by Leonora Ross

All rights reserved. No part of this publication may be reproduced, stored or transmitted in any form or by any means, electronic, mechanical, photocopying, recording, scanning, or otherwise without written permission from the publisher. It is illegal to copy this book, post it to a website, or distribute it by any other means without permission.

This novel is entirely a work of fiction. The names, characters and incidents portrayed in it are the work of the author's imagination. Any resemblance to actual persons, living or dead, events or localities is entirely coincidental.

Leonora Ross asserts the moral right to be identified as the author of this work.

Designations used by companies to distinguish their products are often claimed as trademarks. All brand names and product names used in this book and on its cover are trade names, service marks, trademarks and registered trademarks of their respective owners. The publishers and the book are not associated with any product or vendor mentioned in this book. None of the companies referenced within the book have endorsed the book.

First edition

ISBN (paperback): 9781069082800
ISBN (hardcover): 9781069082817

This book was professionally typeset on Reedsy.
Find out more at reedsy.com

For Dad, who taught me a deep love and appreciation for our natural world, for M, whose words I'll always remember, and for every person who works tirelessly to bring us stories about human cultures worth protecting and about our beautiful planet.

He had no sense of responsibility towards the beautiful and the graceful and the intelligent. They could find their own way. It was the face for which nobody would go out of his way, the face that would never catch the covert look, the face which would soon be used to rebuffs and indifference that demanded his allegiance.

GRAHAM GREENE, 'THE HEART OF THE MATTER'

Contents

Acknowledgments		iii
1	A BOY'S DREAMS	1
2	MOTHER OF INVENTION	11
3	AN OBSESSION IS BORN	16
4	THE GIFT	31
5	FACING LAWRENCE BUSHER	43
6	WATCHING METEORS FLY BY	48
7	THE WAITER-PHOTOGRAPHER AND THE MADONNA	54
8	AN UNFORTUNATE SETBACK	65
9	WHAT COULD BE EATING LEJF?	72
10	A BRIGHT STAR ON THE RISE	82
11	A DANGEROUS DECISION	91
12	THE SEED OF DOUBT IS A PRICKLY THING	102
13	RAILWAYS AND REGRETS	111
14	YOU'RE A SCREWED-UP MAN, LEJF BUSHER	123
15	FLEEING TO THE DESERT	132
16	BONDAGES	137
17	THE RED-PAINTED WOMEN	146
18	GETTING READY FOR SINAI	158
19	AN OPEN-EYED DREAMER	162
20	SOMETHING ABOUT HOPE	169
21	THE LAND THAT WAS SUNG INTO EXISTENCE	179
22	WOMEN WITH SOUL	186
23	SEEING THE LIGHT	194

24	AN UNEXPECTED CALL	200
25	THE LITTLE PEOPLE WITH BIG HEARTS	210
26	THE UNSEEN TRUTH	219
27	IN SEARCH OF HIS INNER GHENGIS	222
28	NOMAD'S LAND	227
29	AN UNRAVELLING TAPESTRY	235
30	WHEN THE PANTHER ESCAPES	242
31	ON A STRANGE JOURNEY	249
32	WORDS BURIED IN THE SAND	258
33	AN UNSHAKEABLE SHADOW	265
34	HER WORDS	272
35	THE FOG AND THE DUNES	278
36	THE REASON AND THE REAL REASON	288
37	WHERE HE WISHES TO BE	300
38	THROWN TO THE STARS	308
About the Author		312
Also by Leonora Ross		314

Acknowledgments

This book wouldn't have been possible without the expertise and support of people I wish to thank from my heart. Two of those have been with me from the start of my writing journey: my editor, Jill French, whose gentle and constructive guidance is invaluable in helping me to grow as a writer, and my fantastic cover designer, Siski Kalla, who always comes up with the perfect cover for my novel.

My family and friends, thank you for putting up with me when I talk about my fictional world and when I make you read my stories. Your encouragement and forbearance mean everything to me. I love you!

1

A BOY'S DREAMS

In a backyard of the small Namibian town, Otjiwarongo, lay two young figures side-by-side in the dark. They were obscured in the shadows cast over the lawn by trees and hedges – only the occasional sound of their voices gave their presence away.

A dog's bark echoed and lingered for a moment in the cold night air. Here and there, someone called out or whistled to a pet, and a door or a window closed, signalling the end of another day. Human sounds faded into the night, now dominated by the monotonous chirping of crickets and the sweet lullabies of fiery-necked nightjars singing to each other in the trees. Stuck to heaven's roof were the constellations, untiring in their pursuit to captivate the mind of the dreamer.

Ten-year-old Lejf Busher drifted back and forth between reality and imagination. His brother Erik's voice pulled him towards consciousness; the crickets and nightjars pulled him back into his dream state, here he roamed beyond the restriction of borders and time. He resisted the heavy-eyed feeling coming over him. Part of him wanted his bed, but the other part wanted to stay up all night and marvel at the starry spectacle, thinking about his secret.

The boys lay stretched out on a blanket with a tarp underneath, and they were covered by two more blankets. The nip of the brisk evening air crept over Lejf's hands and toes like a lizard and he shivered a little. Erik, chilly too, vigorously rubbed his arms, then, growing tired of the effort, stopped and sighed. He tucked the warm covers around his feet and arms so only his head peeped out.

They spoke in hushed voices, there being no need to talk louder as they were so close together. Besides, it created a sense of mystery and camaraderie, like they could tell each other anything in the world. Except, Lejf didn't share his secret with his brother. He held his hands over his chest as if protecting it.

Their mother had called out, 'Half an hour, boys,' about ten minutes ago. Their father would already be fast asleep. He went to bed early but woke up before sunrise. Lejf and Erik knew their mom would give them their last time check five minutes before calling them inside. On any other night, that wasn't a school night, they'd be full of mournful complaints and excuses. Tonight, they would oblige with less resistance.

It had been a milestone day for the boys: their father had taken them on their first hunt. Living where they did, this was a common skill to learn, and many kids did. However, knowing how to handle something as dangerous as a rifle was critical. Their dad, who was an expert shot, had taught them the ins and outs and dos and don'ts, just as he'd done with their older brothers, Torsten, Søren and Ingve when they were Lejf and Erik's age.

'Safety is the number one priority – yours and everyone around you. Never go near a rifle without responsible adult supervision. Are we clear, guys?' had been their father, Lawrie's first words of caution to the youngsters when they'd started their training.

'Yes, Dad,' they'd said in solemn agreement.

'Remember, boys: killing another living being is no light-hearted matter. It should be done with respect and precision, to avoid suffering. We never kill for sport; it's for food only. Pay close attention, don't try to be heroes, and above all, appreciate what we take now will have an impact on nature, even though it may not be visible,' Lawrie explained.

Lejf touched the sensitive spot on the front of his right shoulder where the rifle butt had kicked back and left a bruise. He and Erik had each shot a springbok ram. Lejf's had been the hunter's dream shot: a perfect headshot between the eyes. It seemed as if the young ram looked straight at him as he was peeping through the telescopic lens in that split second before pulling the trigger. He could still see the animal's innocent brown eyes, oblivious to his impending death. Lejf felt sick over what he'd done.

His dad had been ecstatic. 'Great job, son. Excellent job!' Lawrie had beamed as he hugged Lejf around the shoulders.

Erik had been supportive, as always. 'Geez, you're a hard act to follow. Great job.' He had shot his springbok an hour later. Clean behind the ear. Their dad took a picture of the boys holding their lifeless trophies by the horns. Erik had a victorious smile. Lejf too smiled, but there was no satisfaction in him. The two dead animals lay in the back of the Cruiser, eyes open, staring into the void.

Their father had been on cloud nine until Lejf robbed him of his proud moment. 'I'm not doing this again.' His frustration was disguised as stubbornness and moodiness.

'What do you mean, Lejf?' Lawrie frowned.

'I'm not killing an animal again.'

'What's this, now, lad? Are you upset?'

Lejf didn't answer; he kept staring at nothing in the distance all the way home.

Erik babbled over the icy silence between Lawrie and Lejf.

'We did it, Morsa!' Erik exclaimed when the Cruiser stopped in the driveway. He jumped out and ran to meet their mother and brothers, who'd been waiting outside to greet them.

Their mom, Signe, smiled and hugged Erik, then Lejf. 'They are lovely,' she said, eyeing a sullen Lejf. 'We'll have the skins treated, and you can put them in your room.'

'You should have seen how beautiful they were out there in the veld, *alive*, Morsa,' Lejf said as he held her gaze.

'Lejf feels he's had enough of hunting. He could have spared me the trouble if he'd told me ahead that he didn't want to do it,' Lawrie said in his all-knowing way.

Signe didn't say anything. She held her son's hand until his dad drove off to have the animals skinned, and the meat processed at the butcher's shop. Lejf could see in his dad's body language that he was disappointed in him.

But something had happened inside Lejf in the veld after the rush of adrenaline. In the deafening silence that followed the gunshot, his horror at what he'd done was replaced by a calm understanding. He knew what he wanted to do with his life: he wanted to shoot nature through a lens, to capture it on film, not to kill it.

* * *

As they lay looking up at the stars, Lejf asked Erik, 'Do you think animals have souls?'

'I don't know. It's kind of hard to tell since they don't speak.'

'That doesn't mean they don't. Besides, they communicate with each other; we just don't understand what they're saying.' He was quiet for a bit. 'Dad thinks everything I do is to oppose or annoy him on purpose.'

'You are two hard stones grinding against each other. It's because you're so alike,' Erik said, too wise for his nine years and not the support Lejf was hoping for.

'I'm not like him; stop saying that!' He immediately felt sorry for taking his irritation out on Erik, who understood him and, as usual, let it be. He considered telling Erik about his secret but then decided to wait. His brother was his best pal and they shared everything, but this was something he needed to process first. He would tell him, but later. 'I'm not going to eat meat again,' he said.

'Not ever?' Erik asked. 'That's hard to imagine. I don't think I could do that.'

Lejf's mind was roaming. He made a pretend lens with his hands. Through this imaginary scope, he saw much more than the glittering stars. He saw the world he dreamed about and longed to travel to.

'When I'm grown up, I want to travel the world.' He spoke his thoughts out loud.

Erik said, 'Hm. You better get a good job to pay for all of that.' A practical conclusion.

'You sound like Dad,' Lejf said.

'Time for bed, boys,' Signe called them inside.

Yet, not even with all the dreams in his eyes on this starry night could Lejf have known that it would be his destiny to travel the world.

* * *

The next morning, Lejf was brought back from a breath-sucking adventure in a far-off place in his dreams by his brother Søren's agitated voice down in the hall.

'Morsa, please stop! God, I want to die ...'

Throwing the covers off, in a half-attempt to get up, Lejf turned an ear toward his mother's voice coming from the kitchen. He thought he heard her say, 'There's nothing to be ashamed of min älskling.' The bedroom door was closed, so he couldn't hear well. Lejf was accustomed to hearing one of his brothers disagreeing with their mother, but Søren, this excited was unusual. His second eldest brother wasn't prone to arguing. Although their mother, Signe, was oftentimes a little too inquisitive for her sons.

Søren was in his first year of high school. It wasn't so much that he lacked self-esteem (he had their mother's striking good looks) but he was simply a typical fourteen-year-old with an awkward gait who mumbled when he spoke. The one person who seemed to understand what he said most of the time was their eldest brother, Torsten, perhaps no coincidence since the two were close.

A while later, Erik came in, closed the door behind him and sat on his bed (he and Lejf shared a room).

'What was that all about?' Lejf asked.

'You missed a good one.' Erik grinned. 'Morsa discovered a wet spot on Søren's bed when she removed the sheets to do laundry!' he exclaimed wide-eyed.

Lejf was puzzled. 'Did he wet his bed?'

'No. Morsa said it's because he's a man now, and she's proud of him, and then Ingve said he's only half a man. He's such a smart aleck,' Erik said of their middle brother.

Lejf rolled his eyes in agreement and said with a sniff, 'Just like Dad.' In his opinion, Ingve inherited their father's special trait of being a know-it-all.

'Torstie told Ingve he shouldn't tease; it will happen to him too when he goes to high school. Girls do that to you. I guess it must have happened to Torsten too.'

Lejf sat up, more confused. 'Huh? A girl made Søren wet his bed?'

'Ingve said it's called nocturnal penile tumescence. It happens in a boy's dreams.'

Lejf couldn't conceive what he was hearing. A girl could make a boy wet his bed!

The report from Torsten and Ingve on this female with such

mysterious powers was that she was the kind of pretty that made your eyes tear.

As could be expected, Torsten sided with his pal. 'Poor Søren; he has it bad.'

With a chuckle, Ingve said, 'Must be; it's pouring out of him.'

Erik and Lejf talked about it more and Lejf kept wondering about the nocturnal penile tumescence that had poured out of their lovesick brother. Their curiosity about the cause of Søren's consternation was answered a couple of months after the incident, when they were afforded a glimpse of the dark-haired beauty at an athletics tournament. They could at least see that a girl that pretty could lead a boy to some unspeakable embarrassment.

Lejf would be reminded of the frailty of emotions, and cruel betrayal of a teenage boy's own body, when he was halfway through his first year of high school, four years later. He would foolishly think that he'd been better prepared through years of watching his older brothers stumble through their trials and errors with the opposite sex. What he discovered instead was that his confidence was an illusion. In the meantime, there were other important lessons to learn.

***

His parents knew he could carry a sulk around longer than necessary to prove a point, and Lejf was aware of how this agitated his father, since he was unable to speak his mind when his son avoided him.

Lawrie cornered him in the kitchen a few days after the hunting episode. 'I don't understand what's going on in that mind of yours, Lejf. You wanted to go on the hunt; I didn't force you to do it. I wouldn't expect you to do something you didn't want –'

'Yeah, right,' he wanted to shout, swallowing back tears of frustration.

'And we are not people who hunt animals out of waste. That's not the way I've raised you. You know that.'

It was hard speaking to his father about what he thought. His dad was right about not raising them as ignorant individuals. But his judgement of Lejf's choices was tough to defend when he had an unequivocal belief that he was right in every situation.

His dad could distance himself from his respect for nature and hunting for food. When Lejf felled that poor creature, he realised he couldn't separate the two. It was inconceivable to kill the thing he loved (although he later changed his mind about not eating meat again).

If Lejf had told his father how it had made him see what he wanted to become, his dad would have shrugged it off with the excuse that he was too young to know what he wanted to do with his life.

Lawrie had prepped his boys. They were aware that he expected them to all get a proper education. The field of science was, in his opinion (and which he stressed often), the most noble profession to apply a good mind to. Although Signe contended, with a roll of her eyes, 'That's a very hoity-toity bias. There are plenty of noble professions. Teaching, for instance, is one of the most honourable since, without a solid start, children couldn't pursue further education.'

Her logic did little to persuade her husband. He kept reminding his sons about the importance of living meaningful, productive lives. 'It is the individual's contribution of talent and skills which leads to research and innovation, and ultimately, collective success in any society.'

Lejf knew the one thing their dad had been most afraid of was that they (but mostly he) would choose a career that would leave them dependent upon others for help. To Lawrie, that would be a grave sin.

His favourite line was, 'You boys have all the opportunities at your disposal.' And how he liked to remind them.

Lejf had time on his hands. If he had to admit to being like his father in one way, it was that once he'd made up his mind, it stayed made up.

The hunting experience had been a defining moment. With the epiphany, had come the realisation that not everything his father taught him was true. Not that he thought his father was a liar, but he grasped, for the first time, that truth could have a different meaning for people; it just depended on how you looked at a situation. Perhaps with this new knowledge came a certain loss of innocence, too. Knowing that his father, whose physical and mental capabilities to Lejf were unparalleled, could have weaknesses was confusing for the young boy to grasp.

It was clear that Lawrie loved having his boys with him when he was out working. To the Busher boys, being out with their father was their remote classroom. It was the place where they learned invaluable lessons about life and manhood from the man who guided their decisions, but he was a tough tutor. He expected a lot from his sons. Lawrie was as unshakeable in his morals as the hard earth of the Namib Desert. His reputation, however, was impeccable, and it was this ethical standard he seemed to struggle to impart to his growing boys.

His parental love and pride could sometimes be conveyed in such a way as to leave room for misinterpretation, especially by the child who bore his resemblance and nature the most. It was often the areas such a parent wished they could change about themselves that they saw reflected the strongest in the developing version of them. Stubbornness worked both ways, and those who were most similar seldom wanted to admit to those similarities.

Whether Lawrie intended well and too much got lost between misinterpretations was another matter, and it would take Lejf many years to arrive at this truth among all the truths he would discover. The boy saw only one thing when he faced the rock that he couldn't move out of his way: his father expected the impossible from him.

So, he nurtured his secret, and it grew into a dream as big as the world. And the stronger his own discovered truth grew, the weaker Lawrie's truth became, and the deeper the struggle between their opposing wills.

2

MOTHER OF INVENTION

For the Busher boys, their coming-of-age years were filled with an odd mix of awe and disquietude over their mother's eccentricities. Signe believed in honesty and to her teenage sons, that dreaded word, transparency. Nevertheless, they indulged her unorthodox methods.

Signe Nyberg's ideas stood out to a conservative farming community, much like an acacia tree on the arid plains. She was her husband's companion and an indispensable part of their mutual success in work and life. Lawrie desired a solid, secure existence, which was the life he had always known, while she had the heart of the constant traveller and free spirit, which none of their five sons embodied more than Lejf.

Signe came to Namibia as a twenty-seven-year-old backpacking tourist nineteen years ago. She met the serious, passionate thirty-one-year-old wildlife veterinarian on a game drive, became love-struck with him and the land where he was born and raised, and she stayed and settled down to form a life with him. From photographs on the wall in his study, it was easy to see how Lawrence Busher became instantly and forever infatuated with the leggy Swedish beauty from Stockholm.

Signe's otherness (perhaps in part because she was Scandinavian, but more likely because of the force of her personality) sometimes caused consternation for her boys. Yet, they came to respect her approach to things as an important guide for their lives and the choices they made. What she wanted to instil in them above anything else was the value of individualism and standing true to your principles, even when faced with scepticism and social rejection.

One of her many quirks was that she preferred that her sons called her by her name, although only Ingve did. She was, to the community she'd adopted and who'd come to accept her strangeness with cautious affection, a mystery they didn't know how to solve and, due to mysteries' nature, kept them wondering. That her men dearly loved her was no secret.

Inspiration struck after the heated debate she had with Søren about him reaching his manhood, and Signe wrote a manual – the A-to-Z of what a man should know about a woman and sex. It wasn't the kind of knowledge gained from a school-level biology textbook. That was her whole motivation behind it because academic facts, so she reasoned, couldn't replace life lessons to become a complete person. And her job as their mother was to guide her sons in the areas where school education fell short.

Her manual started with, *'Sex is a natural part of being human, and no maturing young person should be made to feel guilty or shy over wanting it and thinking about it.'* However natural their mother may have perceived her children's carnal urges, the older boys chose to read her manual in private, away from any possibility of probing questions from the author.

Lejf displayed a mild curiosity in it, while Erik took a real interest and even read it at school during recess. It caused quite a stir in the Otji community when talk of a book called *The Manual* started circulating among the juveniles. Signe was called into the principal's office.

'I find myself in a predicament, Signe,' Jonathan Baxter said. 'I have to explain to baffled and concerned parents something I can't put a finger on to categorise, let alone solve. Is it worth all the concern, or is it an overreaction that will blow over? I'm not sure.' He thought the last part out loud.

If Signe were guilty, it was only that she was her boys' champion. There was no fault in her motives. She never meant to embarrass her boys or anyone else. Her objective was for her young men to enter life equipped with the knowledge she knew they wouldn't get in school, and she didn't want them to seek it out from random sources either.

As she explained to the principal, 'These are awkward years of self-discovery for a child, Jonathan. It's 1995, not 1905. Kids are curious and are exploring sex much sooner but it makes them vulnerable. There's an abundance of low-quality information out there in contrast to substantial content. Just because some people object to speaking openly to their children about sex, doesn't mean everyone shares that view.'

'I agree, Signe, but there is the issue of the appropriateness of Erik reading it here at school,' said the principal.

Mr Baxter took pride in uplifting the standards of the Otjiwarongo Primary School to near private school-level (as he liked to tell people). Signe thought that perhaps made him more cautious. He wasn't an unreasonable man. They were dealing with common mindset in a community that held on to conservative values. Neither the principal nor she had control over that. She understood where he was coming from: he had seen many of Otji's children pass through his school, and with each child, came a story.

He'd praised her and Lawrie for their role in both Torsten and Søren's academic success when they were students at his school, but Principal Baxter glowed when he spoke of Ingve, the shining star, who he said (with passionate emphasis) was *brimming* with intellectual promise'. The last two representatives of the Busher clan didn't display the same zeal for learning as their older brothers – something the principal also expressed to Lawrie and Signe. 'Erik does what is expected of him. His progress is satisfactory, but I can't help but think he could do more if he made the effort.' Of Lejf, he said with a sigh, 'Lejf is a bright boy, but his head seems to be in a cloud. It's like he is barely here …'

It was a strange human phenomenon: parents often loosened the reigns by the time the youngest ones made it to school, and it became the task of the education system to help steer the wobbly wagon through the drift. Signe and Lawrie were aware of their second youngest son's lack of academic interest and for Lawrie this was a sensitive topic. Signe wanted Lejf to figure things out for himself; Lawrie wanted to guide their wild horse away from the cliffs.

However, Signe did leave the principal with a solution to his dilemma over *The Manual*. 'How about we try this: you may tell concerned parents that anyone with questions is more than welcome to speak with me. I think people may find it interesting and helpful. I'd be happy to offer them a copy of *The Manual* for free. I'm not going to ask Erik to stop reading it at school, since I don't think he's doing anything wrong, but I will ask him to be more discreet in who he shares it with.'

Principal Baxter nodded. 'There's nothing wrong with trying. Hopefully, this will blow over, otherwise I'll have to re-evaluate my position.' He held out *The Manual* to her, but she shook her head.

'You keep that. Consider it a gift.' Shrugging, she added, 'Even when it blows over, and it will, something else will come up for people to worry and complain about.'

Signe later relayed the sequence of events to all her curious men at home, including to Lawrie. 'Mr Baxter and I came to an agreement. You may continue reading it, but be wise about who you share it with, okay, min älskling?' she said to Erik. He nodded in earnest agreement.

There were no further complaints to the principal. In a small town like Otji, people preferred to discuss such controversial matters among themselves. They weren't inclined to confront someone they were talking about in person. There were, however, numerous anonymous requests for copies of *The Manual* from all over town, and Signe had to start asking for a printing fee. It became a cult classic of sorts.

Through this Erik was unperturbed. One purpose drove him, as he confided in Lejf as they lay on their beds, talking about all the great things they'd like to achieve. 'I can't wait to reach the forbidden land of women and unspeakable pleasure, and I hope it won't be too long now,' he said, hands behind his head and staring at the ceiling.

Lejf turned to look at him. 'That's a little ambitious. Don't you think?' Erik shrugged.

***

A while after the hype over his preference for leisure reading at school had abated, Signe stood looking at the carefree expression on the sleeping Erik's face. He had a maturity beyond his years and a resilience that would serve him well in life. Her instincts told her that whatever Erik faced, he'd be all right, she didn't have to worry about him.

Looking over to Lejf sleeping, she felt a pang in her heart. How different to her other boys he was; her dear, serious, intense dreamer. He absorbed and internalised things. Lawrie worried about what would become of him. She couldn't help but wonder, too.

3

AN OBSESSION IS BORN

Laia Ackermann longed for independence. Small-mindedness frustrated her, and in a small town like Otji, it was difficult to avoid that. Some people were too concerned about labels; comparing the good church goers (like her parents) to the bad non-church goers. Or pointing out the vices of the haves (like her parents) and the have nots. She didn't want to be associated with any of that, didn't want any label stuck to her, yet it seemed that was how some people perceived her. She wished she could be more assertive and set them straight. Instead, the eighteen-year-old lived vicariously through her sister, Iben, who was three years younger and was born with an audacity that wouldn't be constrained.

Iben made no secret of her contempt for 'archaic rules', as she put it. This, on several occasions this year already (and the year being only halfway through) had resulted in her having a cup of tea with *Schulleiter* Vos at Deutsches Schülerheim, Otijiwarongo, to discuss her attitude. Principal Vos was patient with Iben's wayward ideas. Laia thought that this was not coincidental as their father was a major sponsor of the prestigious private school his daughters attended.

Laia's life felt humdrum and unemotional in the same way as her parents expressed themselves to each other and their daughters. Iben was the only one who was willing to challenge the status quo, and she was Laia's heroine.

It wasn't a question of whether she loved her parents. Of course she did. She just wondered why it didn't seem to bother them to go through life, day after day, without stopping to ask themselves if they were happy. Were they? They didn't argue. Sometimes, she wished that they would at least disagree about something. What troubled her most was the unattended feelings that lay beneath their silent tolerances. This was especially true of her mother, who, on the surface, was the exemplary dutiful wife. If it weren't for Iben, there'd be no conflict at all, not to mention no excitement.

Iben had caused another shockwave last night during dinner. Their father, a cardiologist, had rambled on about the complexities of the heart surgery he'd performed on an elderly patient (a conversation they'd heard many versions of) when Iben jumped in and declared, 'Mom, Dad, I've decided to lose my virginity.' She looked from one parent to the other.

Laia almost choked on her food and watched the scene with wide-eyed anticipation.

Both parents looked at their youngest daughter aghast before Dael said, 'Iben, *really!*'

Gerhard said, 'Well, I hope you'll reconsider before doing that, young lady.'

'And why should I?' Iben challenged.

'You are fifteen years old,' Gerhard said.

'Yes, you're only fifteen!' Dael added, sounding distressed.

'So? In your grandparents' time, girls got married at fifteen and no one in church complained about underage girls having sex then. I don't know what the big deal is.' Iben shrugged.

Gerhard wiped his mouth with a napkin and took a sip of water.

'You could become pregnant, for one, and there are multiple venereal diseases,' he explained as he looked at his youngest daughter with concern.

'That's what condoms are for, aren't they?' Iben rebutted without blinking.

Gerhard opened and closed his mouth, searching for the words. Then he said with resolution, 'You are too young for sexual intercourse, Iben. I hope it won't be necessary to have this discussion again.' He seemed to contemplate and, shaking his head, pushed his plate away. 'I've lost my appetite.'

'Oh, Iben, now you've upset your father. Could you please not do this during dinner?'

There, Laia thought, there was the problem. They never discussed anything upsetting or controversial. Did her parents believe they could shield their daughters from the realities of a world they would inevitably be exposed to? And perhaps her mother had something to say on the matter (Laia would have liked to believe she did), but Dael never spoke her mind.

It wasn't that their father was an unkind or rude man; Laia thought he just suffered from a kind of ignorance. For all the intelligence he tried to inculcate in them, he lacked emotional awareness. Was that typical of all strong males who made decisions on behalf of their women and children?

Alone, Laia had asked her sister, 'You're not serious, are you?'

'Of course I'm serious! It's blatant hypocrisy that church people can't make up their minds about when sex is acceptable for a girl.'

'I mean about losing your virginity.'

'And give away my trump card? No way. Besides, for something I can only lose once, it will have to be worth it. I thought I'd spice up the dreary atmosphere. You looked so bored,' Iben said with a wicked grin.

AN OBSESSION IS BORN

'Well, that spiced it up. Be careful; you're going to give Mom and Dad heart attacks one of these days.'

'Look on the bright side: at least we'll know how to perform open heart surgery,' Iben said and sniggered.

And that, Laia thought, was her sister's strength: even at fifteen, Iben displayed a certainty of knowing who she was and what she wanted from life. Her game was shocking both their parents and Otji's most shockable residents – it was pure impishness – but she wouldn't compromise and settle for choices that would undermine her future. Iben was the voice for the things Laia wished she could express.

As for herself, she was happy not to be a part of the dating scene. Everyone seemed to be dating. Apart from a few guy pals, there were no boys at Deutsches Schülerheim who interested her. Her best friend, Ilze, who attended Otjiwarongo Secondary School, had started dating a guy in her class, Søren Busher. Laia had to admit, he was the first intriguing guy their age she'd spoken to, and the best one Ilze had ever dated. Since she'd grown breasts, Ilze had never been without a boyfriend. Søren and Ilze seemed in love, but they were going to separate universities next year, so it would be fascinating to see when the flame would burn out, and Laia was certain it would.

Søren was good-looking and intelligent, but she doubted he was ambitious enough for Ilze, who had a fatal kind of ambition: she wanted a man to take care of her, so she would have a comfortable life (Iben would have had a fit if she'd heard that). Ilze's parents had modest financial means, and she said Laia was ungrateful for what she had. It was true that she didn't know what it felt like to be so tight on everything and not be able to buy something you liked, but she didn't think she was ungrateful. Money wasn't a silver bullet to happiness. Had Ilze learned nothing from Laia's mother over the years?

It was 1999, and if the world was changing toward women's financial and emotional independence (albeit at a snail's pace in a place like Otji), why would a woman who had the opportunity to show her worth settle for subservience? Wasn't *that* being ungrateful?

She just wanted to get out of these stuck ideas. Six more months, then she was off to Karlsruhe, Germany. Freedom, at last.

***

As for fourteen-year-old Lejf his life was as complicated as a boy of his age's life could be: homework, thinking about girls and avoiding the embarrassment of speaking with a breaking voice. Summed up, his biggest concern centred around the harrowing task of getting through the second half of his first year of high school.

Søren had started dating a girl named Ilze, in his class. Lejf had heard him speaking about her over the phone to Torsten (who was studying at UCT in Cape Town) but it took some time for Søren to summon up the nerve to ask her out. Lejf couldn't even conceive of how you asked out a girl who was as stunning as Ilze. She looked like the supermodel Cindy Crawford. Søren had a big poster of Cindy and photos of Ilze up in his room. Lejf sometimes saw Erik in there, staring at them when Søren wasn't around.

The routine was for Lejf to bike home from school with Søren (Ingve had piano practice), but Ilze told him he could pick up notes she'd helped him with for an assignment due the next day. Søren was to meet her at her friend Laia's house, and Lejf decided to tag along out of curiosity. It was in the affluent part of town. Lejf had only ever biked through the neighbourhood, nothing more, but he felt the impulse to join his brother. What were the Ackermanns like as a family? He knew of Dr Ackermann; everyone in town did, but he'd not met him or his family.

The cardinal rule of a conformist society was clear: the lower and middle class mixed with their kind, and the upper class mixed with theirs. In a town like Otji, the same went for the churchgoers and the well-born. They were welcomed with open arms by the leaders of all the church denominations, for their generous coffers, Lejf assumed. The more influential a person's position was, the closer to the podium they would sit – one could argue because they'd paid, and it made them feel entitled to receive the message first. He concluded this not because the Bushers were reputable people. In fact, they didn't sit in church pews, but he and Erik had been curious to find out what went on behind those heavy doors after the church bells rang so loudly on a Sunday morning.

When they'd told Signe about their findings, she'd said, 'You shouldn't judge, boys. If you do, you'll be no better than the hypocrites.'

* * *

Lejf had no idea how his life was about to change as his brother pressed the Ackermann's doorbell.

Mrs Ackermann opened the door – an attractive, soft-spoken woman with kind, sad eyes. She was different to how Lejf had imagined her, proving what Signe told her sons, 'Don't form opinions of people until you meet them in person.'

In the corner of the living room stood a beautiful, shiny black Bechstein grand piano. It must have been worth triple Torsten's university tuition, and Lejf thought of Ingve, who had to practice his genius on a second-hand Yamaha (not a bad piano at all but not this grand).

Ilze and Iben were doing homework at a polished cherry wood dining table big enough to seat twenty people.

'Sit down, guys. I have sandwiches in the kitchen; they're still fresh, and I always make too many.' Mrs Ackermann waved them to the table.

Søren introduced him. 'Iben, this is my brother Lejf.'

'Pleased to meet you, Iben,' Lejf said, extending his hand. 'Hi Ilze,' he added. She greeted him with a nonchalant wave, eyes only for Søren.

'Nice to meet you, Lejf.' Iben looked him over.

Iben was a beautiful girl. What Lejf noticed was the wilful gleam behind her clear blue eyes. She looked like her mother, and that's about where the resemblance ended. As he came to know her better, he realised that he and Iben were similar in some ways: headstrong, and neither liked being told no, or you can't. Unlike him, Iben also had a fun, mischievous nature, which made her quite likeable.

Mrs Ackermann set the plates of sandwiches on the table with napkins. 'Please help yourselves, boys. The girls have already eaten.'

'Thank you, Mrs Ackermann,' Lejf said. Like Søren, he knew full well that they'd have a second lunch with Signe when they got home.

Søren and Ilze were going over the notes for their assignment and playing footsie under the table. Lejf looked around the room, indecisive about whether coming here was a good idea after all.

Laia walked into the room, and all thoughts swimming around in his mind dissolved, and only she, the long-unsolved mystery, stood there, like truth itself. Her eyes held his captive. Pushing back his chair and rising to greet her, he noticed she was tall but not as tall as Signe (who was a little over six feet). Even though he was four years younger, he was already taller than her. He cursed fate for the age gap between them.

Søren introduced them. 'Hi, Laia. This is my second youngest brother.'

'Hello, second youngest brother.' She extended her hand with a smile.

'Hi, Laia. Lejf's the name. Pleased to meet you,' he said and tried not to stare.

He puzzled over the exact colour of her hair – not quite blonde, yet not quite brown – and she had it pulled back in a ponytail. Her features were unusual. Striking, but not conventional. Dark greyish brown eyes, like the bark of a black walnut tree, their colour and shape made them one of her loveliest features.

Reminding himself to breathe, Lejf stood there, a wordless fool, in that vacuum at the beginning of time when she started to exist for him as the only woman. And along with this pivotal moment in his life began the awkward process of trying to conceal the unbearable strains inside pants and the incessant fantasising behind closed doors that plagued this love-struck teenage boy.

* * *

Laia watched Lejf as he was looking around. Did he know that the things he was looking at were clues about her life – symbols of a world she wanted to escape? For instance, she saw him staring at the decorated plates with farming scenes and windmills on Delft porcelain sticking through the sterile white wall where they hung: not colourful, unmatching, like her insipid, colourless world. From the comment he made about the craftsmanship of the antique grandfather clock ticking loudly in the corner of the dining room he did not see it as she did. How Laia hated that morbid old thing that stood there like a stern patriarch keeping a watch over everyone's movements. It was a reminder of the filiation she and Iben shared with their mother and of most women in Otjiwarongo and other towns throughout Namibia – a conservative sisterhood whose lives revolved around the men who always seemed to stand at the centre of their women's lives.

The objects around the house were themselves devoid of character. Or was it she who was without a soul? She understood that people liked following patterns. They put them up on walls or wherever they would be reminded of their traditions and why they clung to them – whether they made sense or were of genuine spiritual or emotional value was less important. She also knew that for some people, like her parents, those things provided a distraction from the issues they didn't want to address. Yet those issues seemed to linger. They took possession of the objects; they ensconced them like spirits of the dead.

Lejf made an innocent comment, 'It's a fancy-looking home. It's very different from ours.' Søren gave him a look prompting him to explain, 'Our mother is Swedish, so there are plenty of Scandinavian influences.'

Laia didn't know why but she wanted to meet Søren and Lejf's parents. Of course, she'd been to other people's homes, but she wanted to see the parents behind these boys and whether Ilze's opinion that she was ungrateful was justified.

She met Signe, Lawrie, Ingve and Erik a few days later when Søren invited her and Ilze over to have a barbeque with him and his family, and she fell in love with them on the spot. Signe personified the ultimate woman who was who she chose to be, not to mention the persona she brought to her vibrant home. It was obvious that her men adored her. The most palpable thing Laia noticed was the energy so different to that of her own home. She mentioned this to Lejf, with whom she enjoyed talking. His insightful answer surprised her. 'Perhaps it's because our house is full of males and only one female, where in your case, your father is the outnumbered gender.'

To some, the friendship that developed between Laia and Lejf could be seen as strange for high school children, due to their age gap. Perhaps one of the things which drew them to each other was that neither was concerned with other people's opinions. They weren't popular or unpopular – they were simply comfortable in obscurity.

Laia felt she'd found a confidant in this strange, serious boy with a beautiful, artistic heart whose depth seemed unreachable. Yet he was the sounding board she needed besides Iben. Although, at times, he displayed typical signs of an insecure fourteen-year-old boy (and now and then she caught him staring at her with puppy eyes), she attributed his overall maturity to Signe's remarkable influence over her sons. She liked Lejf Busher and his family.

***

What did a boy who fell head over heels in love with a girl who, he was certain, didn't feel the same about him, do in the days, which felt like light years, between seeing that girl? He fed his lustful thoughts by obsessing more.

Obsession was about collecting as many details of the person you were obsessed with and hoarding them in your mind like a million tiny love letters written on Post-it notes. It required careful manoeuvring when your mind became too overwhelmed with trivialities, and you had to discard those which were least beneficial to your obsession.

Lying on his bed and thinking about Laia, Lejf remembered overhearing a conversation between Torsten and Ingve (not long before Torsten had left for university two years ago). They spoke about Torsten getting caught having sex with a girl against the gymnasium wall. Ingve had said, 'Well, what did you expect would happen? You had sex with her outside the gymnasium. Did it occur to you that you could get caught, or were you too consumed by lust to care?'

'Nobody else saw us, I made sure,' Torsten replied.

'Yes, but *I* saw you fucking her, although, for the love of my sanity, I wish I hadn't.'

Signe had walked in at that moment. 'Please don't use such uninventive and crass language to describe an intimate act between people, älskling,' she said to Ingve.

'Sorry, Signe, but I'm surprised at your eldest son's lack of discretion.

He *made love* to someone in public.'

Sitting back with his arms folded across his chest, Torsten said in a monotone, 'Don't be a twerp, Ingve.'

Signe looked at Torsten in disbelief. 'In public?'

'There was nowhere else, Morsa.'

'Oh, älskling, why didn't you bring her here?'

'She's not my girlfriend. We just had sex.'

'She's everybody's girlfriend.' Ingve sniggered.

Signe gave Ingve a disapproving look before saying, 'Torstie, no girl deserves to be treated as an object to be used. If you don't want to bring her here or go to her home, you shouldn't be with her. I'm assuming you had the sense to use a condom.'

'Yes, Morsa, I did.'

'You know that condoms don't protect against all STDs, don't you?' said Ingve.

'You're wise for someone who's never had anything but his own hand job,' Torsten said, not in the least bit upset by Ingve's remarks.

Lejf switched off the bedside light (Erik was asleep), and staring into the dark, he could see Laia's face. Sex with Laia. He could only imagine what it would be like, although most definitely *not* with an audience. His mother wouldn't mind them having sex here, in his bed, but that would be way too awkward. He understood why Torstie hadn't wanted to bring a girl home either. Geez, how would he look his dad in the eye? Would Laia even want to have sex with him? Damn, these insane urges!

The beauty of imagination was that anything was possible in your dreams. The faint rustling of bedsheets broke the silence of the dark room, and the adolescent boy pressed his face into his pillow as he cried out in lechery's despair.

Not all his thoughts about Laia were impure. There was one moment out of the vast collage of moments throughout Lejf's life that would come back to him time and again. He would replay it as often as he wished, and it would always bring him the same amount of joy as when he'd first experienced it. He would go about his tasks, absorbed in the stream of events that followed one after the other in the day. Somewhere in that flow was that moment, like a secret waiting to be told, filled with immeasurable beauty, semi-awake in his subconscious, anticipating the slightest prompt. It was that perfect moment when he saw Laia for the first time.

＊

Lejf was looking for any opportunity to spend time with Laia; he knew he didn't have much time left before she'd be off to Karlsruhe to study. He loved how comfortable their friendship was. Everything about her self-expression felt natural. It was wonderful; he could be honest and tell her anything. Well, that which didn't include his carnal yearnings for her.

Laia was book smart. She loved literature – the kind he had no interest in reading himself, because it was too complex. He found it hard to concentrate on the language, never mind the hidden meaning, something he never understood. Why didn't you say what you meant?

Lejf liked forming details in pictures, not words. Words were hard to construct into sentences, which was why he hated playing word games like Scrabble, where his inability to find a word hit him from all angles. With visual objects that he photographed – an obsession he immersed himself in – he could capture exactly what he wanted to, without the complication of words.

Whenever he was on a mission with his camera, Lejf felt like he was the odd one out. The loner, looking in from the outside, anticipating stories. He used Signe's old Fujifilm she'd given him. It was basic and didn't have a separate lens but took decent pictures. When he had the camera in his hand, when he looked through that lens and focused on an object, something inside him became alive. It was a language he understood and he knew how to express.

Laia became a staunch supporter of his work from the moment he first showed her what he was passionate about. 'Lejf, you're amazing. You have a natural feel for the mood of a scene you want to capture … I can't even do it justice in trying to describe how it makes me feel. It's beautiful. You're a great artist; someday, you'll captivate the world.'

Even though Laia was respectful with her parents (she wasn't rebellious like Iben), Lejf discovered that there were undercurrents to her relationship with them. He wondered if the tension he sensed in her home life had anything to do with why she didn't seem interested in dating. To his shame, he had to admit; it was an enormous relief.

Laia did, of course, notice how he rubbed shoulders with his father. She said, 'At least there's emotion, Lejf. You may not agree about everything, but love doesn't have to be about perfect synergy every time we engage with someone. Sometimes we can communicate love stronger in our disagreements because there's less of a compromise.'

Much later, her words would come back to haunt them both.

Lejf felt sorry for her. Her yearning was so great. Did she also think that she couldn't please her father? What he observed about Gerhard Ackermann was that he didn't express emotion. He was a man of few words, but from what Lejf saw, Gerhard was a loving father – despite his youngest daughter's shenanigans, which tested his patience to the limit. Laia's mother, Dael, didn't walk with her heart on her sleeve either, but she was kind.

Laia became a natural extension of Lejf's family when they became friends. He didn't mind visiting her at her home; he wasn't bothered about where they hung out, but she insisted they go to his house. She adored his parents.

'I love your mom. She's so real and she knows who she is,' she'd say to him.

As he grew older, Lejf enjoyed having an eccentric mother like Signe. She was what many kids craved in a parental figure. Children sought out her advice as if she was some kind of guru. It was interesting how many came from conservative, religious homes, and Laia was no exception.

Random friends of friends would show up at their house, and it was common to see a strange kid sitting in the kitchen, having a cup of tea with Signe. There may have been resentment from parents in the community but Lejf and his brothers never knew of any. His mother didn't involve herself with gossip. Like the wind, Signe blew wherever she wished to. She abided by the laws of society while staying true to her own personal morals and principles.

Lejf sensed that Laia received emotional fulfilment from his parents. It seemed less laborious to let people in when they weren't close. Perhaps presenting others with your unfamiliar self was easier to manipulate. You could control how much they got to see, whereas there was seldom that luxury with family.

This didn't reassure Lejf that Laia found emotional fulfilment from him. He couldn't get himself to tell her how he felt about her. She felt too far above him.

He held on to her words of becoming a great artist someday; they were all he could cling to. She was embarking on her life journey into the adult world, where she'd have exposure to cultural experiences beyond the limitations of nugatory Otjiwarongo. Her mind was going to broaden. She would meet men and one or more would become her lover. Would she forget about their friendship over time? He wanted to ask her but was too afraid. She would have been kind and answered something like, 'Of course, I won't forget.' Lejf feared the strong possibility that maybe she would. He was the intense boy she'd met a few short months ago and with whom she could talk about serious matters, neither of them with any clue about life – him least of all. They connected for a moment in time. And yet it also felt as if he'd known her all his life. He hoped she wouldn't forget.

It weighed Lejf down. He couldn't stop thinking how Laia would soon be gone from his life – not for good, but her absence would be painful. He couldn't control fate. And only a miracle could make him grow into a man overnight.

These immediate circumstances he could not change. But time changed situations and the age difference between them would become insignificant, however much he dreaded facing four agonising and slow years of catching up with her now.

Of greater impact would be the opportunities offered to him later, which he would fail to take.

4

THE GIFT

The year 2002 would be a momentous year for Lejf. It started off with a bang, quite literally and left the teenager walking around in a daze for months afterward.

Laia turned twenty-one on February 10th, four months before his seventeenth birthday, and she was home for the occasion since her parents were throwing her a party and had booked an entire lodge in the Waterberg Plateau area, just over an hour east of Otji. Although Lejf and his brothers were all invited, Torsten was working and had commitments, and Ingve was studying in England.

Søren was home from Cape Town for the weekend, and Erik and Lejf drove with him to the lodge. Laia dominated Lejf's thoughts, as did the alarming possibility that there might be a guy with her. She'd been coming to their house for sleepovers during her breaks from university. With his three older brothers having spread their wings there was plenty of room, and Lawrie and Signe loved having her over. She hadn't come home for Christmas a couple of months earlier which had left him panicky. He'd made himself believe he still had a small hold on her. Could it have slipped away, and had she grown tired of their friendship as he'd feared? He had no idea what to expect when he saw her again.

Erik was in his element among the women. Not even sixteen, though appearing a few years older, because of his height and maturity, he was eager to get acquainted with Laia's girlfriends from Karlsruhe. The unfailing optimist that he was – the age gap was no problem to him. Although the girls spoke excellent English, he was dishing out his irresistible charms in German (many people in Namibia, like Lejf and his family, were fluent in German). And boy, was he the shining star among those wise women of the world? They flirted back with him in equal amounts of English and German.

'Be careful; you're not old enough to consent to solicitations. It would be illegal and somebody might end up in jail.' Søren cautioned Erik.

'I won't tell if they won't,' Erik said gloating.

Watching Erik, Lejf longed for his confidence and as he took slow sips of a fruit punch he followed Laia's movements from a distance, *ohne deutschen Freund*, to his great relief. He wouldn't have been able to cope well if Laia had brought a boyfriend. Pretty in a summer dress, she looked radiant. It was good to see her so happy.

Some people danced, some played games in the pool, and others hung out with a drink. Lejf saw Iben's father taking her aside and whispering something in her ear.

'Lock me up in a dungeon if I'm such an embarrassment... since when is having fun a crime, Dad?' she said, hands on hips and loud enough for everyone nearby to hear. She made eye contact with Lejf, giggled and strolled off; presumably to perpetrate some mischief in defiance.

There was something about Laia's demeanour as he watched her. She seemed carefree, playful and sultry in her movements as she danced, closing her eyes and giving herself over to the moment and the music: a ballerina, a mellow Rastafarian, a headbanger. She let every mood wash over her as she lifted her arms in the air or ran her hands down the shape of her body, which he visualised underneath the thin material of her dress. Her girlfriends fussed over her all evening, and although she wasn't one for the spotlight, she indulged them. Lejf liked seeing her like that: unapologetic about enjoying herself, embracing her sensuality.

After dinner, a bit tipsy, Laia pulled him by the hand and said, 'Come, you haven't danced with me yet.' She studied his face. 'You've been quiet this evening. Everything all right?'

'I'm always quiet.'

A little laugh. 'You are when you choose to be, but not always.'

Lejf felt out of breath holding her. 'I like your hair shorter. It suits you,' he said. She'd had it cut to just above the collarbone.

'Thanks. I'm mad about your gift by the way. It's beautiful and original and my favourite. You're amazing, and you have no idea how good you are. I'll put it where I'll be able to see it to remind me of home.'

It was hard to focus on what she was saying; he was aware of her warm, feminine body against his. Her left hand was cradling the back of his neck. She had to reach up, standing on her toes. It made him feel wild inside when she looked at him with those black oyster eyes in the glow of the tree lights around them.

He'd given her a framed photograph of a desert rose. It wasn't a rose in the true sense of the word but rather a rose-like formation of crystal clusters comprised of gypsum. They were rare and took hundreds of years to develop. He'd captured the image at Sossusvlei a few months before her birthday.

After Laia had invited them to her party, Lejf had been walking around, wondering what to get her. What did a teenage boy get a twenty-one-year-old woman? Then he remembered the photograph and knew she'd like it because she was fascinated with desert roses.

Signe had helped him pick out a frame. It was one of the best close-up desert images he'd taken, and, considering the likelihood of encountering another this unique, it was one of his most cherished photographs. Now, he would always associate it with Laia.

'You're welcome,' he replied, satisfied that it pleased her.

They danced without speaking for a while, and then she said, 'There's something I want to talk to you about, but not here. Will you meet me in your room in about fifteen minutes? Just make sure no one sees you going there.'

Lejf shared a room with Erik on the lodge's far end. A soft knock and she locked the door. She stood leaning against it with her hands behind her back for a moment with a guilty smile.

'I guess you want to know what the secrecy's about?' she said, cheeks flushing and eyes sparkling. He sat on the bed and nodded. She walked over and sat down next to him. 'Lejf.' She hesitated, then took his hand. 'Have you ... had sex with a girl yet?'

No question could have bowled him over more than that one. Swallowing, he said, 'No. Have you?' Of course, it was a stupid question; she was twenty-one years old. And she no longer lived under the scrutiny of small-minded people. She lived in Karlsruhe; she was grown up and free to do as she pleased.

But Lejf didn't know that shaking off the old stigmas wasn't as easy as simply moving far away from them.

'Do you mean, am I still a blushing virgin?' She laughed, and he felt ridiculous. 'Yes, I've had sex. For your information, I don't put myself on parade. It's on *my* terms.' He didn't comment, and she asked, 'Does it change your opinion of me? Do you think I'm a bad girl now?'

'No, I don't think that at all, Laia.'

He stared at her fingers, tracing the palm of his hand, light as feathers, as she spoke. 'I think when you share your body with someone, it should be because you are drawn to their soul. Sex would be more meaningful instead of being some random event between people.' She shrugged. 'Well, it's my decision to have sex; I won't pretend to be a saint.' Lejf looked at her, and she held his gaze. 'I wish I'd saved my first time for you. It would have been amazing to be each other's first sexual experience. Don't you think? I guess that's water under the bridge.' He blinked, a speechless dolt. 'You are something else, Lejf. Do you know that? I knew from the day we met you're different. You are so wise and deep. I love that you don't just look at things as they appear on the surface; you examine them. Your genuine interest in uncovering truth and beauty is something I admire. Our friendship is valuable to me. I trust you.'

Things started to string together somewhere in his befuddled brain. He understood the meaning of her words spinning through his mind in a loop, yet he still found what she was saying unbelievable.

She paused for a moment. 'Would you like me to be your first, Lejf? If you want to.'

'Now?'

'Yes, now. Right here. Do you want to?'

Of course, he wanted to. It was the one thing he'd been wanting more than anything in life for nearly three years now – to make love with Laia. God, how he wanted that! Still, he couldn't blurt the confession out to her. It was something that lived inside the mind of the foolish boy sitting next to her on the bed when he was in his room, in the dark, where no one could see, where it was nothing more than a fantasy.

She must have realised he wouldn't make the first move, that he was too paralysed by disbelief. She touched his cheek and kissed him, and Lejf dreamed, eyes wide open, how the real him floated up to the ceiling and watched his surreal self with his clumsy arms holding her.

That sublime passage from boy to man; it was nothing like the way he envisioned it would be. Although it was incredible, he had none of the confidence he'd had in his fantasies of them together. It was lustful, yes, but also shy and innocent; awkward, not knowing where and how to touch. He had an embarrassing premature climax. Yet somewhere between wanting and fumbling toward ecstasy, Signe's words from *The Manual* returned to his memory and he explored her while she coaxed him. He wanted it to be perfect for her, knowing it wasn't, not yet, but the moment was too beautiful for it to be of consequence.

After, lying in each other's arms, they kissed and it began all over. There, in the room at the lodge, with the glow of the table lamp on their young limbs, intertwined like the roots of old trees. And Lejf witnessed the most exquisite thing he believed a man could behold: when the woman you embraced opened up like a delicate lotus flower, and she drew him in, and he drank from that sweet cup until so drunk, he didn't know whether he was alive or not.

Laia came to him on her twenty-first birthday, and she gave him the most glorious gift, and then she left to continue her studies in Germany.

And Lejf: though he longed to do so, he couldn't follow her. Fate gave him a bittersweet pill to swallow. He still had two more years of school.

***

As much as he would have liked to, Lejf couldn't hide that something transformative had happened to him from Signe. A mother's heart knew things and she orchestrated a clever way of getting the truth from him.

Lawrie planned a weekend hunting trip for him and his boys. Ingve was home from Cambridge for summer break, Søren was on winter break at UCT, and Torsten flew in from Cape Town for a week's vacation. Lejf and Erik were eager to hear news of their brothers' exciting lives, which would have been more exciting than theirs even if they didn't live in fantastic world cities.

Of course, Lejf didn't go on the trip with the guys. As Lawrie had done with all the hunting trips since his son's renunciation of killing animals, he told Lejf, as a poignant reminder, 'There's no reason for you not to join us. You may have chosen to be a hunter no more, but you are welcome to accompany us. I wouldn't want you to feel left out.'

Great. To hear them boast about their accomplishments? No thanks. There was a blatant hypocrisy to Lejf's argument. He ate meat again, after all.

'The selective blind eye of the conscience is willing to overlook many forms of indiscretions.' Ingve liked to tease him about his self-imposed moral dilemma.

Nevertheless, he'd determined not to participate in those kinds of pagan rituals. A classic situation where he was over-proving one point and missing the opportunity of spending time with his brothers, whose company he enjoyed.

Signe suggested, as an alternative, that she and Lejf go camping for the weekend at Namutoni, in the eastern part of Etosha National Park. Lawrie looked sour over her being so ready to come to their son's rescue.

Lejf was torn. Part of him wanted to be with his father and brothers. Pride, alas, was a strange thing: it had a way of sticking its head in the middle of reason and, like a thorn embedded in the flesh, it wouldn't budge without intervention.

Signe, for whom the friction between Lawrie and Lejf was excruciating, didn't take her usual role as arbitrator, and Lejf soon discovered why she chose not to. He loved the idea of camping with his mom. She was a great companion.

Camping in winter was preferable to summer. The days were in the mid-to-high 20s Celsius. Far more bearable, even though the nights became cold and could fall well below zero. The stargazing was extraordinary. Namibia had some of the best starry nights on the planet – it was a photographer's dream.

Lejf was using a reputable Nikon D3500. A beginner's camera, but it was the most he could afford and miles better than taking pictures with the old Fujifilm. It was tricky to develop adequate skills to capture the night sky. As with every stage of the experience curve, he had to learn through trial and error.

'The rule of thumb for getting clear and exact pinpricks of light is to use manual focus, set the white balance to daylight and set your shutter speed to a maximum of 20 seconds since stars move because of the Earth's rotation.' He demonstrated this to Signe, whose curious mind was eager to learn something new.

'I'm fascinated with how the solar system connects with life here on Earth – the way the moon and stars illuminate our world, not just in an obvious way but on a spiritual level too. They seem to pull us out of our thoughts and the internal worlds we create for ourselves,' he'd told her on one of their camping excursions. They'd spoken about the energy of the moon phases.

'Ah, yes. The new moon makes us look closer at the stars, and it makes us more conscious of the moment,' his wise and wonderful mother had said as she viewed the world beyond Earth's boundaries through his camera lens. She'd taken a beautiful picture of what she was describing.

'You're a natural, Morsa,' he'd said, and she'd smiled.

Lejf realised from early childhood how much he depended on her, and as he grew older that awareness increased. She was the channel through which he could communicate with his father, but more than that, her wisdom and presence were a salve to the rough edges of his soul.

THE GIFT

Etosha lay 170km north of Otjiwarongo, and it was an easy drive for Namibians who were accustomed to driving hundreds of kilometres in a day. The camp was centred around an old German fort and, for its remote location, had a few decent facilities to cater to the needs of the hungry and thirsty traveller. Out here, it could feel like the middle of nowhere to someone from a big city, but that was part of the charm.

Etosha, meaning Great White Place in the Oshindonga language, lived up to its name in every respect. The Etosha Pan covered most of the park. It was dear to Signe's heart.

They'd packed a six-person tent, high enough for Signe to stand up straight, stretchers equipped with mattresses, plenty of blankets and their swimsuits for a mid-day cool off in the swimming pool.

'Here in this place, nature won't be denied her glory. And she hides nothing from view. She presents us with her open-armed gift,' Signe said, gesturing and staring out over the barren earth where optimistic animals gathered around a life-giving waterhole.

It never ceased to amaze Lejf how his mother, who'd grown up in an opposite environment, had adopted Africa with her whole heart. It was the home she loved. Numerous times when he was out on one of his expeditions, and he lifted the camera to his eye to focus on an object, there she would be in his mind: her diamond blue eyes squinting as they gazed over everything.

At the Rietfontein waterhole about two hours' drive from their camp, sitting in Signe's four-by-four truck with the windows down, she asked, as she viewed the scene through a pair of binoculars, 'Tell me what happened to you, Lejf. There's a change in you.' She turned to look at him behind the steering wheel.

Tapping with the fingers of his right hand leaning on the door, he watched six oryx as they walked to the water and lowered their necks to drink. They were lovely antelope. Their straight, black horns looked like long peace signs. Far on the horizon, it was hard to see them, they blended with the colour of the earth and sky. Up close they were a joy to photograph, and he loved their big, brown eyes, framed by thick eyelashes to protect them from the blowing desert sand.

There were a couple of giraffes who squatted to drink water, their awkward legs bent low. The wonder of those animals: it seemed impossible how they sucked the water up their long, straw-like throats. Humans swallowed down. It was easier for them, but they managed to choke on the slightest thing, as he did with his words, pondering his mother's question.

He turned his head and looked at her for a moment and sniffed, thinking how well she'd timed it, so he couldn't escape her searching gaze. 'I'd been with someone, a girl – a woman.' She didn't reply but was watching and waiting. 'It was with Laia. It happened a few months ago, at her twenty-first birthday party.' It wasn't an easy subject to have with your parent, no matter if she was the most open-minded person you knew. His throat felt dry, and he reached for the water and took a few swallows. 'It was my first time.'

Signe took his hand in hers, smiling. 'That's wonderful, min älskling. Are you not happy about that?'

'I am ... but ... it was nothing more than that. She lives in another country, in another world, far above mine. I am a boy and she is a woman.'

'You are a man, Lejf, not a boy.'

'I'm seventeen years old. That doesn't make me a man.'

'You are more of a man than some men twice your age and older.'

'I try, but I can't stop thinking about her. I know it's ridiculous,' he said as he looked at the animals gathered around the waterhole again. Whether his mother could sense it or not wasn't clear to him, but he didn't tell her how his longing for Laia was driving him mad. He felt desperate and frustrated that he couldn't do anything about it.

'Love can be like that. There isn't any logic when the passions rule.

Don't be so hard on yourself, my love. None of us starts out knowing how to handle complicated things. This is life teaching you a valuable lesson; your heart will find a way to work it out. Be patient and give it time.'

'I will soon be required to apply for university,' he changed the subject. 'Dad's going to explode when I tell him I don't want to go.' Lejf had told his mother some time ago and discovered she knew, but he'd asked her not to tell his father, knowing how hard it was for her not to. He needed mental preparation before he faced that hurdle.

'Hmm,' she said, thinking about it. 'Ja, well, it's your life and your decision, Lejf. He will need to accept that, and he will. Give him some credit, won't you?'

'I think you give him too much credit where I'm concerned, Morsa.'

She didn't press the topic further, and she didn't ask about him and Laia either. They drove to the Chudop waterhole. It wasn't too far from their camp, and they spent the last part of the afternoon there. An eerie quiet buzzed in Lejf's ears, and it didn't take long to understand why. Faint specks in the distance grew into two magnificent male lions walking toward the waterhole, as if by wizardry they appeared from some mysterious hidden place in the savanna desert.

He photographed them as they squatted side-by-side to drink, their mirror images on the water, with the setting sun hovering between them like a big, red ball. Their amber eyes looked straight at him and his mother as they lapped the water with long, pink tongues. It was a beautiful shot. When they had drunk their fill, the lions found a shady spot underneath a tree and lay down, camouflaged to the untrained eye. The only thing that gave their presence away was the flicking black tips of their tails every now and then: a signal that they didn't appreciate Signe and Lejf's presence. They were unwelcome on their terrain.

Signe gave a satisfied sigh. 'Don't you just love this place? Let's go back to camp. While I pour myself a glass of wine and get our barbeque things together, you can light the fire. We'll hear those two later tonight.'

They did hear them. The kings of the desert woke them at four in the morning, thunderous, glorious.

Lejf thought of his dad as he looked at the picture of the two lions again – the same blood, but not the same.

5

FACING LAWRENCE BUSHER

They received the paperwork at school for applying to university, along with their report cards, near the end of grade 11. Lejf didn't bother to take the application home. Instead, he summoned the nerve to confront the man he knew would resist his quest to conquer the world his own way.

'Your grades are good. Could be better, but they're good,' Lawrie said as he studied the report card. He put it down and looked up at Lejf. 'So, what's your move for the future, my lad?' It was an open challenge, as if he didn't know his son's plan already.

Lejf's knees felt like they were about to buckle underneath him, and he took a seat opposite his father at his desk. Signe was doing things around the house, but he sensed that she was tuned in to their discussion.

'I know what I want to do, Dad, and I don't need a degree.'

'You're not going to apply for university at all?'

Since the day he and Erik had gone on their hunting initiation with their father when he'd realised he wanted to become a photographer, Lejf had been putting into action a plan for reaching his goals. It was a fire fuelled by everything around him that had the potential of a story, and the more he was doing it, the stronger that fire burned.

He'd been delivering newspapers on his bike early in the mornings from age eleven and did every available job that offered pay. When he started high school, he submitted a portfolio of photographs he'd been working on, to the local newspaper, for special features. In those days, he had to rely on the Fujifilm Signe had given him since he couldn't afford a professional camera, but this only compelled him to work harder and be more attentive to get the perfect shot. The editor liked the portfolio and asked him to do freelance work for him. In his spare time, around schoolwork, he read everything he could about photography and photojournalism.

When he was sixteen, he did a feature called 'Unsung Hero – Story of a Wildlife Veterinarian' during his winter break and went out with his dad while he was working for three weeks. Lawrie supported the idea because he couldn't resist having one of his boys around him. It caused its fair share of conflict: he expected Lejf to be more of a helping hand than a bystander taking pictures.

It worked out well in the end, and Lejf entered the story in a competition held by *Africa Geographic* magazine. That was his first major entry, and he won first prize in the amateur category. It enabled him to buy the Nikon, and although still not the real McCoy in terms of professional grade, the quality of work he could produce with it laid the foundation he knew he would need for outside interest in his projects once he became a full-time photographer. It also affirmed to him that the human journey was something he wanted to continue exploring.

His father saw these things, yet he chose not to believe them, or so it appeared to Lejf. Lawrie clung to the idea that Lejf would still get his academic training. To him, that was paramount.

He drew the hard truth out of his son like pus from a wound. They were in his study as Lejf sat opposite him and they eyed each other.

'No.' Lejf sounded glum. Shouldn't he feel upbeat, considering he had a clear vision of his life? Having to contain his enthusiasm for something so important was what irked him.

His dad didn't see it that way. He leaned back in his chair, both palms flat on the desk – how every ounce in him must have resisted that word. 'What is your big plan for your life then?' Although Lawrie sounded calm Lejf knew he wasn't. A vein next to his right eye throbbed when he was upset, and it was going bonkers. You could tell what he thought; he didn't need to speak.

'I want to become a professional photographer. You know that.'

'A professional photographer. Yes, that is what you've been saying,' Lawrie said, as if he'd only then registered what Lejf meant by it. 'So, you don't want to get a degree and have something to fall back on at least?' It sounded not so much like a question as an accusation. 'Tell me, Lejf, do you know how risky that is? How you're gambling with your future? It's one thing to win a local photographic competition, but it's different doing photography for a living. There are a lot of good photographers out there who battle to scrape by. The competition in that field is fierce.'

'It wasn't a local photographic competition; *Africa Geographic* magazine covers the whole continent. I know it's a tough industry, Dad, but photography is what I want to do. Nothing else makes me as happy as when I'm taking pictures. I have ideas, stories that I want to tell through my lens.'

'You can do that, son, after you've obtained a degree. It would give you peace of mind for the future.'

'I don't want to waste time studying something I won't do anyway. Through hard work and commitment, I can earn a decent living at the least. Besides, there are plenty of successful photographers out there.'

'You're romanticising it. Those who make it are a small percentage. It's a hard and uncertain life. What if you fall ill or have an accident and can't work? How will you support yourself then?'

Explaining himself to his father felt like being on trial for a heinous crime. Of course, he'd practised the conversation, trying to go over all the possible stops his dad might throw at him. It wasn't easy coming up against your most formidable opponent, who had plenty more counter-arguments than you could have prepared for. And his dad wasn't afraid to add in the drama for effect either. The grim picture Lawrie painted made it seem as if Lejf was about to jump into the lion's den without thinking of any consequences.

'The way everyone who works for themselves does, Dad: I'll put money aside.'

When straightforward didn't work, Lawrie's strategy was to switch to reverse psychology. 'Ah, I see. All the money you think you'll be making. Listen, I think the pictures you take are good; you have potential. Won't you please think about this before you make your final decision?'

'I've already made my decision six years ago, Dad.'

Lawrie watched his son with a frown, searching for an angle. 'You may think it's your life to do as you please, and yes, I suppose you may. Just consider how your mother and I will worry about you –'

'You mean you will worry about me and resent me because you choose not to believe I can do it,' Lejf interrupted, impatient and angry.

Signe walked by and stopped for a moment to communicate with Lawrie in their silent language. Lejf hated when they did that because it felt like his dad somehow gained the upper hand.

'The choices you make do affect us, Lejf, no matter how independent you may think you will be from us,' his father said.

'It kills you that I won't have a higher education. You're ashamed to think one of your sons won't have a university degree.'

'Don't put words in my mouth. I'm proud of all my children. I only want the best for you, and to see you reach your potential.'

'And that's what I want to do. I don't want to go out there and do crazy shit, Dad. Photography is my passion, and I'm good at it.'

The father was trying to find a way of penetrating his son's mind. Yet, like a mirror, their wills reflected the other's thoughts. It had always been that way with them.

'You are young and you have much to learn in life. I'm only saying that, before you do what you feel passionate about, build in some security for yourself, a safety net. If that means you'll need to take a slight detour before you reach your goal, so be it. Do your photography part-time as a hobby in the meantime. Giving up a few years is a small sacrifice. In the bigger scheme of things, it won't make a difference. Is that such an outrageous thing for me to ask of you?'

Lejf didn't answer and they sat staring at each other.

There wouldn't be a compromise for Lejf, who had a clear idea for his life. Lawrie's resistance became the thing that drove him forward. He was determined to prove his father wrong. It had also pushed the Great Rift Valley between them. Like two stubborn tribal kings, they were perched on their high mountains, watching each other's moves with suspicion.

6

WATCHING METEORS FLY BY

Laia was becoming increasingly frustrated and torn between the two worlds she lived in. She'd been in Karlsruhe for almost four years, and she wasn't acclimatised yet. She loved her academic course and would graduate in a couple of months. Yet as excited as she'd been to get away from Otji and that environment, her first year in Karlsruhe had been an emotional rollercoaster. Going out with men seemed more daunting than driving on the right-hand side of the road.

When she'd told Iben over the phone, 'I miss Otji', her sister's reply had been, 'Oh, my God. You need to get out and have fun. Have sex, for crying out loud!' How did Iben even know she wasn't having sex?

She thought she was homesick, and perhaps she was. Still, four years? Shouldn't fear of the unknown have become a place and culture that had grown on her by now? She was half-German and very much so in her reserved nature. Her timidity was what frustrated her. The irony was, now that she *was* having sex, it all seemed so banal at times.

Part of her missed her parents and wanted to see them, but she felt emotionally weighed down whenever she was in their company. She'd been home for a few days, and she was already at her wits' end. Her father talked about his work because there was nothing else for him to talk about. And her mother was the paragon of self-denial.

Iben, who was her saving grace, was in Cape Town (she didn't want to study in Germany and opted for UCT). Once Iben had tasted freedom, there was no stopping her. Gerhard hinted on the fact that he was paying for the flat in Cape Town, where Iben lived, but her response was, 'Okay, Dad, fine. If you don't want me to live here, I won't. I'll find somewhere else. I have plenty of guy friends who wouldn't mind me living with them. There's no way I'm spending my vacation time in Otji. I work hard in my studies, and I'm entitled to enjoy my free time however I want.'

Unlike her, their father's emotional blackmail had no effect on Iben, and she was right: she was indeed doing well in her studies; their dad had no advantage there. Laia marvelled at Iben's ability to unravel their father's schemes. She could never be as bold or do that to him, although she wished it wasn't so.

She resorted to Lejf, who was halfway through his final year of high school and on a break. Though she spent time at Lejf's house, she sensed that it hurt her mother's feelings, so she thought of a neutral alternative.

She called him. 'Let's get out of here. I can't stand being cooped up in this place. I told my parents you want to go to Sossusvlei and asked me to go with you since you don't have a driver's licence. Your parents won't mind. Will they?'

'Okay. No, they won't mind at all. I do have my driver's licence, by the way,' he said.

'Then you can drive,' she chuckled.

***

Lejf was ecstatic when Laia called and suggested they go away for a few days. They drove down to one of the campgrounds near Sossusvlei in his mother's truck. He fantasised that it was their romantic getaway of glorious freedom, uncensored coitus and that their minds were as wide open as the desert with its mysteries and sky filled with unexplored galaxies. He feared that the truth was that she wanted an escape from her parents, and he was the perfect excuse. He knew Laia resented being dependent on her father for financial support, though she had no choice but to accept his full assistance. He also suspected she was conflicted about spending her holidays in Otji, and felt obligated because Gerhard was using it as leverage.

'I can't wait to cast off my reliance on a man for help. Nothing will give me greater pleasure than being my own woman. He says he doesn't mind, but my father loves reminding us how he's the provider, as if he's doing us a huge favour. Well, he won't have to for much longer,' she said.

Lejf was the benefactor of her conflict. That didn't make him feel like a hero, but he got to spend time with her. They had sex, and there was their friendship. It was something, at least. But she didn't tell him she wanted to be alone with him because she needed him. And he hankered for her, though he didn't tell her. Every time he attempted to sum up the nerve, it felt like the words got stuck in his throat.

He tried to find the spot where he'd taken the photograph of the desert rose – the one he'd given her as a present on her twenty-first birthday – but it had disappeared underneath the shifting sea of sand. In the evenings, they lay on their backs with their sleeping bags spread out underneath them, looking up at the stars and the flickering lights of aeroplanes that flew high overhead, trying to guess where they were flying off to. Now and then, a meteor streaked past and each time one did, Laia said, 'I'm making a wish for world peace.'

'I'm sure the world will be war-free if all your wishes come true.' He grinned.

'Wouldn't that be marvellous?' She sighed. 'Nowhere else on Earth are the stars more beautiful to me than in our Namibian sky. Look how dense and bewitching they are; I feel drunk looking at them. They make you forget the world's filled with chaos and misery.'

'Hmm.' Laia had the same effect on him.

They spoke of his going to Cape Town soon and how a whole new world would open up once he started photography full-time.

'Everyone's excited for me except my dad,' he said.

'He doesn't want you to struggle through life, that's all.'

'I don't intend to struggle,' he said, appearing more defensive than necessary.

'That's a naïve thing to say, Lejf. Everyone struggles to some degree, and so will you.'

'If that's so, why does he try so hard to stop it from happening to me then?'

'Because he loves you.' She was pensive. 'Your home is a joyful place to be.'

'I wouldn't call arguing with my father joyful.' He could have asked her: what about your own home? He knew better than that.

'No matter how perfect someone's life may seem, we don't see their troubles when we view them from the outside.' So Signe told Lejf and his brothers.

He'd met people with similar backgrounds to Laia and Iben's, who seemed self-entitled or narrow-minded. He'd met only a handful who didn't want to associate with that privileged world. Laia was part of the latter, seeing it as a cause for unhappiness. Iben was in neither category since she didn't associate with people based on their social ranking but on how far they were willing to challenge the system of patriarchy. If Lejf had to venture a guess, that was perhaps Iben's sole goal in life. Part of Laia's conflict was that she shared many of her sister's views, yet she didn't state them – except with him.

She kept staring at the stars and he could hear the sadness in her voice. 'Our home is too polite to be joyful. There's no passion. In your home, love and an individual opinion are valued. The frustrating thing is that nobody gets to say how they feel when everyone is careful not to offend. Everyone besides Iben. At least she has the nerve to stand up and say, "I'll express myself, whether you like it or not."

'I want to be a rebel and scream at the world, at my father. I want to yell out loud: you don't have to be so civilised and immutable! Show some emotion, shout at me, ridicule me for whatever petty offence you can devise. I'm too obliging myself. My father, my mother and I are the same. All three of us have our emotions tucked away. Aren't we neat?' She was quiet for a while, and Lejf turned to check if she was alright, but she continued, 'In truth, I don't know if my parents love each other. If they do, they're concealing it well because I can't feel the love between them, and I never hear them speak that way. I think my mother is so sad because she longs to hear that from my father, but he doesn't know. Funny, for such a smart, educated man, that's the one thing he doesn't seem able to do. What an antinomy. I will never let a man tie down my thoughts and emotions. I refuse to let him.'

She turned her head and said, 'Your parents are crazy about each other and make no mystery out of it. And your father expects a lot from you Lejf, but his resistance proves his love.'

'Some parents prove their love by supporting their children, Laia. My mother does.' Nevertheless, her words made him think about the kind of man his father was: strong and stubborn, but they knew where they stood with him. Unlike Gerhard Ackermann, his dad didn't keep his emotions stored away in a secret garden. However, Lejf thought his father's expectations of him were unrealistic, regardless of whether they sprang from love. And he wouldn't say he loved Lejf in so many words; that was not his dad. It wasn't easy telling his father he loved him either, but he did. And his mom and dad were happy. Signe

Nyberg could somehow appease Lawrie Busher without giving in to him.

It was a skill Lejf still needed to acquire.

7

THE WAITER-PHOTOGRAPHER AND THE MADONNA

When he arrived in Cape Town in early 2004 after graduating from high school, Lejf moved in with Torsten and Søren in their flat in Newlands. He experienced a twitch of panic – a bit like a dog with two new masters. His uncertainty soon eased and he settled in with his easy-going brothers. The flat had two bedrooms, and he slept on the pull-out sofa in the living room where he was responsible for ensuring his space was tidy. They took turns doing the cleaning. The agreement was that he'd start contributing toward groceries and rent once he found a job and received his first pay cheque.

The whole thing was a cover-up. Their parents had no idea he'd moved in with his brothers. He told his mother he would be living with a friend. Signe would have been thrilled that he was staying with Torsen and Søren, but she couldn't be trusted with keeping secrets from his father.

As Lawrie was adamant that Lejf learned how tough life could be without a university degree, he'd said, 'I wash my hands. You want to be so independent; there you have it: you're on your own.' As far as he was concerned, his son didn't need financial assistance and, with a stoney face, Lawrie declared Lejf liberated. That was the end of the story.

Torstie worked at a pharmaceutical lab in Pinelands while studying for his master's in biochemistry part-time at UCT. Søren was in his final year of a BSc, also in biochemistry. He depended on their parents for financial assistance, but Lejf and his brothers were aware of their parents' sacrifices – although they grew up with enough, there was no excess. Søren didn't want to burden them more than necessary and worked as a waiter at an upscale restaurant in Rondebosch, not too far from the flat, three nights out of the week, including most weekends. He earned great money. Lejf was sure his good looks were an advantage.

Both Torsten and Søren had cars, which benefitted Lejf as well. Neither of them had girlfriends. Søren's relationship with Ilze had run its course sometime during their first year at different universities. In his brothers' lives, between work and studies, there didn't seem to be time for getting serious with women, but Lejf had to make himself scarce when either brought a woman over. To his relief, that wasn't often. He deduced that a lady preferred her own place, where it was less crowded. He discovered women were more sensitive to that than men. Whatever the reasons, the brothers didn't discuss technicalities surrounding their love lives.

Lejf's love life seemed dismal. Søren tried hooking him up with some of the girls at the restaurant, and Lejf indulged him, but after a few awkward dates, he gave up and told him, 'Thanks, bro, I appreciate it; they're great girls, but not what I'm looking for.'

He didn't tell his brother that he was interested in one woman: Laia. She lived far out of his reach, but he couldn't stop thinking about her. Although they spoke over the phone and sent the occasional text, his obsessive self couldn't bullshit around the truth that it wasn't a real relationship. It was too platonic, even though they had sex when she visited Otji on her breaks from university. What a strange unreality that was. Lejf knew she was fond of him, and there was an amazing connection between them, but she made no love declarations to him. And he didn't have the guts to tell her how much he longed for her; he didn't dare.

Laia was enjoying the autonomous life she'd craved, and with each passing year, it was becoming more apparent. Whenever she was in Otji, she'd tell him how she loved not being accountable to anyone else. He too, was a grownup now and free to make his own choices. Yet here he was, a lovesick fool and a heartbeat away from tattooing her name on his arse. His emotional state could be summed up in two words: desperate and pathetic.

He enrolled in a 10-week online photography course through UCT. Although it was more expensive than he could afford, Lejf had the sense to recognise that he would need some credentials – it looked better on paper. He protested, but Signe insisted she and Lawrie pay for it. She told him the reason was that since they'd helped all three of their older sons in their pursuits, it was fair to help him. His dad was silent on the matter, and Lejf suspected his mom had put her foot down. It left an uneasy feeling in his gut, knowing his dad didn't support him, and Lejf was determined not to depend on him for financial aid, convinced Lawrie would use it against him in an argument. To his dismay, he had no choice but to swallow his pride and accept their help.

Through Søren's connections at the restaurant, he got a six-day-a-week waiting job. The evening shifts suited him since he could do his photography during the day. It felt great paying his share but his focus was saving money to buy a reliable second-hand runabout and a proper camera. His parents gave him a high-quality lens to attach to his camera for his eighteenth birthday. It had been an expensive gift and no doubt his mother's initiative. It made a huge difference, but he needed a professional camera, like a Canon or Nikon DSLR type. They were around 5,000 USD each, which was more than 50,000 South African Rand. His father would have a fit if Lejf told him.

He was a long way from his goal. On the positive side, if there was something he knew how to do well, it was taking good photographs, with or without an A-grade camera, and that was where he needed to put his energy and focus for the time being.

***

About six months after he moved in with his brothers, there was a knock on the door, and there stood Laia with a big grin. She was a sight for his sore eyes.

'Hello, stranger.'

Lejf managed a flabbergasted 'Hi,' and she chortled at his awkwardness. 'How ... When did you get to Cape Town? I thought you were in Otji.'

'I was there for a few days, but all the fun is here, so I chucked that sad lot and told Iben I'd be coming to her place. And that's where I've been for the past few days. Are you going to let me stand here all night?'

Iben's flat wasn't too far from there and was close to campus. Lejf had been dying to see Laia. She'd mentioned to him that she was thinking about moving to Cape Town after she was done with her studies, then added that it was just an idea she was playing with. Of course, he hoped, against all odds, she would and started visualising their incredible, happy life together.

The thought that she'd been in town for a few days, but didn't seek out his company right away darted through his mind.

'What am I thinking? Of course not. Come in. I can't believe it. It's good to see you.' He hugged her for a while. 'We're about to have dinner. Why don't you join us?'

'Sure, thanks. Iben's out tonight, and I was on my way to pick something up to eat but I thought I'd pop by and see if you were home, and lucky me, you are.'

'Lucky all of us,' said Torsten, who gave Lejf a sly grin.

Lejf kept staring at her in disbelief. It was no secret that the two of them had been having a 'rather awkward thing', according to Ingve, the wordsmith. Erik's classic response (on discovering that it had started in the room they'd shared at the lodge and that it had been Lejf's first sexual experience with a woman) was, 'Epic!'

Laia being in Germany posed a considerable obstacle. Seeing her only once or twice a year wasn't close to being enough for his love-crazed heart and aching body, but he pined for those few visits. No woman could hold a candle to her. That bias had been augmented since he transitioned into manhood two years ago. The person who appeared to have taken note of that, and didn't discourage it, was Signe. And since his father liked voicing his concerns or displeasure about his choices, Lejf took his silence as either ignorance or disinterest. He had no intention of enlightening his dad on the subject.

Torsten and Søren excused themselves after dinner under the pretext that they had to study at the library.

'How's the great photographer holding up?' she asked.

'Cape Town's great. Torsten and Søren are putting up with me crowding their space. I realised something the other day: if people ask what I do for a living, I must tell them I'm a waiter-photographer. That's so cliché. The waiting bleeds me; I wish I didn't have to do it, but it helps pay my way, and I'm trying to save. I'm focusing on that.' He ran his hand through his hair, a longtime self-conscious habit Laia's penetrating gaze induced. 'I'm also discovering how hard it is to put yourself out there; the scepticism. It's funny; everyone tells you to pursue your dreams when you're a kid, and the moment you're grown up, the tables turn and you become competition they'd like to get rid of.'

'As long as you don't allow it to discourage you. Show me what you've done so far.' She sat down on the sofa, kicked her shoes off and tucked her legs in to make herself more comfortable.

'Okay, let me get my laptop.' He took a seat next to her and opened his website. 'It's categorised; you may select what you want to view. Don't feel obligated to look at all of them.'

'Obligated? Don't be silly; I want to look at them all.' She scooted closer with a tut, her body pressed against his. Her hair smelled like sweet pea flowers. He studied her face as she clicked and paused. With some, she lingered: fishermen repairing their nets in Fish Hoek harbour, elegant little Cape Bluehood flowers along a misty trail on Table Mountain. A Saturday market with vivid stalls selling anything from flowers to baked goods and coffee to artisan beer, jams and arty handmade jewellery. Blurred human forms weaving about in the colourful bazaar made her stop for a moment. 'There, but not there, like ghosts. A perpetual state most of us operate in,' she commented, staring long at the image as if to make a connection with something or someone in that scene. She tittered at some photographs, biting her lip with a frown of contemplation at others. Her reactions were thrilling to watch.

'Have you sold much?' she asked as he closed the laptop.

'Yes, somewhat to travel magazines as promotional material, but it's small fry and doesn't pay enough for the effort. I've started covering weddings and events; they're an easy way to make money. I didn't realise how many people are getting married all the time. The reviews so far have been favourable, and my weekends are becoming booked up. It's not my thing though; I won't do it for long, but it's helping me improve and experiment with techniques, which is great. I'm on track as long as I'm learning and getting better. Now, I'm working on ideas for themes. What I need is a car and more money to be able to travel. Torsten and Søren have been great about me using their cars, but it's inconvenient to them and a short-term solution. I'm feeling a bit frustrated, like I'm moving one step forward, two steps back.' It sounded like he was telling her he wouldn't remain a loser. He was terrified that she'd think he was.

'Your photographs tell beautiful stories, Lejf. You have an eye for every peculiar detail, and as you said, you're learning and getting better. Someone's going to notice your work not too long from now. They will, because it's exceptional. I'm not saying it to be kind; it's the truth.'

'Thanks, Laia.' He stared at her, longing to hold her, mad with desire, hesitant about the timing as well as her expectations, and then she was the one who leaned closer and kissed him. He wasn't worried about his brothers walking in on them; he could have locked the door and put the latch on. He didn't want to put Laia in a position where she'd feel awkward. She didn't look uncomfortable, though.

'May I offer you something to drink? I'm not sure what there is. I'll have to check.' he said, not eager to pull out of her embrace.

She noticed him glancing in the direction of the front door. 'Sure.'

'Boxed merlot, okay?' he asked from the kitchen, holding the box up in apology.

'Perfect. I'm here for another two weeks. You should come to visit me at Iben's flat.' She had a wide inviting smile. 'Thanks,' she said as he handed her the wine. 'I'll make us something to eat. I've had lessons from a chef and have become a decent cook, and Iben has a few bottles of excellent white and red on hand.'

Lejf was tempted to ask if the chef was male. Instead, he asked, 'No boxed wine?'

'No wine in boxes, and my sister knows to text before barging through the door. She's considerate that way.'

'So you've tested it out then.' It was meant to sound funny and came out more like fishing. She laughed, kissing him again and reached underneath his T-shirt, holding her hand on his thundering heart.

'You can take photographs of me in the nude,' she whispered in a husky voice against his mouth.

His resistance couldn't hold up against such torture, and he caved, thinking let his brothers see what they would see. He was relieved that their studies kept them busy long enough.

Lejf thought about how Laia hadn't dismissed his comment about testing out her texting arrangement with her sister, and it made him realise how naïve he'd been about her life in Germany.

***

She lay on her side with her head resting on her outstretched arm, legs stacked and a fraction bent at the knees, her other arm draped along the arc of her hip. An opal-eyed Madonna in a Renaissance painting, watching him as he viewed her in full focus through his camera's lens. His big Cyclops eye devoured her from head to toe. She was at ease as if she'd done this a hundred times before although she swore that she hadn't posed naked for anyone but him. Lejf had a sickening flash of another man looking at her lying naked and inviting, on her bed in Karlsruhe. He wondered if it was the chef.

Iben's flat had two bedrooms, and Laia said he should stay with them until she returned to Germany. Lejf welcomed the change from sleeping on the pull-out, as he was sure his brothers would enjoy a break from him sprawled out in the middle of the living room.

'Don't get too accustomed to the luxury,' Torsten teased.

The thought of her going back gutted Lejf. He stayed over, and they alternated between borrowing his brothers' cars or Iben's, and Laia went on excursions with him and watched as he took photographs.

She dropped him off at the restaurant in the evenings and picked him up after his shift. Sometimes they ate the boxes of untouched seafood platters and drank the half-empty bottles of expensive wines left behind from the rich customers he'd served (he was allowed to take the food and wine home and it was a huge perk for a man on a tight budget).

At other times they ate the delicious meals she cooked for them while he was working, and they drank wine from Iben's impressive collection. And afterwards, they made love until their bodies were spent, and while she lay in his arms, they talked about him visiting her in Karlsruhe – someday soon – and of him becoming a world-class photographer – one day. Sharing their thoughts felt natural and made Lejf cling to that flicker of hope.

As she lay there, posing for him, Laia asked about his relationship with his dad. It was something that troubled her. Lejf knew she longed for a deeper relationship with her father, but she and Lawrie had a close bond.

'I don't think he'll warm up to the idea that I won't have a degree. That's his Achilles' heel, or he may think it's mine,' he said, adjusting the settings on his camera and raising it again to get her whole body in scope. 'He's convinced I've chosen a poor man's profession and that a life filled with misery will ensue.'

'You and your father remind me of Aesop's, *The Ant and the Grasshopper.*' He lowered the camera again, and she explained, raising herself so that her head rested on her hand, 'In the fable, the hungry grasshopper, who'd danced the summer away, finds itself without anything to eat when winter arrives. The ant refuses to help the grasshopper, saying it should have made the proper provisions.'

'And you think the story relates to me and my father? Although I think he might agree with you.' Lejf contemplated.

'Not all of it does. Your work ethic and natural talent are much too strong to imply you squander precious time. I see a hint of a resemblance to the diligent ant, which – gathering without seizing – resents the fact that the grasshopper could live in the moment and not think about the future.'

'I *do* think about the future.' He frowned. 'My father's the one who's convinced that I don't. He never considers that there's more than one way to do something. If it's not his way, then it must be wrong. Besides, is living in the moment such a bad thing? Who's right and who's wrong?'

'I don't think there is a right or a wrong side. It depends on which angle you're viewing it from. Is it the carefree grasshopper, expressing its artistry, or the conscientious, practical ant who's storing up for the leaner times?'

'Which side are you viewing it from?' he asked as he moved closer and stroked her arm resting on her side with his finger. Ticklish to the soft touch, it gave her goose pimples.

'Both.' When he lifted his brow, she said with a devious smile, 'You want me to feel sorry for you, that's all.'

He squatted in front of her, running his eyes over her body. 'Oh, I don't think you're as impartial as you would have me believe, Laia. Admit it: you feel sorry for the headstrong, judgemental ant. Tell me, will you not sympathise with the lowly, hungry grasshopper?' He placed his hand on the curve of her hip.

'No sympathy at all.' She pulled his head closer, his mouth toward hers, warm and sweet.

Laia's laughter sounded like a melody. Lejf wished he could bottle and store it, so she would be with him when she wasn't around. He'd also need a bottle for her voice and smell. It seemed she wasn't around enough.

He had it figured out from the wrong angle, but Lejf was slow at discovering certain truths.

Laia returned to Karlsruhe again too soon, and he didn't take the opportunity to tell her how his heart ached for her.

8

AN UNFORTUNATE SETBACK

It was time for Lejf to find his own space. Sleeping in the living room of his brothers' flat wasn't a durable solution. Besides that, his mother had shown up without warning and found him there (he suspected she had an idea about what was going on and came to investigate). He'd made up a quick excuse that his flatmate had family over and he was crashing at Torsten and Søren's place.

To everyone's relief, Erik finished school in time before nerves started unravelling, or their intuitive mother discovered the sham, and it caused the old geyser to blow up in a fit. They found a flat near Torsten and Søren's place. Erik had enrolled in engineering at UCT, which pleased Lawrie. Søren was working, and Lejf was financially independent, so his dad didn't make a fuss over Erik and him living together. Erik and Ingve were the only two under their parents' supportive wings.

Erik wanted to go home for winter break. Lejf had been working non-stop and needed a change from the restaurant scene, so he joined him. By then, it had been a year since Laia had been to Cape Town, and every sight in and around the city reminded him of her. Taking a break from photography was as easy as cutting out sleeping or eating for a while. He couldn't do without it.

Lejf took Erik along for a drive late one afternoon on a game farm.

Namibia was a land of game hunting on a big scale, and there were many game farms in the Otji area. It saddened Lejf to think how much emphasis was placed on trophy hunting when, in a glaring paradox, the country had some of the largest national parks in the world. *Where was the logic?* He wondered. Sure, governments passed legislation to conserve nature, but how did you protect wildlife in your parks while animals were slaughtered on the other side of the park fence – not for food, but for their magnificent heads to be put on a hunter's wall?

Lawrie said with a shake of his head, 'It's a pity that you don't understand how economics works.'

This was coming from a wildlife vet, although Lejf had to admit his father's hunting didn't have anything to do with his ego. His dad liked to contradict him for argument's sake.

'You discredit yourself by throwing your support behind the wrong argument, Dad,' he said. Then he added a melodramatic rant. 'I may not understand everything about economics, but I do understand that trophy hunting's sole purpose is to stroke the ego of a certain so-called civilised man. His victims are the innocent who cannot outrun his fast vehicles and high-tech weaponry. Men like that also like to hunt in packs; they call it *male bonding*. I suppose if he did it by himself, there'd be no one to applaud him when he killed the strongest ram or bull of the herd, who'd fought and overcome his rivals to ensure the most successful genes would be passed on.' Lejf's sentiment didn't elicit a verbal response from his father. Lawrie gave him his signature look. No guesswork was needed to interpret the meaning.

Two years ago – when Lejf was still a naïve kid who didn't understand that not everyone saw particular things as important – he'd told a wealthy Swiss tourist, who'd been on his way to a game farm for a five-day hunting expedition, 'There's so much to discover about the wildlife here. For instance, when you drive through the Namib and encounter springboks springing high in the air, heads and tails tucked in, backs bent like a San man's bow, and legs straight then you'll know how enchanting those graceful little gazelles are to watch.' He'd demonstrated with his arm and hand. The damage done in five days by a single huntsman, not to mention a group.

The tourist's dismissive grin had told Lejf enough to know that his words had rolled off, like water down a duck's back.

He and Erik turned off onto a gravel road past an entrance sign that said *Vrede*. The farm belonged to a friend of their father. It was a beautiful game farm where single-track roads with grassy middles meandered through the bushes as the tall, dry grass screeched against even a high four-by-four truck's suspension. Lejf regularly went there whenever he was in Otji. Sometimes his parents joined him and most of the time, he went alone. His dad's friend knew the purpose of his visits, but as a courtesy, he phoned ahead if he planned on being there. During the hunting season, it was critical to let him know.

The dry winter veld always had something interesting to give to his lens, and the sheer pleasure of walking in the bush late in the afternoon – that magical time at sunset when things quieted down for a moment – was enough of a reward.

Erik was driving at a slow pace as the roads were rugged and bumpy. Lejf stood on the truck bed in the back, holding on to the frame. Standing like that wasn't the safest practice, but nobody would have thought it unusual; that was farm life in Africa. It afforded him a great panoramic view, and he could breathe in the dusty, wild smell of the veld: clean, not like the dust and smog in a city that smelled grimy and like suffocating misery. Now and then, he banged on the roof, indicating to Erik to stop so he could take a picture.

As they were driving along, the Cruiser came to a sudden stop. The jarring impact knocked Lejf over the side of the truck, and the camera fell from his hands. How fate could revel in playing games with you: that *one* briefest moment he didn't have his camera strap around his neck. And what comical scenarios the mind could conjure up. A few seconds could hold the longest aeon. There was no escaping the collision that awaited as he flew, a flightless bird, a ridiculous spectacle of arms and legs too long and heavy for such a short distance. His left shoulder and the left side of his face hit the ground with great force, and for a minute, he had no idea what had happened or where he was.

He heard Erik speaking to him from afar before the words became clearer. 'Lejf! Lejf! Are you okay?' Erik's eyes were like saucers.

Sitting upright on the dry hard earth trying to find his bearings, Lejf shook his head, but it hurt, so he nodded. That hurt too. His shoulder felt like it had been crushed underneath steel, and there was blood on his fingers as he touched his throbbing cheekbone. He could feel the warm, sticky liquid running down his neck. Trying to catch his breath while spitting sand and grass from between his teeth, he asked, 'What happened?' His tongue felt mauled, and he poked around in his mouth with his finger, testing to ensure he still had all his teeth, which he did.

'Aardvark hole, sorry mate. I didn't see it until the front wheel had already gone in. Shit, bro, your face looks bad and you're bleeding something awful. We need to get you home,' Erik said.

Aardvarks and burrowing animals dug deep holes that could damage a wheel and suspension. The rule of thumb was to try and remember where they were. The tricky part was spotting new holes in time.

'Have you seen my camera?' Lejf tried to push himself up, but pain shot through his shoulder, and he sat down again.

Erik found the camera a couple of metres away.

'Oh, fuckity. This is the last thing I need.' Lejf inspected the mangled, dusty thing. The lens was cracked, and there was so much dust on the power button and inside the camera that he couldn't switch it on.

AN UNFORTUNATE SETBACK

'Damn, I feel terrible.' Erik apologised.

'It's not your fault. I should have been more careful.'

'Will you be able to have it fixed, do you think?'

'I may but I can't tell for sure.'

'What about the memory card?'

'Don't know.' Lejf took it out of the camera. 'Seems to be okay.' He put it in his bag. A couple of days' worth of hard work was stored on it.

'What are you going to do now?'

Lejf grimaced as Erik helped him up. Something felt wrong with his shoulder, and he could see his swollen, bloody cheekbone in his peripheral vision. With each throb, it seemed to be getting bigger. 'I'll have to see how much damage there is on the inside. It may not be as bad as it looks, but the lens is done for. That's going to set me back. Do me a favour, don't tell Dad.' When Erik gave him a puzzled look, he said, 'Please, Erik, I have a lot on my mind, and I don't need him lecturing me.'

'Mom would help you to buy a new lens.' Lejf grunted. 'First, we need to get you home,' Erik said, helping him into the truck. He struggled to find a comfortable angle where his shoulder didn't press against the seat.

'I know she would,' he said, grimacing again. 'But she won't keep it from Dad. You know Morsa and her honesty policy. Don't mention it to either of them. I'll think of something. Boy, my shoulder hurts.' He searched the glove compartment and found wet wipes to clean his neck and held some against the bleeding wound. Erik helped him as much as he could.

* * *

Signe was horrified when she saw him. 'Aw! What happened, my love?'

To Lejf's relief, his father wasn't around. She took out a medical kit and cleaned the dirt from the cut on his cheek. She winced as much as he did. 'You'll need stitches; the cut's too deep for a dressing.'

'I'm sure I'll be fine.' He didn't sound sure.

As Erik explained about the aardvark hole, Signe helped Lejf take his shirt off and, taking one look at his shoulder said, 'We need to get you to the hospital right away.'

Lejf was admitted for surgery. He had twelve stitches on his cheekbone and had to have a shoulder arthroscopy because of torn ligaments. It was a pain in the butt and another setback he didn't need. His mind was working overtime, trying to calculate the costs of hospitalisation and physiotherapy. What paltry amount he had saved up evaporated in an instant. It was a double blow: he couldn't work, and there wasn't a repair shop in Otji that specialised in camera equipment. He had no money to buy a new lens. He was in a shit hole.

Despite all that, nothing was as painful as seeing his father's I-told-you-so face. Lawrie didn't know about the camera and Lejf didn't intend for him to find out. That was problematic with Signe, who had a sharp sixth sense and didn't like keeping secrets from her husband.

While Lejf was recuperating at his parents' house, an excruciating six weeks of pent-up frustration and uncomfortable physio, Signe asked, 'I notice you haven't been taking your camera out, älskling. Has something happened to it?' Her voice held such delicate nuance he had to chuckle.

Of course, she'd noticed. In fairness, his mother had plenty of reason to be suspicious: she had a keen interest in his photography, and the technical elements of the camera and its features fascinated her. It was their thing – her sitting and talking with him as he cleaned the camera and attachments. He mumbled an evasive answer, and she let it be.

It turned out the damage was irreparable. Lejf felt like hollering out his anger and self-pity. Letting it all out might have helped him feel better, but it wouldn't have changed anything. He had to be realistic and think of his recovery plan. The only solution was to continue his waiting job in the evenings and find another daytime job until he'd saved enough money again to buy a new camera.

It was a massive blow to his plans, yet he had no intention of asking his father for his charity. Lawrie would have been waiting for something like this to happen so he could proclaim his son's doomed career, and Lejf didn't want to deal with his smugness. If the camera had been his sole problem, he wouldn't have minded; he'd bought it with his own money. The lens had been a gift from his parents, and one they had to scrape the cash together to afford. He felt terrible about that. Erik kept his word. It didn't bring Lejf peace of mind: he knew he was buying time until the inevitable.

9

WHAT COULD BE EATING LEJF?

Laia was starting to enjoy her life in Karlsruhe. It was 2005. She was twenty-four years old and nearly finished with her master's in bioengineering at Karlsruhe Institute of Technology. She had a cosy flat in the Oststadt, a vibey young up-and-coming neighbourhood, and the support of her father's brother and his family in Mainz, about an hour's drive north. It was her growing independence that was causing this big change in her, though. A shift towards happiness and the freedom she'd been longing for.

She'd been thinking a lot about her future lately and what she wanted to do after university. It wasn't a complicated decision if she had to be honest. Karlsruhe was a city of technology and she was in the best place for the profession she'd chosen. More than that, she was embracing the freedom to be her own person and she felt alive.

Iben had called earlier for a weekly check-in. She was studying human resources at UCT and, unsurprisingly, loved life in Cape Town.

'Wie ist Karlsruhe?' Iben asked.

'It's great. I'm starting to enjoy it. I mean, I've always thought it was cool, but now I'm starting to like it more.'

'And all it took was a short six years. Does that include the men?'

'It saddens me to say that the men I've encountered in the dating field are self-righteous jerks.'

'You have to play them at their game.'

'What if I don't want to? What if I just want to have someone to talk to, to be my friend and lover? Does it have to be about games, Iben?'

'Oh, my Lord, you're so serious. How often do you have sex? Is it at least three times a week?'

'Three times a week!' Laia burst out laughing. 'No. It's about three times a year.'

'*Nun, da ist dein Problem, meine Schwester: sexuelle Frustration.*'

'Promiscuity is not my thing, Iben. I like intelligent men and I enjoy sex, but sometimes it feels as if it's hard to get both at the same time, which, in an ideal world, I would like to.'

'We don't live in an ideal world. You can't always kill two birds with one stone. Don't be so picky.' Iben paused for a second. 'What about Lejf? You two seem to have a good connection and, not to mention *ernst* steamy sex. Don't deny it; I've heard you, you saucy thing.'

Laia sniggered. 'That would be the three times a year I'm having sex because that's how much I see him.'

'You're not having sex with him only, are you?'

'No …'

'Are you and Lejf on the same page? He seems taken with you, Laia. Are you leading him on, or is there more?'

'No! I'm not leading him on. He's my best friend, beside you.'

'Your best friend you happen to sleep with three times a year. You do see how there's room for misread expectations …'

She was quiet for a moment, wondering if Lejf thought she was leading him on. There was something about him. She felt as if she could but also couldn't understand Lejf. He was just near enough to touch but not to reach fully. It was as if he was carrying things he couldn't bear to express. Not in words. She could see what he wanted to say in his photographs.

'The way he looks at the world around him is remarkable, Iben, and so is his work. You should see what he's doing. He's going to be big, memorable; I feel it in my gut.'

Laia thought about the two weeks Lejf had spent with her in Iben's flat a year ago and the disappointment in his silence a few days ago when she called him and told him she was staying in Karlsruhe. Although she tried to keep it light, it was awkward. He didn't say he was disappointed, but when he told her he was happy for her, he didn't sound happy. She felt torn about Lejf. He was the only man with the things she wanted in a man. He was two birds with one stone. Perhaps she cared about him more than she was willing to admit but a relationship wasn't what she wanted right now. She couldn't give up her independence. Not now.

***

Lejf found a job at a second-hand bookstore and liked the owner, old Mr Thyssen, who never spoke much but knew his store inside out. Soon after starting there, Lejf became convinced from talking to the old man that he must have read most of the books on the shelves; his knowledge was incredible. He didn't ask Mr Thyssen whether he'd liked travelling at some stage in his life. There were many books on travel and photography, and he studied them whenever he had a moment to spare.

The job turned out to be one he enjoyed as it provided him with an ample supply of knowledge. The store was right in the centre of Cape Town, amid colourful shops and markets selling mid-eastern fabrics, aromatic food and spices. The area was a goldmine of photo opportunities. And it was within a short distance of the Company's Garden, a beautiful place filled with history. He sneaked off to go there during lunch to take pictures of people and their habits.

Despite his shoulder giving him grief and it being exaggerated by the cold and damp winter weather, he continued waiting tables at the seafood restaurant, but he loathed it. The owner was a two-faced arsehole who liked sucking up to the wealthiest clients, while he treated the servers like they were the lowest form of life crawling. The tips were great, and on Søren's advice, Lejf used his best charms whenever he served a table with women, and it paid good dividends. There'd been a few notes saying, *call me* and with a phone number, slipped in with the cheque now and then, but his mind was preoccupied with getting back on track and finding a way to see Laia more often.

He missed her no end and had no idea where they were going, or if they were going anywhere at all. He began listening to the voices in his head that told him to wake up to reality: she was way out of his reach.

It was an inescapable fact that his mother would have told his dad about the camera episode. He wished she hadn't. Signe was Signe and true to her nature, too honest to keep it a secret, and his dad wasn't dull-witted. Lawrie's reaction came when Lejf was home a couple of months after the incident and still without a new camera. There were no surprises.

Lawrie didn't hesitate, but shot straight to his point. 'Perhaps this indicates that you should do something more consistent with your life.'

'More consistent? You don't get it, do you, Father? You don't understand what I'm about at all.'

'I get you much more than you realise. The stress is grinding you down. Look at you. You're twenty years old and walking around as if carrying the world's weight on your shoulders.'

'And you think I'd be happier doing something else?' He intended to sound ironic, although his dad didn't see the humour. 'It's not my work I'm unhappy about, Dad.' Lejf didn't feel like explaining how holding two jobs was wearing him thin. And he did not want to tell his father he had to continue until he had enough for a down payment on an R50,000 camera.

Lawrie was crafty enough not to mention the camera outright. It was more effective for him to play his mind games. Lejf had overheard his parents talking about him living with Torsten and Søren, and how betrayed his dad felt that his sons concealed things from him. Laia was another subject Lejf didn't want to debate with him.

'You're selling your soul for a handful of Monopoly money. It's not too late. You can still go to school. I'm worried about how you'll support yourself eventually. You need to start looking to the future; otherwise, how much will you have left in the end? Do you want to live hand-to-mouth for the rest of your life?' Lawrie asked.

It was the same old, regurgitated argument. 'This is my future,' Lejf said, holding a *National Geographic* magazine and shaking it for emphasis. 'Do you see this? This is all I care about. The thing is, you don't want me to do this. If other people are struggling photographers, that's fine, just not Lawrence Busher's son.' Agitation stoked the fire; it was of no help in an argument with his dad.

'Please don't patronise me, Lejf.'

'I'm not patronising you, Dad.'

'I know what it sounds like.'

'Can we please drop this?' he asked through a clenched jaw.

'What's going on, Lejf? Why are you so unhappy then?'

His dad couldn't leave him alone. 'Nothing's going on.'

'Nothing? It looks like something to me. You seem intent on hiding things from me. I have eyes and ears.'

'God … you should have studied drama,' he mumbled the last part.

'Excuse me?'

'Nothing.'

'Ah, everything is nothing. Is a father not allowed to ask his son what's making him unhappy? Do I not have a right to know what's going on with you?'

'No, you may not because you'll judge me as you do with every other thing I do.'

'That's a lie, and you know it,' Lawrie said, angry and for a second, Lejf had a glimpse of himself a few decades older. Talk about a sobering thought!

'It feels as if you do. I don't want to talk to you about it, okay Dad? I'm going for a walk.'

'Now? It's the middle of the day. You'll die of heat stroke.'

'Tough break.' He walked out and felt his father's eyes burning in the back of his head.

Of course, he reconsidered the walk when the heat outside hit him full force, so he asked Signe if she'd drop him off at the golf club instead.

Otjiwarongo Golf Club was an unassuming place where sport met the desert, but in Africa, water was scarce, and you learned to play the game around nature's rules.

Inside the bar, Lejf greeted a couple of fellows whose loud laughter and rouge complexions indicated their time already spent at the waterhole. He bought a draught, turned to hold it up in cheers to his happy comrades, and turned his back on them again. He had no intention of conversing with anyone and drank the beer in a few long swallows.

Since no person in their right mind would play nine, let alone eighteen holes at this hour, he bought a bucket of balls for the driving range, but even that felt like a suicide mission. Heatwaves danced like frantic silver ribbons above the dry ground, with no hint of a breeze. The birds, too, were quiet. They seemed to be taking a break from the scorching heat under the shelter of leaves, sitting with beaks wide open to try and cool off.

Sweat was streaming from every pore of Lejf's body, and the buzz he'd felt from the beer a moment ago had evaporated. It reminded him that playing golf here required a certain level of skill. He had to do his best to place the pin on a grass poll, but pickings were slim, so he hit the ball straight from the ground.

The dust burned his eyes as he smacked the first few high-flying balls. Distracted by his thoughts about Laia, he didn't heed the discomfort. She'd called and mentioned, 'By the way, I'm not going to Cape Town after I'm done with my studies. I've decided to stay in Germany. I feel it would be best for my career. Besides, I'm starting to get into the vibe of my lifestyle here. Plus, there's no one to hassle me. Ha-ha,' she'd said joking.

Did the joke include him? He struck a ball with such force that he had no idea where it landed and did the same with a couple more until the intense heat won the battle over his rage. It was pointless, all of it. He capitulated, returned to the bar, handed the bartender the half-bucket of balls, and ordered another beer.

'Better luck next time, mate,' the chap said as he pushed a draught across the counter. He must have recognised the defeat on Lejf's face.

'Thanks,' Lejf said with a false grin and sat brooding over his beer. He had no idea what to do about it. Laia was staying in Germany and he had no right to tell her not to. There wasn't a place for him in her world. He was a nobody, a wannabe photographer without a damn proper camera. He had loser written all over him.

At that low point of feeling sorry for himself his phone buzzed in his shirt pocket. Erik. 'How's the golf?' he said, too cheerful for Lejf's sour frame of mind.

'Fantastic.'

'Game or bucket?' A chuckle.

'Bucket and I may have lost a couple.'

'The balls in the bucket or your head?' He laughed out loud.

'Is there a point to this call?'

'Mom said to come to get you; she wants you off the streets and home for dinner, young man.'

Erik brought a rush of hot air in with him as he opened the door to the bar and closed it with an apologetic wave when he received a couple of scornful moans. As he removed his shades and eyed Lejf, he tucked his lower lip in a grin. It was a typical Erik thing when he was about to poke fun. He exchanged cheerful greetings with the guys at the table in the corner and walked over to where his brother sat hunched over on a bar stool.

'What in the world could be eating Lejf Busher?' He sat down on a stool next to Lejf and indicated to the bartender that he'd like the same.

Erik had the gift of lifting anyone's spirits. He had the best upbeat nature; remaining gloomy in his presence was impossible. Lejf wasn't ready to relinquish his sombre mood to indulge his brother's unique touch of benignity. 'I hope you haven't come here to play shrink with me. Don't you have something better to do?' He sipped his beer and stared at the bottles at the back of the bar, contemplating going for something stronger.

'Can't a man be concerned about his brother? I've already done all my chores for the day. So, golfing in unbearable heat's your newest crazy thing.' Lejf ignored the comment, and Erik said, 'I heard you're feeling a bit low, so I thought I'd cheer you up.'

'Did Dad tell you to come to find out what's wrong and then run back and report to him?'

'Hey, don't be a wanker to me because you're angry with Dad,' he said, less offended than he had a right to be.

'Sorry. Dust balls just seemed an attractive alternative to Dad getting on my nerves.'

'You knew he would have found out about the camera.' Lejf shrugged, and Erik said, 'Mom would help you. Why don't you ask her?'

'That would be like handing Dad a case full of bullets. I'm not going down that path. Thank you, but no thank you.'

Erik shook his head and laughed. 'Is the camera the only thing that's grinding you?'

'No, Erik, it's the same thing that's been wearing me out since childhood: our father's displeasure with me.'

'C'mon, you're being hard on the old man.' He looked at Lejf. 'That's it?'

After a pause, Lejf said, 'Laia's not coming back. She's staying in Germany.'

'A-ha.'

'Ah, well. So much for hoping. Here's to nothing.' He lifted the glass in a toast.

'You have to admit, there aren't many options for her here in Otji.' He couldn't help throwing in the joke, but Lejf didn't laugh, so he said, 'It was bound to happen, bro. You can't blame her.'

'I know and that's what's killing me. If she were in SA – it doesn't have to be Cape Town; it could be Johannesburg – she'd at least be closer.'

'Closer to what? You're not going to be in Cape Town forever. You'll be travelling and pitching a tent in some godforsaken place somewhere, taking one award-winning photograph after another.'

'You have much more confidence in my future success than Dad.'

Erik was right about Laia, but Lejf was desperate for her. The problem was that he couldn't see himself not living in Namibia or at least somewhere in Southern Africa. Not that he'd been elsewhere much, and he hadn't even been to Karlsruhe. The most unsettling thought was that he wasn't sure how Laia would feel about him living there, supposing he could.

'I guess we'll have to see what happens now,' he said, taking one last big swallow to drain the glass.

Erik gave him an affectionate slap on the back, drank the remainder of his beer and said, 'Come, I can't drive with more booze in me. Morsa said she's keeping a few cold ones in the fridge for us. We can play darts, and I'll let you win out of the kindness of my heart.'

On the way home, Lejf asked Erik to detour and drive past Laia's parents' house. Erik looked sceptical but indulged him. He imagined her there; what she'd be doing, how she'd be moving about in her quiet way, reading.

He couldn't let go of her. Karlsruhe felt like a universe away, yet he loved her and was willing to take what he could get, however much or little that was.

Those were the assertions of an inexperienced heart.

**

Lejf's first big-league breakthrough was a Sony World Photography award two years later, when he won first place in the professional competition and a handsome amount in prize money. The bigger reward was that it publicised him to the world. He made it to the big league, a *somebody* in his field and people started paying serious attention to his work. But there was the animal inside that kept pushing him harder, bigger projects, more awards until it seemed he'd convinced everyone. Everyone that was, except one man.

10

A BRIGHT STAR ON THE RISE

Gabrielle Joseph readjusted her navy blue suit. The turquoise shirt underneath looked striking in comparison and complimented her burnt-umber complexion. She felt satisfied that she looked professional but confident. It was important that she made a good impression today.

Her scheduled interview for *The New Yorker* magazine, where she worked, was about to start. It was with a young photojournalist who was making big waves in the world of photojournalism: Lejf Busher. She wanted to do the interview not only because she admired the gritty, soul-baring content of the work Lejf did but also because she'd seen the exceptional quality photographs by the twenty-seven-year-old from Namibia. He was extraordinary.

It wasn't easy getting him to respond to her calls; Lejf was notorious for avoiding interviews and she had to try several times, but Gabby wasn't one of the magazine's most successful reporters for nothing. When she'd called him to set up the interview, he was doing work in Europe (he was vague about the details). Now, three months later, he was in New York City to meet with her. Her persistence paid off.

She studied his photograph for a moment. He had a strong,

handsome face, chestnut hair and light hazel eyes. There was something tragic behind those lovely eyes. These silent types, with their dark, impenetrable souls...

When Lejf walked into her office, Gabby stared at him, dumbstruck for a moment. 'I'm sorry,' she said with a girlish giggle when she noticed his awkwardness. 'I don't mean to stare but I didn't expect you to be so tall!' She extended her hand in greeting. 'Gabrielle, but everyone calls me Gabby. Good to meet you Lejf.' She also did not expect him to be this good-looking in person.

'Pleased to meet you, Gabby,' said Lejf.

'Do have a seat.' She indicated. 'Did you have a good flight? You've been to New York, I assume. How do you like it?'

'Yeah, flight was good, thanks. I've discovered that New Yorkers really love their city,' he said and pulled his mouth into a tight smile that could have meant anything.

'Is that an indirect way of telling me you *don't* like New York?' she asked in disbelief.

'I'm not much of a big-city person, to be honest. I could be the worst person to ask whether I like any big city.' He ran his hand through his hair.

Registering his uneasiness again she said, 'May I offer you bottled water?'

'That would be great, thanks.'

She handed it to him with a reassuring smile. 'You're probably right about New Yorkers; we do tend to boast about our city. To each his own. This brings me to why you are here: I've heard so many good things about the work you're doing – wow! There's quite a buzz about you in the world of photojournalism. How do you feel about that?'

Lejf shifted in his seat and shrugged. 'I appreciate the recognition, but there are many journalists out there doing great work. I'm just one voice, trying to do something meaningful...'

'Well, your work makes a difference and it's great that you're being recognised for it. Let's get started. I'll record you if you don't mind,' Gabby said. 'If you need me to stop or change anything, let me know.'

'Yup, sounds good. I'm ready.'

She sat back and pressed the button on the digital voice recorder. This was going to be interesting. She felt a tingle of excitement.

* * *

This wasn't Lejf's comfort zone. He'd much rather be out in the field, working. It was the name of the game, as they say. Gabby was professional and she seemed intuitive. He took a sip of water.

'You grew up in Namibia, a place I confess I haven't been to, but would love to visit,' she said.

'I recommend that you do. It's amazing. But then, I'm biased toward my land of big open spaces.'

'Hmm. So that's why big skyscrapers don't do it for you.'

'My idea of big skyscrapers is the dunes of the Namib desert,' he said and chortled.

'You make it sound idyllic. Let's talk about that, and what influenced you to become a photographer,' Gabby said, crossing her legs. 'How did that first big one happen, the shot of the fog over the red desert that set you on the map?'

'It was five years ago, and at the time I was struggling to get a breakthrough...' He watched her swinging foot in a high-heeled shoe – a delicate ankle peeping out from under the hem of her trousers – thinking about those tough times in Cape Town. 'Sossusvlei: that's the name of the place. The grey-blue morning fog comes swirling in from the Atlantic Ocean about an hour to the west. It's an incredible sight to see. I don't think a picture can ever do it justice.'

'How often do you go there?'

'Whenever I'm home. It's a place that beckons me.' He switched the focus from himself, not desiring to share with Gabby why it was so important to him. 'That part of Namibia has become a popular tourist destination, but people often underestimate the desert. It can be scorching hot and freezing cold, depending on the time of the day or season.'

'Can you describe what you felt when you took that photograph?'

In his mind, he was there, breathing in the fog, damp and cold. Droplets on his eyelashes and brows. The smell of the wet sand, and the rushing sound it made when his boots walked over it. Peace and an aching longing intermingled. How did he express all those feelings? They were hard to put into words, and words felt redundant. He answered with a half-truth, 'I don't really remember what I felt in that split second, but being there, I knew something special could happen at any moment. As my mom would say, it was a gift from the desert.'

'Do you consider yourself a restless person? Is that why you became a photojournalist?'

He twisted his mouth. 'My profession suits me well, I guess. As a child, I dreamed of roaming the world. The paradox is that there's the longing for freedom, yet my heart seems chained to where I was born and raised. I grew up in Otjiwarongo; that's in the middle of somewhere and nowhere. No matter where I go, Namibia will always be a place that draws me back.'

'Odjiwa...'

'O-tji-wa-ron-go. It's kind of tricky to say quickly for the first time. Otji, for short.'

'Otji – I like that. You work all over the globe. What kind of projects do you enjoy most, and do you have a preference for working in Africa or abroad?'

'I did a lot of work for *Go*, *The Great Outdoors* and *Getaway* magazines in both Namibia and South Africa when I started. I enjoy doing projects that inspire me as an artist and journalist to tell the human saga. The most satisfying assignments are the special edition features for magazines with a strong focus on environmental and social issues, like *Africa Geographic*, *National Geographic* and *Time*. Wherever the story is, that's where I want to be.'

'I imagine it can be easy for people to perceive your life as the enviable life of a roamer. What would you say to them?' Gabby asked.

'In a way, it is. I'm free to come and go as I wish, and I can experience world cultures. The unseen exigencies of the job, however, are far from glamorous: long hours of backbreaking work, often fruitless days and no voice but my own to encourage and keep me company – not the most stimulating conversations. I live in a tent or an impersonal hotel room for lengthy periods of time. When you choose this career, you become like a nomad of the desert, packing up and moving around. The way to survive is adaptability. It is either that or burnout.'

He took another sip of water, and she waited for him to continue. 'There are advantages to living like this: it doesn't allow me to grow too accustomed to material possessions, except for my cameras, of course. It has its drawbacks too. It's not great for relationships.' Gabby lifted her brow in anticipation, but he didn't say more. When people he loved needed him, he wasn't around, and likewise, he was deprived of their company when he craved it most. 'For this reason, I call my parent's home mine and use it as a base when I pass through. I lived in Cape Town with my youngest brother for a few years but he's also skidding all over the world now.' There'd been no point in keeping the flat in Cape Town once Erik had started doing contract work across the continent and in the Middle East.

Loneliness drove him to bear many situations he'd otherwise avoid, like living under the same roof as his father. On the other hand, there was Signe. His mother had always been a great source of comfort to him. He doubted he would opt for his dad's solo company, no matter how lonesome he felt. Even so, his dad had his moments; he had to give him that.

'What drives your passion for what you do, Lejf? What is the "why" behind it all?'

'To a large extent, it's the stories: the purpose behind every hour I spend with my camera pressed to my face.' Seeing the concentration on her face, he continued. 'Suppose all of us are individual stories and those stories merge to form what we call culture. In that case, it's reasonable for me to assume that what's happening to the world due to capitalism's influence is counter-cultural.'

Gabby sat forward in her seat, elbows on her thighs, fingers intertwined under her chin and her eyes on him. 'Okay, I'd like to hear where you're going with this …'

He looked down at his shoes. 'I wrestle over the individual's sense of self, which is inveigled into becoming homogenised. The media has too much power and people lose confidence in themselves. They follow ideas presented to them, without questioning: Is this me? Is this what I want? Or more importantly, is this what we as humans need? If there is a middle ground, then art and creativity are it. They play a fundamental role in shaping culture.' He looked at her again when he said, 'Artistic expression makes us aware of ourselves and the world around us.'

'That's such a cool take; I've never thought of it that way. Tell me where this is coming from.'

Shaking his head, thinking, he said, 'Art makes us look at life in a different way. Great philosophical questions have been born through art. Creative expression can reveal astounding truths about ourselves and the things that motivate us. It confronts us with why we do anything we do. To be part of that creative energy is the heart of this passion inside me. That's why I think a photograph has such mysterious powers.'

'What do you mean by "mysterious powers"?' she asked.

'Because of how it can transform space, time, notions and ultimately, the viewer's ability to observe something both private and inexpressible. At the same time, it makes a shared public statement. That's the essence, and I believe, the necessity of all art, and my instinct as a journalist wants to convey this vital message.'

'Why the passion for photography? Where did that start?'

'I was drawn to the medium of photography from my early childhood. It has always been the mode through which I could best express my convictions. I'm not a great verbal communicator of my feelings.' A slight smile curved around Gabby's mouth. Lejf continued. 'What pulled me in, was that what I captured remained somewhere, even if the physical thing would be gone later. It's about conceptualising the placement of an object into an eternal vacuum, to immortalise a person as they are in the moment when you capture them. I never tire of being mesmerised by that. It's as if there's a communication without words in the space between myself and what I'm witnessing.'

'That's lovely.'

'Photography is incredible. You look at a captured image, but there's so much more to it. When I photograph someone, that person's past and future linger there with them. So, I observe and become aware of something beyond the image of that person I have in view. It isn't just wanting to show what he or she looks like but that they *think*, that they *feel*. So, my narrative through my camera lens becomes more than a technical ability: it evolves into a spiritual journey of a sort.'

'Explain that to me, please,' said Gabby.

He thought about it for a while. 'The hypothesis of the influence I exert through my visual story is to bring culture back to the viewer's subconscious mind, to present them with information so they can recognise and identify with the voices of my subjects.'

'We all have an inherent need to identify with something or

someone,' she said.

'Exactly. And nothing makes you more aware of how fleeting it all is – this life and what we hope for it, what we want from it – than seeing our mortality and how the things we cling to are an illusion. That's the beauty of art: the self-reflection that comes when we observe these human emotions in another person as a still object. And we can recognise how we are mirrors of each other. In that sense, a photograph possesses magical elements: it holds you captive for a moment to make you realise that a moment is filled with a lifetime of experiences and a future yet to be discovered. How can anyone not think that mind-blowing?'

Gabby took a moment and a sip of water before she asked, 'What defines a winning photograph for you? What defines Lejf Busher, as many suppose, as a great photographer and the next big thing on the broader visual arts scene?'

'I don't know; it's hard to define such a subjective experience. There's a list of answers for aspiring novices about what makes a photo great; they can tick them off, and, chances are, they'll become a good photographer. This is no guarantee they'll be the flower that will grow taller than the rest.' These were his father's words.

Lejf knew he was such a flower, nothing more than an extra tall dandelion who had so far managed to avoid getting chomped up or trampled upon. He'd been fortunate.

'Believe me, there's nothing special about me as a man.'

Gabby did not take her eyes off him. Lejf thought it was his obvious discomfort in talking about himself, which was why he avoided looking at her when she stared at him so intently.

'Do you think people are born to do what they do in life?' she asked.

'I think that's a relative question, Gabby. Not everyone on the face of the earth is in a position to do what they desire. I'm one of the lucky few; I realise that.' On the other hand, he also knew about the hidden struggles when the longing to succeed was there, yet the scarce resources and unforeseen trouble hit him from the blindside. 'If I know one thing for sure, it's that photography is all I've ever wanted to do. I have no ambition for anything else.'

Yes, photography was the force that spurred him on and it was also the source of his most significant conflicts both internal and external. And there were many such battles, which he didn't share with Gabby.

'This is going to be a wonderful feature, Lejf. Thank you for doing the interview,' she said after they wrapped up.

'You're welcome.'

'I hope you don't have plans for this evening. I'd love to take you out for dinner, and hopefully change your views about New York, or at least soften you to it a tad.'

'No plans. It would be my pleasure to join you.'

She paused for a bit, weighing something. 'Please don't think I'm prying, but are you involved with anyone?'

Gabby was a good-looking woman and her smile revealed the deep dimples Lejf had noticed during the interview. He recognised the look in her eyes; he did not need to be on guard for its meaning.

There was someone he loved, but he didn't have a claim to her. However, he wasn't going to explain that to Gabby. He sensed that she understood what this was about and that she wasn't looking for a relationship with a restless travelling photojournalist anyway.

'Nope,' he said with a grin and Laia's face lit up in his mind.

11

A DANGEROUS DECISION

Upon reflection on where he stood with Laia, Lejf struggled to find a definition for it. He didn't think that even she knew. Either way, it could be called love but not a relationship. She'd been travelling with him for the past six years (ever since his career took off in 2007). There were places he didn't want her to go with him, and Laia didn't like that. He was aware, but it was a murderous world out there and he wasn't prepared to risk her safety.

He was on his way to do an assignment in the Democratic Republic of the Congo and he knew she wouldn't like what he had to tell her.

'I miss you. I haven't had you in ages,' she said over the phone, and from the luring tone in her voice, he imagined that she was lying on her sofa or on her bed.

He felt the fire in his belly and groaned. 'I wish I could be there too ... Soon. I first need to go to DRC. It's a story for *Der Spiegel*. I'll swing by from Hamburg when the project's finished.'

'Oo, I could – ' She sounded more alert.

'No, no. Not this one,' he cut her short. 'It's much too volatile there at the moment.'

'Lejf, c'mon!'

'No, Laia, it's out of the question. You've seen the news. The rebels are waging war against the government, hundreds of thousands of Congolese have been displaced; it's chaos over there. I refuse to expose you to the danger.' The situation in DRC was scarcely the place for a nosy reporter.

It was impossible not to become affected by what he captured on film, but not everyone would be able to endure seeing such human suffering. This job wasn't for the faint-hearted. And Laia? Suppose he could ensure she was protected from harm; it would torment her. She might disagree on how much she could handle, but it was easier said than done.

She was pissed off. 'Excuse me. *Refuse*? As if you have a right to decide what I may or may not do. There are women journalists who go on such assignments, Lejf. I'm under no illusion you've had a woman accompany you.' He chuckled; it was uncharacteristic for Laia to be bitchy. Did he dare to imagine she was jealous? Her voice told him she didn't find his amusement amusing, and she said, more defiantly, 'Tourists go there to see the mountain gorillas. They go on guided tours. I'd be safe in a group.'

'No, you wouldn't; a group is no guarantee, Laia. Besides, I won't be in Virunga. We'll be working in Kivu. I wouldn't be able to live with myself if something happened to you. No way. There's a civil war going on.' He didn't budge.

'Just stuff it then, Lejf!' She was out of good humour for a while after.

Laia, for all her soft-heartedness, could be passive-aggressive and obstinate; Lejf had discovered that aspect of her personality in varying degrees. It wasn't inconceivable that she would bypass him and decide to go by herself. He hoped she wouldn't.

A DANGEROUS DECISION

* * *

His mission to DRC wasn't to cover the wars and infighting but to check out some of the cobalt mining activities in Rubaya, in North Kivu, an area notorious for its staggering crime rate.

DRC mined over 70 per cent of global cobalt, a raw material used in electronic devices, rechargeable lithium-ion batteries and electric vehicles. About 50 per cent of the output from these cobalt mines was from foreign-owned firms, and the majority were owned by Chinese investors, whose rechargeable battery industry accounted for more than half of the worldwide cobalt demand.

His investigation had two threads: one was the horrible practice of child labour at the mines. It was illegal in DRC, but state officials allowed it to slip underneath the radar. The other was the incongruity of cobalt as a vital component in renewable energy versus the negative impact the immediate mining of the mineral had on the environment because of excessive carbon dioxide and nitrogen dioxide emissions.

There was a right and a wrong way of doing things in life. It pained him that his father failed to understand why he was so driven to do this work, but Lawrie agreed, at least to an extent, when Lejf told him, 'Companies are aware when they cross the line, but who speaks up when they do? They become untouchable gods in their inflated minds and need to be held accountable. For-profit organisations look at balance sheets to increase the value of shares, but who looks at the value of an individual's life? The mining industry has appalling statistics when it comes to ethics. I feel compelled to bring these things to light; as a journalist and as a thinking and feeling human being.'

'Yes, that may be so, but should you place yourself in harm's way to do it, Lejf?'

'How else will consumers be informed, Dad? Big tech firms are under pressure from humanitarian and environmental groups, and that's a good thing. Journalists can go into inaccessible places and shine a light on how the global demand for technology, which the tech companies fuel, comes at the expense of innocent people and the earth, and then consumers can make better decisions regarding their technology usage.'

Lawrie said, 'I agree that innocent people are the ones who suffer, and that's a shame. Don't you think it will be one more accusation against unfair practices pinned up against a notice board that no one will stop to read? Will those people's lives change from you being there?'

'It won't outright change their lives. In time, it will. That's why creating constant awareness is important.'

'But it changes you. You are changed every time you come back from such an assignment. Are you aware of that, Lejf?'

'Yes, I suppose I'm changed. How could I view anything with the same criterion when confronted by realities that shatter this illusionary world?' He gestured. 'As long as there's the hope that people's lives will be changed for the better, I'll continue doing what I do. The only way to change their circumstances is to prompt awareness, and that's what I'm doing, Dad.'

'This so-called illusionary world you're referring to has real people living in it too,' Lawrie said, and they left it there.

It was 2013 and things looked bleak, at least from one perspective. For a photojournalist commissioned to uncover sensitive issues in a place of political upheaval required discretion. They couldn't simply stroll in with notepad in hand and a camera slung around their neck, asking questions left and right.

A task force gathering information about acquiring resources in DRC allowed Lejf and his colleague, Andrew Watson, a seasoned and respected British photojournalist, to travel with them. They had fabricated job titles, and the agreement was that the company wouldn't be named. The task force was aware of the journalists' assignment and the prestigious magazine they represented. Lejf would have liked to believe that his and Andrew's presence in their group was weighing on their conscience. Reality was seldom in line with naïve hope. They had two opposing objectives: the acquiring company had to find the money tree, and any problems could be fixed later. On the other hand, Lejf and Andrew had to expose the gaffes they were willing to overlook and report on those indiscretions.

'Do you think humans are all mad – our need for money and the lengths we would go to for it?' Lejf asked Andrew. The humidity was suffocating and with every pothole they struck, his head banged against the roof of the car they were travelling in as it manoeuvred over the rugged roads. They couldn't see ahead because of the dust from the car in front of them carrying the task force. He and Andrew sat in the back, absorbing the scene of the inverted human termite mounds with thousands of people scurrying in and out like ants.

'In an ideal world, we'd all get by through each other's generosity. Unfortunately, we don't live in such a generous world. Capitalism has made some royalty and most slaves,' Andrew answered.

Lejf liked Andrew. They'd been on a few assignments together and shared the same views. Andrew was much more experienced and, as he described it, 'beyond the point of being surprised by bullshit'. He was the kind of journalist Lejf hoped to be: straightforward and he had integrity.

'How many kids do you think work in these mines, Andy?'

'The officials would say none. However, statistics show that around 16 per cent of small-scale miners are children.'

'Look at them; they're barely older than toddlers. What a life for a child,' Lejf said.

'As a father of a six-year-old son, I can't imagine that. He's the same age as many of these kids.'

Lejf indicated with a lift of his chin. 'Tell that to the lot in the car in front of us who are willing to look the other way. So much for international standards that require supply chain due diligence. What a travesty.'

They walked around, never leaving the group, and Lejf and Andrew took photographs with their phones. They could only speak to people here and there. Basic questions. The workers didn't speak English, and although Andrew spoke French and could translate for Lejf, they had to remain cautious.

'What is your son's name?' Lejf asked a man.

'Nsombe.' The child was a skeleton-like figure who, like everyone else, was covered in mining dust from head to toe and whose tired, vacant eyes seemed not to register the strangers' presence.

'How much money do you make from working here?' he asked another man, with Andrew translating.

'Two dollars a day,' the man answered, and he looked relieved, if not grateful to reveal this.

Andrew said, 'He says he is one of the fortunate ones. He can feed his family.'

The ill-fated children and pitiful men and women's stories spoke for themselves. It didn't need verbal or printed words: misery was one of the most identifiable of body languages; it was a cry for help from one human soul to another. When he closed his eyes, Lejf was haunted by them. It was a shame that many people chose to avert their eyes from such realism as if it would make it disappear, like if they switched the thought, the problem would be gone.

His father said he was the dreamer. Ironic.

**

After they completed the assignment in Rubaya, Lejf sent Laia a text:

A DANGEROUS DECISION

I know this isn't what you'd hoped for, but I'm offering a consolation and a truce. I'm on my way to Virunga to film them for you. Friends again?

She replied:

It's bittersweet. Hurry! I need you here to accept your truce and to show my appreciation.
  P.S. Sorry for the bitchiness.

Flying over the dark green Congolese jungle to Virunga National Park, thick mist hanging between the canopies of trees, he regretted that she wouldn't experience it with him. In Goma, they had to take ground transportation to Bukima, a tented camp on the perimeter of the Mahura forest. The views of Mount Mikeno and Mount Nyiragongo were incredible. Laia would have loved that sight. Virunga wasn't that far, but it felt like a great distance from the harsh truth they'd experienced in Rubaya.

Lejf's decision to go to Virunga could be interpreted as unfortunate or unwise. That he could have brushed with death, in a politically tumultuous place, wouldn't have been unusual. The hand of fate was an altogether unpredictable matter.

In the dense, lush environment of the Congo, a silent threat loomed in the shadows everyday: the jungle was the perfect habitat for venomous snakes. Although the guides took care to move the brush out of the way as they walked along, Lejf, out of a group of ten people, had the misfortune of crossing paths with a cobra. He was a tall man. The size of his frame and boots must have intimidated the snake into striking.

He managed to yell out, 'Forest cobra! This one's not a heel-biter; feisty bugger got me in the thigh.' He reached into his backpack for the emergency kit before falling into a useless lump of flesh.

There was a great commotion as the guys sprang into action around him. He saw it all through a strange lens, as if he was filming them in slow motion. Sweaty faces, low voices and fearful eyes looking into his; like they saw death there.

Forest cobras were lethal killers, capable of injecting their potent neurotoxic venom faster than black mambas – a grown man could die in 30 to 100 minutes if left untreated. A few critical things saved his life that day: they hadn't walked too far into the forest, he always carried polyvalent antivenom with him in remote places, and Andrew, who had decided last minute to join him in Virunga, was able to administer the antivenom and kept him breathing through artificial resuscitation.

It must have been hell for those men to carry his paralysed lumber log of a body back to the vehicle as quickly as they did. Thanks be to adrenaline, nature's wonder drug for emergencies. Lejf had read that, in a case of such neurotoxic envenomation, the victim appeared dead but could hear everything, and he discovered that truth for himself.

At the camp, he was given oxygen from a tank and rushed to a hospital in Goma, where he was put on a respirator. When he awoke, two days after an induced coma, his father was sitting beside the bed. It took Lejf a while to register where he was and what had happened. His dad's brow was creased into a deep frown, but Lejf couldn't tell if it was out of concern or agitation.

'Andrew called me,' Lawrie explained.

Lejf managed a croaky, 'Oh.' His throat was sore, and his voice was hoarse. Lawrie held a glass of water for him to sip. 'Hi, Dad.' He felt like crying at the sight of his father, and Lawrie, too, wiped his eyes like he wanted to get rid of something bothersome.

'Hello, son.'

Lejf supposed the rush of emotion was to be expected after a near-death experience, but he felt grateful that his father was there. 'I didn't get to see the gorillas after all,' he said, attempting a smile.

'Ah well, I checked and at least the snake's all right. A little shaken over the ordeal, but he'll be okay.' Lawrie looked down, wringing his hands – an all-too-familiar sign when he brooded over something.

The doctor told Lejf, 'You are a lucky young man. Not many people make it after a forest cobra bite. We need to keep you here for a few more days for observation; then, you may go home. But no running around for a while; you'll need plenty of rest.'

Lejf saw the vein near his dad's right eye throbbing like a red light. Lawrie ended up staying in his hotel room. Andrew gave him Lejf's camera equipment and bag he'd kept for safety.

They flew back to Windhoek, and the 253km drive to Otji felt longer than driving non-stop to Johannesburg. Lejf knew what his dad was thinking. Of course, in his mind, he linked what had happened, to Lejf's job, disregarding that snake bites were a common occurrence anywhere in Africa, even where they lived. Lawrie didn't say anything, but stared at the road ahead, gripping the steering wheel and moping.

As they approached the outskirts where the satellite dishes on the rooftops of houses shone like a brilliant cluster of stars, illuminating the small planet Otjiwarongo, Lawrie broke the silence. 'I hope you understand what this kind of thing does to your mother, Lejf. She's been beside herself with worry.'

Lejf knew his mother would have been worried, and he felt awful about that, but hearing his father's words, and how he spoke them, made the old stubbornness stew. 'Do you think I stepped on that snake on purpose, Dad? Is that why you're throwing the guilt card at me?'

Lawrie pulled over to the side of the road and turned to look at him, eyes blazing. 'It's far more than that, and you know it. What do you think happens when you go off on assignments to those places where people get kidnapped ... murdered? Do you think your mother and I have a peaceful night's rest? She tells me how proud she is of you for the work you do and for your courage. When we received the phone call that you'd been hospitalised, the doctor had told us to expect the worst – the *worst*! I had to beg some sense into her not to go to DRC with me, and I thank God she didn't see you lying there on the brink of death.'

Lejf swallowed a biting remark. 'I'm sorry if I've made you and Mom worry, Dad. This is what I do, and not everything about it is dangerous, but there are situations that can be. If you could have seen those young kids whose childhoods are wasted away digging dirt for the profit of big corporations ... If I had to lose my life in bringing awareness about their plight, I'd do it. Those poor people in DRC die a little every day, under burdens they didn't choose, and one day, when they're dead and buried, there'll be no one to mourn them. Doesn't that make you want to weep?'

His father turned his head to look out the window, a faint sob escaping as he said, 'And don't your mother and I deserve to have you alive instead of mourning *your* death?'

His words crushed Lejf, but he didn't answer. What kind of response would have satisfied his father?

Signe stood at the door when they stopped in the driveway. She held his face between her hands, her blue eyes swimming with tears as she ran her thumbs over the dark circles under his eyes.

'Close call. Sorry, Morsa,' he said and hugged her tight.

She sighed long. '*Ja, alldeles för nära* ... much too close, my love.' She hooked her arm in with his, pressing her face against his upper arm. 'This is Africa: a wild place. You are here now, and that's what matters. Come, let's get you comfortable.'

His mother had called Laia to let her know what had happened, and she called once while he was in the hospital. He told her not to bother since the reception was too poor.

He called her and she was distraught. 'Oh my soul, Lejf! Are you okay?'

'I'll be fine. Sorry about not delivering on my promise …'
'Don't be daft. I feel terrible; that's why you almost – '
He interrupted. 'Please stop feeling guilty. Raincheck, okay?'
'Just get better.'

All he could think of was, thank the stars above, she hadn't been there to see him taking a hit on that jungle path, or worse: it could have been her. After that, he was more adamant about her going with him on specific trips.

In bed after a shower, Singe sat next to him and fussed like a mother hen while he ate something. 'I'm okay,' he reassured her. He felt less than great, but he didn't want to admit that out loud, since his dad's silent presence loomed like an ominous shadow down the hall.

'He was shaken by this, älskling.'

'You don't have to play mediator for us, Mom. Dad and I sort things out best by not talking about them. You know that.'

'I'm not. It wouldn't hurt to show some compassion, Lejf. You have your way of dealing with things, and your father has his. Just remember he is still your father.'

To his relief, he and his dad avoided each other during his recuperation. The incident opened his eyes to how much his parents worried about his safety. His dad had told him years ago that the consequences of his life choices wouldn't be his alone; as his parents, they would also carry the burden. He understood what his dad had meant. He couldn't ease their fears, and he battled with himself because he didn't know the solution or how to reassure them.

His trip to the DRC was one Lejf looked back on with mixed feelings. Not only had he come close to losing his life, but any chance of winning his father's support for what he did for a living – so he would believe for many years.

12

THE SEED OF DOUBT IS A PRICKLY THING

In 2018 – the year Laia turned thirty-seven – she exhibited signs of early-onset midlife anxiety. Lejf wasn't aware, but through a string of unfolding events, he was forced to acknowledge the reality. The long periods of distance between them and the expectations he didn't feel he had a right to impose on her took their toll.

He'd outgrown the childish notion that she was living a chaste life when he wasn't around or that she was saving herself for him. As a result, he too, had taken the survival route of sex without commitment and consequences during years filled with excruciating absences from her – the body's betrayal of its own heart.

There had been a shift in their relationship when she started travelling on assignments with him; there was an intensity when they connected. They said the words, 'I love you.' They behaved as people did when they were in love. The problem was that the physical separation between them widened the space connecting those feelings and expressions of affection. What else could you do to kill the time with so much latitude?

Saying, 'I love you,' wasn't enough. People said all kinds of things in the heat of passion, which made 'I love you' a watered-down phrase. They loved for the short time they were together, and then went their separate ways.

Yet Laia was the woman Lejf wanted, and if he was honest with himself, his biggest failure was that he couldn't admit that to her. He didn't dare to consider that she needed him body and soul. For how could she? She liked her independence. She would not allow a man to hold her down. Why would he be an exception? What could he offer her? And so he rationalised: they were in love but didn't place demands on each other. That was the story he told himself.

It became a conviction when he told himself the same story for long enough.

He'd made peace with the fact that she'd decided to stay in Karlsruhe. It made sense; there were many more opportunities there than she would have had in either Cape Town or Johannesburg. These were her real options in Southern Africa. She'd been working for a research company that created biomechanics since graduating and was happy there.

They saw each other when Lejf was somewhere in Europe, when he visited her in Karlsruhe, or when she was in Otji and, on occasion, they hooked up in Cape Town. Those times were few, but he longed for them as much as he longed for the burn of the Namibian sun.

The way he thought of Laia in her world was that she had stability. Everything in her daily existence was bundled together in the place she lived and worked. She needed that life of anchored security, her habits and routines. That was Laia: steady and where she could ruminate and plan her day.

On the other hand, he moved around. His life consisted of variables; a planned day could bring disruptions. Not everything went according to schedule: the weather could change, a broken-down or stuck vehicle could cause hours of delay, his camera and equipment could fail while he was filming, working with people, who were by nature temperamental, and many other unforeseen factors. Of course, he had to plan for certain projects months in advance, but there were plenty of times he went out on an assignment spontaneously. The fluidity and inconsistency in his existence were the fuel that spurred him on, and he needed that.

He and Laia each valued their independence, but the significant difference between their needs was that Laia's compact, sheltered world was her oyster, while the big wide world was his. They couldn't find a permanent way to each other through the vastness between them. Despite all the uncertainty that kept them apart through the years, there was always a pull toward each other. Always that pull.

Lejf visited her in Karlsruhe not long before a North American project was due to start, which he'd asked her to go on with him. He loved her little haven. Everything in Laia's place was arranged with purpose. It was a rich, well-organised mini-space; her private world, and whenever he was there, he felt like he'd merged and become a part of that.

When he first mentioned the colours, she said, 'It's simpler to express how I feel by using colours – they're often easier than words.' He nodded with a grin, and she explained, 'I wear my mood to the office, but I find that too dull. Here in my home, I can be in every mood without fearing judgement. It's like a colourful rebellion.'

'Who would judge you for being too colourful?' he asked.

'I don't know, mad colourphobics.' She shrugged, laughing behind her wine glass as they sat on a Tabriz rug he'd bought on a trip to Iran, two years prior, for her thirty-fifth birthday. It was one of the off-limits trips for her, and it had been a heated issue. The subtle blue and brown hues blended with everything else. 'They remind me of you, Lejf. You are the colours of the earth and sky, of freedom.'

He remembered that moment: side-by-side, with their backs resting against the sofa, he'd had his fingers in her hair while her head relaxed back against his hand, her eyes half-closed. He'd leaned over and kissed her at the base of her neck, a warm, wet kiss travelling up to her chin, and her chuckle-groan vibrated against his lips. It was one of many tiny moments he had stored of them.

There were bright colours everywhere around her space. They weren't frantic collisions and clashes; instead, every object was placed with care. In a way, they looked like still-life compositions, ready to be photographed. He picked up a minute blue glass jar on a counter. 'I don't know what it's for, but it was just too darling not to have,' she told him when he studied it – pretty, round, petite.

'I'll pick some of your neighbour's flowers to put in it.'

She giggled. 'They'll have to be the littlest ones.'

Her kitchen was accented to perfection: Pots and bowls of red, turquoise blue, deep orange and sap green. Lavender and soft green teacups and mugs were there when you open the cupboard. He looked at her selection of flowery aprons, and he asked, 'Why so many?'

'They're sort of a fetish.'

And, of course, books. On shelves and tables or lying around as if they were having a casual outing. It was like being on a vibrant, decorated cultural trip with Laia as his guide.

During this visit, there were subtle hints he didn't register right away.

'Lejf, would you please write a few things down for me? I need to pop in at ALDI. There's a notepad and pen right by you on the counter,' she said, going through the cabinets to see what she needed.

'Sure.' He tore off the top sheet and placed it on the counter, frowning as he was trying to decipher what was written on it because it wasn't Laia's handwriting.

While she cooked them dinner, he took wine from the fridge and studied the label. 'Hm. You've started drinking cabernet? What about your migraines?'

'I'll have some of the white, thanks,' she indicated with the spoon, not answering his question directly.

And later, when they got ready for bed and she emptied the clothes from the hamper to sort and put away, Lejf noticed the plain black socks, the kind men often wore with formal clothes.

He started to put the clues together and an icy chill came over him. Studying her face while she folded the laundry, he couldn't read her. Or he didn't want to search deeper. No, he didn't want to ask; didn't want to know. So, he tried to ignore it and to adore her for the time that remained. Whoever the stranger was, Lejf didn't want him to exist while he was with her. Despite his attempts to brush the truth aside, it consumed him on the inside: the realisation that Laia had another man in her life.

* * *

Laia met Ravi Ettlinger when her boss introduced him to the staff as a new shareholder. She didn't pay any particular interest to him, although he noticed her. He called and asked her out, but she was reluctant; not only because he was eighteen years older than her (she'd looked him up: he was fifty-five and had never been married), but she didn't think they'd have much in common. He wasn't at all bad looking and he had a certain kind of charm she found appealing, but he was also a bit of a smooth talker, and not what Laia would have considered her type.

He wouldn't take no for an answer until she agreed to go out with him. She gave in, and to her surprise, she enjoyed his flirtatious company. He told her that she was the game-changer. She sniggered at his choice of words.

Ravi was a man who was used to being in charge. He decided where they went – he took her out to elegant restaurants. He also decided with whom they hung out – tight-lipped influentials who watched and listened carefully to what was being said and liked when someone stroked their egos. Laia felt no connection to any of that. It reminded her too much of the world she'd escaped from.

She had to admit that it felt good to have someone around who fussed over her; although to a degree she wished, he wasn't so persistent. He insisted on more of her time, but she wasn't ready to commit. She knew she had to tell him about Lejf, the main reason she didn't want to commit to Ravi. She broke it to him while making dinner for them. He was sleeping over at her place more. She wanted to set the record straight before he decided to move in. He had also brought up the subject of them being exclusive.

'I know you like your little flat, your space and independence. Believe me, I know. I also think we could be good together, Laia.'

'Ravi, it's not that simple. There's someone else …'

If he were going to storm out, this would have been the time, but he stayed. He was surprised, and she thought she saw a flicker of jealousy, or it could have been annoyance.

'You didn't mention this before,' he said.

'I'm mentioning it now, because you insist on us having a relationship.'

'Is he someone important to you?'

'Yes, he is, but we have an open understanding. He doesn't live in Germany. He's from Namibia. He travels a lot and we don't see each other often, but we try to whenever we can. Sometimes I go with him, and sometimes he comes to me.'

He thought about it. 'Okay, so you have someone else who's important to you. I'm not thrilled about that but I appreciate your honesty. I'd like to be important to you too. I want to show you how much you mean to me, Laia.'

And Ravi made good on his word. Laia knew he wasn't comfortable with the idea of her being with another man and she made sure never to call Lejf or take his calls when Ravi was around.

Her problem was that Lejf was barely around and that was at the core of her conflicted state. She was always waiting for him. Waiting to make short junctures gigantic. And time with Lejf was wonderful. There was breathing space in their communication. Sometimes, the words were not words at all, but like his photographs, they were beautiful moments that spoke in silence. She and Lejf lived in a phantasmagorical world when they were together until one of them had to leave.

The leaving part was inevitable. Still, it felt like being awoken from a dream you wanted to stay in, but couldn't remember when you opened your eyes. In between the dreams was the big, black void of loneliness.

So, she let Ravi in to fill those voids. She gave him more, and he took every ounce of it until it felt as if he'd taken her over.

He was eager to introduce her to his parents. When Laia met Frau Ettlinger and the dignified lady asked questions about her family, she said, 'It's Ackermann, with a double n, Mrs Ettlinger.'

'Oh, I see ...' she said, flicking her gaze in Ravi's direction.

Laia knew she'd burst the dear woman's bubble that her son had found a Jewish girl still young enough to bear him children. She wanted to reassure Frau Ettlinger that she didn't have any plans on marrying him, but realised it would make matters worse. She opted for the familiar path of not expressing her feelings to avoid confrontation instead.

Ravi kept steering toward a permanent exclusive relationship, and she said, 'Us dating is bothering your mother.'

He waved it off, 'I'm not concerned, and you shouldn't be either.'

'You are her son. I don't want to come between the two of you, Ravi.' The truth was, she didn't want to talk about marriage, and she could feel it heading in that direction.

'Laia, I don't care about your ethnic background. I care about you. My mother will have to accept that. I'm not a child that I will be told what to do and whom to love.'

No, Ravi was a man who would never be told what to do.

However much she tried to ignore it, she couldn't dismiss the growing need inside her. Everywhere she looked, she saw pregnant women and happy couples pushing babies in strollers. During her lunch breaks she went to a park close to her work to sit and watch mommies and nannies play with their charges. She had to admit to herself: she wanted a family.

Yet Laia couldn't help feeling that something was missing. She liked Ravi but there were times she was so exhausted from being with him that she retreated and told him she had to catch up on work so she could spend time alone. Then, there were times she felt loneliness coming over her like a dense fog, and she would search for the warmth of his company.

He asked her to move in with him and she said, 'No. I'd like to keep my flat,' which, to her, symbolised her independence. It was a screaming contradiction: the simultaneous longing for autonomy and company.

'Okay, then I will move in with you,' he said.

She was running out of escape routes. She didn't tell him no but said, 'Wait, please.'

'Marry me,' he said.

She immediately wanted to say no but paused. She told him, 'I can't give you an answer now.'

'Why not? Is it because you don't want to get married, or you don't want to marry me?'

'Ravi, I need time to think.'

'How much time?'

She thought for a while. 'I want to go on a trip first.'

He looked at her and she thought he might retract his proposal. Instead he said, 'Okay, go on your trip. Do what you must do, then come back and marry me.'

She didn't tell him where she was going, but he knew who she'd be with. She wished she could be as confident as Ravi about her decision. The uncertainty frustrated her.

13

RAILWAYS AND REGRETS

The Freight Railways of North America project was a four-week trip, split into two: the first leg in Canada and the second in the United States.

Laia could only do the Canadian part of the trip with Lejf. It had been six months since he'd visited her in Karlsruhe, and he was aching to see her. She was curious about the fascinating history of the North American railways and excited to see Canada from East to West, as was he since he had not been there before.

They met up in Montréal, where they stayed for two days and explored the cobblestone streets and historic buildings of Old Montréal like young lovers seeing the world together for the first time. On their first evening they went to one of the city's renowned jazz clubs where they ate delicious, decadent food (a little too much). Laia drank dry martinis and Lejf drank local beer (enough to make them regretful the next day), and they flirted with each other, laughing at each other's embellished stories. They gave a stroke on the arm or thigh until neither of them could hold it any longer. Stumbling to their hotel room, they made love with half their clothes on.

Was he able to deny what he saw in her eyes in that maddening bliss?

Was it that she was holding something back? Did he feel, in her body's response to him violence in her longing? It was easier to reason over doubts and tell himself it resulted from his growing paranoia over her lover in Germany. Lejf didn't know what it was, and he was too scared to ask, so he went into default mode and pretended it was nothing.

Laia wanted to stay longer in Montréal, but he reminded her they had over 4,500km to cover. He didn't have much flexibility for long stayovers.

The route he'd mapped out took them through some of the cities on Canadian Pacific Railway's rail network, which it shared with Canadian National Railway: Sudbury, Thunder Bay, Winnipeg, Calgary, Campbell Creek – Kamloops and finally Port Coquitlam.

'They sound like the names on atlases and from Jack London novels I read as a boy, and imagined travelling to. Faraway places in the far north, where people are drenched in fur and ride over lakes and tundra on sleighs pulled by barking dogs,' he told her and she took his hand in hers, smiling at his boyish expression.

Vast distances lay between destinations, and they were on the road sun up to sun down from one city to the next. As they drove Lejf told Laia about the history of the Canadian Pacific Railway, the first transcontinental railway in Canada, and their biggest competitor, the Canadian National Railway. It was early summer, and although there was still a bit of snow on the ground in places, patches of greenery were starting to show. The cool morning air soon turned into a mixture of warm, bright sunlight as the hours progressed, transforming clusters of dark-shaded trees into vibrant splashes of green. The lovely scenery made Lejf's stories sound more believable.

Canada had so much water, and it was hard to wrap their minds around the scope of it: the great lakes that connected to the Atlantic Ocean through the St Lawrence River. Gigantic Hudson Bay to the north drained an area of close to four million square kilometres.

The hundred thousand lakes of Manitoba. Rivers were thousands of kilometres long. The blue and green glacial lakes of Alberta and British Columbia. The Yukon's lakes with mysterious names, like Spirit Lake, Quiet Lake and Hour Lake, to name a few. A world of water surrounded by prairies, forests, tundra and mountains. Sharp contrast to the world of high sand mountains, hard white roads and dry riverbeds they came from.

Throughout the journey, Lejf stopped in several locations to photograph the passing trains: some through a view of field grass, others at rail crossings or trans load facilities where he spoke to site managers, locomotive engineers and shipyard workers – the backbone of the business of hauling grain, coal, engine parts and intermodal goods through the ever-hurried system of freight transportation. The drivers had fascinating stories about the land they covered back and forth and the towns and cities they passed through, and they were eager to give Lejf and Laia great pointers on where to stop for the best scenery.

One such a fellow was Jerry Peterson, a locomotive engineer with a family history of train driving. His great-grandfather had experienced the end of the age of the great railways after the First World War, when passenger rail transport started making way for the automobile and aircraft industry.

Listening to him, Lejf couldn't help wondering whether Jerry had chosen this profession out of his own free will or was living up to his father's expectations. He seemed contented. Either that or else, like many people, he'd accepted, without questioning, what fate had preordained for him.

Lejf wasn't sure if avoiding conflict with your father or yourself was easier. It seemed conflict was a constant that remained, and it mattered not who its subject was.

'Of course, the freight industry wasn't gonna go anywhere with the changes happening, 'cause there's stuff that can't be shipped with an aeroplane, and boats don't sail on dry land,' Jerry told them in a thick Manitoba accent, as he'd informed them, that was where he was from when they were curious to know. In his peculiar Prairie tongue, he explained, 'My great-grandfather and grandfather lived through pretty tough times with mergers and takeovers, but here I am today, living proof that the industry has survived.' He lifted his arms emphatically.

Jerry possessed a naivety Lejf envied. Accepting your fate brought peace. Some things were not worth sleepless nights.

'I'll tell you, folks, there's nothing like feeling the vibration of steel on steel as you're slicing up the miles. Rail is in my blood. I don't have to sit in no stuffy office all day; I see this.' He gestured around. 'There's nothing I'd rather do. You two prepare yourselves to see a country that'll blow your minds.'

Whether Jerry was following his great-grandfather's legacy out of tradition or pure passion didn't change the fact that he was happy. Lejf understood his passion; he couldn't imagine doing anything other than photography.

Jerry didn't exaggerate. The most fantastical rail shots Lejf took on their journey were in the high mountain passes of British Columbia: square-eyed locomotives, bursting with a resounding whistle through the entrance of a tunnel or snaking their way across high bridges – dragging along their cargo loads with CN or CP, and the logos of international companies printed on the containers; bright graffiti on others.

Later, back in Otji, he told his parents about the great rivers and waterways of Canada, the oxygen-giving arteries of that enormous country. He also told them about Jerry's stories; of how he was happy to follow in his father's footsteps. Lawrie had an intense expression in his eyes, and he listened with what Lejf could have sworn was envy.

*　*　*

In Banff, they stayed at the Fairmont Banff Springs, formerly the Banff Springs Hotel, for two days. It was one of Canada's earliest grand railway hotels, opened by the Canadian Pacific Railway in 1888. Lejf knew when he'd made the reservations that one night would be inadequate. Laia was ecstatic that they stayed there at all.

They ambled around the busy tourist town and took a boat ride on Lake Minnewanka, surrounded by the Rocky Mountains. Lejf relished in Laia enjoying herself; it was as phenomenal as it had always been between them.

Much later and alone, he would see with greater clarity how she'd wanted to imagine everything was all right, as he did, and she avoided confronting him with the truth for as long as possible. How could they not have wanted to hold fast to such a moment, ignoring reality, when surrounded by immeasurable beauty, themselves so in love?

Soon after they crossed the Alberta-British Columbia border, the long and winding road took them through the Continental Divide at Kicking Horse Pass toward Golden. From there, they climbed up the Columbia Valley, entered Rogers Pass in the Glacier National Park, and drove through the majestic Selkirk Mountains.

'This is the boundary between Pacific and Mountain time zones, and we're travelling back in time, so to speak,' he said with a grin.

'Oh yes. Could we do that, please?' she asked.

He didn't miss the flash of melancholy in her eyes, but he talked over it. 'Rogers Pass was founded in 1881 by a surveyor, Major Albert Bowman Rogers. CP Railway needed to find a route through the Selkirk Mountains, and he was the man who delivered a plan for them.'

They got out to stretch their legs at a lookout point and for Lejf to take pictures.

'Unbelievable to think they'd pathed a way through this massive rock,' Laia said. 'This is amazing to see.'

'And they did it in four years. Can you imagine the backbreaking work, and that for a few pennies?'

'I wonder how many really lost their lives. I mean, if you think about it: they had to blast through these mountains with dangerous explosives, unprotected, carrying all those heavy railway ties and equipment, malnourished, freezing in winter, alone in a strange country and longing for their families and loved ones. That's so heartbreaking.'

'That's capitalism's trade-off.' He stared out over the vastness and said in contemplation, 'One of the greatest engineering feats of our modern era, built on the ideals of the leaders, and some would argue, with the blood of the immigrants. It seems our awe clouds our memories of history. When people look at this network of activity that fuels such an enormous part of the economy, do they remember what it cost in lives?' He turned to look at her. 'There's no mercy for the little human, Laia. Men in power are too corruptible. I see it everywhere I go.'

Of course, he took plenty of photos of Laia looking at everything, and then that perfect shot of her turning to look at him, hand in her hair to keep it from blowing in her face, big, glorious smile. Laia: beautiful and happy.

Sitting beside him, clutching his arm, she said, 'Show me what you've taken.' And he showed her, watching her reaction.

'It's going to be an incredible feature, Lejf. I'm proud of you.' The way she said it, the look in her eyes ...

From Kamloops, the drive to Vancouver was a welcome change from long days on the road for two weeks. Lejf wished she didn't have to go back so soon. Alas, everything has a beginning and an end.

The last item on his Canadian itinerary was Port Coquitlam, 27km east of Vancouver. They spent most of the afternoon at CP Railway's colossal rail yard in the city centre. He spoke to a site manager and then took photographs of the busy loading activities. Laia followed him around, never complaining, waiting for him to finish. They were eager to call it a day.

A sleepover in Vancouver and a few sights in the city the following day before taking the ferry to Victoria on Vancouver Island. Laia, head resting against Lejf's shoulder, was lost in her thoughts.

The ferry passed the islands along the way as his eyes followed the streaks on the water where other vessels had passed a short while before. All carrying travellers, some embarking on journeys, making fond memories, others returning with shattered dreams.

It could be that he'd willed his mind to believe the clock had slowed down when the truth was, the years with Laia had sped past at the speed of light, and he desired to hang on to her for dear life. Except, he felt clueless. He didn't know how to cling to her, slipping through his arms.

* * *

Their room in the stunning Hotel Fairmont Empress overlooked the Inner Habour, and the location was a short walking distance from the British Columbia Parliament Buildings and the Royal BC Museum. They spent some time there, but Laia had her unconventional idea of collecting memories, and they meandered through the streets and entered obscure stores where the concept of time stood still when they crossed the threshold. In a bookstore, he followed her as she took her time walking through the aisles, pulling out a book here and there and reading a passage to him in a low, soft voice.

She wanted to see Victoria's Chinatown. 'We must see it. I saw in a brochure that it's the second oldest Chinatown in North America next to San Francisco's,' she explained.

In a tiny shop, a tiny figure sat behind the counter and eyed Lejf's frame with suspicion. He appeared enormous in proportion to the surroundings. They were careful as they manoeuvred around the shelves full of kitschy merchandise. Laia bought a bauble to add to her colourful collection in her flat. Lejf smiled, imagining where she'd put it, then wondering with a sickening twitch of doubt if he'd get to see it there.

When he awoke that last day, he resolved to take their time together in languid sequences, adding the pearls onto the string, one by one and savouring them. Laia started stirring next to him, pulling the covers over her leg and shoulder that had been cold outside all night. She scooted closer, searching for his heat – a satisfied groan of discovering what she was looking for – and he inhaled her, wanting to be a part of every detail of her existence. His eyes and hands ran over her, loving her. She was a playful, graceful dolphin in the waves. Her hair falling in her face allowed him mere glimpses of her eyes now and then: sultry and evasive.

'Let's get a big breakfast before we go out,' she said, collapsing next to him. 'I'm starving!'

They rented a car and spent half a day at the Butchart Gardens. Lejf's senses were on high alert. He noticed everything. She wore a lilac-coloured summer dress that hugged her calves and flat leather sandals tied with straps around her ankles. When Laia moved, she floated. He could spend all day watching her, as she turned walking into an art form.

Like the butterflies and bees drinking the sweet drug of their hosts before they flew off drunk and with engorged bellies, he was the love-struck Puck, stoned by the beauty and sweet words of his Tatiana, there in that enchanted paradise. Only the two of them existed; he was cognisant of no one else. And he captured the perfect moment of his Fairy Queen, sitting on her throne bench, looking around and then at him with love shining in her eyes.

'Come sit here with me for a while, Lejf.' She extended an inviting hand – a truce for what was to come.

At last, the magical juice from the love-in-idleness flower didn't have permanent sway over them and wore off.

'Here's to all our trips,' Laia said as she lifted her champagne flute during dinner.

'To all our trips, past and future.' He took a sip. She looked into his eyes for a brief second, then looked down with a rueful smile. He heard himself saying without much conviction, 'There'll be more.' The sip of champagne went down like a big glass marble that got stuck in the middle of his chest where all the fear and paranoia had been stewing.

A moment's silence. 'There is someone; we've been seeing each other for a while now, Lejf.' At last, an admission. He nodded and she added, 'He knows about you.'

'Why are you telling me this now? A bit late, don't you think?' He struggled to get the words out.

'I'm sorry, I wanted to, but I didn't want to spoil our trip.'

'And now that the trip's over? What does any of this mean for us, Laia? Are you going to go back to him? Will he allow you to see me again? Is that the arrangement?' His heart was pounding in his ears.

'He's asked me to marry him, and I haven't accepted his proposal, but I'm considering.'

The marble hit his stomach with force. 'He's asked you to marry him, yet he's allowed you to come on this trip with me. How generous of him,' Lejf said, blowing out a slow breath to try and calm his racing pulse.

'I told him I wanted to come before I gave him an answer. I wanted to be sure it's the right decision.'

'And are you sure now?'

She nodded and said, 'I think so, yes.'

Lejf poured and drank a full glass of champagne. The air didn't circulate well through his airway; it was too tight, and his clothes felt wrong and uncomfortable. He wanted to be outside to catch his breath, throw off his clothes, dive into the dark ocean and live there. Or die there.

She took his hand, and her eyes were tragic. 'I'm sorry, Lejf. I didn't want to hurt you like this.'

'Good God, Laia. Why didn't you tell me you couldn't come on the trip in the first place?'

'Because I wanted to come on this trip with you.'

'Why?'

'For old times' sake, I suppose.'

'Why did you withhold telling me?'

'Would you have let me come then?'

Would he have let her join him? He didn't answer.

'Do you love him?' Did he somehow hope she'd tell him his love – the fragmented version he'd been giving her for years – surpassed whatever this unknown man would give her? The truth had caught up with him.

'He has stability, and he loves me.'

'That's not what I asked. Do you love him? It's a reasonable question, Laia.'

'I care about him. I could grow to love him.' She turned, and looked at something somewhere in her mind. 'It's this growing old alone thing.'

'You're not alone. We have each other.'

'What about each other is it that we have, Lejf? And that for five, maybe six weeks out of the year. It's not enough. I thought I could do that, but I don't know if I want to anymore.'

'You said you wouldn't let a man tie you down. Are you tired of us?'

'I didn't say I won't allow a man to love me. You're putting words in my mouth. It's the loneliness I'm tired of. It feels good to have someone around who … who's around.'

'We could work something out, Laia. Find an alternative.'

'How? What? You'd hate living in Germany, and I like my life there. And I wouldn't expect you to give up your work for me. You *have* to do what you do. There's no question about that. I've been thinking about this a lot, Lejf. We aren't kids anymore, and I can't see how we'll be together. Not permanently. We need to be realistic and move on with our lives.'

'That's impossible! You and I can't stay away from each other, and you can't deny that.'

'Are you not hearing me? I'm saying to you that we are not together enough, and I'm lonely, Lejf. It gets unbearable. I may be presumptuous, but I don't think you feel it as much as I do when you move around. It distracts from the loneliness. The emptiness surrounds me; it reminds me every day. And I'm a woman, getting older. The rules are different for women; they are.'

'Of course, I feel lonely Laia, but not so much that I'd compromise.'

'No, you shouldn't compromise, not for me or anyone else. It would change you.'

'Change *me*? I'm talking about *you*. How will it change you Laia, being married to someone you don't love?'

The thought of Laia married to someone else. The marble was ricocheting off walls now.

She looked down at her hands. 'Well, it's impossible to settle for anything less than this, so I may as well try.'

The awful, unbearable silence between them lasted three billion years. Here he stood under the spotlight: his inability to communicate what he felt highlighted in this brutal moment. And another truth was revealed: Laia had decided on happiness, and she was willing to find it without him, crushing the illusion he'd been living under that being somewhere in her world had been enough. But it had been his pipe dream, not hers. He'd looked at the two of them through the wrong side of the telescope lens.

'So, Laia, we're going to finish the champagne, then we're going to go up to our room and make love one last time, and tomorrow you're going back to Germany to get married. Is that the plan?'

'Yes. That's how I'd like it to be. One last time. Could you do that for me, please?'

Lejf already knew it was possible to die more than once. He'd died many small deaths in Laia's arms. This was a different kind of death.

14

YOU'RE A SCREWED-UP MAN, LEJF BUSHER

Events flowed one into the other in a blur. Lejf had two weeks in the US to complete the second leg of the Railways project, and all he wanted to do, was to get the hell out of there. A great weariness had taken hold of him, shrivelling him up as if his body was collapsing into itself like an inflatable doll with a slow puncture.

Nat Geo had assigned another photographer to work with him. Lejf had seen what stuff she was made of in articles and exhibitions before: she was first-rate. He'd been thrilled at the prospect when they'd planned the project. Timing was everything, as the saying went.

He met up with Natalia Bencivenga, a pretty, petite Italian with dark Mediterranean features, in Spokane, Washington and, to his shame, his attitude wasn't warm and inviting. She seemed unfazed, neither curious nor sympathetic about his moody silences. They had a job, and she might have been more than willing to see that they did it in time and in a professional manner.

Despite his funereal aloofness, Lejf was able to muster up the strength to produce high-quality photography of the northern rail routes operated by BNSF and Union Pacific Railways, running from the Pacific Northwest through the upper Midwest to Chicago in the east. That was the thing about the camera in his hand: it became his brain and took control of his senses and motor skills. All it needed was for him to hold it to his eye.

Each day they trekked from west to east, he traced the imaginary line separating the US from Canada – going back to meet Laia at the starting point. To undo the wrong. To make a new beginning. He was running to stand still.

His heart was a mangled mess, but he wasn't planning on unloading his emotional burden on a stranger. It suited him that Natalia appeared disinterested in the reason behind the storm clouds in his eyes.

Yet, when he was on the road and found himself at an inn in Essex, Montana, a town with a population of less than fifty and an average age of sixty-five, and he had plenty of time to spare when the sun went down, Lejf became much more aware of the physical attributes and wily ways of his female colleague. All of a sudden he noticed the seductive look in her eyes and the way she circled the glass of bourbon with the tip of her finger while licking her lips. How she spoke with an accent that seemed way too exotic for the surroundings but fitted her whole vibe to a T. He allowed the spicy, amber liquid to burn its way down his throat, numbing the pain for a while. He didn't consider how it clouded his judgement.

Natalia – true character revealed through the gift of fermented mash – wasn't the kind of woman who beat about the bush; her intentions were laid out on the round wooden table between them: she wanted him and told him so plainly. 'I want you, Lejf.'

'I thought you were ignoring me because you couldn't stand me.' He sniggered, his warm breath fogging up the glass.

'You don't know anything about women; I can see that. I was only playing hard to get,' she said and laughed, tracing the veins on the back of his hand with her fingernail.

There wouldn't be any rejection here tonight; he could see *that*. With a lift of his brow and leaning closer to her, he said, 'As a matter of fact, I know quite a bit about women. My mother wrote a manual for me and my brothers when we were boys: the A-to-Z of what a woman wants and all that. We learned things they don't teach in school.'

'How in–te–res–ting... You sound like you have an amazing mother.'

'Yup, I do. I can show you if you like.'

She frowned. 'Do you carry this manual around with you, or are you going to pull out pictures of your mother?'

He laughed. 'Neither. The knowledge is all in here.' He pointed at his head.

She sat back, arms folded, and said, 'Okay then, show me this A-to-Z knowledge of yours. Let's see if you can teach me something new.'

So, as per her request, Lejf unburdened his wisdom on her, and she took him in, loving and cradling him. And he cried out for Laia and all his wasted opportunities with a sob.

The fog cleared away, with it the dread that he may have unbosomed too much in the heat of passion. His handling of the situation was poor the following day. He didn't know if Natalia wanted to keep things light, without strings, but his sombre state lacked decorum, and he couldn't afford her the opportunity. He was the classic jerk. Unsurprising, it made her sullen with him and left the air between them intolerable for the rest of the trip. They worked in complete silence, speaking only when necessary and avoiding each other at the lodgings. He also avoided all other female interactions. He wasn't on a winning streak.

After finishing the project, he and Natalia parted ways with her sweet words, 'I think you're the most talented photographer I've worked with. I can see big things for you, Lejf. You're a beautiful but screwed-up man. I hope for your sake you sort yourself out. Life's too short to carry shit around.' To the point, honest, practical. He couldn't have agreed with her more on the screwed-up part.

Nat Geo was over the moon with the results, and then he went one short of a dozen.

* * *

The plan was for Lejf to visit Erik in Dubai, where he'd been working on a two-year contract after the Railways project was finished. He bought a ticket to Karlsruhe instead. Erik wasn't happy that he ditched him, but when you were on a self-destructive mission, the last thing you considered was how your disregard for pre-arranged plans affected others.

Obsession could trick you into justifying any dreadful thing under the sun. And so, he convinced himself that he would watch them from a distance, that's all. See what the man looked like, what they looked like together, and then he'd leave.

It seared, like a red-hot poker thrust into his heart, seeing them coming out of her building, holding hands, laughing. He was older than Lejf had imagined: his hair was thinning and he had a slight midlife paunch. With her high heels on, Laia was a fraction taller than him. He kissed her long, his hands on the small of her back, pressing her against him, before getting in his car and driving off.

His Laia, holding and looking at that man with such affection. Were they married? Possibly. He hoped they weren't. He had no idea how he expected to change things with zero strategy.

While you were doing something like that, the knowledge that it was wrong was in your mind. Watching her this way was an abhorrent invasion of her privacy, but Lejf couldn't stop himself, and he didn't want to stop himself, so he pushed reason aside, as he had done many times before. Like a loathsome, slimy creature crawling out of the gutters, he sat with his twisted insides, nurturing his self-pity and misery, and watched them, not bothering to shave and barely eating. In the morning, they left for work – Laia in her Volkswagen, her lover in his expensive Mercedes Benz. She got home around 6 pm. Her fiancé's car pulled up in front of the building past seven.

Vivid scenarios played through Lejf's mind of what was happening behind the walls of Laia's flat. She would have cooked for them; she seldom ate at restaurants. Laia was a house mouse who liked her comfortable nooks where she could put her feet up. She didn't want noisy crowds. She and Lejf were both unsocial and valued each other's company for that reason.

He walked around the building to the side, where he could see their faint shadows passing behind the drapes. Her bedroom light went on after she got home from work – when she liked taking a shower – and then it went on around ten before bed. Lejf visualised them making love, her lover's hands on her, her cry of release. It stoked the madness, and he wanted to break through the window and yank the git's heart out as his had been ripped out. Someone peeped around the corner of the building and gave him a dubious look when they saw him hovering around. It could have been a neighbour, and he left.

He drank into a mindless stupor each night in his hotel room to anaesthetise the pain and rage. Nobody knew where he was, and he ignored Erik and Signe's calls and texts.

On the thirteenth night, unable to hold it in longer, he called Laia at eleven thirty, drunk and miserable. 'Hi, Laia.'

She didn't speak and he could hear her breathing into the microphone, perhaps collecting her sleepy thoughts. The rustling of bedsheets and a soft, *'Es ist Iben, ich nehme es in der Küche. Geh wieder schlafen.'*

Why did it please him that she told a lie? He heard her close the door behind her.

'Hello, Lejf,' she almost whispered.

'How are you, Laia?'

'I'm fine, thank you. Is something wrong? Where are you?'

'No, nothing wrong, nothing wrong.'

'Lejf, where are you? Your mom and Erik called to ask if you're here with me. What's going on?' There was genuine concern in her voice.

'Don't worry. Nothing's going on. Miss you, ish all.'

She took a few seconds. 'How much have you had to drink?'

'A little. More than a little.'

'Lejf,' she groaned. 'It's late, and I have to get up early for work tomorrow.'

'I know you do. I'm sorry. Just wanted to hear your voice, Laia.'

'Oh, Lejf. Where are you?'

'I'm here in DC.' He made up a quick lie.

'How did the rest of your trip go? Nat Geo must be pleased.'

'Everything went great. They love it.'

'When will it be published? I can't wait to see it.'

His sweet Laia. He knew she meant it. 'It will be out in January's issue. Full spread.'

'That's wonderful. You should take some time off now; clear your mind. Didn't you say you were going to visit Erik?'

'That was the plan ... is the plan. In fact, I'm on my way to warm Dubai.'

'You didn't tell me why he and your mom were looking for you.'

'The project ran past schedule. We were working in high mountain passes with no cellphone reception. I forgot to let them know, but they do now, so no worries.' The lie begat many lies. After a long silence, he asked, 'Was that him you'd spoken to earlier?'

'Yes, that was Ravi.'

'Ravi. A bit old for you, don't you think?'

'What do you mean, too old for me? How would you know?' She sounded wary.

'I don't. I'm being impertinent. Are you married, then?'

'No, not yet. We shouldn't be talking about this, Lejf. I don't want to cause you any more pain.'

'I can't believe you're going to marry someone else, Laia. I messed up, didn't I? Tell me, have I wasted all my chances?'

He heard a voice in the background, and she said, *'Alles ist gut. Ich bin fast fertig.'* In a hushed voice she said, 'I must get to bed, so I'm saying goodbye now.' There was a pause. 'Please take care of yourself, Lejf. Will you? Goodnight.'

'Goodnight … Laia, wait!' he yelled, but she'd already hung up. He wanted to tell her he loved her. He drank until he passed out on the bed with his clothes on.

The next morning, he was again parked across the street from Laia's place. Ravi came out and looked around. He must have felt Lejf's eyes on him because he turned his gaze and looked him straight in the eye. Laia came out of the building, and they spoke as Ravi nodded in Lejf's direction. Her demeanour changed in an instant to tense and on guard. Ravi took out his phone, but she stopped him. Lejf could hear them talking.

Ravi was agitated. *'Nein, ich rufe die Polizei. Dein Nachbar im Jahr 204 hat ihn herumschnüffeln sehen. Sie beschrieb einen Mann, der wie dieser Typ aussieht,'* he said, pointing at Lejf. *'Er ist ein verdammter Stalker!'*

So it was a neighbour who'd seen him.

'Das wissen wir nicht, Ravi.'

Although Laia kept trying to get him to calm down, Ravi didn't seem convinced. Lejf was uncertain whether he should get out of the car or stay where he was. Ravi tried to make a call again, and Laia said out of desperation, *'Bitte nicht! Ich kenne ihn.'* Lejf froze with his hand on the door handle.

Ravi looked at Lejf, surprised. He and Laia argued for a while. She used considerable effort to stop him from walking over to Lejf.

'Ravi, *nein!*' she said something to him; it was too soft to determine what it was. He shook his head, indecisive, staring at her with his hands on his hips, then over at Lejf again. She didn't budge. They stood glaring at each other in silence.

Finally, Ravi said something that looked like he acceded. He turned to Lejf and said in a loud voice, '*Scheißdreck!*' He got in his car and drove off. Laia stood watching with her back to Lejf until Ravi's car was no longer visible, then turned around, her breast heaving. He'd never seen her so upset.

She crossed the street to where he was sitting in the rental. 'Lejf, what the hell are you doing here?' she asked. He was dumbstruck. 'Well?' she asked again.

He slowly got out of the car. 'Laia, I know this looks bad –'

'*Looks* bad?' she cut him short. 'What the fuck, Lejf? My neighbour told Ravi she saw someone walking around outside my flat. Please tell me it wasn't you. Have you been stalking me?' His silence gave her the answer. '*Stalking* me. Have you lost your mind?' She was nearly hysterical.

He leaned against the car, his wordless mind light with air, so tired. All he wanted to do, was to embrace her and tell her he loved her, but he couldn't speak.

'I can't believe you've done this.' She had her hands in her hair, shaking her head. 'You told me you were in DC. You lied to me. I was sick with worry last night after you called, but this is inconceivable. Do you understand the mess you've created here? I had to beg Ravi not to call the police, and I'm not convinced that he won't. You could go to fucking jail for this!'

'I know. I'm sorry.'

A couple of people looked at them wide-eyed as they got in their cars. Laia ignored them, but Lejf felt bad putting her in that position.

'Why would you do something so preposterous and reckless, Lejf?'

'I don't know.'

She looked him over. 'You look like hell. When was the last time you had a shower or ate something?'

'That's exactly where I've been: hell.'

'Lejf…' She turned around, hands on her hips, then back to him. Remembering the time, she looked at her wristwatch and said, 'I must get to work. You will have to pull yourself together. This is no good, and I can't deal with this; with Ravi…'

'I'm no good without you. Are you happy with him?' She didn't answer right away, and the desperate fool that he was, he said, 'Maybe you need our friendship. I need our friendship, and I need to be your lover also.'

She clenched her jaw. It was an unjust demand, and it angered her again. 'Damn it, Lejf. No. If I choose us, I choose loneliness. It's shit being alone all the time, and I can't do it anymore. I'm trying to make Ravi and I work. It's so hard, but I'm trying. Please let me.' She paused, gathered herself, and then said, 'You have to leave the country now. If you don't leave, Ravi will report you to the police. It will be the end of your career, and I won't have it on my conscience. Leave, Lejf, please.' She looked at him with the saddest eyes before she turned around and walked away, her body shaking.

15

FLEEING TO THE DESERT

When Lejf walked through the door of his parent's house after Laia had sent him away, Signe's eyes expressed her horror at his sorry state, but she didn't probe, knowing him too well. Lawrie was shocked too – that was evident from the look on his face, but it wasn't a total surprise; Lejf was accustomed to his dissatisfied reactions, both verbal and non-verbal. He showered, washed his laundry, and told them during dinner, 'I'm going to the desert for a while. I'll leave early in the morning.'

He alternated campsites near Sesriem and drove out to Sossusvlei, walking up and down the dunes in search of Laia's desert rose, a maniac, stumbling across the sand mountains, trying to find redemption. He spoke to her in his desolate asylum, at last telling her everything he had failed to say until his voice became so hoarse it dried up, and he couldn't utter even a whisper. Plunged into the terrain of his thoughts, where his voice still existed, Lejf carried on his conversations with Laia.

Yeats fled to the mountains, hiding his face amid a crown of stars, pondering his Maud. Did the poet's soul feel a rage, a madness threatening to tear him apart? Something on the inside that he wanted to tear out? Or did he accept that he wouldn't have the one woman he loved?

He'd been so careful not to impose on Laia's independence, but how had that helped either of them in the end? His fear of saying how he felt had resulted in him and Laia adapting to circumstances neither of them had wanted. And now it was over because she didn't want that anymore.

The tricky thing about hindsight was that you could see the truth that had eluded you *after* the fact. You could see it, but that didn't mean you had insight on how to move forward. It was a twisted catch-22 life played on you: to give you the knowledge you needed when you've already screwed it up.

Three weeks later, Signe found him at the Sossus Oasis campsite. Cellphone reception was spotty, not that she would have forewarned him anyway.

'Come, älskling, help me set up this tent. That one of yours is too small for both of us.'

Lejf watched her as she worked with total concentration and with precision. His mother tree – the sturdy camel thorn who'd survived many desert droughts, yet she had enough reserves to rescue her sapling from himself. She was fearless, tougher than most people he knew. The life-giving nutrition she brought was much more than food and fresh clothes. She also came to tell him in her way, 'You've dealt with this enough on your own'. He didn't know how his mom managed to do it, that formidable inner strength that refused to give in. If he was sure of one thing, it was how happy he was to see her.

Signe didn't probe. They spoke of other things, and she made sure Lejf ate enough. They drove to Meob Bay, about 121km from their camp.

There were no roads in or out; you could access the beach with a four-by-four vehicle and lots of experience driving through thick sand.

It was a breathtaking, unspoilt piece of heaven on Earth. Lejf drove at a slow pace to keep in sync with the thoughts running through his mind. The sea breeze raised dust clouds off the dunes, reshaping them. The beach stretched forever, littered with Cape fur seals and thousands of migratory shorebirds searching for food at low tide. Oryx appeared like ghosts on the crests of the dunes, and when he blinked, they were gone. Black-backed jackals trotted next to the Cruiser in search of a meal – their tongues hanging out of their mouths – then, all of a sudden, they dashed off in another direction as if they'd heard some inaudible signal. These familiar and beloved scenes felt dull to him, as if there was a clamp on his emotions.

Signe walked with him as he captured a cluster of cotton ball clouds with the sea and dunes as backdrops. 'The sky is such a deep blue in winter,' she said.

He also took a couple of photos of her, one where she looked straight at him through the lens, and he smiled. His mother's beauty was as ageless as her soul. They had leftovers from the night before for lunch in the Cruiser, watching the seabirds plunging into the deep and then reappearing with wriggly silver treasures.

'Today is a good day to be here. The sky is clear and perfect, but those little clouds will bring thick fog tonight. We'll need to bundle up; it will be cold. I can feel it in my joints,' she said, pouring coffee from a flask and handing Lejf a cup.

'I want to drive to Sossusvlei tomorrow morning to capture the sunrise with the fog. Would you mind? You don't have to go with me. It will be early.'

'Of course, I want to go with you. It's been a while since I've seen a foggy sunrise there,' she replied.

It was cold that night, as Signe had predicted, and the Milky Way lightened up the heavens like the stairway to the gods. And all the undiscovered diamonds of the Skeleton Coast that have eluded prospectors for millennia were shining in triumph at their clever deception above the heads of the awe-struck humans below. Lejf took a couple of photographs he knew would make publication. It wasn't difficult under such a night sky. All he needed to do was adjust his lens and press the button.

Out of the blue, looking up at the colourful spectacle, Signe shivered a bit as she pulled a blanket tighter around her, and said, 'I didn't want to marry your father.'

Lejf threw two more logs on the fire and lifted his gaze in surprise. 'What do you mean?'

'It's true. I would have been happy for us to be in a loving relationship. But your father's parents were people with traditional values and beliefs, and I didn't want to disrespect them or cause a rift between them and him.' She exhaled a long, 'hmm', thinking about it.

'And are you sorry you compromised?'

'You have to choose your battles in life and decide what you want to achieve. That means making some compromises.'

'Dad probably pushed for you to get married,' he commented with a sarcastic snigger.

'It may surprise you that your father isn't altogether conventional in his thinking, Lejf. He had no qualms about remaining unmarried, but there were other practical things to consider, like my becoming a Namibian citizen. In the end, I had to do what I could to be with him here in his world, which is the world I'd accepted. I've never been sorry for my decision.'

'Are you telling me I should have accepted Laia's world? Would that have saved us?' Signe didn't answer. Lejf hadn't told his parents he'd been in Karlsruhe. His bedraggled looks must have been enough for them to deduce that something upsetting had happened. When he told them he was going to the desert, he mentioned that Laia had decided to get married, not to him, but to someone else. If they'd been disturbed by the news, they managed to conceal it well. Signe must have been pacing up and down; Lejf was surprised she'd let him be alone for so long. She did call to hear if he was all right. His dad would have found out from her how he was doing if he was interested in knowing. Lejf imagined Lawrie would have said something like him, always running away from the *actual* reality. His father wouldn't have been far off with such a claim.

'Laia doesn't love the man she's with and doesn't want to be alone, so she compromises, and I can't blame her,' he said.

'And what compromise have you made to have her? You can't have it all, älskling.'

'I'm aware of the disparity between what I want and my choices, Morsa.'

'Lejf, you're a grown man. This is no great mystery; there is either one way or another. It's yours to choose, and until you do, it will remain a burden; I wish I could take it from you, but I can't.'

'It's too late for me to choose – I've wasted my chances. She's going to marry him.' Signe was sympathetic to him because she didn't have all the facts. He was too much of a coward to come clean with her, and he changed the subject. 'A project has been on my mind for a couple of years, and I've been formulating the details of it these last few days. The time has come to implement it, and I want to speak to Nat Geo and start my research. It will be intensive, but I think this has the potential of being impactful.'

She turned her head to look at him. 'Ah, see, the desert has revealed its pearls to you. Then we can't stay here much longer. We'll watch the sun chase the fog tomorrow morning, and then go home. Your father has been worried about you.'

'And me working on an elaborate new scheme will set his mind at ease?' he asked with biting mordacity. She waved him off like a child who'd made a silly remark.

16

BONDAGES

The brain often ran on a programme independent of what the body needed. It could be a cruel master: creating a reality of its own. Absurd as it was, the body couldn't function without the brain's instructions, so it tagged along on an ever-escalating treadmill which couldn't go anywhere except to a dissolution.

In his mind's eye, Lejf saw Laia's face before him as she confronted him on her street. He saw how she stared straight into his madness. Did she recognise it, and did it frighten her? He heard her telling him how lonely she was, and he saw her laughing and smiling with Ravi, desperate for happiness. Her heartbreak as she walked away from Lejf. He'd picked up his phone a hundred times or more and not made the call. He kept his distance, trying to channel his energy into researching the new project. The torturous thoughts seeped into the pages of his explorations. Through the details and planning and putting together of itineraries, there was the unbearable urge to share it with *her*, as it had been between them.

It was futile; she didn't belong in his world anymore. She'd gone in search of a new universe. So, he functioned in the cage of his mind, doing what it told him to do. There was an obscene comfort in swimming around in his woe, drinking that bitter cup until it liquified his reasoning.

Erik nagged him about coming for a visit. 'Lejf, come see Dubai. It's high-tech and fantastic to explore. We can do dune bashing and camel riding; it's the thing to do among the yuppies. They pay big money for it. I know a guy who can organise something.'

'I can drive to Swakopmund to ride over dunes, and I'm certain I'd be able to avoid the yuppies.'

'Good Lord, you're grumpy. Okay, we can skip that if you wish.'

'Well, you keep telling me how I'm like Dad. I'm busy with research. Now's not a great time for me, Erik.'

'Now's the best time. If I don't get you here now it won't happen. You've let me down. I'm not letting you off the hook this time.'

Lejf didn't know if Erik knew about him and Laia. Signe may have told him. He was too ashamed to tell Erik or Signe he'd stalked Laia in Karlsruhe. There wasn't a likelihood either of them would have been sympathetic to his cause. What would his mother have done if he'd told her when they were out camping? He couldn't bear the thought of her condemnation; that was the truth. Erik was a lot like Signe in that way: easy-going as both were, they weren't prone to support behaviour that crossed criminal boundaries. Neither would a judge, if Lejf had been caught.

And his father wouldn't have bailed him out, that he knew for sure. He'd burned that bridge years ago when he was in his final year of high school and was arrested for getting into a bloody fracas with a boy at a picnic area. There'd been drinking involved. It happened because he took offence over a comment the guy made about Laia and her 'free for all' sister. Someone called the police and he and the boy he had fought with were loaded in the back of the police van and taken into custody. Long story short, his dad told the constable to keep him there overnight to sober up and think things through.

Being jailed for an inebriated brawl was a lesser sin than flying to another country and invading people's privacy, no matter if you could claim temporary insanity. His dad wouldn't have bailed him out, no matter if it was Laia whom he'd stalked. Lawrie may have been more adamant because it was her.

Erik pushed on to try and convince Lejf. 'Or if you prefer, we can go out for a fancy dinner and talk about women, and why we love them and they us, even when they think we're full-of-shit bastards. I'm willing to give you some excellent tips.' So he did know about Laia. This was his kind of cheer-up pep talk.

'On why women think you're a full-of-shit bastard?'

'Ah, now. I may not get everything right, but I always try to be a good listener brother. You have to make her feel wanted, valued. Sometimes you need to read between the lines.' It was impossible to offend Erik. Lejf didn't want to tell him how close he was to the mark. Reading between the lines where Laia was concerned had been an area he had failed in. How could we excel in some areas of our lives and become defeated in the most important ones?

'How many women have you pissed off to know so much?' Lejf asked with humour this time.

'I'm a lover, not a fighter. Stop being such a wise arse and come. I'll buy your airline ticket.'

'I can buy my own, thanks.'

Erik could fire up Lejf's enthusiasm as few people could. He talked over issues in general and kept things light, but there was the underlying sense that he knew more than he let on. Behind the laid-back exterior lay a sensitive soul. Lejf doubted he'd admit to being deep, but when you knew yourself and were comfortable with who you were, it didn't matter. Erik considered what he was doing a good-natured game in which he had to come up with plans to solve problems as if he was building a real-life Lego set.

On the other hand, he viewed what Lejf was doing as sagacious, something extraordinary. He had no idea how much Lejf admired him. He wouldn't; he was among the least self-absorbed people Lejf knew.

'So, I've been to Cape Town to meet Torsten's new woman, Hannah,' Erik said as they were having drinks at a lounge on the 154th level of the Burj Khalifa, with views over Dubai.

Signe had told Lejf that Torsten had met someone, and they were serious, but he'd been out of touch with everything around him and hadn't spent much time thinking about it. Erik, here in Dubai, was more in tune with their family matters than he was. He felt increasingly out of tune with reality.

'Yes, Morsa told me he met someone. Will they get married, do you think?'

'Yup, I believe so. I like her; she's good for him. He's moving in with her.'

'Søren's going to be by himself, poor dude. A new era.'

'True, but you know our fate will either be that we'll all die lonely old bachelors, or we'll become Dad.'

'Heaven help us.' Lejf snorted.

Erik chortled. 'Speaking of a new era: I ran into Iben there.'

'Did you? How's she doing?'

'Pretty well, I'd say. She works for an IT company; an HR manager. Says she's devising a system of changing their corporate culture, and I quote, "from sexist prigs, to nimble-witted chicks". That one has some wayout ideas,' he said with a sly look without elaborating, but Lejf's perception was too fogged to see through the mist.

'I believe she'll make good on her promise. Did she mention anything about Laia?'

When he and Signe got home from Sossusvlei, Lejf started delving into the research for his project right away. She'd been walking around for weeks, giving him the occasional eye, which meant one thing: she knew something and was reluctant to tell him.

After what must have been intense self-deliberation and her perpetual need to tell the truth, she sat down with him and said, 'There's something you should know, Lejf: Laia got married.'

He could see how it had pained her to tell him, but he was grateful she did. It would have made the blow more severe if he'd heard it from someone else. Unsurprising, he'd missed the talk in town. It was official: Laia was off-limits.

Regret made you see all the things you could have done. Then it punished you by showing you how you wouldn't have been good enough – how far you fell short.

'Not so much.' Erik gave an evasive answer.

If he and Iben had spoken about Laia, Erik was careful not to tell Lejf, who didn't push him for fear of hearing what he both longed for, for her sake and also couldn't bear: that she was happy.

'I'm worried about you, bro. Are you okay?' Erik asked.

Should he admit to Erik that he, too, was troubled by his emotional state and was desperate to escape this black hole? Lejf answered his question halfway through his thoughts, 'This new project will be something constructive to keep me busy, although the research is causing me another form of agony.'

Erik watched him with a deep frown.

***

It was nearly a year after Laia had confronted Lejf in Karlsruhe, and the new project was about to start. Though he'd long since moved back to his parents, he never stayed long. He was on the go non-stop. Yet it was remarkable how his feet seemed to find their way back to Otji, to the comfort of his mother's loving presence and his dad's stoic acceptance of where he went and what he did there. Lawrie was still working himself, although well past what was considered retirement age. His absence during the day made it more digestible to deal with his critique.

Lejf told him, 'If what I do is so pestiferous, why do you hang around when I tell Morsa about it? You don't need to put yourself through the torture, Dad.'

'Pestiferous? The notions you come up with.' He shook his head. 'Might I remind you this *is* my home?'

'It's our children's home too, Lawrie,' Signe intervened, and Lawrie did what Lejf did whenever she chose a side: he moped. Still, his dad was right; it was the home he had built with his mother. Lejf had insisted on his independence, fought for it with tears and shouted the odds, and here he was, back where he'd started.

The incompatibility between him and his father didn't change. Being away often didn't improve matters. It was, in fact, a prodigious contributor to the conflict between them.

Lejf admired his tenacity. He couldn't imagine his dad anywhere but out in the open, where he could do a hard day's work and feel he was paying his dues to society. His father's mind was as tough as his body. His spirit animal was a rhinoceros, Lejf was certain: the animal whose plight, Lawrie said, motivated him to do what he did. His kind of makeup was as endangered as the animals he cared about. He was a stubborn, hard-armoured old rhino.

The nature of their relationship, based on a tug of words and a mordant sense of humour, was getting old too. In a couple of months, Lejf would be thirty-five. He needed change and to find his own place to pin the flag and build something permanent amid the inconsistency.

He ran into Laia's mother in town. Dael was friendly and polite, as was her nature. She asked him how he was doing, and they made small talk.

Whenever he looked at Dael, it appeared as if she was clutching her emotions tight to her body, afraid of releasing them, as if they'd cause harm. To herself or others? He wondered. He couldn't help but think about how Laia had so much of her kindness.

Dael paused for a moment. 'It's a pity we don't see you anymore, Lejf. Why don't you come and have a cup of tea sometime, and tell me about your projects? I would love to hear all you've been up to.' Almost as an afterthought she said, 'Out of everyone, you've been the most important person to Laia. She has a void in her life: she misses sharing in your world.' Perhaps realising she'd revealed Laia's secret, she touched his arm – a brief, embarrassed gesture – and they said goodbye.

Did Laia tell her mother he'd stalked her? It was doubtful; he'd never known Laia to be spiteful and vindictive. It struck him how forlorn Dael seemed. All the charities and committees she was involved in couldn't keep the loneliness out of her heart. Was Laia following in the footsteps of her mother's passionless marriage after all?

Too many men in the world caused women hardship. He'd caused Laia pain. He'd left her with a void. Was it a pardonable excuse to say it was unintentional? How much were women willing and capable of enduring? Even when religious or cultural laws didn't subjugate them, they were bound to their code of loyalty to their men – good or bad. That was something that amazed him about the character of women.

Laia didn't want to be controlled by a man, but her desire for a stable relationship chained her to her longing. She had to, since he didn't fulfil that need. It was a cross he placed upon both of them. His poor Laia. What other option did she have but to find an alternative? From one mediocratiy to the next. She'd told him, that awful night at the beautiful Hotel Fairmont Empress, that it was impossible to settle for anything less. Hanging on to the fragments of them was as low as she could go. How the truth stung.

Perhaps women would be better off without men, after all. Happier. Laia might agree with him. The ugly truth couldn't stop him from loving her, when she'd spoken it; he doubted anything could. He wished he had the nerve to pick up the phone and call her.

* * *

That same evening, after Lejf had run into Dael, he heard his father speaking to someone over the phone in his study. 'Why don't you take a break from all that's weighing you down and come visit? When was the last time you were home? It will do you good, and your parents would love to see you too ... Oh, my girl, you know I'm not one for those big European cities with miniature beds and noise into ungodly morning hours when I'm trying to sleep. Besides, I need the sunshine; this old bag of bones works best when my hide becomes pliable from the heat ... Ha! She would love it. You should ask her ... He's doing all right, I suppose. When I turn, he's off somewhere ... Yes, he'll be going to Opuwo in a couple of months; I think that's what he said ... It's part of a desert project ... Oh, he's been thinking about it that long? Interesting, I didn't know. He never tells me anything ... He seems preoccupied ... Hm, I can't say I agree 100 per cent ... You know how it is, my child: Lejf goes and pours his soul out to other people and comes back with his battle-worn wasteland ... I know you support his work, but I know what it's doing to him and us ... I will do so, Laia. Do me a favour and take care of yourself over there. Will you? I'll tell them both. Bye now.'

Battle-worn wasteland? His father didn't understand anything about his work; Lejf didn't know why he even bothered.

Laia supported him, but she lived in Karlsruhe with her husband, whom he doubted she loved, and now her heart felt empty because Dael said in a slip of the tongue that she missed his friendship. Why didn't she call him then? She called his father and asked about him. Why didn't he call her? Because he was a coward. He felt ashamed that he'd left her to deal with the balls-up he'd created when all she wanted was someone around.

There was a little black spot on his heart. He woke up one morning and felt it there – like sunlight through a magnifying glass, singeing a hole in a piece of wood. It was etching deeper. He couldn't stop the burning.

17

THE RED-PAINTED WOMEN

Lejf's project was about to start. It was a five-part series on desert people and the impact of globalisation and climate change on them. He'd told Nat Geo he could do it in less than five months. It was ambitious; there'd be no time for dallying once the wheels were in motion, but he needed to stay busy so there wouldn't be time to think about Laia.

As with such extensive undertakings, there was a lot to consider: research, budget, permission to work in certain areas, car rentals, hotel accommodation, safety aspects, a guide for some of the countries he'd be working in, and so forth.

'Are you sure you'll have enough time, älskling? It seems a bit tight for all you have to do,' Signe had said.

'I'll be fine, Morsa,' Lejf reassured her. His mother was perceptive; she saw deeper changes in him.

It was fitting that his desert journey commenced at the heart of his existence: the Namib. Much of what he learned about nature as a boy, and that which helped shape him into a man, happened along the arid stretches of what was believed to be the oldest desert on Earth.

The Namib Desert spanned a couple of thousand kilometres along the Atlantic coastlines of South Africa, Namibia and Angola, and from the Atlantic Ocean in the west to the Namib Escarpment in the east. It was a vast area and a harsh place to survive for any living thing.

Opuwo meant 'the end' in Herero. Lejf inhaled a deep breath, dust stinging his nostrils and the back of his throat through the open windows as he pulled into town. In a way, this project signified an end, but it was also the beginning of a new chapter for him. It was the biggest one he'd shouldered. He would just need to get used to things this way: projects without her with him.

The town was unimpressive, but it was a critical hub for the surrounding area. There were some basic stores and many Himba and Herero sold their crafts at markets. Lejf's first instinct was to buy something for Laia, then he remembered. It was a force of habit.

The women sat patiently, engaging with tourists. They sold much of the same thing, and some tourists tried to barter the already low prices down further. It couldn't be easy to make a living and support a family this way. Many Indigenous people worldwide faced the same dilemma: they went to nearby towns or travelled further from home to cities hoping to find work. Their chances were slim with no commercial work experience, and in most cases, no government support.

The purpose of his trip was to meet and photograph a Himba village and witness their traditional way of life. Signe had a deep affinity and respect for the Himba's natural existence and had visited remote villages several times with the services of a guide. She'd encouraged Lejf to do it right and seek out an authentic experience when he told her of his planned series on desert people.

'Lejf, your work is your visual voice; use that voice judiciously. Cultural tourism is threatening to erode the Himba's uniqueness. How would they be able to remain who they are amid an onslaught on their traditional ways? It's a noose that's tightening around them. On the one hand, you have certain tourists who treat them as objects of amusement; on the other, some in society are dead set on making them good moral citizens. Ask yourself what is ethical here? Destroying a beautiful people and their culture would be an unconscionable act,' she said.

It was easy to understand people's fascination with the Himba. Their red-painted skin, striking features and intricate adornments made them intriguing and easy to recognise, and they had become a symbol of Namibian tourism. Signe was right: there was more to their story. They had found a way to survive in a place where most humans couldn't. They deserved to be admired, not exploited.

There were several Himba villages around Opuwo, and many of them had already succumbed to the lure of the tourist dollar. Who could blame them when they had few other alternatives? Lejf was going to an inaccessible part further north where there remained a handful of Himba villages who hadn't had much (if any) contact with tourists.

Opuwo's streets were paved, but not well maintained and overblown with dust. Somewhere a water pipe must have burst, leaving a stream across the road, splattering muddy streaks over cars. In a water-scarce area, one noticed such a waste. Lejf parked at a grocery store, rolled up the windows just enough to let some air through, and got out and stretched his stiff arms and legs from sitting still for 489km.

His Land Cruiser wasn't an unusual sight there, kitted with the essentials for travelling anywhere in this vast country with a sparse population: two extra tyres, a repair kit, a pump and lots of water. Another essential for the Opuwo area (and the northern regions of Namibia), was antimalarial medicine and mosquito repellent. He couldn't risk getting sick with his tight schedule.

Cellphone reception was limited to the town. He checked last-minute emails and sent Signe a quick text: *In Opuwo. Getting supplies and will hook up with my guide soon. Anything urgent, let me know within the hour, otherwise it will have to wait.*

He bought food, metal cups and pots; blankets; fabric and craft beads, which he would present as gifts, and filled cans of petrol, since there were no filling stations outside town.

Lejf's guide was a Himba man who introduced himself as Paul, a name he'd taken when he left his village to pursue an education and an economic life that would keep him connected to his people.

'Good to meet you, Lejf,' Paul said. He had a firm handshake, and Lejf liked his jovial, open face.

'Good to meet you, Paul. Let's find a spot to put your bag.'

Lejf moved things around on the backseat, and Paul grinned. 'I see you didn't take any chances.'

'You think it's over the top?' Lejf asked, looking at the pile of supplies.

'Nah, don't worry.' He chuckled. 'It will be much appreciated. Nothing will go to waste, I assure you.'

They passed villages – some big and some smaller – and after driving for nearly two hours along dirt roads and past mopane trees, Paul indicated where Lejf should turn; he knew the area well. They arrived at their destination early evening, as the sun rested on the backs of the Baynes Mountains in the distance, close to the Angola border.

The *onganda* was an enclosure made of long sticks. The Himba built their villages in the open, not underneath trees, which would put themselves and their livestock at risk of predators. The women constructed the huts from mopane trees and covered them with a mixture of clay and cow manure. Some huts were dome-shaped while others had thatched roofs. This provided shelter from the scorching heat during the summer days and cold winter nights. The layout of a typical village had the main hut of the chief, a couple of huts for the rest of the tribe and a *kraal* – an enclosure also made of long sticks for the cattle.

Paul said, 'The men aren't here; they're at the outposts to tend to their cattle. I'm sure you've read that many of them have wives elsewhere. The women aren't without recourse; they have boyfriends too. Think of it as a free and sharing society.' He grinned. 'So here, the women are the ones in charge. They take care of everything in the village.'

A free and sharing society. Conventional wisdom couldn't seem to grasp this practicality.

Lejf parked the Cruiser underneath trees. He and Paul unloaded the supplies and there were eager hands to greet and help them carry it to the onganda. Paul introduced him to Uatika, the chief's first wife. Her sun-weathered face looked old, but her eyes were tender. Bashful kids eyed Lejf from behind their mother's legs, while bolder ones peeked into the bags of supplies. Paul spoke with Uatika to explain what Lejf would be doing. After Lejf had called him to hire his services, Paul had been to the village to ask for permission to spend time there on Lejf's behalf.

Uatika nodded in acknowledgement and welcomed Lejf with a wave and a grin. As Lejf presented the gifts he'd brought, they all stood closer. The women held the colourful fabrics up with excited tuts, rubbing them gently between their fingers to inspect the quality and pressing their noses into them to smell the newness. Talking and laughing, they opened the containers filled with beads, allowing the children to stick their hands in them to swish the balls around as they squealed with delight.

'*Hoku heppa*,' they thanked Lejf, and he was moved by their sincerity.

'It's my pleasure.'

They had the traditional porridge for dinner, which they ate by the fire. Lejf asked permission to take photographs. Paul explained he would need to do that each time he wanted to take pictures, and the women had to be comfortable with it.

Long 'ahhs' circulated as they agreed.

As the smoke of the *okuruwo* – the holy fire – rose in the air, Uatika implored Mukuru to watch over their husbands and sons and to 'bless the time with the tall stranger', as Paul translated for Lejf. She spoke of her husband and their sons with him at the outposts. She elucidated the challenges they faced when the rains didn't come and how difficult it was to dig for water in the dry soil. Her calloused hands demonstrated in the glow of the fire.

While the mechanical clicks of his camera were making a memory in still frames, Lejf's eyes captured the hardship and the resolve behind the endearing smile and gestures. And when she told him about protecting their goats from predators, he was struck by the verity of their world inside and outside the onganda – how it was a regular part of their survival; there were no guns to defend themselves with. They had to use sticks, stones or whatever weapon they could forge. They would even use their bare hands. Sitting around the fire with the black African sky above them, Lejf felt as if he had become a small man in the presence of these larger-than-life women.

This world here was the quiddity of their existence. They didn't hang around the village, braiding each other's hair and looking after the children. They did that, but there was more to it. There was much at stake, and they needed to be diligent and proactive to safeguard themselves, their homes, and their animals. Their wealth and their food.

Not knowing if it was the right time or appropriate to bring up the subject, Lejf hesitated before saying, 'Tell me what your heart says about the big water project.'

This was a proposed hydroelectric power plant between the Angola and Namibian governments at Baynes in the lower Kunene River region. The Indigenous people were fiercely opposed to it.

During his research Lejf had told Signe, 'It seems a common thing in such elaborate deal-makings that the voices of the people who live and depend on the land are spurned by those who see them as sunk costs that raise investment stakes. And how long has this one been going?'

'For decades. They rationalise their argument that such projects are essential in the face of water and energy scarcity. But the potential consequences are dire for the Indigenous tribes. And don't forget that the Himba are among Namibia's most independent people, Lejf. They have been able to sustain themselves without depending on modern intervention. It is right that they should fear the loss of their livelihood and displacement, which *will* happen, not to mention the environmental damage that flooding will cause to the area,' she said.

These poor people didn't benefit from such big schemes. Did that mean their voices mattered less? Were their apprehensions as unfounded and embellished as the advocates for these kinds of projects claimed in their propaganda campaigns? Were they as outdated and ignorant as they were made out to be? As his mother had said, their knowledge of the earth and their sustainable farming practices suggested otherwise.

Lejf wanted to hear it from Uatika's mouth. She was the most influential woman in her tribe. She was a mother, a grandmother and a voice for the other women sitting around the fire, observing him. There was an atmosphere of trust. He, the stranger, was welcome in their inner circle.

She was silent for a moment, thinking with a frown. 'This is the land we know. We know nothing else. We have our goats and our cattle, and when the grass becomes few, we must move our animals to other parts so the grass can grow again. Those people who tell us we must move don't live out here. They do not know about the fire that burns within that will make you die for the sacred things you wish to protect. The dam will destroy this area. The earth will flood, and many animals and plants will die. They speak as if it will be something good for us. How will it?' She shook her head. 'We want to live here.

We ask them to listen to us, but they don't want to understand our way of life. They say we must become like them. What will happen to us? Where will we go?' She looked at him, eyes filled with pain and uncertainty.

His answer was a simple nod; what could he tell her? He agreed with her. She was the one who carried the burden for herself and on behalf of everyone she loved.

As in most of his other outdoor trips, there were no facilities for ablutions. Lejf washed his face and essential body parts and brushed his teeth away from the village, where he parked the Cruiser. Water was sacred to the Himba. They didn't wash themselves with it.

He and Paul were invited to sleep in one of the men's huts. It smelled of smoke and the cowhides they slept on. It was a small hut, but Paul told him, 'A hut this size would sleep five to seven men.' It was a tight fit and hard to imagine with five others.

Lying on his back, and staring at nothing in the darkness, he told Paul, 'One of the biggest revelations of my travels has been how we live in the modern world and squander space and time as if it's limitless. We take it for granted and become offended when someone else encroaches on the invisible boundaries we place around ourselves. These people here know everything about each other and they want it so.'

Chuckling Paul said, 'You're preaching to the choir, my friend.'

A while after Paul had drifted off and Lejf could hear his deep breathing, he lay thinking about what Uatika had said. He was moved by her guileless words and disturbed by the frustrating reality of fighting the system. It reminded him of something he'd read. Or had his mother told him? It was two Himba proverbs: start your farming with people, not cattle, and he who has people will not perish – it went along those lines.

Signe's own amazing heart had been drawn to the overflowing

generosity of these lovely people. That's why she had come back. Unconditional love seemed like a luxury in a world filled with marginalised thinking.

The Himba held on to community and sacred things. They possessed a level of being in tune that made Lejf wonder about the sophisticated, technological and hyper-material-driven world outside of this harmonious existence. That was the odd world, out there, not this one.

***

Early the next morning, Lejf was awoken by tiny hands running over the stubble on his cheeks. When he opened his eyes, two sparkling brown eyes were watching him, and the face of the pretty little girl turned into a glorious smile.

'*Wapenduka nawa?*' she asked. Meaning: did you wake up well?

'*Ah, nawa. Hoku heppa,*' he answered in a sleepy voice, saying yes and thank you. He knew only some basic phrases. '*Ennaroe?*' he asked her name.

'Ennaranje, Kauukua,' she said.

'Kauukua,' he repeated. '*Moro morinawa.*' Beautiful. Shy at the compliment, she stood with her hands behind her back.

The adorable five-year-old followed Lejf everywhere and sat, quiet as a mouse, beside him, holding his camera bag whenever he was busy taking photographs. They had porridge again for breakfast. Part of the food he'd brought were two big sacks of maize, a welcome gift in an area of scarcity.

The woman started their daily smoke baths, a cleansing ritual of crushed twigs and leaves from the Commiphora tree and herbs burned over hot coal in a bowl. The process involved throwing a blanket over themselves, and the heat from the smoke then caused them to sweat, thereby cleansing them with aromatic smoke. The bitter, resinous vapour drifted up Lejf's nostrils; the smell reminded him of topical cold medicine. After that, they applied *otjize* to their bodies and hair, this an ochre and butterfat mixture gave them their distinctive red colour. He tested a dot of the oily mix on his skin, which was pale in comparison, and it looked almost bright red.

'It protects them from the sun and insects but also acts as a perfume,' Paul said as Lejf took a close-up photograph of a woman grinding a piece of hematite on a large, smooth stone they used for the purpose, then mixing it with the sticky warmed butterfat in a separate bowl.

Lejf asked, 'Why do only women paint themselves?'

Paul smiled as he translated for him. 'Because how then will women be beautiful to men if they look the same?' Indisputable logic.

The women loved telling Lejf in detail about their jewellery and adornments, which, along with their hair and headdresses, symbolised their social status. He noticed how everyone laughed a lot. It amazed him: in this barren, harsh place, they were full of joy.

The warm sun baking on the earth, the peaceful sound of the women working while their children played. Occasionally, Paul would say something to one of them, and they'd giggle. Lejf couldn't understand what they were saying, but he liked the sweet tone of their voices.

How was it for these women when the men were around? Were they as carefree as they were now? What was the love between a Himba man and his women like? Did he have a favourite? Did they display their affection in public? Did they hold each other after they made love? With a certain kind of woman, when you held her, it felt as if you were holding the universe with all the brightness and darkness of space and time in your arms.

A woman smiled at him as if she'd seen his thoughts and took pity on him.

'Do you miss having the men around?' he asked the question in general. Paul didn't have to translate their answer. They shrugged it off with grins. Life was what it was, with or without the men.

Lejf thought about Laia and the years she'd had to do without his presence, except, she didn't have a village of women to support her.

It was the rainy season, but the rains had not come. The river was dry, and the women had to dig deep holes in the sand to access underground water which they had to carry back in buckets – it was excruciating and laborious work. Firewood had to be collected in the veld, tied together in bundles and carried home. Lejf couldn't balance the load on his head without using both his hands; it was challenging to walk with it because it was heavy and awkward. The women made it look effortless and moved with grace, as you wouldn't find even in royal courts.

One young woman made a remark in a teasing way, and Paul translated with mischief. 'She says how can such a big man not carry a few sticks?' All he could do was acknowledge that he was in superior company. The Himba women made him aware of how they were ready to support each other, the strong sisterhood between them, and how tough their mental and physical endurance were.

They sat by the holy fire on Lejf's last evening in their company. Little Kauukua inspected his camera in between him taking pictures, and Uatika spoke to the ancestors through the rising smoke, imploring Mukuru through them to send blessings and good fortune. 'Especially for you on your journeys,' Paul whispered. Lejf thought they would be pleased in heaven by what they witnessed down here.

His heart was wrestling with many things, but he couldn't deny how being in the company of these women had a soul-altering effect on him. From the central woman in his village he had learned important lessons – and many unusual ones, too – about life. It seemed proper to dedicate the first part of his desert project in honour of the extraordinary Signe Nyberg.

No matter how much he tried to resist the urge, it was Laia's thoughts he longed to hear. She had always played a big part in the motivation for his projects and research. He'd forfeited the right to share his news with her. He agonised over it.

18

GETTING READY FOR SINAI

Lejf met Amun Abaza at the V&A Waterfront in Cape Town for coffee. They shook hands; Amun's black eyes and broad, white-teeth smile were radiant. He had a slight build, as many Egyptians do and he was young; Lejf guessed early to mid-twenties. His sponsor had a friend in Cairo who'd recommended Amun as travel agent and would-be guide on his next desert project in the Sinai Peninsula in Egypt.

Their connections arranged for them to meet at Lejf's request. He didn't know how much Amun knew about the kind of work he did. Amun also wished to visit relatives in Cape Town. When Lejf told him about his research, and intention to cover the impact of various socio-political factors on the Sinai Bedouin, he listened with interest.

Amun's English was excellent. 'I will send you the details of my uncle's travel agency in Cairo and email the itinerary to you. The Bedouins are hospitable and are eager to answer questions about their tribal life and traditions. The police become suspicious when you start asking questions that sound political of random people, so be careful about the kinds of questions you ask.'

What he said matched what Lejf had read in his research. Follow the rules, and don't get caught.

'We will fly to Sharm El Sheikh, and from there, we will do a desert tour with Bedouin guides. After that, we will go to Dahab, back to Sharm and then fly back to Cairo. And then, my friend, you can return to your desert home in Namibia and share your interesting story with the world.' He grinned.

It was a good, uncomplicated plan. Amun was a modern Egyptian. He was Muslim but didn't hold extreme beliefs. Like most young men his age anywhere else, he wanted to carve a life for himself by working hard. His uncle owned the travel agency, and from the way he'd spoken about his family, it was clear that they were close-knit.

Life was hard for most Egyptians. All sorts of pressure infringed on their freedom of speech and movement. It just wasn't that obvious to the outside world.

The Sinai Peninsula was a triangular shape between the Mediterranean Sea in the north of Egypt and the Red Sea in the south, and it formed a land bridge between Asia and Africa. The northern part was dangerous and unstable. South Sinai was one of the most peaceful parts of Egypt, especially toward the interior where the Bedouins lived.

'The Bedouins aren't really integrated into Egyptian society. They're perceived as the "other people,"' Lejf told his mother while discussing his research.

'Why is that so?' asked Signe.

'Because of stigmas. Sad to say, Sinai trafficking had done little for their cause. The military government had made sure they'd clamped down on the trafficking, but it had tarnished the image of the Bedouin. It's easy to start stereotyping a group when something like that happens; it's a universal flaw that does nothing other than create resentment.'

'And that leads to all kinds of social problems,' Signe added.

'Exactly. They've never been allowed to own land. So, with the boom of the resort industry in the 1980s, the government started selling coastal properties that Bedouins once inhabited. They went from freedom as nomads to living in confined areas. It makes me think of the Himba: the predicament of displacement they also face to make room for development.'

'Their situations are different, but their realities are the same.' She nodded.

'There aren't many jobs like cab drivers, tour guides and café managers available in a small area. As you said: it becomes a breeding ground for socio-economic issues. At first, unemployment drove some of them into the drug trade and weapon smuggling, and the next thing you know, human trafficking. And the pressure keeps mounting on them to change their traditional ways. The Bedouins in northern Sinai are feeling most of the political pressure. I can't help feeling sorry for them. Bedouins are people with an introspective view, but it makes them vulnerable to extremists.'

'What is at the root of their grievance, älskling?'

'In essence, the government's counter-terrorism stance, which appears discriminatory. The definition of terrorism is so broad that anyone who voices their critique is subject to questioning.'

'There is no middle ground, is there?'

'No, there isn't. I've checked but couldn't find official numbers on terrorist-related charges and arrests in Egypt. There are no formal statistics available. They don't want to advertise what's happening, but the information from underground media sources indicates a huge disproportionate figure.' Lejf didn't tell his mother that, in many cases, these people of interest vanish from sight, only for their families to discover they've ended up in one of the dreaded prisons with no chance of a fair trial. Many journalists had been jailed, tortured and sentenced to death or life imprisonment.

'It makes me livid, Morsa: such systems of brutalising and vilifying the slightest discord. Yet, Western leaders are all too eager to sell their weapons to the Egyptian government so that it might wage war against its own citizens. Where is the humanity? All it does is stir bitter, silent hatred that leads to more bloodshed.'

'Violence breeds violence.' Signe tutted as she contemplated.

Lejf hadn't noticed his father standing by the door as they talked. Lawrie understood well enough that the kind of journalism Lejf was drawn to didn't involve just taking pretty pictures. And though he may have liked his settled existence, Lawrie wasn't ignorant about world affairs.

'There's a lot of conflict there. One reads about attacks on security forces and civilians. The terrorist threat is ever present on the surface, and there are travel advisories,' he said, leaning against the door frame, arms folded across his chest.

'Most of it is localised in northern Sinai. I'll be travelling in the south.'

'According to the newspapers, the advisories are for southern Sinai. Besides, do you think the terrorists' reach can't extend there? Do you forget what happened between 2004 and 2006? Those resorts that had been bombed were in South Sinai.'

'The army has a strong presence there, Dad. Many people travel to South Sinai without encountering problems.'

'Yes, but they don't go around asking questions, Lejf. At least not the type of questions you ask.'

'I'm not going to ask those kinds of questions, Dad, so relax. I want to learn about people whose way of life is under threat of disappearing.' Lejf looked at his mother for support, but she and his father communicated non-verbally. Then Lawrie looked at Lejf like he did when he disagreed.

His father's silence was more unbearable than his words; Lejf couldn't refute it.

19

AN OPEN-EYED DREAMER

The flight from Cairo to Sharm El Sheikh was an hour. The turquoise-blue water of the Red Sea was a beautiful sight from the air. So much beauty amid so much turmoil.

Lejf and Amun stayed in budget accommodation in Sharm for the night and met their first Bedouin guide, Mantsur, and driver, Attayeq, early the next morning. The men seemed prepared with their Land Cruiser kitted out.

In the interior desert, the images of wind-carved hills and rocks, high dunes and plateaus, a maze of mountain canyons, wadis and, on occasion, a green oasis filled the scope of his camera's lens. Lejf watched Mantsur and Attayeq, observing their quiet, respectful ways.

Later he told his mother, 'The Bedouins' build is suited for the severe conditions where they live: small and thin to help lose body heat. They have a characteristic love for freedom and being unbound. Amun told me about the Bedouin term, green hearted. It describes the attitude of being joyful and unburdened by trivial matters and instead preferring adventure and risk.' Signe had asked him to repeat this, so that she could write it in her journal. She walked around, saying it over and over with a smile.

The number of true nomadic Bedouins was shrinking. Centralised government and land borders had impaired their natural inclination to roam and trade for survival. Roads had brought them into contact with the outside world, and now they had to live in it, but did they feel a part of it? Were authentic souls who craved freedom able to accept human-made borders? Through his talks with them Lejf discovered it was a concept they battled to grasp.

He understood their perpetual need to move around and couldn't conceive the thought of being constricted, but then he had the resources to travel when he wanted to alleviate his yearning for freedom.

It was hard to wrap his mind around their complex customs of legendary hospitality on the one hand and the need for revenge on the other. The conflict arose in his heart – that desire for retribution, which to an extent had led them to do unspeakable things against innocent people. No, no. To say *they* seemed unjust, for it wasn't the Bedouin as a group, but specific individuals who'd perpetrated those acts. Unfair as it was, they were targeted as a group. Justice was a term wide open for interpretation and abuse.

Mantsur knew the area like the palm of his hand. As he spoke and pointed, he had a gleam in his eyes, and Lejf saw his father's face in his mind. He would have liked this place and these honest, hardworking men.

There were roads in the desert, and they had to stop at each checkpoint. Security was tight, and the military presence sent a clear message: follow the roads and follow the rules.

'You're a good driver, Attayeq,' Lejf complimented him, and his permanent smile grew wider. Driving in the desert required careful manoeuvring, and they were surprised and curious to learn that Lejf too, grew up in Namibia, a country of deserts.

They drove to an area where the landscape looked like a town of gigantic boulder-shaped houses and dry riverbed streets. Then out of nowhere, the red granite erupted into the green canopies of acacia trees.

They all helped to set up the tent under an acacia tree for the night. 'The *sayal* is precious and sacred to the Bedouin,' Mantsur said, looking up at the tree. 'We call this place Namibia because so many of them grow here.' He chuckled when he saw the surprise on Lejf's face.

'Sayal shares its riches with the Bedouin. Our camels eat the flowers.' Mantsur picked up a puffy yellow flower that had fallen to the ground, and Lejf photographed his sun-weathered hand cupping it; so delicate, it looked like it could break. 'Our goats eat the seeds, and to us the sayal provides its cool shade to gather under.'

With the stars out and the crisp air carrying with it the sounds of the night creatures, they sat huddled around the fire, drinking their sweet and minty after-dinner tea as Mantsur and Attayeq told stories they had heard from their fathers and grandfathers; stories particular to their tribes.

Amun must have noticed the contented look on Lejf's face. 'This is why many Egyptians from Cairo and other cities come to Sinai. It is like an oasis for the soul. When I bring guests here, they tell me they want to return, and many of them do,' he said.

'There's a place in Namibia that I like to go to; it's close to the coast,' Lejf said. 'It's called, Sossusvlei. The sand is white and hard around the salt pan, but all around it, there are high dunes – some of the oldest and highest in the world – and their colour is similar to when the sun shines on these granite rocks. In that place, I feel that all the things that attach to me like thistles, are stripped away. This is the feeling I get here now.'

Mantsur said with a deeply furrowed brow from many years in the hot, bright sun, 'You are a Bedouin in your heart, Lejf Busher.'

'I consider that a high compliment; thank you, Mantsur.'

Lejf remembered something he'd stumbled across in his research and had written in the front of his journal. He took it out of his backpack and read it out loud. It was a famous quote by T.E. Lawrence:

All men dream: but not equally. Those who dream by night in the dusty recesses of their minds wake up in the day to find that it was vanity, but the dreamers of the day are dangerous men, for they act their dreams with open eyes to make it possible.

He closed the journal and said in reflection as all four of them stared into the flames, 'My father fears that I am such a dreamer.' The three men looked at him, but no one said a word.

Lying awake, looking at the Milky Way and the uncountable luminous specks across the heavens, Lejf thought of when he and Laia had camped out near Sossusvlei years ago when they were young, and their eyes were filled with glittering hope. She'd told him nowhere were the stars more beautiful to her than in her Namibian sky. If she'd been here with him, she'd have agreed that this desert sky cast another kind of irresistible spell on you.

'Should I wish for the confidence to speak to her? Would you grant me my desire? You have not acquiesced in her requests for world peace, so perhaps you will afford me this as consolation,' he whispered to the silent meteors flying across the sky.

A few years back, she'd texted him when he was out in a place without reception (he'd only gotten the text a week later). She might have been overworked and frustrated from missing him. She wrote:

I literally don't know how to reach you, Lejf. I don't know whether you'll get this text – you can't seem to be in a place I can reach you. I want you to pick up when I call; I want to hear your voice and speak to you, but there's nothing.

You are the distant planet, Neptune. But no, you are not cold. You are the Red Planet, Mars. What am I, then? Perhaps I am the inhospitable Venus to your temperate Mars, and Earth is the world between you and me.

Somehow, somewhere, between her eloquent words, he'd missed her clues.

He dreamed of Laia's eyes with the constellations behind them and awoke early and noticed she'd changed into Venus, hanging in the air until she dissolved in the light of day.

* * *

They came across a Bedouin family of the Mizena tribe. Gamal, the sheikh, invited them to have tea and lunch with him. Gamal's grandsons were curious and came and sat with them by the fire as he prepared the tea and proceeded to make flatbread, called *farasheeh*, over a dome-shaped hot iron plate. The young girls, tending the goats, couldn't hide their interest from a distance. Gamal was good-natured, and his patience with the youngsters around him was infinite.

While they sat on colourful carpets underneath the shade of a tree, Gamal explained as he poured the tea into small glasses, 'You will discover, Lejf, that the Bedouin love both their coffee and tea. We used to drink far more coffee, but good coffee comes at a high price.' He smiled. 'So we drink a little more tea.'

The women didn't sit with them around the fire. They performed their chores in their area of the tent, called *maharama* – place of the women. Lejf took photographs of the men and boys. The women too agreed and although he wasn't permitted inside their area, he took a few beautiful close-up portraits of inquisitive, kohled-eyes behind veils, sun-creased lines around them.

His mother was on his mind while he was observing them. He wondered what they would have thought about her ideas. Would she have asked them what it felt like to do everything separate from men?

She may have; she's curious about other cultures – women's roles in particular – but she wouldn't say anything disrespectful or unkind.

'The women in Bedouin society have a strong position,' Amun said as if reading Lejf's thoughts when he saw him looking at the setup, and taking pictures of the women talking and working in their small group. 'This may surprise you, but here they are equal to men. Each woman has her job and may keep the money she makes from selling her crafts. They wear veils in the presence of strangers, but these women enjoy many more freedoms than most Arab women in cities do. Life is freer out here.'

They stayed until late afternoon but agreed to meet with Gamal and his band the next morning to watch a camel race at a place Mantsur and Attayeq knew. Gamal's ten-year-old grandson would represent his family.

The number of trucks gathered at the racing spot early the following day caught Lejf off guard. The racing field was nothing more than an open stretch with one prominent tree in the distance to signal the finish line. The atmosphere wasn't tense but hyper-excited. Everyone was in high spirits after a few coffees to get the adrenaline rushing.

'Boys make better riders than men because they weigh next to nothing,' said Amun.

Attayeq had a wicked smile. 'Hold on to your seat, Lejf.'

It was good advice. Mantsur and Amun sat in the back and held on for dear life. It was an insane mix of dust and noise. Lejf had never witnessed anything like it. With their boy riders spurring them on, the camels were bailing as if there was no tomorrow. Vehicles drove next to them as people shouted their encouragement and even the camels seemed to reply with their take on the matter. How Lejf got a single photo in focus was a mystery to him. He held the camera up and pressed down on the button.

He did manage to get a couple of decent shots and a brilliant one of the dusty-faced victor, sitting with a triumphant smile on the back of his camel. When he wondered out loud if a camel could smile, a chorus replied, 'Of course!' They debated his incredulous question over more coffee for some time after.

Attayeq peeped at his camera's screen to look at the photos and grinned. 'Hm, not bad, Lejf.'

'The same to you, my friend. Those were some wicked driving skills.'

When they set up camp in the desert for one more night, before heading to St Catherine, Lejf couldn't help but feel sorry they didn't have more time. He longed to linger here, where life felt freer. Just for a little while longer to ease the growing heaviness inside.

20

SOMETHING ABOUT HOPE

The village of St Catherine was home to the Sacred Monastery of the God-Trodden Mount Sinai and lay at the mouth of a gorge, right at the foot of the mountain. Here Amun and Lejf said goodbye to Mantsur and Attayeq.

At the monastery, they had to follow the prescribed itinerary that led them from the gate to Moses' well in a courtyard, to the Catholicon, the Burning Bush and ending at the sacristy. What struck Lejf was seeing so many of the Bedouins in and around the monastery.

'There's a great feeling of charitableness here. An indisputable mutual support,' he said.

'This is the norm, Lejf,' Amun explained. 'The Jebeliya tribe are descendants of soldiers and their families who were brought here in the ninth century from the Pontos of Anatolia, and from Alexandria by Justinian, to guard and assist the monks when he built the monastery. In the seventh century, they converted to Islam, but the monastery remains an integral part of their day-to-day. They devote their lives to maintaining it. Here they are respected and loved, and they accept the archbishop of Sinai as authority over their tribe. It's not just the Christians and Muslims who coexist here. This is a sacred place for

Jews too, and they join in the celebrations during the day of pilgrimage.' He paused. 'It makes one believe it's possible, doesn't it?'

Lejf looked around. 'The pilgrimage must be a sight to see. Laia would think so too. This is her kind of religion,' he mumbled to himself.

There were rooms to rent in the monastery, with dinner included, and they made it an early night since they had to get up just past 3am to meet their local Bedouin guide for the hike up Mount Sinai (having a guide was compulsory for security reasons). It was cold at the high altitude, and they were dressed warmly. Before proceeding, they had to go through a thorough military security screening.

At the base of St Catherine's Monastery, Lejf chose to take the 3,750 Steps of Repentance. Somehow, the opportunities to reflect on his choices have been popping up at every turn on this desert journey so far; Lejf couldn't escape them. He had plenty of time to repent (if only to Laia) during the 1.5 hours it took to reach the summit.

They had some time to spare before daylight broke and bought hot chocolate at one of the Bedouin tea houses. Warm drinks in hand, they climbed the last few steps to sit on rocks while waiting for the sun to peep over the horizon.

Lejf caught his breath when the first slither illuminated the mountains in the distance before it exploded toward them in a wave of blue, pink, orange and yellow – one of the most incredible sunrises he'd ever captured. He wasn't religious, but sitting there, on top of the world with what would be God's view to many, he experienced a pang of melancholy for something he couldn't put a name to, aching for Laia to see it with him.

Not intending to, he said out loud, 'If there is a God out there, it seems that He received the short end of the stick, looking down at the mess we're making of everything, not to mention our own lives.'

Amun looked at him for a moment, thinking about it and shook his head. 'No, my brother, He sits on top of this mountain, and He watches these people who live here, and then His hope for humankind is restored. That is why this place has survived: so that people may come and see a world as God intended.'

'Do you fear that it could disappear one day?'

'This mountain is unshakeable. It is made of more than granite, Lejf. Human hands and evil intentions cannot move it.'

They stayed there for a while, exploring a Greek Orthodox chapel beside the Rock of Moses, the ruins of the Justinian Basilica and a small Muslim mosque still in use.

So much religion in the world and so little peace. Lejf didn't share these thoughts with Amun. There was something about having hope: it was the energy behind the actions of those who believed in it. Hope, like love, was a powerful emotion, and it took a strong heart to carry it as a beacon through the darkness in this world. Amun had hope. What right did he have to deny him that?

He stopped and photographed strings of people making their way up the hill. They were looking for something, not knowing what they would find, and it might not be what they hoped for – it almost never was – yet they too, had hope.

He gave their Bedouin guide a handsome tip and thanked him for escorting them. They bought coffee and waited outside on the street to meet their new guide, Isra, who took them on a tour of Al-Milga, the Bedouin settlement in the valley, including some of the orchards still operating in the St Catherine area.

'How many orchards are there?' Lejf asked Isra.

'I don't know the exact amount, but there are hundreds,' he said. 'Only a few of them are operating. There are efforts to bring back Beduins who can't find jobs in the cities. Living expenses are too high there.' He shook his head.

'Some people feel there aren't enough tourists here. Do you think that will change?' Lejf asked.

Isra shrugged his shoulders. 'Come, I will take you to a great and wise man, and you can speak with him.'

They drove to a well-kept orchard with a busy farm stall where people bought fresh and dried fruits, nuts, preserves, herbs and all sorts of cures for ailments in bottles. Isra introduced Lejf to Dr Ibrahim (Amun knew him, and they exchanged happy greetings). When Lejf shook his hand and Dr Ibrahim looked into his eyes, he had the unnerving feeling that the man before him saw far more than he wished anyone to know.

Dr Ibrahim took them on a tour around his orchard with its surprising variety. 'Not all our summer fruits are ready yet. The pomegranates and apples take their time. We make trail mixes with the dried fruit and nuts,' he said as he picked a couple of lemons, tangerines and apricots and put them in a bag he carried with him. He picked herbs and held them under Lejf's nose. 'Wild oregano – smell,' he said with a smile. The fragrance lingered on Lejf's fingertips.

He photographed a glossy, bright blue bird hopping on the plants in search of insects. The bird inserted its curved beak into the flowers to draw nectar. 'That is a Palestine Sunbird. Beautiful, isn't it?' said Dr Ibrahim. It was a wonderful place with an air of calm and well-being.

Dr Ibrahim invited them for lunch. They drank tea and ate the fruit he'd picked while he prepared the meal. How like their names they smelled and tasted: tangy, juicy tangerine and sweet, soft apricots you could pry open gently with your fingers – there in the centre, the bare dark seed from which a future tree would grow in this or another orchard in the valley. Lejf looked around and imagined the love and careful hands that nurtured them.

Dr Ibrahim showed them where to put the seeds. He talked about his passion for helping to revive the orchards that have fallen into neglect. 'It is a slow process, but this is about cultivating a sustainable way of life that has benefitted the Bedouin. Many people who have left have returned because they are not making enough money and struggle to support their families. Here, life is much simpler. People can live from what they grow and sell to earn a living. It's a shift back from being consumers to being producers. It empowers them, but they need to learn the skills first. I believe in this community. They are loving, joyful and hardworking people,' he said.

For lunch, they had roasted chicken with vegetables. *'Bismillah al-Rahman al-Raheem* – in the name of God, the Beneficent, the Merciful,' said Dr Ibrahim.

The chicken was some of the best Lejf ever had, infused with citrus and herbs; everything tasted wholesome.

While having their tea, Dr Ibrahim changed the focus to Lejf. 'May I speak with a free tongue, Lejf?'

He nodded, feeling a bit uncertain.

'Your eyes gaze far in the distance – for answers, perhaps?'

'Don't we all search for something?' His uneasiness at being uncovered was apparent.

'You don't like to confront the issue; I see that. You look at it through your camera's lens; that way, you keep a distance between the thing you fear and yourself. Am I right?'

Lejf took a while to digest what he'd said. All three men at the table waited with forbearance for him to respond. No one seemed to be in a hurry.

'I feel that I cannot measure up. I try, but I fall short somehow. With my father, there is a war between our wills. He has never supported the work I do. He fears it will either leave me hungry or dead. He resists me, yet his opinion of me – not just whether he thinks I take good pictures, but what I strive to accomplish – drives me the hardest to prove myself to him, knowing it is impossible to please him. But I cannot seem to stop myself from trying,' he said.

Dr Ibrahim shook his head. 'Nothing is impossible. And who is the other person you are thinking about?'

'It's the woman I have loved since I was a boy, but we live in separate worlds. I couldn't give her the life she needed, and now she's married to someone else.'

Dr Ibrahim was silent for a few minutes. 'It could be that you are looking at these situations from the wrong angle.' Lejf waited for him to explain.

'It is obvious that you love these two people, but suppose what you have been giving them is not what they need from you.'

'What do you mean by that?'

'Maybe they need something else.'

'But *what*?'

He shook his head, laughing. 'I am not clairvoyant, my friend. Only they can tell you that.'

Dr Ibrahim had the kind of light in his eyes that shone from his soul. A man of profound wisdom, yet he was modest. Before they left, he indicated to Lejf to lower his head and pressed his forehead to his as a sign of friendship and acceptance. Then he stood up straight and said, 'There is a Bedouin proverb that says: when a guest comes, he is a prince. When he sits down, he is a prisoner. When he leaves, he is a poet. Go now poet and find peace for your troubled soul.'

* * *

At Sharm International Airport, they checked their luggage and, while they waited to board, Lejf thought of the last few days in Dahab: how commercial and unsatisfactory the experience had been. It was difficult to loosen his mind from such a rewarding experience as they'd had in St. Catherine. He felt a stab at the thought of the Bedouin's immense pressure. How much outside influence could a culture withstand?

They boarded, and Amun talked, jumping from one topic to the next without stopping to breathe. After a while, not wanting to be rude, Lejf checked out of the conversation. Later, when he went over it in his mind, he could see the hints.

The doors to the aircraft closed, and the flight attendants did the pre-departure checks. The engines started, and they were moving along. Then an abrupt stop, no announcement. The doors opened again, and two security police officers spoke with the captain. Walking down the aisle, checking the row and seat numbers, they stopped at Lejf and Amun's row. They said something to Amun in Arabic. He got out of his seat and collected his things.

'Don't worry, Lejf, this is standard procedure,' Amun said, but Lejf saw the fear behind his eyes and felt it gripping his own throat.

The policemen asked to see Lejf's passport, eyeing him with suspicion, as they inspected every page. After what felt like forever, they spoke to each other, looked at him and handed the passport back without a further word.

What did Amun mean? Standard procedure for what? Lejf opened his mouth to ask him, but Amun shook his head; it was almost imperceptible. His eyes told Lejf it would make matters worse. He felt helpless as he watched them escort Amun out. No one in the cabin said a word; it was silent as the grave for the whole hour back to Cairo. Lejf had chills running down his spine and felt rage for what seemed like a terrible injustice.

When they arrived in Cairo the atmosphere was the same. The place was teeming with military police, armed to the hilt, watching every passenger who came through the gate. It was meant to be intimidating.

He called Amun's uncle at the travel agency from a pay phone. 'Mr Abaza, this is Lejf Busher. I'm here at the airport in Cairo. There's been an incident; Amun's been taken away by the security police. It happened in Sharm. I'm sorry I wasn't able to call you sooner.'

If he was shocked by the news, the older man gave no indication. 'You must leave right away, Lejf. Take the first flight you can get. Thank you for letting me know. *Ma'a Salama.*'

***

Lejf completed the editing and layout of the Sinai trip and was ready to move on to the next one, yet, he had mixed feelings. He'd called Amun's uncle several times to hear if he'd been released from prison, but the answer was not yet. Signe loved the photographs he showed her and asked endless questions, hungry for details. She too, was disturbed by what had happened to Amun.

His father was agitated for other reasons. 'I'm certain it is not necessary to tell you that it could have been you.' Lejf ignored the comment and didn't tell his dad how close it had been.

An article in the *New York Times* online caught Lejf's eye, and his heart sank. The headline read:

Another Egyptian Citizen Pays With His Life For Telling The Truth

... An unidentified source told the Times *that Amun Abaza, a man suspected of having sympathetic ties to a well-known Islamist extremist group in North Sinai, had died after being arrested and detained in prison. According to the unidentified source, the arrest occurred after Mr Abaza had written and published an online opinion about North Sinai citizens' poor and unaffordable living conditions and their growing mistrust of the government. Following numerous inquiries by his family, the Egyptian authorities have confirmed that Mr Abaza died of a virus contracted during his incarceration.*

There is no evidence that he had ties to any political movement.

The fear had been lingering at the back of his mind, but reading the news was a knife in his gut. Lejf felt sick like he would throw up – that poor boy. Amun's only crime had been that he cared about his people. He had known they'd be coming for him and protected Lejf, who could have been arrested if Amun had not ensured his tracks were covered. How does one repay such a selfless act? There would be nothing he could do to bring back Amun's vibrant energy. He was gone. What devastating heartbreak for his family.

Stupefied at the senselessness of it, he sat staring at the screen as if the words in the article would somehow rearrange themselves, making the events undone and that it would instead read that Amun had been found alive, without harm, that he had been reunited with his family. All his wishful thinking couldn't change reality.

Hell wasn't some doomed destination you were cast into because you lived a licentious life: it was the real world here on Earth, where men ruled. The Amuns of this life couldn't say what people needed to hear because their voices were silenced, snubbed out like candles. Amun had seen a world which didn't exist because he had hope. A beautiful world where people coexisted regardless of their race or creed. Who had the right to decide over the life and death of the innocent? Men with their ghoulish agendas had no right to play God – how he despised that foul brood of vipers!

'He was only twenty-four years old. He had done nothing wrong. Nothing under the sun,' Lejf told his dad when he found him. His afflicted state must have drawn Lawrie to read the article's headline on his computer screen. Lejf said, 'Freedom of speech is a luxury that too many who have it take for granted. I know you don't understand but this is why I have to do this. For people like Amun.' They stared at each other in silence for a while.

'I am truly sorry about your friend losing his life. You are right, and we do take freedom of speech for granted, Lejf. Someone has to pay the price so that others can be free. It seems that you want to be that person. Is that what this will lead to for you? Are your mother and I to accept that without question?' His father stood looking at him with grave sadness in his eyes.

The *sine qua non* of being a photojournalist was uncovering the heart of the matter: the human story, which was all he cared about. Telling these stories might come at a price; this was true. Was that what he wanted?

Where did the acceptance lie? With him or with his parents?

21

THE LAND THAT WAS SUNG INTO EXISTENCE

'How much time have you got? I hope enough to join me for a game of football before we head out to the Outback, mate,' Lejf's longtime friend, Graham Townsend, said when Lejf called him to let him know about the desert project and his intention of doing a segment on the Australian Aboriginals. Graham was a personal tour guide, and Lejf wanted to support his business. He couldn't imagine a more ideal person to travel with through the Australian Outback.

'The Waratahs are playing against the Chiefs from New Zealand in Sydney, and since you'll be coming from that way, we might as well use the opportunity,' said Graham with much enthusiasm. 'I'll forgive you for not barracking for either team, but I'll have to support the Tahs since someone's sure to spit the dummy if I don't.'

Graham was from Canberra, and the Brumbies were his rugby team of choice. He used to play Aussie Rules football in his twenties until a knee injury forced him to the sidelines, where his ardour for rough sports had intensified along with his strong and flavourful opinions about environmental issues.

He was the same age as Lejf, though he looked at least ten years older. Hair bleached white by the sun, face, arms and legs dark as leather, he was a genuine Aussie who loved and lived life to the fullest – he played as hard as he worked. His passion for his country and deep respect for Australia's First Nations people made him change gear from a white-collar career to an Outback adventurer and advocate for sustainable tourism in collaboration with Indigenous Australians. His energy and good cheer were boundless.

Feeling more than the regular out of sorts than he was willing to admit to anyone, Lejf was looking forward to Graham's company. There was a queer vibration on the inside; it was hard to identify, let alone define, what he felt. It could have something to do with a higher-than-usual irritation toward the invisible forces behind the sadness and turmoil in the world, exaggerated by what his research uncovered. The project itself was intense. He contemplated extending the deadline but decided against it, figuring it would be better to get it over and done with.

Laia was running in the background of his mind like a throbbing joint pain, as was digesting the trauma of Amun's death. Reliving that day on the plane when he was taken away plagued his thoughts, not to mention his dad's growing fear and concern over his safety, which he couldn't dismiss. These things slowed him down when he didn't have the luxury of time.

If Lejf were frank with himself he would recognise that he was overwhelmed. But he was his father's child: stubborn and unbending (Erik would have loved hearing him admit that).

Trying to stay focused and tame his fragmented thoughts and emotions, the incessant and unrelenting questions and self-talk drove him mad, and he was caught in a compulsive, obsessive spiral. No amount of research could provide him with the answers he craved, yet he was desperate to do the project well. No, it had to be something extraordinary because deep down, there was the underlying fear of disappointing Laia. He couldn't disappoint her again.

Chuckling at Graham's Aussie expressions, he said, 'Well, my friend, until Namibia joins the big league, I'll have to be a fence-sitter.'

'Too right, mate. I'll have your ticket ready and see ya in Sydney.'

* * *

Lejf was deeply affected by what he learned about the First Nations people of Australia, whom he hadn't known much about. As much as he was intrigued and enlightened, his emotional state felt like it was deteriorating, but he didn't speak to anyone about this.

'I am blown away by the Australian Aboriginals' whole outlook on life and living,' he said to Signe when they discussed his research. 'Their lores, respect for one another and a connection to country is what guides them. They have a completely different view of ownership. They don't consider themselves owners of the land, but believe that they belong to the country and owe it their deference. What a profound perspective. We are brought up to praise individualism and to define success by ownership of material things.'

'Perhaps this otherworldly soulfulness they possess intimidates people and prevents them from learning about their stories. It can be difficult to persuade people who have been raised to believe that any religion outside of their own, is wrong,' she said.

Signe loved their Dreaming Stories in particular, as did Lejf; these spoke about how the Creator Beings walked the earth and sang everything into existence.

'Aboriginal people dwell in and form a part of this labyrinth of life; to them there is no separation between the spiritual and the real world. It's an unfathomable, intricate bond. No wonder the clever historians had branded them savages and heathens. When you don't understand you default to judgement.'

Sitting back in her chair, arms folded across her chest, she said a long, drawn-out 'Uh-huh.'

'I am amazed by how much we can learn from Indigenous people's practices. Australian First Nations people understand the connection with, and their responsibility toward, protecting their country. It's a simple, yet far-reaching philosophy: if you use too much, the earth will suffer and, as a result, humans will suffer too. Even when the colonialists came and took the choicest spots with the best water resources, Aboriginal people have managed to survive because of their knowledge and respect for the land. How can one not admire them?'

'What about the destruction of their holy sites by the mining companies? I saw something about that on the news the other day and was so upset,' she said.

'It's a loss we can't grasp Morsa because we only see the tangible loss, but it's far more significant to them than losing precious rock art or artefacts. They were the Songlines, the Creator Beings or ancestors followed across the land. There's a fragmentation of their culture and it causes wounds that couldn't, and still can't, heal for many of them. Just one more consequence of the civilised man's obsession with bringing disaster and taking what doesn't belong to him.' Lejf looked at his dad. 'I suppose you don't agree with me.'

'What concerns me Lejf, is your preoccupation with things that can't change,' Lawrie said.

'Preoccupation – is that it? No, Dad, I can't change the past. From where First Nations people are now, no amount of rewritten laws and attempts to reconcile can undo what has been done. Should they be forgotten, though?'

'Heaven knows, nobody is saying they should! But you are not the one who brought these things upon them, Lejf. A dose of perspective will do you good.'

'When you stand on the other side from theirs, it's impossible to understand the pain and distrust Aboriginal people must be feeling toward those in society who tolerate them with a silent disregard, in some cases, with open antagonism. And I am aware that the media and individual journalists contribute a fair share of the negativity. I'm trying to think about how to approach this project because I don't want to repeat the same critical bias; that would be pointless. No wonder it makes them feel disparaged to hear all that; it doesn't reveal the story of what makes them unique.' Lawrie stared at him in silence.

The more he tried to explain himself, the less his father seemed to understand. The more he uncovered through research and the further he moved along on the desert project, the tighter the underlying tension between them was becoming. His mind was glutted; he didn't have the energy to spell out why the project meant so much to him, why these people, whose stories deserved to be heard on every social channel and news network, weighed on his heart. His father was wrong. If people knew, they would care. There had to be *somebody* out there who would care about the fading worlds of Indigenous people, about the terrible injustice.

These overwhelming thoughts ... Amun ... Laia ... Laia ... Laia ...

***

Few champions of Indigenous Australians' voices were as energetic as his friend Graham Townsend or Townzie, as he was called with much affection.

They flew to Darwin, the capital of the Northern Territory, and from there, made their way South to Alice Springs.

'The Northern Territory Government has grand plans for Darwin. To make it world-class and unlike anything Australia has had, so they say. The hope is to bring in more tourism and for new developments to spur growth. Darwin has a young population on average, which isn't a bad thing, but I reckon they also want to keep older people from retiring elsewhere. The tug of war that keeps going on,' Graham said as they drove around the marina area.

'It should do a lot for the city, and I'm inclined to agree with them.'

'It's an ambitious project. They need federal and territory funding to fill the gaps and a lot of it.'

'You don't sound enthusiastic about that,' Lejf ventured.

'Yeah, nah. The waterfront upgrade: sure, it can lift the city; I get that. It's a double-edged sword. You know me: I'm not too keen on decision-makers' motives; they have to prove my doubts wrong before I clap my hands, all excited over their ideas. I don't know if you've heard, but a huge subsea optical cable system is also underway, linking Oz to Asia and the US.'

'I've read about that.'

Graham looked over at some of the residential developments. 'They're bargaining on creating jobs and infrastructure through the data centres, but I'm sceptical about how much it will benefit the locals, the First Nations people particularly. I'm chuffed it should give Darwin a much-needed boost. I wish they'd invest more into developing people who could do with those kinds of jobs. I hope I'm off the mark and that it won't be just a handful who'll skim the cream.'

'That's the way it always ends up being, Townzie.'

'Bloody oath.'

Graham parked the car, and they walked around. There was plenty of construction happening. He pointed out some of the areas around the city centre. 'A few First Nations communities use pockets of land. Do you know much about the Larrakia People who live around Darwin?' he asked.

'I know they were the original people here and that they've battled to get a claim to the land.'

'Yeah, it took them twenty-one years – the biggest land claim in the history of Aboriginal Rights. The court ruled that 600 square kilometres be handed back to them. Ha! What a joke. Then the federal court turned around a few years later and said, "No way, can't have it," because they couldn't find sufficient evidence that the Larrakia People had a continuous connection to the land, quote unquote.

'It was handed back to them, but the important thing the courts, and many other people, have missed for their convenient arguments is what Indigenous Australians are about. It's effing impossible for them *not* to have a connection to the land because they and the land are one.' He demonstrated with his hands in the air. 'Whether they live 5 or 10 or 5,000km away, it doesn't matter. You're not less of a Namibian when you're not in Namibia, right?'

'Right.'

'Listen, I know I'm stepping on many toes, but I'm not anti-progression. I think development is necessary; people have to live somewhere. What about the people who already live here who don't fit in with the glitzy new neighbourhoods they're building? There's always a high price to pay with any kind of development, be it people or the environment. No matter how much they say they'll put back, developers' number one objective is making money, not the welfare of people or the Earth. I've yet to find an honest one among the lot of them – and they're biding their time to scoop up every morsel of land they can get their hands on. The Larrakia Nation Aboriginal Corporation provides services to the Darwin region and does a great job supporting its communities. Even so, a helping hand from the federal government would go a long way. Things are changing for Aboriginal people, but in some areas, it's still too slow.'

'It's a universal problem, my friend. Nobody in government wants to claim responsibility.'

Graham nodded. 'Anyways, you'll meet a few people who will blow you away. Their kind is the heart of this country.'

22

WOMEN WITH SOUL

'So, what have you been up to? Dare I ask the dreaded question: how's the love life?' Graham asked with a chuckle.

Lejf shrugged. 'Work is my love life.'

'Crikey! That doesn't sound too sexy to me. You all down in the dumps over a woman?' He looked at Lejf askew, as if he couldn't conceive that it was true.

'You can say that my bubble burst, and she grew tired of see-you-later, so she decided to get married. And that's the sum of it.' It twisted his insides to admit to the truth out loud.

Graham whistled through his teeth. 'Bugger. Sorry about that.'

'One of those things.'

You didn't pay attention until one day, you found yourself alone in the desert, walking in circles and talking to yourself, and then you realised you couldn't stop having those conversations. The windmill of the mind kept you in its sweep. You didn't know how to break free from it, and it made you afraid because what you imagined felt more and more real and, above everything, more comforting, and made you feel connected to her. So, you let her stay because you ached for her. You told no one about this. It became your secret: yours and hers.

'Isn't that the truth? Relationships: I swear I can't figure out how people even do it. Our parents' generation believes you stick it out, come hell or high water. For many of them, their strategy was to have a bunch of kids in the hope they would act as buffers so those parents didn't kill each other – and you wonder how so many of us turned out normal.' Townzie cackled. 'Nowadays, there's a trend not to have any kids. Pets have become the new children. The more advanced we get, the more we can't seem to cope with each other's complexities. What are we bloody coming to as a species?'

'I'm beginning to think pets are better at relationships than we are,' Lejf said, laughing more at his life's ironic, miserable truth.

Darwin to Katherine was about a three-hour drive. Graham pointed at mining activities. 'Gold mine. This is one of eight major mines in the Northern Territory. There are a couple of smaller ones too. Mining is big business over here.' He pulled a face and shook his head. 'Eighty per cent of Australia's mining activities occur on Aboriginal people's land. They'll rehabilitate, so they say, but when the mining companies begin using words like rehabilitation that sound fancy-schmancy on paper, I can't help but want to scratch the itch crawling around underneath my skin. They've sucked the life out of the earth, and now they're going to cover the holes up with heaps of dirt and hand it back to the First Nations people, as if they'll be doing them a huge favour: here ya go, take this dead thing, it's of no use to us anymore.'

'What's the solution, though, Townzie? Even in Namibia, mining is the leading economic sector. Governments argue it's the greater good versus the interests of minority groups, yet you and I know it's far more than that. The essence of what's at stake is that people and their cultures, worth more than all the gold and diamonds in the world, are being squeezed into thin glass jars without proper ventilation. You go out there with that message, and chances are you'll be met with resistance; not everyone wants to see it that way. It's not profitable to think like a human.' Lejf paused and inhaled. The shortness of breath was becoming bothersome. 'I worry about society's perception of time: people think there's much more of it. They don't think there is a cut-off time for everything within our control to turn around. It seems the only way for some people to understand what will be lost is after it's lost forever.'

Didn't he know that from experience? The sounds and images in his head were irritating him. Round and round, the windmill turned as a die bounced from one arm to the next. It didn't fall to the ground to show him how many chances he had left. He didn't need to look to know the answer anyway: it was the same wasted chance, bouncing and bouncing down the sails of the windmill.

'Right, you are, mate. Governments would do a hell of a lot better in making sure they look out for those minority groups if they didn't have a particular fondness for puckering up to rich investors.'

'Well, as Lord Acton's famous quote goes, "Power tends to corrupt, and absolute power corrupts absolutely. Great men are almost always bad men."' Lejf looked out the window at the dust clouds from the mining trucks. It was no coincidence that the quote didn't say 'bad women'. Perhaps the whole problem with Mother Earth's dilemma was that her sons had never learned to share, and like in any unfair play, there were a couple of bullies throwing their weight around. The more sophisticated a culture deemed themselves, the bigger the bullies.

'Katherine isn't a big town, but it can get busy. It provides important services to the surrounding area. Tourism is a major sector and it's the central hub of the Savannah Way. You'll see plenty of motoring tourists here. The First Nations people make up about a quarter of the town's population, while the larger communities are spread out. They use the town as an important meeting point, and tomorrow we'll go and visit some of them. First, we need to get ourselves settled in, and then we can search for something to eat and drink,' said Townzie as they pulled into their hotel's parking lot.

The town sort of bulged out on flat plain dominated by tropical savannah (a parched winter landscape much like parts of Namibia) and sat on the banks of the Katherine River. It was dry season, and temperatures hovered around the mid-20s Celsius, but it was much less humid than in Darwin.

Driving toward a Barunga community of the Jawoyn people, the scenery changed into dramatic and breathtaking gorges.

Graham introduced Lejf to three women elders in their community: Pattie, Joy and Susan, whom he called aunties. He explained that the term aunt or uncle wasn't limited to blood relatives within Aboriginal people's communities. Younger people addressed older folks this way as a sign of respect. Using it as a non-Indigenous wasn't appropriate unless such a relationship was established. 'I'm sort of like the prodigal son who shows up now and then. He-he.'

Lejf wondered how his friend managed to keep up his high spirits.

'G'day, aunties, this is my mate, Lejf Busher, the world-famous photographer I told ya about.' He handed one of them a box of Lamingtons he'd bought at a bakery in Katherine. 'This is to have with our tea.'

'I wouldn't put any stock in the world-famous part. Pleased to meet you, ladies.' Lejf extended his hand in greeting.

'Good to meet you, Lejf. Boy, a tall one you are. You look like a decent chap. What ya hanging around this rascal for?' said Joy, giving Townzie an affectionate shove with her elbow, and merry laughter erupted from all three women.

Over a cuppa, enjoying their sweet treats, they told Lejf about the enterprises run by the Jawoyn Association. Barunga was a small and vibrant community. It reminded Lejf of some of the towns in Namibia – most of it was farming activities with a definite tourist flavour. The women's passion for their country spoke to him.

'You've probably read plenty of negative things. The internet's full of that,' said Susan, shaking her head. Lejf nodded, and she said, 'Ya going to get the sceptics. Nothing you can do about that. The only way to silence the knockers is to prove them wrong. We're not where we'd like to be, but I'm proud of how far we've come. As elders, we must lead the way so that people will have a place they can come to for support, and to learn a few things about life from us old ladies.' She winked at Townzie.

'Too right, auntie Sue,' he lifted his cup, giving her a bright smile.

'To Sue's point,' Joy added, 'that branches out to our community who supports each other through initiatives that raise money. There is help from the federal and provincial government, but it's not always enough, and we need money to fund projects and services to create employment anywhere, Indigenous skills and knowledge of the land are needed. No one understands this country better than we do. We labour in love.'

Lejf made notes and took photographs, looking around at the surroundings. They were in Susan's home. Family pictures hung on the walls, and cultural objects stood in the corner of the living room, where he imagined many gathered on the well-worn sofa and chairs. It was a place where a soul could find comfort. Gazing down the hall, sunlight flooded through an open kitchen door, which led to a dry winter backyard. A sleepy dog lay basking in the warmth on the kitchen floor, flicking off flies with his ears. It could have been anywhere in Namibia.

He'd expected the women to be more guarded, yet the opposite was true. They were full of humour and positive energy. He didn't sense bitterness, only a hopeful longing to be recognised as a people.

What did people desire more and gave them greater security, than being loved and having a sense of belonging? Across the oceans and spanning continents, humans displayed these desires through symbols and traditions. That's what made them inherently the same, but also distinctive in their cultures. One culture wasn't more important than another; they were just different. And yet so many people feared the differences, instead of recognising the humanity behind it all.

'We are finding ways of reaching out to the greater community of Australians and people from other parts of the world through festivals, through tourism. The Barunga Festival is gaining popularity. We had great attendance this year,' Pattie said.

'Yes, I'd read about that. I'm sorry I missed it,' Lejf said.

'These cultural events are important,' Pattie continued, 'When people see and experience our connection to country with their senses, their emotions become invested. It changes the dynamic from they-versus-us to we. After all, this world we inhabit is a living part of all of us. Everywhere we humans go, we walk with our feet planted into the earth; we are connected to it and to each other.'

***

'Here at the Banatjarl Strongbala Wimun Grup we strive to empower Jawoyn women and their families. It is about sharing culture, working together and learning from our elders,' said their guide as she walked them through the facilities. 'Our doors are open to those who need support, and also for visitors who are curious about Jawoyn culture.'

The cynical voice in Lejf's head was drowning out her words, saying it was a beautiful sentiment lost on the ignorant of any land without the desire to learn. He was feeling hot and strangely irritable and tugged at his collar.

She took them through the bush garden. 'We're getting ready for the wet season,' she said, pointing at the women working with spades and trowels, pulling weeds and planting seeds. 'Our garden is expanding.

We started it in 2012, and it's thriving in the care of loving hands. Women who come here, gain traditional knowledge for growing plants for bush tucker and bush midijin.'

As the guide was explaining the ancient use of native plants for healing, much of the serenity at that moment – the women working together in harmony – reminded Lejf of the Bedouin in St Catherine, when he'd visited Dr Ibrahim at his orchard. It should have made him feel tranquil. He should have been happy, but there was a sinister storm brewing. He felt as if he was in a straitjacket when all he wanted to do was go out and plunder with this surge of rage inside.

Voices in his head kept repeating that it was all too much. Perhaps his father had been right all along when he said this profession would be the end of him. Lejf was sure his dad would love hearing him admit to that. Stubbornness didn't want to give him that gratification.

Witnessing so much kindness and goodwill among these lovely people, everything felt wrong outside the barriers of their existence. They were engaged in a never-ending fight for a right to something that belonged to them. They had to battle to speak in their cultural voice, to speak for themselves. Many people had been dictating what they should and shouldn't say for far too long. Who would listen now?

And where was Amun's voice? How in the world did a kid with a head on his shoulders and a genuine heart in his chest end up tortured to death in prison? He imagined his screams, those kind eyes filled with horror and pain. Why didn't those who had the power to do so change things? Bureaucrats with their screw-you attitudes. No, they wouldn't do anything. They liked to revel in suffering; it made them feel untouchable. They were sadistic snakes.

Was Laia's husband one of them? Lejf hated the guy's guts. The way Ravi looked at him with contempt. His assertiveness when he spoke to Laia, the way he held her arm: the strong man, in control. Yet Ravi hadn't been the imposter there; *he* had. His Laia. She was trying to make a life for herself, and he came in, a lunatic with no words in his mouth. He was no better than any of the germs in society whom he wanted to spit on and grind down underneath the sole of his boot.

Where had his thoughts run off to this time? The heat was burning him up. He tugged at his collar again.

'You okay there, mate?' Townzie glanced at him.

'Sure. A little hot. I'll have a drink of water.' His heart was racing from a lack of oxygen. What the hell was the matter with him?

23

SEEING THE LIGHT

'During Buwurr – known as The Dreaming – the Creator Beings created the land, rivers, gorges, plants, animals and humans. And they bestowed each with its unique word. They gave the country its language and laws, so people should obey them. Buwurr isn't something that happened in the past. It is today as well. It is everything. The Jawoyn people means the land, the lore, the Songlines of The Dreaming. We are the country, and the country is us,' said their Aboriginal guide, Mick, as they walked along the trail in the Nitmiluk National Park.

Townzie introduced him and Lejf in his colourful way. 'Lejf, I'd like you to meet my partner in crime: Mick – Mick, this is Lejf. He's from Namibia, so he swears he'll be able to handle the heat, although I've seen signs that he's burning up. Good thing he came in winter.' They both laughed at the joke.

'How ya goin', mate?' Mick said, extending his hand in greeting. He had a skewed smile and a way of looking at you the same way, a most likeable chap suited to his profession.

'Pleased to meet you, Mick.'

'You ever been to Nitmiluk?'

'I've never been to this part of Australia.'

'Well, I haven't been to Namibia; there ya have it. Reckon it would be pretty deadly to see those red dunes of yours and compare them with ours.'

They followed Mick on their hike as he continued the story. 'Nabilil, the crocodile, came from the sea with his firestick. At the entrance to a gorge, he set up camp and there he heard a cicada song. So, he named the place, Nitmiluk, which in the Jawoyn language means the place of the cicada.'

They followed Nitmiluk Gorge along the Jatbula Trail, a network of sandstone gorges carved by the Katherine River. It was stunning, yet Lejf was troubled that his overcast mood dominated something as beautiful and transformative as this place. He took a deep inhale to try and refocus his attention.

'The Jawoyn have walked this trail for many generations. It was named after Peter Jatbula. He was instrumental in securing land rights for our people. It was a long and hard battle, and we won our land in 1989. This is the route he walked with his family.'

The place had a strange effect on Lejf. He thought he heard voices speaking together in a language he didn't understand. Or was the heat and continuous cracking pops made by grasshoppers in flight messing with his senses?

At a lookout point, they sat down, and, staring out over everything, Mick continued, 'Bolung, the Rainbow Serpent, rests in the deep water at that gorge over there.' He pointed. 'He is both the giver of life and the destroyer of it; therefore, he must never be disturbed or spoken to. But the most important figure in our Dreaming is Bula, the creator of Jawoyn land. Bula left his image in some places, painted on rocks. North of Katherine, there is an area known as Sickness Country, where no one must go, for if Bula is disturbed, terrible sickness and calamity will result.'

They sat quiet, each lost in his thoughts for a while. Lejf wiped the sweat from his face and neck with a bandana. He turned his head to try and establish where the piercing sound was coming from.

'Do you guys hear it too?' he asked.

Townzie looked around and said, 'Can't hear anything besides the racket the insects are making. I guess all creatures have a right to express themselves.'

Lejf didn't tell them he thought he heard voices. 'That must be it. They're rattling my mind,' he said with an embarrassed little laugh.

* * *

Walking along the riverbank, he tried to follow the location of the whispering voices. He listened, straining to hear. No, there was one voice after all. The moon shone on the water. He stood still and stared, hypnotised by the widening ripples on the surface, and a terrible fear gripped him, but he couldn't run away; his feet had sunk in and were stuck in the mud. He wiped off some of the sweat pouring down his face and neck but was soaking wet again as soon as he did.

'You must not go into the deep pool where Bolung lives,' he heard a voice – Mick, say. The form of the serpent rose out of the water. Lejf was paralysed. Slithering up the riverbank, it circled him; its beady eyes followed him with intent. He didn't realise it had coiled around and constricted him until its face was on his eye-level. It struck quick as lightning, plucking both his eyes out of their sockets, and, for a while, everything was total darkness. He didn't feel the burning in his eyes; the pain was in his heart, but he couldn't move his arms to press his hand on it. The serpent placed two glistening marbles into the sockets where Lejf's eyes had been. For a moment, all he saw was blinding white light, then his vision started to return, and everything was more transparent than before, a world once hidden from plain sight, a marvellous feeling of enlightenment.

He heard the whispering voice, turned his head, and saw her: Laia, radiant and beautiful, standing at a distance with her arms open wide. 'Come to me, Lejf,' she said. He leapt into her embrace, at once free from bondage.

A kingfisher perched on a tree branch outside the tent brought him back from his dream reality into a world that felt less authentic. He closed his eyes for a moment to try and recreate the dream, but it was gone. In the distance, the unmistakable ochre shape of Uluru stood with its hidden mysteries. *It is our secret. We will tell no one.*

'The whole area from here at Uluru to Kata Tjuta holds spiritual significance for the Anangu people. There are more than forty sacred sites and almost a dozen Dreaming tracks,' said Townzie, as Lejf took photographs of the red giant against the arid landscape.

They'd gone there at sunrise and sunset for the effect of the reflected sunlight that caused Uluru to glow as if a raging fire from the inside had lit it. There was something about the island mountain. A strange magnetic pull made Lejf want to climb to the top and float down to earth like a grass seed in the breeze, light and free from the stone inside his heart.

'The Anangu people live in scattered communities in this part of the Outback, and they hold on to their traditions and care for their country.' Graham contemplated something before he continued, 'Globalisation and consumerism have come at a high price to the First Nations people and diverse ecosystems. It has been a painful lesson for these people with a natural inclination to trust.' He plucked a dry grass stalk and chewed on it in deep thought. 'Take this big fella over here.' He indicated to Uluru. 'How long has the Anangu pleaded with visitors not to climb it? And what did the government do? They put up a bloody rail to make it *easier* for people to climb and they added a sign saying "It's not illegal, but we'd prefer it if you don't climb it". Effing hell! They might as well have built a cable car that led to a bar at the top. It's sacred to Aboriginal people, don't they get it?' He shook his head in disgust, then looked Lejf in the eye, and for a brief second, there was a flash of concern as if he'd seen something there. He added, 'Australian Aboriginals have to fight the forces on both ends.'

'In what way?' Lejf asked.

'Well, first of all, you hear enough about mining companies destroying sacred sites.' Lejf nodded. 'This is in part because they don't do enough research about indigenous land, and let's not forget that our government approves their permits. It's a double-edged sword: the location of sacred sites is known only to Aboriginal people. They're torn between their religious obligation to keep the whereabouts of those sites a secret and disclosing their location to prevent them from being bulldozed. It's forcing them to compromise on beliefs so sacred to them that they don't talk about it.

'And then there's the role of information technology, which can be a blessing and a curse. Tech can help them map out their territories but proving that the land belongs to them throws them onto another battlefield. They have found allies in activists, and that's great, but to prove their rights, they must give up sacred knowledge and endure long, expensive court battles. What must they do? I ask you, mate,' Townzie said.

'They are smack between Scylla and Charybdis. Whichever one they choose, they lose,' Lejf said in reflection.

Had he and Laia not been caught by those sea monsters themselves? The choice of the one was the ruin of the other. Had she chosen the lesser of the two evils for herself? And by not speaking up, had he not taken the course that would send him on the most destructive path? The erosion of cultural values. The demise of emotional well-being. It was all the same.

Graham spat out the grass stalk with a slight nod. 'The Australian government has at long last pledged to do more to help preserve ecosystems under threat, and they've realised they can't do it without the knowledge of the First Nations people. I suppose one must look at it as progress.'

Lejf's soul felt sick at the thought of all the sadness brought upon Indigenous people caused by the irreparable damage from the decisions of others.

'We need our First Nations people to keep us from destroying the earth and ourselves,' said Townzie, and sat down on a rock.

Lejf took photographs. He saw an Aboriginal man walking in the distance. He didn't walk over to ask for permission to photograph him as was the protocol, but instead zoomed in and captured him. The man was painted white, and he carried a long walking stick. He stopped, turned and looked straight at Lejf. He put the stick down, touched his hands over his eyes and then moved them to his heart, picked up the stick again, and continued. Lejf glanced at Graham; he seemed oblivious, and Lejf followed the man with his gaze until he disappeared on the horizon.

Staring at the lonesome soul's image on his camera, etched against the bush and the blue sky, he held his camera for Townzie to see. 'Have a look at this.'

Graham looked at it for a moment. 'What am I looking at?'

'You don't see him?'

'See whom, mate?' His look was a mix of curiosity and concern.

'Never mind,' Lejf said. Perhaps it was a spiritual message intended for him, and Graham couldn't see it.

The voices in his head sounded like deafening screams.

24

AN UNEXPECTED CALL

After all the maddening thoughts about Laia accumulated like the tangled-up mess of a fishing line, and Lejf couldn't figure out the beginning and the end of it – the rationalising, the self-condemnation, the self-pity, the denial, the anger, the swallowed-back tears of frustration and regret – the answer arrived. As he suspected, it was the dream he had about her in Australia. He felt relieved: it was a good omen. Her soul had found him and called to him there, where it had been full of anguish in that spiritual place. His Laia came to his rescue as he hoped she would.

It was a different kind of revelation to those who knew Lejf. They didn't understand the reason behind his sudden joy and renewed energy. How could they? They hadn't gone through the dark corridors of the abyss. His mother at least seemed pleased to see him with lifted spirits. His dad was eyeing him with more leeriness than ever.

When Laia called, Lejf was stunned into silence for a moment at the sound of her voice. They hadn't spoken since that fateful day she'd told him to leave Germany. He'd been yearning for news from her, although he had no interest in knowing about Ravi. All he cared about was to know her mind and her heart again. It was an awkward start.

All the unspoken words of the long months between them hung in the silence.

Laia broke the ice. 'I heard you've started the desert project. That's great, Lejf.'

'Yes, I have. It's going to be good, meaningful. I want people to be inspired.' And he wanted her to be proud of him.

'Of course, it will. I'm thrilled that you're doing it. How far are you?'

'Almost there. There are two more to go. Between research and editing, there's not much time in between. The next project's in Botswana – the Kalahari, to be precise. I think it's one you'll like.' He smiled, knowing her answer already.

'You're going to do a feature on the San? I'm envious!' Lejf didn't miss the unmistakable excitement in that sweet voice. As long as he'd known Laia, she'd had a soft spot for the San.

'You could go with me.'

She paused before she answered. 'That's a wonderful thought.'

'How are you doing, Laia?'

'I'm not too bad, I guess. Work's busy; it has its fair amount of interest, but it's not as exciting as yours.'

'And otherwise?'

'It's okay, you know: two people from different cultural backgrounds and a big age gap sharing a life. There's bound to be friction. Ravi's set in his ways. I am too, I suppose, but it feels like I'm caring for a big baby.' She sniffed.

'Men are all big babies.'

'I've been questioning myself. It could be me, and I'm not doing it right, or I'm not cut out for this marriage business after all.'

What did you call it when you experienced concurrent fear and hope? Was there a word for it? Hope seemed so ambiguous compared to fear sometimes. What was he hoping for? That Laia's marriage was a failure? For her to tell him she'd made a mistake? He didn't want her to feel as if she was a disappointment when she was everything but, to him. She had the courage to try, and there was no failure in that. 'No, that's not true,' he reassured her.

'That's kind of you to say, Lejf, but you don't know that for certain.'

He wanted to ask her many questions at once. But their first steps were cautious, reading each other's moods at a distance and on different wavelengths, testing the other's vulnerability. It took a while to become synchronised again. She felt like his Laia, though her voice sounded muffled, as if she spoke behind a shroud. How muted his voice must have been to her all those years. Did she notice this new change in him? Perhaps she wouldn't because she hadn't experienced what he'd been like for the past year they'd been apart; before she'd rescued him in the dream.

Uncertain whether he should ask her about her personal life, she said, 'I've missed you, Lejf. It's good to hear your voice. I can't tell you how happy it makes me that we're speaking again. It has been awful not to be able to communicate with you when I've craved it so much.'

How could he give her anything but a hopeless confession? 'I've missed you too, Laia.'

**

Two weeks before his Kalahari trip, Laia called to say, 'Lejf, is the invite still open? I've thought about it; I want to go with you.'

'Of course!' he said, elated and not knowing the situation between her and Ravi or where it would leave them. All he could think of was seeing her again.

His mother commented, 'Oh,' when Lejf told her Laia would join him. She perceived Laia's husband wouldn't be a third wheel on the cart. The only times she'd stated her opinions were when she disagreed. Lejf took her silence in this instance as grasping how important it was to him, that she wanted him to be happy. His mother understood him.

His father didn't conceal his disapproval. 'What does Laia's husband think of this?'

'Are you all of a sudden concerned about what Laia's husband thinks? I assume she's told him she was going away with an old friend.'

'An old friend. Is that what you were hoping this would be? The rekindling of an old friendship?'

And his dad liked to accuse *him* of being patronising. 'I'm going to interview and photograph the San in the Kalahari, and Laia had asked if she may join me. She's eager about this project and about the San people.' Lejf didn't tell Lawrie he'd invited her, nor did he tell him Laia was having marital problems; it would only fuel his father's argument. He didn't know for sure that she was having problems; it may only be a bumpy spot, and she needed a break to clear her head.

Yet there was the mysterious dream that led her to him.

'Lejf, you and Laia are two consenting adults, and you know I love her like a daughter. Forget what others may have to say for a moment and think: is this the path you want to take?'

'We haven't done anything wrong, Dad.'

'No. Can you tell me without a doubt that you would be strong enough not to?'

He ignored his father's question and looked at Signe, who remained silent.

On the morning of their departure, Lejf drove to Laia's parents' house to pick her up. The awkwardness was palpable when he greeted her parents and even between the two of them. There was no emotional show – perhaps for Gerhard and Dael's sake. The weight of a year's worth of turmoil was underneath the surface in their reserved greeting. He longed to embrace her.

Gerhard and Dael were curious when he told them about the trip, and Dael invited him in for coffee, but he was eager to get on the road and excused himself. Laia greeted her parents with a casual wave. She looked keen to head off too.

'We're glad you stopped by. It was good to see you, Lejf,' Dael said. 'All the best with your project. We know it will be a huge success, as always.'

'All the best, Lejf,' Gerhard said with a handshake.

Laia was waiting for him in the Land Cruiser. She was married and they were friends, nothing more, he reminded himself. 'Ready?' he asked.

'I am,' she said, and he couldn't interpret the meaning behind her smile.

***

They entered Botswana through the Mamuno border at Ghanzi. Lejf refuelled the Cruiser, checked the tyres and water, and stocked up on water for drinking, cooking and bathing, and to buy supplies; their last chance before entering the Central Kalahari Game Reserve. From Ghanzi, it was another 100km to New Xade, a Basarwa settlement. As far as modern life was concerned: there were pathed roads, a clinic and a school.

Lejf parked and they got out. He wiped sweat from his face with a handkerchief. There was no breeze to alleviate the intense heat. Although it was still winter, daytime temperatures remained high. The thermostat in the car read 31°Celsius.

'Are you okay to wait a bit? I'd like to talk to a few people. You don't have to stay out here in the heat; you can sit in the car and I'll turn the engine on for air conditioning,' he said.

'Of course I don't mind waiting. I'll walk around.' She cupped her hand over her brow, scanning the scene.

The merciless sun baked the dry earth. A few people were congregated under the shade of a tree, their cattle and about ten goats seeking the same relief some distance away. There was no visible grazing for the animals. A few dead cattle lay in the distance – the faint stench of their decomposing bodies still lingered, although their dried-out hides covered nothing but empty trunks and skulls with grisly smiling teeth and hollowed-out eye sockets.

'Look, there are traditional huts,' Laia pointed. 'They look out of context, don't you think?'

They did indeed stand out, not so much because they were interesting compared to the bare concrete buildings, but because they looked forlorn.

Lejf approached an old man smoking a cigarette. 'Good day, mister, how's it going?'

'Not too bad, sonny. How about yourself?'

'Same here, sir. I'm Lejf,' he extended a hand.

'Good to meet you, Lejf. You can just call me John,' said the old man, who looked like a child next to Lejf's tall frame.

'I was wondering if you'd mind if I take a couple of pictures and ask you some questions, John? I'm a photographer and I'm doing a project for a magazine. It's about the San. It won't be for free; I'll pay you,' he said with a reassuring smile.

'A photographer, hey? No, Lejf, go ahead; I don't mind,' he waved and took a deep drag. 'Your plates say Namibia. Where are you from?'

'Otjiwarongo.'

'Otjiwarongo, hey? I haven't been to Namibia in some time. I wouldn't mind visiting the Skeleton Coast. Ah, the cool breeze and the rough sea,' he said and stared into the distance, perhaps remembering something or someone there.

'Pretty dry in this whole area. We noticed a few dead animals,' said Lejf while he took photos from different angles.

'It didn't rain much in summer, and it's been a tough winter.' John tutted.

'Where do you take your animals to graze?'

'The nearest grazing's about 5km away. There's not much but it keeps them alive. We go early, before it gets too hot.'

'That makes sense. Do you have family in the reserve?'

'No, we're all here.'

'Do you miss it?' Lejf asked cautiously, watching his reaction.

John thought about it for a bit, finishing his cigarette. 'When the government wants to make decisions for you, there's nothing to do but to accept it.' He shrugged. 'So, your spirit fades away bit by bit ... You heading off to the reserve then?' he asked.

'Yes, sir. I'll be filming there. It's part of the story I'm doing.'

'That's what I thought. It's popular with the overseas photographers. Xade or Tsau Gate?'

'We'll enter at Xade.'

John peeped around Lejf with a frown. 'Ah, yes, that's not too far to go from here, only 50km, but with the roads, a bit of a drive,' he said.

He didn't tell John he was familiar with the game reserve from travels with his parents when they took their boys on adventure camping, and he and Erik let their childhood imaginations run free in the wild, barren land. His mom and dad experienced the San in their natural environment when more of them lived in the reserve. In his father's study was a photograph of Signe, five-year-old Torsten, three-year-old Søren and Ingve – a baby – sitting with a San family, broad smiles on all their faces. Only Torsten talked of faint memories of that.

Lejf paid him, 'Thanks for your time, John. Take care.'

'All the best to you, Lejf,' said John with a wave.

A cluster of girls was playing under the shade of a tree, and Laia watched with a contented grin. Lejf offered them some of the fruit he'd bought in Ghanzi. She looked happy there among the children. Joy amid hardship – something about seeing that felt wrong. Unlike these Basarwa, he couldn't accept the unfair hand that had been dealt to them. And looking at Laia, he felt wistful about having dealt her an unfair hand too.

They'd been on the road since 7am and their bodies were aching from sitting still by the time they pulled into the campsite at Xade in the early evening. Laia had offered to relieve Lejf from driving for stretches, but he assured her he was used to it. She hadn't done long-distance driving in Africa for a while; these roads could be challenging.

They set up their tent, unfolded the camping chairs and Lejf opened a beer for each of them, which had kept cold in the chargeable cooler box during their drive. From the camp's vantage point on a hill, he watched a group of animals gathered at the waterhole below, and Laia came and stood next to him.

There wasn't much water, but it was enough to draw wildlife closer. Elephants ripped out the water pipes from time to time; it was the luck of the draw to have pumped water here, the reason why it was so critical to bring your own.

Black-backed jackals were calling close by, their melancholic voices harmonising with that beautiful peace which descended, pulling a slow, glittering dark blanket over everything. Lejf hadn't experienced anything like it anywhere else in his travels, as he did in Africa.

Sitting with her head resting back, Laia turned to him and said. 'It feels like I've come home after a long, tedious quest.' He wasn't sure if she meant home to Africa or home to him.

* * *

There's a degree of separation between us; I can't penetrate her thoughts like I used to. I don't want to speak to her about the distances between our lives, or the small day-to-day or about her and Ravi's marriage or even about our fathers. I want it to be the way it used to be when she travelled with me and we were disconnected from the faraway world where reality kept us apart.

I told her about the San on the way here, and she listened but didn't speak. I couldn't see her eyes; she kept staring out the window. Still, I felt her sorrow – it is mine, too. She knew their story, how their government had sold them out for diamonds. It's the same tragic story of greed and loss I've seen over and over: people forced out of places where they were free to become enchained because of capitalism's insatiable thirst for more, no matter the cost.

I wonder if there's something else troubling her besides hearing the harrowing tales and witnessing the desperation on those poor Basarwa people's faces. Could it be her marriage? Perhaps she's still angry with me about what happened in Karlsruhe. I want to tell her about my dream in Australia, but I will wait for the right moment.

He closed his journal, turned out the gas lamp, and lay watching her sleeping form in her sleeping bag on the other side of the tent until his thoughts melted into dreams.

***

Lejf was up when there were still plenty of stars visible, to take photographs of the sunrise and morning vistas. Though the winter veld had a subdued beauty compared to summer, the stark contrast between the earth-and-sky landscapes made for fantastic photography.

By the time Laia appeared, he'd made a fire and brewed a pot of coffee. She pulled a blanket around her shoulders and shuddered with a giggle. 'Brrr.'

The air was crisp, and a thin layer of frost covered everything. He indicated the coffee. 'That will help for now. The sun will start warming you up soon.'

One of the things Lejf admired about Laia was her lack of self-consciousness. They'd camped together many times over the years, and she'd never fussed with her appearance, which to him made her lovelier.

'As soon as we've had breakfast and are all packed up, we'll head to Bibe, set up our tent, and then drive out to meet a few of the San,' he said.

There was one other couple in a rented camper van some distance from their tent. They kept glancing in Laia and Lejf's direction. 'They must be impressed with our organised setup,' he told Laia with a chuckle. Camping was second nature to him, and Laia herself was no slouch.

On the way to Bibe, they saw two cheetahs lying in the shade of a tree. He pulled to the side of the road, and Laia had to lean over him to get a good view. He wouldn't deny that the sensation of her so close sent a tremor through him, but his father's words were like a spoke in the wheel of his thoughts. He didn't touch her, although he ached to do so.

25

THE LITTLE PEOPLE WITH BIG HEARTS

'It's impossible to imagine this land without the San. It's their home and they belong here,' Laia said.

They were on the way to a traditional San village. She was sitting with her back half against the car door, legs pulled up and her feet resting on the seat so she could face Lejf.

He momentarily glanced at her. She was starting to open up, he thought. 'Yes, I agree, but there's a distinction: for us, to think of the Kalahari without the San is unimaginable for sentimental reasons. For the San, to think of life without the Kalahari is spiritual death.'

'Yet their government is adamant about making them modern and educated. Knowledge ought to be measured by what we know in relation to the world we live in. Out here in the Kalahari, the San aren't less educated and experienced than a CEO in the company they're in charge of.'

He thought about that. 'True. I've observed something interesting: when globalisation penetrates the world of Indigenous people, there's a common conflict that arises within those communities, between traditions that are upheld by the older generations versus the desire of younger generations to learn new things and to become modern. When I spoke with the Basarwa in New Xade, they told me they wish to live the way they have done for thousands of years. I don't know if they would feel different about it if their lives weren't so hard – if they had better opportunities. Perspectives change with circumstances. Yet they speak of their longing to roam the Kalahari. I can't help but wonder if it has something to do with who they are; how something in their spirits will always remain free and untouched.'

She rested her hand on his leg, and he took it. It was pure impulse. 'That's why I knew you had to do this project, Lejf. People need to hear this; see your beautiful photographs telling these remarkable stories of survival. Will you tell me about the others you've done so far?'

'Of course I will.'

The San family stood in front of three dome-shaped grass huts, watching Lejf's car pull up with curious expressions.

He greeted them and explained his purpose for being there. 'Good day, I'm Lejf.' He waited for Laia to introduce herself, then continued, 'I'm a photographer. I'm doing a story on the San for a magazine and was hoping we could spend some time with you. I'd like to ask you some questions about your life here in the reserve and take photographs. Would you mind? We've brought supplies and I will pay you generously for your time.'

They peeked in the car and conferred with one another. The tallest of the group stepped forward. He had an approachable, easy demeanour. 'I'm Albert. No, we don't mind. Of course you are welcome here,' he said, shaking Lejf's hand.

Albert introduced his family. His brother, Daniel, was his friend and hunting partner. He was shorter and more muscular and didn't make much eye contact. During their time there, as they got to know him, Lejf and Laia discovered Daniel, with his gentle nature, was a talented artist. He made delicate necklaces and bracelets from hand-carved animal bones (he painted San art on these), porcupine quills and colourful seeds, which he strung on kneaded strips of hide and sold to tourists.

Betsie was their sister. There was a melancholy about her, and they learned she'd been married, but her husband walked off because she'd been unable to bear children. Miriam was Albert's pretty, shy wife, and they had three children. Last, but not least in any way, there was Little Bit, their mother, a tiny, wrinkled figure whose eyes were filled with a mixture of mirth and sadness.

Laia fell in love with them all at first sight. Lejf, himself, wasn't invulnerable to their gentle onslaught.

It was later in the afternoon, and although the camps weren't that far apart, the roads were not conducive for driving at night. Laia and Lejf sat with them around the fire for a while longer, listening to their stories. They spoke in the Afrikaans language, which most San understood. Lejf and Laia spoke Afrikaans too – it was understood throughout Namibia.

Laia whispered to Lejf, 'Ask Little Bit about her name.'

The old soul paused a moment before she answered in her slow, calm voice, 'When I was born, my mother could hold me in her hands like this.' She cupped her hands together. 'So, she called me Little Bit. I was named after no one but myself. My granddaughter is named after me. Children are never named after their parents; only their grandparents or relatives, and sometimes, after no one.'

Lejf didn't know whether it would be appropriate to ask about her husband, but Little Bit brought him up and said he had died during the removals. The water supplies were destroyed, and many people couldn't make it out in time because of heat exhaustion.

'After the high court ruled that removing our people from the reserve had been unjust, some lucky ones, like us, could return, but we are just a few. Many couldn't bring their families because the government decided only those who'd brought the suit could return. And they are scared to leave the reserve to visit their loved ones because they don't know if they will be allowed back. We were fortunate that we could stay together,' said Little Bit with a rueful smile.

'Who is the leader here?' Lejf asked.

'You can say that I am the leader,' said Albert, 'but we all partake in decision-making. There is no hierarchy. A woman can also be the leader of her own family group and have the claim to waterholes and foraging areas. We rely on our elders' experience and wisdom,' he said, looking at Little Bit. It was clear that she was an important influence over them all and they addressed her with respect and affection as 'Klein Mammatjie'.

'Everyone has their role in San society,' said Little Bit. 'Women gather the food and, sometimes, they go on the hunt. Now I'm too slow for all that; too much pain in the joints,' she tittered.

'What about the children? Where do they go when everyone is out hunting or foraging?'

'Children must have fun and play; that's very important,' said Little Bit, 'but when they are young, they go out with the women to gather food. Dries has already started going out with his Pa and uncle, and in a few years, Jessop will be old enough to join them.' She indicated to her grandsons.

Underlying these individual and group functions was their connection during leisure, which was a high priority for the San. Lejf and Laia felt privileged to witness this time of bonding.

Albert made music with his bow by plucking it with a piece of wood, creating a vibrating sound. He held one end near his mouth, changing the shape to alter the sound produced. Daniel and the women's rhythmic voices and clapping created the melody and beat. The sound carried clear in the cool evening air. The trance dance – perhaps one of the symbols associated most with the San people –

was a deep and significant experience for them; Lejf and Laia didn't witness this.

Little Bit explained, 'The trance is for healing and to get rid of bad energy. We also call to God to ask for rain and guidance for the hunt.'

The lines of the San's religion have become blurred. Albert and his family were an example of that intermingling of shamanism and Christianity. Sitting there with them, Lejf watched Laia's face aglow in the light of the fire as she clapped along.

When they were alone, Lejf told her about his visit to Australia. 'We have moved away from our most basic and important needs as a species – how we live and the choices we make. Graham and I sat with Mick around a fire in Nitmiluk National Park. He told us stories about Australian Aboriginals, beautiful and real things to those who can look at them with an inward gaze. It is easy for our eyes to be deceived by what we think we see, and they cloud our understanding. Mick spoke about some of Indigenous cultures' core qualities; the things that help them survive: their patience, how they embrace ownership as a community, and how they work together for the benefit of the group. I thought about this. They are not merely primitive people who live in wild places. They collaborate with intelligence and purpose. They think, dream and have joy and sorrow, just like we do. When we see ourselves through their eyes, we see our need for the things our souls hunger for.'

'I see one thing beyond question, Lejf: this project was meant for you. These people need voices on the outside who can speak for them.'

'I hope to be their voice. What I wouldn't give to have a heart like theirs. Indigenous people are like the bright stars in a desert sky – unfathomable, unreachable through conventional thinking, but they have been the ones who've shown travellers the way to go. What would we non-Aboriginals be without these beacons, Laia? We would burn out like artificial light bulbs because we have no natural energy to sustain us. We have lost too much of our connate values.'

When he closed his eyes, he saw the San family around their fire, clapping and singing; desperately holding on to their culture; hanging on for humanity's sake.

Over the next few days, they kept returning to visit with the beloved group. Lejf's strategy was to capture the men and women performing their daily roles. They first went foraging with the women and children and spent peaceful hours in the cool, dry Kalahari winter veld, something Laia enjoyed with glee.

The women carried the plants and firewood they gathered in a *kaross* made from animal hide slung over their shoulders. In a larger kaross, Miriam had her baby daughter, whom Laia called Little, Little Bit. The two boys, aged five and nine, demonstrated their extraordinary knowledge of the plants and herbs they collected for medicine.

Laia was perceptive and whispered, 'Make sure to take an equal number of photographs of Betsie.'

She'd noticed Betsie's glances when Lejf paid attention to Miriam and the baby. Miriam was a beautiful woman, and although it wasn't intentional, he did focus more on her; she was photogenic and bashful, which made for lovely photos of her and her child. Betsie beamed in the spotlight, making him realise how a woman paid much more attention to certain situations than a man.

***

The hunting expedition with Albert and Daniel was thrilling. It wasn't a persistence hunt, where they tracked an animal for days until it succumbed to exhaustion.

'It's a good thing; we probably would have faltered before the hunt even began,' Lejf told Laia and laughed.

Albert and Daniel searched for easier prey like spring hares, turtles and smaller meat sources. They found a nest of ostrich eggs, and after first kneeling down to press an ear to it, took two of the twelve eggs, careful not to disturb the remaining ones. It was a big prize for a hungry San family who consumed the egg protein and used the eggshell to store water. During the winter months, insects made up a significant portion of their diet. Lejf wasn't as put off by the idea of eating grasshoppers as Laia was.

'Trust me, when you're hungry enough, it will taste like honey,' he said.

She shuddered. 'Ugh, I'm not there.' And then she added, 'I hope I haven't offended them.' The two men watched Lejf with intense gazes and appeared unaffected by her remark.

He gained a new respect for what it took to bring a meal home by observing these patient huntsmen. They took what they needed, nothing more, but hunting was illegal in the reserve.

'What do you do to avoid being caught?' Lejf asked Albert.

He clicked his tongue. 'We cannot stop hunting. How do you change the way you are born to be? We watch out, but we will not go without a fight if we get caught. If I must die resisting, let it be here, then at least my spirit will remain in this place, and it will be at peace.'

With the San, it was hard to read their expressions. They carried permanent smiles, but that didn't allow Lejf to see what was going on inside their minds. They were as deep and mysterious as the Kalahari itself. Daniel didn't affirm his brother or express his opinion.

Lejf couldn't picture either of them living elsewhere: these little people with their enormous hearts. They moved erect and with elegance. Their steps were light, as if they were careful not to disturb the shape of the sand that the soles of their feet trod over, and when they stopped at intervals to speak to each other in clicks, it sounded like the desert's music. He turned to Laia, and she was watching them with quiet reverence.

Sitting by their campfire, he told Laia, 'It's laughable: the excuses people come up with to justify their actions. The San have been exiled under the pretext that the government wants to protect the fauna and flora, yet they allow mining activities in the reserve – there's the true damage done.'

'The San were made scapegoats for their agendas. It's tragic,' she said.

He nodded. The moment made him aware of a weighted feeling in the air, the avoided subject that could no longer be ignored. 'I haven't apologised for what happened in Karlsruhe –'

She interrupted him. 'No need. Neither of us has done right, Lejf; I was as much to blame for springing my news on you the way I did, but I was so desperate. I thought it would solve things. You didn't deserve to be cast aside. You, least of all people. You're my best friend; you know that, right?'

He would have gathered all the stars above their heads and given them to her if he could. 'You felt we couldn't work something out. Nothing at all?'

'I couldn't see how. I still can't. Look at where we are; what you're doing here. This incredible gift you have that you're sharing with the world. You said you want to be their voice, and you *are*. You speak for people like Albert and Daniel and Little Bit, and those like them. Your work is significant because it isn't a job but a labour of love.'

'And what can I labour on to give you what would satisfy the need in you, Laia? I haven't ever asked you that. I'm aware I should have but haven't.'

She paused. 'You told me in Karlsruhe that you needed to be my friend and lover. That is what I need from you too.'

'Are you going to stay with Ravi then?'

'I don't know. It's better than being alone.'

Light from another world shone through the perforated black sky.

She rose over him, a divine creature from that luminous place beyond, taking possession of his body and soul. A drop of sweat fell on his cheek. He reached up and touched her Plender gap, searching for the source of the moisture as his hands moved up her neck to her face. It was wet.

'Laia?' he whispered.

She shook her head and bent down to kiss him. 'I'm okay, Lejf. I'm okay,' she whispered against his lips. He felt his own wet face.

26

THE UNSEEN TRUTH

Driving back to Otji, Lejf occasionally turned his head to watch Laia as he listened while she told him of things that had happened during the past year. Yet she didn't speak of her and Ravi. With a stab of love in his heart, he realised Laia's longing for companionship and her commendable effort to make her marriage work had not been enough after all, and it had led her back to him. It was inevitable. 'That's why you came back to me there in the Outback: you wanted to tell me how much you needed me,' he thought out loud, and when she gave him a puzzled look, he told her about his dream.

This time, she didn't come to him as a hopeful innocent as she'd done on the evening of her twenty-first birthday long ago. No, it was wrought with doubt and uncertainty; with caution from hard lessons, learned through experience.

There was too much that was unresolved. She was married, and Lejf could not judge her decision to stay with Ravi. He had no better alternative to offer her. His father's voice sounded in his ears, and Lejf pushed it to the back of his mind; it would be another disappointment for him.

Desperation – such a frightful trap. He didn't know how he and Laia would be able to overcome the barriers between them. The answer eluded them both. He knew of one undeniable truth: it didn't matter that they were apart; their souls remained together.

Signe was eyeing him when he got home. Her demeanour was quizzical, but she was delighted when he showed her the photographs of Albert and his family.

'Their lives are simple and pure in that world where they feel they belong, Morsa. Their way of life is fading away, and I don't know if anyone will be able to rescue them.' Then he thought of an endearing moment out in the veld with the women. He smiled as he showed his mother the photographs of Miriam and the baby. 'Laia called the baby, Little, Little Bit. Isn't she adorable?'

His mother looked at him in surprise. 'Laia?'

'Yes, she went with me. You knew that,' he said with a baffled expression.

She shook her head and replied, 'No, I didn't.' She looked into his eyes, searching for something. Lejf didn't like her probing gaze. 'That's impossible, min älskling.' She was careful. 'She couldn't have gone with you.'

He sniffed. Was she making a joke? 'What do you mean that's impossible? She was right there with me. Mom, I know it's hard for you and Dad to accept, but Laia and I ... the fact is, we can't stay away from each other.'

She looked at him with a deep frown. 'Lejf, I spoke with Dael Ackermann the other day. She mentioned that you came by their house before you left on your trip. She said she thought you weren't yourself. Are you feeling all right, my love?'

'Is this an interrogation? There's nothing wrong with me. You know as well as I do that Dael is a frustrated, lonely woman. What would she know about whether I'm feeling myself or not? I was there to pick Laia up, not to talk to Dael about how I'm feeling.'

'Pick Laia up? That's not possible, Lejf.'

'Why do you keep saying it's not possible?' Signe flinched at his raised voice, and he apologised, 'I'm sorry. I'm sorry, okay, I don't mean to get upset, but I don't understand why you keep saying that. Laia had asked to go on the trip with me Morsa, and something happened between us. Yes, she's married, but we're going to find a way. I know we'll find a way.'

She looked at him a long time before she answered with worry in her eyes. 'Lejf, your father spoke to Laia over the phone while you were in Botswana. She *couldn't* have been on the trip with you, my love. She couldn't have.' She took his hand. 'Laia hasn't been to Otji in months; she's in Karlsruhe with her husband.'

He pulled his hand out of hers. Wounded by the worst betrayal: his mother refused to believe him. Signe, of all people. Has his dad at last gotten to her? To hell with what they thought. He and Laia weren't children, and he was done trying to justify his actions.

The constriction was back in his chest and in his gut. It sucked the air out of him – an intolerable suffocation. He needed to go for a physical; it had been a while since he'd been for one.

He'd go after Mongolia he decided.

27

IN SEARCH OF HIS INNER GHENGIS

Mongolia's capital, Ulaanbaatar, lay at the centre of the province, Töv, but it didn't form part of the province; it was an independent area.

Viewed from the air, the city looked grim and unimpressive. It conjured images of ugly grey Soviet buildings from the Cold War era as the aeroplane circled before landing. Flanking this unattractive concrete mass to the north, it was impossible to miss the sprawling white horde of the *ger* district.

Lejf's guide, Batbayar, was a squat, round-faced man with a thick knob of black hair. He wore a shiny purple jacket with LA Lakers written in yellow on the back over a flowery blue Hawaiian shirt, and carried a smile almost the size of the sign he held up with Lejf's name. He was as quirky as his outfit.

He explained as they drove from the airport, 'It's growing fast. About 60 per cent of the city's population now lives here, and the government hasn't figured out how to deal with it. Only a quarter of Mongolians still live a traditional nomadic life. Many people have been forced to move to Ulaanbaatar in the last few decades after losing all their livestock to frigid winters. The *dzuds* are weather systems unique to Mongolia and cause extreme hot and dry summers and brutal winters.'

'I'd read about that.'

'When the communists ruled, they controlled everything. Most of it was bad for Mongolians, but they at least helped the herders with fodder during hard winters. People weren't allowed to migrate to the city. There's none of that kind of help or control anymore.'

'I've read that it's estimated that pastoral land in Mongolia is degrading twice as fast as the rest of the planet due to climate change,' Lejf said.

Batbayar nodded. 'And over-grazing is contributing to the problem. Unfortunately, there aren't great possibilities for migrants here, Lejf. They don't have the skills and experience to work in commercial industries, and they can't afford rent in the city, so they settle on the outskirts in the tent district where they have no access to services and living conditions are tough.'

Viewing it through an outside lens, it seemed as if hope and despair competed with one another, each holding the other down, hovering in a poisonous, smoggy haze over dome-shaped gers where children played on rusty old cars in tiny backyards, and dogs ran around looking for food. Different from any picture Lejf had in his mind of the self-sustaining and free existence these people had as nomads.

He soon discovered that the overall appearance of the city was deceptive. It was, in fact, rich in culture and diversity. Batbayar drove him around in a dove-grey van that looked like it had seen many long journeys across the steppes. Lejf thought all it needed was a big peace sign stuck to the side to complete the picture.

He captured the charm of it all: small Buddhist temples sandwiched between modern glass skyscrapers. Graffiti art on buildings told the Mongol story. Mongolian and mainstream music blared over car radios passing them by and people walked around in traditional Khalk deels alongside professional businessmen and women, dressed like westerners, all on their way to work.

'Now we will go see the big Buddha,' said Batbayar.

Looking up at the golden Zhang Ranze Buddha at the Gandantegchinlen Monastery filled Lejf with awe, and he sent Laia a photo and a text:

This is a place you would like. It's full of mysticism, and these Mongolians are spiritual people. It is strange to encounter a nation of kind and polite citizens. We can come back here to see this monastery, but I'd like to explore Mongolia with you.

I saw the statue of Genghis Khan earlier, in a square bearing his name. It's gargantuan, and a clear expression of their larger-than-life reverence for him here. I can't help but think how it's an anomaly since the Mongolians are a peace-loving nation, yet Khan wrought such fearsome destruction in his conquests. For some reason, I was swayed by the history and symbolism, and his story has made me think of you and my mother.

Tomorrow we'll drive to a town called Erdenedalai. Cell reception might be off; I'll keep you posted if I'm able to.

Laia's response puzzled him a fraction, and then he thought it may have been that her mind was wrapped up in work:

This is a surprise. It's good to hear from you, Lejf. It's been a while since we last spoke. Well, more than a while. So, you're in Mongolia now – the land of the horse. I can imagine how mind-blowing all those sights must be. I would love to see that one day. I hope your project will be a success, but of course, it will; your work is extraordinary. Tell me about it sometime, will you?

P.S. I'm curious to know how Genghis Khan reminds you of me and Signe.

He chuckled at her inquisitiveness and replied: *I'll tell you tonight in my hotel room.*

IN SEARCH OF HIS INNER GHENGIS

***

Lejf wrote Laia a long email, telling her about his research into the life of nine-year-old Temüjin, betrothed to ten-year-old Börte-Ujin – still teenagers when they married seven years later. When a rival gang kidnapped Börte, Temüjin pursued her captors for months, not relenting until he'd rescued her. This set in motion the path he would follow to become Genghis Khan: formidable force and ruler over all the Mongols, one of the greatest conqueror warriors in history. And at his side, stood his grand empress, who gave him her lifelong allegiance and support.

Of course, Lejf knew Laia would have known the story of Genghis Khan; she was much smarter and the scope of what she read far broader than his. Books were her thing. But it was as if all the revelations he'd encountered at every corner were spinning in his mind, opening up a world of understanding. He merely had to tread on the soil to become saturated by the truth that flowed like a river. He linked it to the First Nations Australians' belief in the interconnectedness of humans with the earth. His new eyes saw it clearer, he felt in his soul how he was changing into an unearthly being. And he was anxious to share what he'd been pondering with Laia. There was so much inside him that he didn't know where to begin.

You said you're curious about why you and my mother remind me of Genghis Khan. I find it interesting that two of the most important and influential people in his life were Börte and Hö'elum, his mother.

Hö'elum had to care for Temüjin and his four brothers when their father was murdered. Temüjin had learned a lot about tenacity from his fearless mother.

And although he had other women, Börte-Ujin was the supreme female in Genghis Kahn's life. Like the meaning of her name, she was his mistress and his voice of wisdom. Her wise counsel saved his life on more than one occasion. Börte was her own woman; she ruled her territory and was the queen of her court as her husband continued his quests. And through it all, her loyalty to him never failed.

You see, Laia, Genghis, and Börte had been bound to each other since childhood, and only death could break that bond, like you and me. Alas, I was no brave Temüjin: I did not go in search of you when you needed to be rescued. I want you to know that I am aware of that now.

The words, like dreams, danced in Lejf's mind, and he moved in and out of them, and they of him. He was on a swift chase over the steppe – his white horse's name was Genghis. He was searching for Laia. Through valleys and over mountains he rode. His heart beat fast in his chest until it felt like it would explode. Then he saw her running in the distance. He could see her fear as she turned to see who was following her. When he'd caught up with her, he scooped her up and rescued her. Her eyes laughed with his.

The alarm clock startled Lejf. He'd fallen asleep with his laptop beside him on the bed. He checked to see if Laia had responded; there was no reply. He grappled with her silence and touched the place in his chest where it felt hollow and cumbersome at the same time.

28

NOMAD'S LAND

It was surprising how the scenery turned into steppe right outside the city limits. Grassy plains stretched as far as the eye could see. Lejf photographed them, clothed in their yellowish-brown autumn coats. There were a few tarred roads and electricity lines here and there, but even Namibia seemed to have more infrastructure in the rural areas than Mongolia did. He loved the simple, clean lines of the landscape which looked like it had been drawn with fine coloured pencils, and left bare enough so the viewer might fill it in with their interpretation.

Erdenedalai was a town in the province of Dundgovi in central Mongolia. To call it a town was a bit like calling Otjiwarongo a metropolitan city. The main street had a few small buildings, but as Batbayar assured him, that was typical of these outposts.

'Mongolia's twenty-one provinces are divided into *sums* or districts. Each sum has a permanent town with basic services like a hospital, police, markets and a school,' explained Batbayar.

'How do kids in the area get to school?' Lejf asked.

'They ride their horses,' he said, as if it should be common knowledge for a stranger like Lejf. Then to qualify added, 'Those who live close enough, of course.'

That made sense. Lejf chortled at the thought of parents sending some tardy youngster off to school on their horse early in the morning. Kids riding to school on horseback in the twenty-first century: what a different kind of life it was.

'And those who don't live close? What do they do?'

'They stay in the dormitory in town and go home for the weekend. If they live too far, a family member moves to the town to care for them for the whole school year. It's standard for grandparents to fulfil that role. Remember, gers are mobile homes so it is doable for families to help each other in need. That's what people do here, Lejf. If they didn't back each other up, no one would be able to survive.'

How the hearts of the people in Mongolia moved him. When you saw so much pain and suffering and your soul felt the crushing weight of it, you allowed yourself to start believing there was no more goodness left in the world, that all people were corrupt. Then you met the ones with untainted hearts who demanded nothing, who knew the art of giving and living with a freedom that originated in a place where no injustice could reach it. They taught you profound truths, mystifying you and making you want to hold on to those intangible, beautiful things for their sake, because you feared for them. Because they stood to lose that which made them free.

***

Batbayar was a seasoned operator and an easy-going companion. It was like witnessing a miracle: there were no road signs for the many obscure roads leading off to who-knew-where in the great beyond, and he knew them all.

There were *ovoos* throughout the country, scattered across the planes, desert and mountains and right next to the road, adorned with the skulls of animals and with prayer scarves flapping in the wind. Whenever they passed an ovoo, they stopped; Batbayar got out, walked around it three times clockwise, added three stones and said a prayer. After each mini ceremony, he returned to the car, smiling. 'Now our travels will be safe again.'

To Lejf's amusement, he discovered that not everyone stopped for this ritual. But his wise guide informed him that driving past an ovoo on the left side of the road was the custom. In the past, they had served as the boundary for a nomad's pastures or as a road sign.

Mongolia was steeped in religious tradition, and although Buddhism was the majority religion, it wasn't the first. Shamanism, known as *Böö mörgöl*, had been practised since the age of recorded history, and over time, it had been incorporated into Tibetan Buddhism.

Batbayar said, 'In shamanism, we believe humans are connected to the universe through mountains and lakes, to each other and our ancestors. The gods – our grandparents – are the guardian angels of their families below, and this love chain between parents and their children is an energy that transcends death.'

During his research, Lejf discovered that Genghis Khan, a devout practitioner of shamanism, was believed to have been of divine origin and that his first ancestor was a grey wolf.

'I was unprepared for how revered Khan is in Mongolia,' he admitted to Batbayar.

'Oh, yes. He isn't just an icon; most Mongolians believe him to be the main embodiment of the supreme God, Lejf.'

Religion was abstract to Lejf. He struggled with the concept of doing good so that you might obtain a reward from an unseen God. To him, people's motives were too egocentric by nature, at least in educated, modern societies and it was hard to imagine that you'd be able to outsmart, even manipulate, God, or the gods, who knew all thoughts and deeds. What would have been the point, then?

The undeniable truth he discovered was a strong parallel between the people he'd met on the desert journey: they lived in isolation and under trying circumstances. For all of them, their religion was at the heart of their existence, and everything else – their family, their animals, their connection with nature – revolved around it. It was the bridge to overcome their privation.

There was something to be said for trusting in something outside of oneself. Laia had told him that years ago when he believed in nothing but her.

***

The generous family they stayed with made room for them in their ger while the kids boarded in town. Batbayar entered without knocking. Seeing Lejf's surprise, he explained, 'This is a welcoming place, Lejf. Anyone may come in.'

Lejf had to bend his head as he entered, careful not to step on the threshold (which was considered a bad omen). Batbayar introduced him to the two women working at the stove: Chimeg and her mother, Narantsetseg. They looked up at Lejf, startled at his height, then waved the men in and quickly made milk tea, pointing at the snacks on a small table and indicating them to sit down and help themselves.

'There's always food ready for strangers in a nomad's home,' Batbayar said.

Lejf had brought bags of carrots, onions and potatoes. Thanking him, the women started chopping and adding some of the vegetables to a mutton stew they were preparing at the stove, in the centre of the ger. They wasted no time with anything. He was fascinated as he watched them use the tiny space they had for cooking.

The milk tea had a salty taste but was satisfying. There were also milk sweets set out on the table.

'Dairy and meat are the Mongolian nomads' staple diet, and they serve mutton with every meal. They dry it to preserve it; that way, meat's available when they need it for the long winter,' Batbayar said and then he pointed things out to Lejf. 'The women process the dairy into cream, yoghurt and cheese. They keep the cheese in a goat stomach. See that leather bag over there? That is where they churn the butter. And in those buckets, they ferment the milk. There's always milk in different stages of processing. Then there's the *airag* – the nomad's favourite beverage. It's fermented mare milk, a little alcoholic but nutritious and good for the immune system and digestion. From mid-June to mid-September, if it's a warm summer, they sometimes substitute meals for airag.'

Lejf asked the women if he might take photographs, and they again agreed with a wave without stopping what they were busy with.

Batbayar said, 'They are 100 per cent dependent on their animals for survival. That is why the dzuds are so devastating. It used to be once in a decade, but now they happen every year.'

'How do they deal with it, those who remain here?' Lejf asked.

'The government helps as much as they can to provide fodder for areas that have been hit hard, and some herders have been taught how to care for their animals when the winters are so bad. The distressing thing is, for the most part, they have to deal with it by themselves. It's a harsh reality,' said Batbayar.

Chimeg's husband, Dzhambul, came inside after putting the animals in their pen for the night. He'd been out in the open, herding their flock all day. It was early October, and the air outside was already cold. How could one not be filled with genuine respect for those who chose to live this life? To do that all day, every day, required tough mental and physical endurance and survival skills.

While they had delicious mutton stew for dinner, they shared their diurnal lives as Batbayar translated for Lejf.

'The women collect the animals' manure to dry out in a shed, and we use it for our fire. There's not much wood here, but we don't have to worry about running out of dung as long as our animals stay alive,' said Dzhambul with a smile that couldn't disguise the truth behind his words.

'How do you get your supplies?' Lejf asked.

'When we know someone with a vehicle will be coming this way, we text them and they bring us supplies. If no one comes this way, I go to town with my motorcycle and get what we need for the week.'

Technology was limited for them, but they made full use of their meagre resources. When they'd arrived, Batbayar pointed out the solar LED panel outside, which was tied to a pole. He explained, 'It's typical for a family to have one. It enables them to charge their phones, the one light bulb hanging in the ger, and often a little radio. They rotate it as the sun moves.'

It was simple and practical. Lejf checked and saw a signal on his phone and thought of texting Laia before bedtime. She hadn't responded to his email yet.

Dzhambul said they would be packing up their summer camp soon to move to a small valley near the edge of a forest before it got too cold. They could pack everything inside, including the ger itself, in a few hours. For families who had camels, they loaded the folded-up house and its contents on the animals' backs. If that option wasn't available, they had to borrow a vehicle.

On their drive here, Batbayar had told Lejf, 'Buddhists call gers the white pearls of the steppe and consider them a symbol of intelligence.'

Lejf thought about how these people's connectedness centred around the 40 square metre space they lived in: their family home. It was much more to them. Symbolism, instead of inner walls, defined each area, signifying their overall transparency. It was where nomads slept, ate, cooked, bathed, made their babies and gave and received love as a family. There was no personal space.

There was an altar with figurines of Buddha and other deities stationed on a dresser, with photographs of the family – alive and dead – and the children's medals and awards and a small calendar to plan their lives.

When he saw Lejf gazing around, Dzhambul explained, 'Our home is shaped like the round Earth with the sun at the top. We call the opening the Sun Gate.' He pointed upward to the smoke hole. 'And the droplight represents the round shape of the moon. In Buddhism, we believe there is a connection between our world inside and the outside world.'

Due to the gruelling winds from the north, the painted wooden door of a ger always faced south. Colourful area rugs for added heat lay spread out over the linoleum floor, which rolled up, Batbayar informed him. There were only a few small chairs, and the stove served as a heater also. Their life, possessions and people – all within the confounds of a compact, round home. What an attitude toward life to appreciate this as abundant.

Before bedtime, Lejf sent Laia a text:

I am sleeping in a ger tonight. We are a couple of people in this small space, and everyone seems contented. I was surprised at how cosy it is here.

In the days of Genghis Kahn's conquests, he used to travel with a golden ger that was never packed up but was mounted on a cart and carried by twenty-four oxen, and there he held his councils with his generals and foreign dignitaries. Can you imagine the sight of that?

It dipped to a chilly minus 8°C during the night. Lejf had brought an ultra-lightweight thermal sleeping bag. He had bought extra blankets in Ulaanbaatar to leave as gifts for their hosts, on Batbayar's recommendation. He used a couple of the blankets but when the fire died in the early morning hours, he felt the frost nipping at the part of his face sticking out of his warm covers. This was nothing compared to the winters they faced in these steppes. He searched for such courage inside himself, but he felt hollow.

29

AN UNRAVELLING TAPESTRY

Scanning the scene around him, Lejf took his phone out of his pocket.

All across the desert remnants of the ancient Silk Road are visible. You can see the caravan tracks; they're etched deep. They conjure up images of merchants who moved at a snail's pace, braving the elements and the mountains as they exchanged information and brought prosperity.
  Those romantic tales of adventure are in the past, Laia. I'm witnessing another sinister element: not old pathways linking civilisations but wide, grotesque tyre tracks brutalising the fragile desert surface, kicking up thick clouds of dust and carrying it over the Gobi landscape. It looks like a futuristic movie set on Mars, where actors in padded suits behind masks could appear out of the gloom at any moment.
  Except, this is no figment of the imagination: people and their livestock live on the perimeters of these mines and have no protection from this ghastly air.

The message didn't send – no cellphone reception. It sat in his message box, unable to escape, like the oppressive feeling inside him. Lejf wiped his irritated eyes with a handkerchief, and there were brown smears on it from the dust.

He looked around again. Mongolia's rich resources of coal, copper and gold had brought in foreign investment, but he did not see prosperity, only the ugly truth of the scars mining left in its wake.

Batbayar pointed out the location of some of the mines. They couldn't enter because of restricted access. 'Ömnögovi used to be the least populated province, and now it has become a large candy factory for big overseas companies. More land is taken up by mining and this is contributing to climate change and drought.'

'Yes, I've read that the Gobi region has the highest rate of desertification in the world. That's a disturbing stat.'

'How long will they wait before they do something, Lejf? There are consequences to all this. People suffer, animals die. There's pollution in the air and water. And where are our lakes and rivers?' He gestured around, shaking his head. 'And still, they cannot keep up with the demand. They ask for more and more.'

Lejf agonised over Batbayar's words and what he was certain disturbed him too: that the candy wouldn't last forever, the jar would empty.

The distance between Erdenedalai and the Gobi Gurvansaikhan National Park in southern Mongolia was 4.5 hours. It took longer with Batbayar's prayer rituals at ovoos, but Lejf didn't mind; it gave him an opportunity to observe his surroundings and take photographs. Much of the Gobi Desert was rocky, but this area had gorgeous stretches of yellow pastures shaped by the Gurvan Saikhan Mountains. They stayed at a lodge in a two-bed ger with a bathroom and warm fireplace – different from the days they'd spent with Dzhambul and his family.

Tourism was an important source of income for Mongolia, and staff wore beautiful traditional deels. How did they feel about acting out the experience of Mongolian life for tourists?

These nomads' real culture was about being one with the open spaces they roamed and supporting each other. He could see how their reality was slipping away from them, as he felt his slipping away from him.

The panoramic views over the plains and mountains were breathtaking. Although October was a dry month, there was a lot of cloud cover at times, which made photography challenging but more interesting in many ways. At other times, there was the Eternal Blue Sky that the Mongols worshipped and believed determined their destiny. Lejf longed to have a faith like theirs.

* * *

At last, I'm in a place with internet access again. I know you find it inconvenient when trying to get a hold of me, but a bit of a disconnect is good. It allows me to think about where I am in the moment; what the purpose of it is. I feel melancholy tonight because it's my last night in this phenomenal place. There is more to it, but it's difficult to define. It's intangible and, in a strange way, familiar. Maybe I'm yearning to identify with a part of Mongol culture and history.

These people weigh on my heart – they and the others I visited during the desert project. They are cut from the same cloth, and a common thread is unravelling, like essential pieces of the Earth's tapestry disappearing. And a part of me feels as if it's vanishing with them.

What's happening in the Gobi tortures me. They're disembowelling the Earth, which has a limit to what it can give. In a few decades, it will be a dried-out skeleton, and for the enormous profit some are making now, it will be worth nothing to the rest, who will have to live here in future. What a heartbreaking inheritance to bequeath to the younger generations.

Anyway, let me not tell you only the morbid news. Gobi Gurvansaikhan National Park was stunning; I longed for you to be there with me. The plains looked like they'd been spray-painted a soft yellow ochre. A real-life picture, etched against the sky and mountains and speckled with horses and, here and there, Bactrian camels and antelope.

To these nomads, there's a spiritual connection to everything. I think it would be for you too; you would get that. For me, nature is filled with drama, and I'm cast under its spell, but I've never come as close to spirituality as during this project. The whole experience has altered me.

And, of course, we went to Khongoryn Els, and I recorded the singing sands as you requested. Sort of freaky in a way: I kept looking up to the sky to try and find the sound in the air – much like an aeroplane when it takes off. They're not orange, like the dunes at Sossusvlei, but golden and they remind me of the dunes in the Sinai Peninsula.

I'd dreamed of you there in Egypt, under the starry sky, Laia. Have I told you that? I don't always remember what I've shared with you. It's becoming blurrier to discern; so many things appear to be losing shape in my mind. Thoughts linger like phantoms, but they disappear when I reach for them to test them.

We climbed the foothills next to the singing dunes and explored the Khavtsgait Petroglyphs (they date back to between 8,000 BC and 3,000 BC – I know you like the facts). Fantastic scenes of horses galloping, hunters, wheeled carts, gers. On the last stone slab was a scene of two wolves mating. A symbol of the animalistic need, or a true depiction? I'll let you draw your own conclusion. Ha!

We arrived here at the Khustain Nuruu National Park this morning. I've been burning to tell you about the Takhi, the spirit horse. They are the only true wild horses in existence; there aren't many of them left – two thousand or so – and the majority are in Mongolia. They are kind of odd looking: a huge head, long face with a white muzzle, short legs that look like they're dressed in black stockings, and their manes are bristly without a forelock. It's hard to believe this animal, with its peculiar shape, has managed to outrun humans for centuries, and no one has ever been able to tame it. Not even Genghis Khan and his formidable army.

You mentioned the land of the horse, and it is that way here. There are more horses in Mongolia than people. The Mongolians say, 'A man without a horse is like a bird without wings.' And it makes sense when you hear them speak about their horses. They equate them to the freedom and well-being they experience in the vastness of this land, and they dream of their mares mating with the Takhi so that they have fast horses.

They have fabulous beliefs – your mouth will hang open in wonder – like when a Mongolian herder dies and returns to the earth, his beloved horse is released so that it can roam the grasslands. And if you should stumble upon a lone horse out there, looking up at the sky, neighing, it may be such a horse who's remembering its master. I want to grab at my heart: the aching beauty of that. Can you say that you've possessed the soul of another living being in such a way? What am I saying? Of course, you have. I am your Takhi.

There's an innocence about these nomads. They are strong as nails, yet their ideology teaches them not to oppose and not to speak ill. But that makes them more vulnerable. I can't stop thinking about how they've persevered until now, to be let down by a flawed world system. Government aid helps them to survive, but it's not enough and the Earth's climate is changing fast. Would these pastoral nomads, who have moved around and enjoyed the freedom of wide open spaces, be able to accept a sedentary life? It's a lot cast on their kind around the globe. I feel deep, deep sorrow for their inevitable loss.

At this moment, I'm looking up at the night sky, and it's no less dramatic than Egypt or your Namibian heaven. My mind is wandering in this space tonight. It relieves the awful heaviness that has been tightening itself around me.

There is another matter on my mind. I have been troubled by my mother's reaction to our love affair. I feel as if I can no longer turn to her for support. Perhaps my father has, at long last, poisoned her mind. I shall have to find a way to confront them both when I get home. The project is complete, and I feel my energy is depleted.

I believe this is the most significant work I have done. As you told me on that last night underneath the Kalahari sky: I can bring a voice to these people. But I am only one voice. True, through Nat Geo, it will reach many eyes. There remains the fear that it's either not enough or, worse, in vain.

I have captured the beauty and the sorrow – they belong to me now, and how they grip me! Now I must show it to a world that is increasingly reluctant to accept truth. Ah, yes, the truth can be painful, and those with a spiritual void do not like to acknowledge its necessity because they would have to admit to their role in contributing to the pain and suffering in the world.

I speak as if I do not know how hollow my own soul is or how painful truth can be. There is the strange, vague feeling that I have transcended into a form of delirium born out of this agony. I can feel it sitting here, on the inside. I wish to be able to cut it out, to be rid of it, but it sticks to me like tar.

If I have one consolation, it is that soon, I'll get to be with you. You know of course, Laia, my love, you are always with me.

30

WHEN THE PANTHER ESCAPES

'How are you feeling, älskling?' Signe'd asked a couple of times since Lejf came home from Mongolia.

He mumbled an answer, not interested in talking, feeling over-emotional and too drained to have a conversation. His mind felt empty and, at the same time, overloaded and the weight bearing down on his chest felt intolerable. His mother knew his routine; it took a couple of days after big time zone changes to return to normal. Of course, there was no normal. He was restless and had trouble sleeping, and in the morning woke up with severe dysania.

He tried to busy himself by doing editing, yet to no avail; he was unable to stay focused. His sponsor called to hear how the project had gone, and he needed to give an update to Nat Geo, which he procrastinated with. His grasp of time and date, or day of the week, was distorted. He was operating in a foggy haze that clouded his senses, lost in a world of unrealities, oblivious and distressed.

At one point, Lawrie stood before him, looking him up and down and shaking his head. 'Don't you think it's time to shave your face and make yourself presentable to the world? How about a haircut? I know it's your mother and me here at home, but do we need to walk into you looking like that? Take a shower. You'll feel better if you take care of yourself, and so will we.' Lejf was too weary to respond.

The razor blade rasped against the stubble, making smooth paths through the foam as he pulled it across his cheek. He held it under his chin for a moment, pushing his jaw forward, stretching his neck so that his Adam's apple strained underneath the surface of his skin.

'It's called the laryngeal prominence,' Laia had told him once as she'd run her fingers down his throat. She liked touching his 'masculine places', as she called them. They'd made love. It had been beautiful.

Lejf stared at the knobby thing. What would it look like inside there if he cut it open? Would the heaviness come spilling out into the sink? The stranger staring back at him in the mirror looked terrifying. Wild hair; tired, sunken eyes. He avoided looking at him.

Categorising photographs into folders and printing some out, he found comfort in speaking to Laia. 'I feel as if I'm adrift on a raging sea. Do you ever feel like that? You know you are the only one who can calm me. It's true. You have a special knack for doing that; you always have,' he said while looking at some photographs on his desk, arranging them like a deck of cards, then moving them again without a clear purpose. 'I don't know what's up with my parents; they are unnerving me. I can't stand it. Why is my mother asking me all these questions? They're not even trying to be more understanding of our situation, Laia. Are they blind to our love?'

Signe knocked lightly. 'Are you okay in there, älskling?'

He whispered, 'See? That's what I mean.' He called, 'I'm fine, Morsa, thanks.'

Lejf was unaware that Lawrie and Signe were waiting for the right moment to voice their concerns over their son's erratic behaviour.

He stumbled along in his delusional state, unable to identify why he felt the way he did. Unable to ask for help. The compression in his chest and his scattered thoughts hindered him from getting work done. He had an awareness of that, and it bothered him the way a tiny stone would if he walked around with it in his shoe, but he was unable to remove it.

The way his parents were eyeing him felt strange, further unsettling Lejf's mood. He gave evasive answers to his mother's questions, more convinced that his father had a hand in her suspicion toward him. Lejf was certain his dad would try and manipulate him to break off his relationship with Laia, fearful that he would convince her to do the same. He didn't mention to Laia how hurt he was that she'd only responded to one of his texts in Mongolia, which he attributed to his dad's meddling, making him angrier with Lawrie.

'These are marvellous. This project is the best work you've produced, Lejf. Beautiful,' Signe said, looking at some of the printed images strewn across Lejf's desk, moving them around, scanning his workspace. It felt like she was checking in on what he was doing more. His eyes followed her movements. 'Don't look at me that way älsking. I'm curious; that's all.' She patted his arm. 'How far are you with the editing?' she asked.

'It's coming along.'

She nodded. It could have meant either agreement or sympathy, but the way she looked at him made Lejf feel as if she saw something – the same way she looked at him after the Kalahari trip when they'd spoken about Laia. He didn't like it.

'Let me know if you need help with anything. Organising, typing, whatever,' she said.

'Thanks Morsa, everything's under control.' It was doubtful she believed him since his desk was not the only area of glaring chaos surrounding him. Nothing was clear in his mind. The way he perceived sights, sounds and objects felt off-centre, as if he touched through things. It was evident in the incomplete and haphazard tasks he was leaving on his trail.

Finally, when sanity's grip slipped at the fateful moment that the pressure could no longer be contained, madness became the cruel emperor over Lejf's thoughts, playing barbarous games. He was a helpless, blindfolded prisoner awaiting his inevitable fate in the arena before the panther was let loose. Yet he was also the panther, escaping from his cage in a terrifying rage while his parents, the spectators, looked on.

'There's something your mother and I need to speak to you about, Lejf,' Lawrie said.

Signe stood by his side in the doorway of Lejf's room. He had a hunch they were teaming up against him, trying to push him into a corner, and it agitated him.

'What about?' he asked.

'I've been speaking to Laia …'

'So I've heard.' Lejf gave his mother an accusing look, which she returned with a frown.

His father seemed to ignore his comment. 'She said you'd sent her some emails and texts while you were in Mongolia.' Lawrie waited for Lejf's response.

'Yes, I did; what of it?'

'She's troubled by them Lejf, and so are your mother and I.'

'What do you mean by troubled, Dad?'

Lawrie and Signe looked at each other for a moment. 'Laia told me you spoke about being together on your Kalahari trip – that you are romantically involved. She says it isn't true, and she doesn't understand why you'd say something like that –'

'What your father means,' interrupted Signe, 'is that Laia's worried about you, älskling. We all are. You've been saying things that don't make any sense. We've noticed you haven't been yourself for a while now. We're not prying into your personal life. We are concerned about what's going on there in your heart, that's all. Are you feeling all right? You look stressed. Tell us what we can do to help you, Lejf.'

His fears were confirmed. 'You have planted ideas in Mom's head. Haven't you? It was you who started this,' Lejf said to his father, pushing the chair back and glaring at him.

His aggressive tone and body language made Lawrie step back for a moment. 'I have no idea what you're talking about.'

'Don't act like the innocent. You have been lecturing me on morals my whole damn life, and I can't live up to your high ones. Can I? Nothing I do is good enough for you. You wanted me to fail in my career, and now you're trying to destroy my happiness further by causing trouble between Laia and me.' He got up and stood in front of his father. In a flashing second, an inkling of clarity, he saw an ageing man who looked much more fragile than he sounded.

'Lejf, please calm down, sweetheart. Let us take you to see someone.' Signe touched his arm; it was a gentle, reassuring gesture. He pushed her away, not intending to be so forceful, and she stumbled a few steps backwards. She gasped; her eyes wide with shock.

'Don't shove your mother. I will not tolerate this kind of behaviour. You are not well, and you need to get help,' said Lawrie. He took Lejf by the arm but he shook him off.

'I need help? See what you did? You've turned her against me. Are you happy now? You want to take Laia away from me too, but I won't let you. I won't let you!'

The cold, grey fog from the sea came over him. He was a tiny desert creature scurrying over the sand, trying to get away from something or someone. Then, before it caught up with him, in an instant, he was running and the Namib dunes changed into the flat, barren planes of the Gobi. Lejf stood in the middle of that frightful scene of dark dust clouds and big monster trucks breaking Mother Earth's heart open. He heard her harrowing screams in the distance, Stop! Stop! For a moment, he had to put his hands over his ears; the sound tore through him.

Something was chasing him – a grey wolf – and it was closing in. No matter how fast he ran, he couldn't escape the animal. His legs wouldn't move, and he couldn't breathe from the thick, suffocating dust. The wolf lunged at him, but Lejf grabbed him, hands around his neck, strangling him. He was strong; he had to use all his strength as he looked into the animal's fierce eyes. The beast snarled, razor-sharp teeth trying to get hold of him. Down, down, Lejf pushed him, fighting for his life.

'You're killing him! Lejf, stop; you're killing him!' Signe's shrill voice came from somewhere, a long tunnel he couldn't see the end of.

Blinding pain made him loosen his grip on the wolf's neck, and he collapsed in agony, holding his leg. He sat down on the floor and watched, mesmerised, as the red, warm blood poured out of his thigh, soaking his jeans and forming a dark pool.

Signe rushed over to Lawrie, lying a few feet away, coughing and heaving as he clutched his throat.

Lejf was confounded. Why was his dad lying there? Why was his mother so hysterical?

'Lawrie, are you okay? My God.' She sobbed, helping him to sit upright.

Why was she crying? His dad had purple welts on his neck and face, and his eyes were bloodshot. Lejf had never seen him in such a state. He was shocked and tried to move closer to his father, but the pain in his leg stopped him.

Signe rushed out of the room and returned with a glass of water, but Lawrie couldn't swallow. 'Don't worry; I'm calling an ambulance. There, there, sweetheart, it's okay,' she soothed him.

'Lejf, stay right there, don't move,' Signe said in a firm voice. She came back with a medical kit and handed him a thick gauze. 'Press down like this.' She showed him. 'I'm sorry, my love.' She was shaking when she made the emergency call, but her voice sounded strong and steady.

'Morsa?'

'Shh.' She stroked his hair with a trembling hand. She was pale as death. 'It's going to be all right. Help is on the way. You're going to be all right, min älskling.'

Lejf looked at his father. 'Dad?'

Lawrie's face bore a sad, pathetic look. Signe went to him and hugged him. Clinging to each other, their bodies shook as Lejf looked on, not comprehending what anything meant.

31

ON A STRANGE JOURNEY

Years ago, when I was the young Adam, moulded from the red desert dirt and given life by the breath of you, my Eve, you told me a story there in the Garden of Eden where we lived, about Tolkien's elves, sailing to the Undying Lands. How you love getting lost in your big books. Do you remember that? I loved that story and the way you told it.

I have also been to that other sombre place where there is no light. It is full of men and their schemes. Men mess everything up. It is in their DNA. The world of men is a dark anti-utopia where they implement the machinery of their destruction. Oh, the things I have seen done at the hands of men, Laia! They don't care what they destroy, only that they have the power to do so.

What was it again that you told me once? Ah, yes. 'The patriarch is a mini version of the big system: he wants to assert his power over his woman and children so he may feel good about himself. Prove how strong he is,' is what you said. You are so wise, my love.

You've never cared for the likes of such a man; I know you haven't. Is your husband not a man like that? I don't know him, but he is not what I would have chosen for you. I would have chosen myself if I wasn't such a weakling.

And now I am on the verge of death, sailing to that place you read to me about – Valinor. I long to be there. I remember you telling me there exists a magical world that is unchanging, and men of the Earth have no power over anything. At last, I will be free from their hatred and malice. Will you come to live with me there?

Blissful in his dream, medication coursing through his veins, Lejf threw himself head-first into the water, floating with his paralysed arms at his sides. And he could see his body, a buoyant vessel, cross over the sea until he came to a luminous place where she was waiting for him.

He heard a voice like his saying, 'Spread your legs, elfin and let me dive into your abyss where a slow, glorious death awaits me. Devour me. You may consume me bit by bit; remember, certain particles take longer to digest, like the shards in my head and my heart; they are stubborn. Your dragon eyes are beautiful, my elfin queen. I don't want to leave this tomb; it is a refuge.'

His mother's voice faded in and out in Lejf's hypnopompic state. 'He's so incoherent; I don't understand a single word he's saying.' She sounded strange. Her voice was low and thick. Then Lejf realised it was his dad speaking to someone he didn't recognise.

The strange voice said, 'The medication will help control the hallucinations. Bear in mind it may take time for them to seize; each case is different.'

When he opened his eyes for a brief moment, his dad's hand was on top of his, not holding it but resting there. Lejf looked into Lawrie's sorrowful eyes before he was lost in oblivion again.

The wound where Signe had stuck a letter opener into him became infected, and he had to go on another course of antibiotics.

'Flesh wound. Didn't nick a bone or major artery,' the doctor said. 'It will hurt for a while but heal over time.'

The wound did heal, but on cold, damp days, Lejf experienced muscle aches in the area, much like the dull throbbing of delayed onset muscle soreness. The thick, pink scar was sensitive to the touch, a reminder of how close it had been. His mother should have stabbed him in the chest to drain the filth inside him. His brave mother, what he'd put her through. Not to mention his dad.

After time spent in the psychiatric ward in Windhoek, Lejf was referred to a small private clinic in London where he met Dr Lang, a gentle father figure who helped set him on the road to recovery. Therapy wasn't easy for Lejf; talking about his feelings wasn't one of his strengths. Besides that, the hallucinations persisted after he went on antipsychotic meds because he was reluctant to let Laia go.

Dr Lang called him out on this. 'The subconscious is powerful – it has a will of its own and rules our behaviours. Our objective here is to bring those underlying things to the surface where you can deal with them, where they won't cause any further damage. Trust means letting go, Lejf. You're holding on because you're afraid of losing. Ask yourself what it is you are holding on to?'

'Laia had asked me the same question on the night she told me she was getting married,' he thought aloud. He didn't tell Dr Lang that she'd seen it had no long-term benefits; she had grown enervated with holding on to air.

It felt like holding on to that nothingness was at least something, a perverse sort of hope. His initial reluctance to speak in therapy was a continuum of what he did: he collected wasted chances like souvenirs and nurtured them. Thrown into that twisted mix were the things not within his power to change. Lejf was aware that holding on to nothing was another way of resisting reality and that clinging to Laia was a chimera.

'Dr Ibrahim was a man I'd met in Egypt. I think his soul is too deep for this world,' he told Dr Lang. 'He suggested perhaps what I've been giving my father and Laia isn't what they need from me.'

'That's an interesting observation. How do you feel about that?'

'About the fact that Laia decided to get married because I didn't give her what she needed from me? I don't know how analysing my feelings would change anything. And what kind of madness could drive a person to kill his father, Dr Lang? I almost did. Sweet mercy, how would I have been able to live with myself? My dad and I battle each other, but I don't want to kill him.'

'Despite your sense of failure and self-condemnation, you show a lot of compassion for other people, Lejf. I believe part of what you are experiencing is a sense of soul loss.' Lejf frowned, and Dr Lang continued, 'It has a medical term: dissociation. It is, in essence, a disconnect, a fragmentation of the psyche; traumatic experiences, as you've had, can amplify that. The mind, under stress, creates coping mechanisms because it wants to avoid pain.'

'And do you think there's a chance I will retrieve my lost soul, Dr Lang?' he asked.

'Of course. However, it will take commitment, honesty and a willingness for self-transformation.'

Ingve lived in Chelsea, a convenient location and close to the clinic. Although he'd studied music (along with an MBA), he wasn't a musician. But he worked as close to it as he could at the Royal College of Music, where he held a director's post. It was a decent position, but the arts didn't pay hefty salaries. He had to settle for a tiny, expensive two-bedroom flat, a small price to pay to have the lifestyle he desired.

Their parents stayed with Ingve while Lejf was an inpatient for psychiatric rehabilitation. Lejf knew his dad must have borne the cramped space, not to mention the noise and smog, with gritted teeth – that was perhaps one of a few things they did agree on. Signe, the Scandinavian, didn't have those prejudices. Once he was discharged, she dragged him with her to anything that had a remote resemblance to culture. Her motive might have been to get him out into fresh air, although he suspected she was starved for a sophisticated, big-city experience.

He liked strolling around museums for hours with his mother. It was therapeutic for his fragile state. Laia had told him once that being in an art museum and walking around in a library were two of the most soul-gratifying places to her because they held a secret world you could disappear in. How he would have liked to be able to disappear from this state of being.

He did lose himself in the beauty of timeless works of art: gods and humans, sinners and saints, animals, nature, still-life objects – a silent world in frames. They didn't seek approval or explain why they were there. Their purpose was to hang on walls and to tell their wordless stories. Would his work also be displayed in a museum somewhere one day when he was long gone? Would he be remembered for his insanity?

His mother knew how to handle his moods. As a child, when he'd gone on reticent intervals after a fallout with his dad, she knew when to approach and when to let him be. His father tried to fix him, his broken son and it had been their core issue. His brothers required minimal effort from his dad. Perhaps they and his mother knew how to handle his dad better than he did.

Lejf could see his father was troubled. Who could blame him? His mental meltdown was a prophecy fulfilled, but Lawrie didn't say this in so many words. Neither he nor his parents spoke about what had happened. Lejf couldn't bear being alone with his father for fear Lawrie would be afraid of him. The thought that there could be reason for it tormented him.

He had to stay in London to continue with therapy. Signe was reluctant to leave him and, before she and Lawrie went back to Otji, she asked, 'What about your project? Is there anything you'd like me to do for you?'

Dr Lang suggested he keep a distance from work for a while. At least until after his in-office therapy sessions, and then take it one step at a time. He'd asked for a postponement from Nat Geo.

He shook his head. 'No thanks, Morsa. I'll get to it once I'm back home.'

She said something to Ingve, they both looked at Lejf, and Ingve agreed with a nod.

'Please don't feel sorry for me and treat me like I can't do anything for myself or, worse, do something typical like quoting Shakespeare.' Lejf grinned.

Ingve patted him on the back. 'Nothing to fear lives here, brother. I'll give you a list of chores and keep Shakespeare on ice for Erik.'

Where Erik had confidence with women, Ingve had an easiness with himself. He seemed almost impervious to criticism. He'd been that way from childhood when Lejf and their other brothers had jeered at his arty flamboyance. When he was young, Lejf mistook it for arrogance. Looking at Ingve, he realised how much he took after Signe. Lejf liked and admired his brother for the person he chose to be. Ingve lived life his own way, liberated from others' opinions and expectations.

Lejf thought he was the free one – there was irony for you – but you could be free to roam the world and be a prisoner in your cage. Unlike Ingve, he was bound by his self-imposed expectations of the world and the people in it whom he couldn't change.

Lejf watched Ingve playing a classical piece on the piano, admiring his skill. 'That's a beautiful piece. You play it well.'

'Thank you. It's Bach's Concerto in D Minor. It's one of my favourite pieces; I like playing it when I want to take my mind somewhere else.' Ingve smiled.

'You were always amazing at playing the piano. Do you ever feel sorry that you didn't become a concert pianist?'

Ingve didn't answer right away and Lejf thought perhaps he was concentrating on the intricate notes. He did a *glissando*, played a silly little ditty, stopped and turned to Lejf. 'No, I have no regrets. I don't think I would have enjoyed the travelling and repetition. That's fine; I'm surrounded by music, and when I wish, I can play it myself. It's good to stick to the thing you're best at.'

'Tell that to Dad. But then, you made a success of your life.'

'And you being a renowned photographer didn't?' Ingve chuckled. 'Do you know who David Helfgott is?' Lejf shook his head. 'It's impossible that you haven't heard of him.' Ingve gave him an incredulous look.

'The name sounds familiar.' It was a weak venture.

'He's a famous Australian pianist. He studied here at RCM and won a number of awards for his performances. He's fantastic, a unique and gifted artist, but he battled with mental illness in the prime of his life when he gave his most memorable performances.'

'I assume this is a comparison. Am I supposed to be flattered?'

'God, you and Dad are so alike.' He laughed out loud. 'The point I'm trying to make, if you'll allow me, is that great artistic genius often takes a big mental toll. When you pour yourself out and over the thing you love, it can consume you from the inside.'

Lejf stared at his brother in silence for a while. 'That must be the kindest thing you've said to me.'

'It's true, and it saddens me to say everything about it is. I do think your work is brilliant, Lejf. You're a phenomenal photographer with journalistic integrity. Those are qualities that seem hard to come by nowadays. Society benefits from voices like yours. It's obvious that your work is important to you; even Dad knows that. You care about the people behind your stories. Remember: you can't save all of humanity from its bondage; no single human has that ability. And there will always be those who will resist your best efforts. Don't let them get to you.'

Lejf thought about what Ingve had said. 'What happened to David Helfgott? Was he cured?'

'He's around. There was a period when he had to step away from everything. He said he needed to find his inner music again, and he did. When he returned, it was with a vengeance, more so because he'd learned to embrace the way he was without apologies.'

'I wish to be in that emotional place where it doesn't feel so heavy … The anxiety lingers; I can't shake it off. I still see and hear Laia. I don't know if it's hallucinations anymore. It could be her memory that haunts me. It makes me afraid. How will I distinguish between being well and being sick? Will I recognise the difference?' They were rhetorical questions. He couldn't expect Ingve to give him an answer. Not even Dr Lang could tell him how to get rid of these feelings.

'Allow yourself to go through the motions. Society's stigmas about mental illness have changed. There's no shame in what you're going through, Lejf. It's okay to acknowledge that you're overwhelmed, heartbroken.'

In a way, talking to Ingve helped Lejf open up to Dr Lang more in their sessions. Sometimes, some other truth is revealed when you go through shit times. He wouldn't have thought that Ingve, of all his siblings, would be the one he would lean on in his darkest days, but he was.

Before Lejf went back to Otji, Ingve gave him a package. Inside was Alexander von Humboldt's five-volume collection of *Kosmos* in the original German and beautifully leather bound. 'This came a few weeks ago. Sorry for the delay; I was asked to hold off on giving it to you.'

Lejf recognised Laia's handwriting on the envelope but didn't open it. 'This will give me something to do for the next while,' he said as he paged through one of the books.

Ingve gave him a CD of a David Helfgott recording. Lejf was touched beyond what he could express, and they hugged for a moment.

'Go find your inner lens. Take all the time you need,' Ingve said.

32

WORDS BURIED IN THE SAND

So much to digest. So much well-intended advice. Settling in and trying to process everything proved hard for Lejf and his parents. Lawrie and Signe were unsure how much they needed to be involved. They and Lejf walked around each other in loops, holding their breaths to see what would happen next. But it wasn't like following a list of instructions as with medication and hoping everything would fall into place like magic because it didn't. That sticky awkwardness was hard to wash down, even with a handful of mood stabilisers. Lejf felt as much a foreigner in his parents' home as in his own body.

When he started reviewing his notes from the desert project and editing and organising the photographs, he was pleased to see how well they'd turned out. The deep, penetrating portraits tightened his insides – as if they'd seen too much of what was happening to him. As if he had been their subject and not the other way around. That had been a prevailing sense he had throughout the desert journey: how those people looked at him with heartfelt compassion and that unsettled him the most. He decided to leave everything until he felt ready to deal with it.

Erik came home for a visit and seemed tentative, not knowing how he should approach his brother. They haven't spoken since the incident. Erik had called and spoken to Signe while they were in London but Lejf didn't know how much their mother told him.

'Quit being so careful. It feels too weird. Be your natural self. I can handle you when I know what to expect,' he said to Erik.

'Let's go to Sossus. You and me.' Erik grinned.

Signe was apprehensive. 'Lejf still has online therapy, älskling.'

Lejf felt sorry for her; she'd been through a lot with him. And she had every right to be concerned; he wasn't in the clear with his hallucinations and emotional stability yet. His confidence was shattered by what he'd done to his father. He didn't trust anything his mind told him.

'Mom's right. Perhaps it's best if I stay here.'

'We won't be away forever, a couple of days max. C'mon, you need some sun and fresh air; it will do you good. Don't worry, Morsa, I'll take good care of him,' said Erik, hugging her.

* * *

Going away with Erik was a welcome break. Lejf sat with his wandering mind tuning in and out as Erik brought him up to speed with what he'd been up to, which were amusing trivialities; the details were not as important as enjoying his brother's company.

'... so I'll meet up with Iben in Morocco before heading back to Dubai.'

'Iben?' Erik had his full attention.

'You haven't listened to a word I've said.' He gave Lejf an accusing look and shook his head. 'Yes, Iben. We've sort of been having a thing.'

Lejf thought about it for a moment. 'This news both surprises me, and at the same time, I can't say that I'm at all surprised. Since when?' He *had* been operating outside of the real world.

'A couple of months now.' He smiled his you-don't-want-to-know-everything Erik smile. 'Iben is way outside the box. She fiddles with my head but in a good way. It's rare to find someone who has something of the pure inner child, yet she explores the world around her with critical thinking. She's the most self-aware person I know besides Morsa. She reminds me of Morsa in many ways. I like being with her. With some women I've been with, they wanted to change something about me. Not at first, but it would creep in gradually. Iben's not like that. She brings herself to the table and says, "This is me. Take me as I am if you dare, and I'll take you as you are."'

Iben and Erik. So, that must have been the shroud of mystery Lejf had sensed when he'd visited him in Dubai. He understood where Erik was coming from, however. His brother was circumspect. He'd known about the situation with Laia and didn't want to upset Lejf, but it didn't seem fair that Erik would consider his feelings at the expense of sharing his own good news. Iben was a great woman; Lejf tried to imagine where it could lead for the two of them.

He'd not opened Laia's envelope. She had something to say, and he wasn't ready to hear it. First, he needed to bury his need for her here in the desert with his unspoken words. How did it work, letting someone go? Did you gather all the memories of all the times you spent with that person and stick them in a hole you dug in the sand? How deep did that hole need to be when more than half your life had to go there? Would the memories remain there and die, or would the wind that shifted and reshaped the dunes release them over time to haunt you?

Lejf poked the burning logs with a stick, causing embers to shoot up like a legion of little electric fairies, then disappearing, poof, into the night. 'Did Mom tell you what happened? How I ended up in the psych ward?' He looked at Erik through the dancing flames.

'She said you had a breakdown.'

'She hasn't told you anything.' He paused a bit. 'I lost it, brother; I tried to kill Dad.' Erik was startled by the news. He shook his head, and Lejf continued, 'It's true; I strangled him. Mom had to stab me with a letter opener to get me to stop. See, here's the evidence – it almost went all the way through,' he said with a self-directed sneer and pulled up his khaki shorts to show Erik, who stared at the protuberant pink scar in disbelief and then at Lejf with questions in his eyes. Perhaps Erik was beginning to understand why their mother had been reluctant for Lejf to go away for a few days. They'd all suspected something was wrong, but no one could have foreseen how severe his psychosis was.

'I had bits of memory but nothing made sense, so I begged Mom to tell me what had happened. She downplays it but I know she wouldn't have had to resort to such drastic measures if it wasn't serious. What if I'd killed him? God, I can't get rid of that nauseating thought. I'd caused them so much pain …' He shoved the red coals around with the stick again, and the tip caught fire. He stubbed it out in the sand. Was he worried he had altered his brother's high opinion of him? That he'd proven Erik wrong in believing in him? Of course, he feared how Erik, who was one of the most important people in his life, would see him. It pained Lejf to disappoint him.

They were quiet for a while; Erik was processing what Lejf had said. He asked, 'How did it start? When, do you think?'

'The psychotic episode, you mean? I don't know; it's hard to say when I couldn't tell what was real and not anymore.' He thought about it. 'It may have started after I went to see Laia in Karlsruhe.'

'When was this?'

'Did Iben mention anything?' Erik shook his head. 'So, Laia didn't tell anyone after all. She's like that.' Lejf smiled to himself. 'It was after the trip she did with me in Canada. She told me she was getting married at the end of the trip.' He swallowed, thinking of that gut-wrenching moment. 'I would have gone to visit you in Dubai …'

Erik finished the sentence, '... but you went to see Laia. That's why Morsa and I couldn't get hold of you.' He contemplated this. 'Wait a minute ... that doesn't make any sense. If you'd gone to see Laia, why didn't she know where you were?'

'Going to Karlsruhe is only half of it. I didn't actually go there to see her ...' Erik frowned and Lejf said, 'I stalked her for two weeks, stuck in a sick nightmare.' He poked around the fire with the stick again, needing something to do with his hands, unable to look his brother in the eye.

'Did Laia see you?' The news was another bombshell, and Erik couldn't hide the shock in his voice.

'Yes, she and Ravi both. Caught out like a criminal, right there on the street for everyone to see. What a spectacle. I messed everything up with Laia, and if it hadn't been for her intervention, my career would have been destroyed too.' Looking up at the stars, he said, 'It's funny, it's not as if I didn't know she was seeing other people, but the thought of someone loving her and giving her what I didn't: that's the part that burns the most. She was so lonely. From there, things started unravelling. All the energy coming out of me felt wrong all of a sudden. It's hard to pinpoint; my mind's still not in a place where things make logical sense, and I fear the hallucinations recurring. What happened with Dad ... I can't assimilate it. We've always had our differences. You know how he's been on about my work or some other thing. But to attack our father Erik, and not recollect doing it. Do you understand how far gone I was?'

'You're going to get better, Lejf. You're talking about it – that's progress. Right?'

'I'm not talking about it with the two people it concerns. I can't speak to Laia. Not after I've made such a gigantic ass out of myself. I hate that I left her in that predicament. Who knows what was going through her mind, trying to figure out what was going through mine when I contacted her during my delusion.' He sighed deeply. 'And I don't know how to talk to Dad. We are like thorns in each other's sides.'

'Dad's always been tough on all of us, Lejf. Say what you will about that man, I'm glad he pushed us. He didn't want us to end up as washouts on a dead-end street. He knew we needed a push, especially you and I. Face it, we weren't model students.' He threw a stick into the fire. 'His methods may have been a bit rough around the edges, but Dad did us a favour.'

'I've disappointed him, Erik. I'd gone mad and then I tried to kill him. Am I any better than those losers who ended up on dead-end streets?'

'You are not a loser! Lejf, look at what you've achieved. You're burned out; that's all. When things feel less overwhelming, you'll see your purpose.'

'I wish I knew how to let go. I want to go back and do it over. Life isn't that kind to us. Is it? It wants us to make the right decisions in the moment or suffer for the wrong ones later.' Gazing into the dark desert night, he said. 'I need to drive to the dunes tomorrow morning to stand there. Process some things.'

'We'll do it together.'

***

Lejf photographed Erik's lanky shape and chestnut hair against the curvy copper dunes. They both looked like their father, but Erik was easier to love than him. When they were young, Signe used to tell people she'd run out of Scandinavian by the time she had him and Erik. Their mother would have adored the sight of Erik right here, the handsome devil: strong and secure, like the pillar he was.

Lejf knew Erik had brought him here to the desert because he understood what it meant to him, and he didn't judge him even knowing about his shame. Could he ever forgive himself?

'I love you, bro,' Lejf said, lowering his camera with a smile and overcome with emotion.

Erik slapped him on the back and, grabbing him around the shoulders, said, 'I don't have to tell you. You know how my heart sits with yours.' He ruffled Lejf's hair. 'You're going to be alright.' Peeping at his image on the screen, he grinned. 'Excellent. I'll send that to Iben to remind her to miss me.'

Lejf realised at that moment that Erik was in love.

33

AN UNSHAKEABLE SHADOW

Of wishful thinking and hoping things would get better, Laia knew enough. It wasn't clear to her anymore whether she was complacent to please Ravi, whom she knew had married her against the wishes of his mother, who told her son it had nothing to do with Laia not being Jewish. Well, even if that wasn't the reason, Mutter Ettlinger, who was never rude to Laia, must have seen more than her son did (but then we often chose to believe what was most convenient to our situation). Or, perhaps she had slipped back into her old habits. One thing was certain: she'd become the person she'd sworn she wouldn't be like: her mother.

Only now she understood how easy it was to become like that. It wasn't intentional; leaving that window open just a fraction was all it took. Her mother's motives had never been malicious. Dael had always wanted to do the right thing, and cultural notions about a woman's role were difficult to change. Ravi's mother was no exception and her advocacy of her son's illustrious professional and social standing was evidence of that.

Could she blame it on a generational thing her mother and mother-in-law seemed to be willing subjects to? Laia wondered what her own excuse would be then, other than supporting her successful husband. Was supporting him at the expense of her emotional well-being? That seemed a bit neurotic. Or wasn't it so neurotic? She couldn't claim it was at the expense of her financial freedom, for she still had her career, and Ravi at least didn't discourage that.

The truth lay somewhere between all the small things that accumulated and became the issues she tried to but couldn't brush aside. She was frightened that all she'd worked to achieve and was proud of was systematically slipping away. Yet her heart seemed to have deceived her. She also longed for companionship, and now that she had it, she felt dissatisfied. Or was it disillusioned about what a real relationship required? Did the fault lie in her expectations? What in heaven's name was it she'd expected or, more to the point, what was it she wanted?

Giving up her beloved flat had been the first step in the process, and one of the hardest.

'*Es ist zum Besseren, meine Liebe*,' Ravi had said (she'd thought with a bit too much compassion). 'We can't live here. We are forming a life together. We want children, don't we? There's not even room enough for the two of us. What about when my parents visit? This was a nice little place for you when you were alone; now it's time to move on to bigger things with me.'

She'd agreed with a nod and a fake smile, while on the inside, she screamed. She wasn't sure if she wanted children anymore or if the reason was because she didn't want children with Ravi. That would involve his mother in their lives more, and the thought was enough to shrivel up her ovaries.

'You are worth more. I want to give you everything your heart desires, Laia,' he said.

Why did the tone in his voice sound so familiar and patronising? She'd looked around the small space as she'd packed up her things, remembering all the moments. Her beautiful haven was now colourless and stripped of a soul. She chided herself for not trying to feel more optimistic about her future.

Laia had seen signs of Ravi's temper tantrums when he stayed over a few days a week at the flat. Being married to him was different; she couldn't make excuses to avoid him. She'd experienced the full brunt of his fury the day he'd caught Lejf stalking them – in the terrible aftermath when she'd had to use all her diplomacy skills to convince him she and Lejf were done and not to report him. Lejf had made a mistake in a moment of weakness, although she'd been furious with him. Ravi she could deal with, but Lejf putting his career at risk like that was unimaginable. Only when she'd agreed to marry Ravi did he let his threats go, but he brought the incident up in every argument as if it were a stain on her judgement of character. The constant effort to reassure him was draining.

What was the point in feeling sorry for herself? Nobody forced her to marry Ravi. He was the man she'd vowed to spend the rest of her life with.

The tiny things that scratched didn't fade as some said they would. Yet, above those small things, was that word repeating in her mind, which scathed more than the overbearing love he smothered her with: manipulation.

It was the recognition of her father in Ravi (although her father wasn't emotional) that made her question herself and her decisions, whether they were driven by acceptance or omission. Was that what she'd seen in Ravi all along: a father figure? The irony. If you tried to run away, it was only a matter of time before your ghosts caught up with you. Still, she'd wanted emotion and she got what she wished for.

'You don't sound like a newlywed. You sound like a tired old woman,' Iben said over the phone.

Conversations with Iben were also becoming exasperating. 'We need to find our groove, that's all,' Laia said.

'Why don't you admit you made a mistake marrying him? I think it's because he's brainwashed you.'

'That's ridiculous.' She'd done that to herself.

'Is it? Look at the things you surround yourself with, the people you hang out with. None of it is you. You've turned into some kind of robot-wife. I've seen how you are when you're with Ravi and his friends.'

'I'm trying to be more social. You were the one who accused me of not being social enough.'

'I told you to go out and have fun. The problem is, you're not having *any* fun. You're not yourself, Laia. You've never been a big crowd person. You're doing it because Ravi pressures you into doing it and it makes him look good while it's making you miserable.'

'You've always had a bias towards marriage, Iben. You don't know the first thing about what it takes. It's hard work and a lot of sacrifices.' She was such a hypocrite.

'Sacrifices for whom? It seems as if you are the only one making them and it pisses me off that you're allowing it. I may be biased towards marriage but from what I've seen of it through our parents' stellar example, I'm not convinced it's the golden path to happiness people make it out to be. And I'll tell you another thing: I'm never going to be Mom and Dad, Laia. To hell with that "supporting my husband" nonsense if it's not an equal partnership. I am so sick and tired of that old-world mentality. Everything has been easier for men. They have great careers; they get married when they've screwed around enough, and when they feel like settling down in their middle age, they don't have to worry about having children. Why would they worry when they could simply choose younger wives? Ravi is an excellent example of an old bore with money who marries a beautiful, younger woman he can control. As for you, you're doing exactly what he's telling you to do. You're turning into an old bore like him. What happened to your self-respect?'

'I don't need you lecturing me, Iben.'

'Have it your way then.'

Laia hated what these conversations with Iben were doing to their relationship and she cringed at the truth of what her sister had said. It wasn't just Iben she was lying to, but herself.

And then there was Lejf.

It was too painful to admit how much she missed him. Her mother had asked about him. Laia wasn't sure what to tell her because she didn't know much about what was happening with him.

Iben had told her more than once, 'You were a fool for giving up the perfect deal: your independence and someone who isn't a twit.'

Sometimes, she sat by herself (those rare moments when Ravi didn't invade her thoughts with his neediness) and thought about her and Lejf's trips together and when he'd visited her at her flat. She remembered their unusual love and how it had left her feeling discontented because it was frustrating to maintain a small portion of such a beautiful thing.

He'd said goodbye to her in Victoria, so forlorn. She had travelled on, thinking she was making the best decision for her life.

She'd called Lawrie after those disturbing, yet moving messages she'd received from Lejf when he was in Mongolia. Lawrie said he and Signe had been concerned about his behaviour, but with him away so often, it was difficult to confront him about what was troubling him.

'I am the one troubling him, Lawrie. It's my fault.' She didn't tell him or anyone else that Lejf had stalked her.

'The coin has two sides, Laia. Nothing is ever one-sided, my child. Lejf has always been complex. He lives in an extremely internalised world. He takes on more than he can handle and puts his physical and emotional well-being on the line without any consideration to how it may affect him or others.'

News of his breakdown had cut deep. Thinking back on it, the signs had been there that day in Karlsruhe: not just the fact that he'd stalked her but the dark and disturbing look in his eyes. She'd been too angry with him at that moment, too upset with Ravi for seeing Lejf so vulnerable and acting superior to him. She'd been too damn angry with herself because the whole disaster could have been avoided if she hadn't broken Lejf's heart. Instead of helping him when he'd come to her, she'd sent him over the edge.

She'd written a letter with the books she'd sent him to Ingve's address in London but she hadn't heard from him. What was going through his mind now? She'd alienated the most important man in her life. She couldn't bear the thought that he hated her, but if he did, she'd brought it on herself.

* * *

'Hello, this is a surprise.'

'Hello, Mama.'

'What's the matter, Laia?' Dael asked with concern.

'I don't know. I had an urge to speak to you, but I don't know what I want to say …'

'We all feel like that sometimes, honey.'

'Do you, Mom? You've never told me this. I guess I never asked, did I?'

They were both quiet for a bit.

Laia broke the silence. 'I've been thinking about my life and choices; about Lejf, what he's going through. And I feel so lost, for his sake and mine.' She burst into tears.

'It's all right, sweetheart. You can talk to me.'

'I keep asking myself why I married Ravi. We want things that are not right for us but we still pursue them. I knew ... I knew he wasn't right for me, but I married him anyway because I was lonely. It's a terrible excuse but it's the truth. It's not his fault; he tries. I blame myself for not being honest with him. I don't know what to do. I'm scared to leave, scared of the loneliness. And yet, staying is another kind of loneliness. Does it make any sense?'

'Yes.'

'Are you unhappy, Mama?'

Dael didn't answer right away. 'I find things to keep me busy so I don't think about that.'

'Do you and Daddy still love each other?'

'In a strange way, we do. Neglect is a fungus: it spreads. After a while, the abnormal becomes the routine you function in.' Dael paused. 'I've always wondered why you didn't choose Lejf.'

'I don't know, Mama, we've navigated differently, Lejf and I. He was looking toward horizons in the distance while I wanted to plant my roots.' She sighed, thinking about something. 'It's an odd feeling when you bid farewell to someone again and again. There's a certain envy toward the person who leaves – that act of freedom. But staying behind, aye, *there* is the problem. And look at the trouble I've made of my staying.'

After another long silence, Dael said, 'You'll have to decide which kind of loneliness you can live with, my love.'

34

HER WORDS

Lejf walked around contemplating reading Laia's letter for weeks, too afraid to open it. Uncertain about how he would react, paralysed by the overwhelming fear of the monstrous thing lurking in the shadows of his psyche, so hard to shake off.

The letter, sealed in the envelope, sat in his shorts pocket, brushing against his thigh through the thinner material of the pocket lining. A silly, repetitive routine: taking it out at the end of the day, tucking it into a new pocket the next day, until the edges frayed and the paper became soft and fragile.

'Fear is a reaction to experiences of pain. When you anticipate that something dreadful could happen again, fear rises to the surface in the form of anxiety, which debilitates your reasoning,' Dr Lang told him.

'How do I prevent that premonition when it's overwhelming, so real?' Lejf asked.

'You can't prevent fear from arising. When it does, there are several things you can do to help you deal with it so that it doesn't leave you feeling disabled. Acknowledge to yourself that you are feeling afraid, and be honest about why you do. Allow yourself to feel rather than fight the fear. Once you confront it, its hold on you will become weaker as you gain more power through understanding why it is causing you to react the way you do. You'll be able to manage your fear and put it in the right perspective. It will become a skill you'll get better at the more you practice,' said Dr Lang.

Laia'd given him the books he hadn't started reading yet but picked up to smell as if they'd bear traces of her. He reasoned she wouldn't have given them to him as an act of kindness, to be malicious with her words. That was, in a way what he feared: the magnanimity from her he felt he didn't deserve. No matter how hard he tried to ignore them, Dr Lang's words kept tugging at his shorts pocket. He had to confront the dread of exposing whatever conjured-up harm he perceived Laia's letter contained.

He drove out early to take photographs of the sun rising over Otji's sleepy houses and buildings. The canopies of trees lit up for a brief moment at an angle of the sunlight. Early morning photography was spectacular for many reasons: your soul roused and stretched out inside you like the day before your eyes. The new day brought fresh anticipation for something extraordinary to meet you on your path.

Many years ago, he had awoken on a similar day with no inclination about what that morning brought. He'd not paid any particular notice to anything. He may have looked at the sunrise for a moment and thought it beautiful on his way to school, but then again, perhaps not. It had been another mundane cycle to complete.

On the other end of his camera's lens, where the yellow sun was perched on the hook of an acacia tree, he saw her dark eyes and wide smile as she walked into the room and into his heart that day. As perfect as any moment could be. He'd long since discovered that perfect moments didn't last forever. In the blink of an eye, they were gone, remaining only as impressions on the memory card of your mind, which you retrieved and caressed from time to time.

He found a rock to sit on and opened the light beige envelope, careful not to tear the fragile paper.

**

My dear Lejf,

Your father told me about your ordeal; that you are undergoing therapy. I am relieved to hear you are dealing with the things that have been causing you distress. My heart has been troubled for your sake.

The knowledge that I've had too great a role in your emotional state torments me. We didn't talk about anything other than that evening on Vancouver Island – what a shock it must have been for you. And I know I could have dealt with the Karlsruhe episode much better. I'd sent you straight into the dragon's lair.

It's easy to think now how we should have spoken more and that you should have told me. Some things have always been hard for both of us to say, not just for you. I assumed it would resolve itself, but our assumptions seldom prove correct. I can imagine you feeling so alone and abandoned in the ashes.

You see, I am aware of how I have failed you too. Compromising love had taken its toll on both of us. We ought to have been much more demanding of each other. Alas, mute, you and I have born our crosses.

I'm not judging you for seeking me out in the ways you did; for your desperation. You have suffered, and scrutiny from me is the thing you deserve least of all. Even so, my sweet Lejf, in your sorrowful state, there under the Mongolian heaven, your words found their mark, and my heart heard yours.

Tell me, when you saw the golden Zhang Ranze Buddha in Ulaanbaatar, did you also think about the Golden Buddha we'd gone to see in Bangkok? Do you remember how the monks believed it was divine intervention for it to fall and for the plaster to crack? How else would the golden statue underneath have been discovered? And so, our inner Buddha is revealed by accident or through pain.

Pain is a lonely voyage our souls must take sometimes.

My soul weeps, not only for what I have put you through but because your beautiful words have made me think about the course I'd chosen. Nothing you have said or done has left me unaltered. You have that effect on me.

You spoke of a world reluctant to acknowledge the truth. Yes, we try to avoid it, and mine has at last caught up with me.

I used to blame my parents, and I blamed Otji and the small-mindedness people succumb to. That is foolish; they are the products of their mental environment and what they've chosen to believe, and if I'm honest with myself, so am I.

It's painful to face what you discover when delving into your own soul. Even when I thought I'd killed my old passive habits, they resurfaced. Now I must consider what my next move will be. In truth, I am uncertain because neither option seems attractive. You know me well; I'm terrible at making decisions – either procrastinating with making or executing them. More than that, I am afraid to be a failure. Or perhaps I'm too proud to admit that I have already failed.

I've been reading about Henry David Thoreau lately and his great work, Walden, *which I recommend you read. I was drawn to his writings and persona because he reminds me of you.*

There are people born into this life who are meant to shake the gatekeepers of mandates and morals to their rotten cores. For these kinds of people, who live with such a firm conviction, the only course of action for them to follow is one of the heart. Yet a path like that means resistance, disillusionment and loneliness. You follow such a heart path. Oh, Lejf, I have always loved you because you do. There is no half-hearted way to do it either; you must express yourself with all the passion inside you.

Thoreau wanted to give an honest account of the human experience, knowing it couldn't be without the inward battle between enjoying his labour of love and the urge to fix the faults in society. That, to me, personifies who you are and what you are about as an incredible man and an artist with an exceptional gift. You must share that gift with humanity.

I know you think he opposes you, but your father is concerned about what this sordid world is doing to you because he understands your heart is too big for your body to carry, and he loves you so much. He does, and so do we all. And we know it is the path you must walk.

Thoreau had his Walden, where he connected with his soul and envisioned his purpose. Whenever I imagine you as you think, Sossusvlei is where I visualise you being. You'll find solace and clarity there; I know you will – it's a good place for solitude.

Once, you told me that the desert sands shift; and you don't stand on the same version of the dunes as the time you were there before. There is a degree of change in your point of view.

HER WORDS

When your heart has mended and you have made peace with yourself, follow your heart's path with all your might. Whatever you do, do it truthfully, don't hold back. Show them the despair, the inequality and the humanity behind it all. Those who love you are standing beside you.

Your friend for always,

Laia

35

THE FOG AND THE DUNES

He wept. This time Lejf allowed himself to grieve over what had happened between him and Laia. It was her beautiful, open letter. The meds too had a part to play in opening those clogged valves, but it was her words, her own vulnerability, which had been the catalyst. There had never been spite; they just didn't dare to speak when they should have.

He wrote in his journal: *The healing is washing over me, and I can feel the dark dystopia where things scratched and popped like messages sent through distorted radio waves starting to diminish. Her voice and her image have settled back into that peaceful space in my mind where fond memories live. I can remember again what Laia looks and sounds like – Laia as herself.*

The therapy with Dr Lang continued online, and Lejf wasn't eager to be rid of it either. It was a peculiar and uncomfortable crutch he somehow needed, and it helped him deal with what had happened between him and his father; the trust he had to build with Lawrie, and he had no idea how he had to do that.

When they were alone together, which wasn't often, there was silence. Not an easy, comforting kind of quietude, as with someone your soul communicated with. It was a voicelessness filled with questions and what Lejf assumed must have been great uncertainty about his mental well-being from his father's side. They were polite with each other to the extreme, and it felt unnatural. He'd have preferred it if his dad was his usual, displeased self with him. But that was guilt, speaking. In his heart of hearts, Lejf longed for them to set aside their differences; the snag was that he didn't know where to start, and he suspected his dad didn't know either.

Reading *Kosmos* opened up his creativity. It reminded him of when he'd begun his journey years ago and had so much to learn about everything: the raw and inexperienced fire that had burned inside him. It was painful. 'Step by step, Lejf,' he heard Dr Lang's voice saying. He started removing the cockleburs and pesky weeds that had gotten stuck in his socks and hindered his progression.

As the electric pulses returned to his mind's pathways, he could remember Uatika, Amun, Dr Ibrahim, the Jawoyn women, Little Bit, Batbayar and all the others in between. Not low, droning voices in his head, but their true and wise words, which became illuminated when he read that remarkable book by Von Humboldt.

I comprehend now what Von Humboldt knew and the people I visited in the desert places also understand: that everything is part of everything. The whole universe is one interacting entity. Nothing exists without having an impact on something else. The Indigenous people I met have a far deeper understanding of what is popularly called ecology and environmentalism. They don't need to be taught the relationship between all living things with their environment or how to live in partnership – or stewardship as the First Nations Australians view it – their practices are already sustainable.

Lejf closed his diary and smiled with the consciousness that he'd climbed his Chimborazo and, at last nearly beaten, stared down into the inactive void of that volcano. He was thinking much about the unity of this inner man and his gift and his conclusion was that the observer of his work was no less subjective than he was. His purpose was clear: to present lucid and honest observations in love and respect for the people he admired and whose stories deserved to be told.

The sun breaking through the dark clouds, he shared his epiphany with his mother, who was pleased to see the improvement in him. 'If a small percentage of people are making decisions for political or financial gain which destroy the Earth, and with it, precious endangered species, as well as Indigenous cultures who bear the knowledge to save fragile ecosystems, then my role is to bring a message to the majority of people whose lives will forever be affected, to stop those decision makers. Can I achieve such a goal alone? No. But if voices like mine rang out in unison, we could be heard. We could create quite a roar.'

'You are an extraordinary channel and your work helps bring awareness. I am proud of you, Lejf,' Signe said.

* * *

The official title of his desert project, 'The Earth Belongs to Them', was featured in a special edition of *National Geographic* magazine in 2021, a year after his mental breakdown. He won the World Press Photo Story of the Year and an Honorable Mention for contributing to social and environmental awareness.

When a reporter asked whether he felt a sense of accomplishment, Lejf paused to think about how he wanted to answer. 'I suppose there is a feeling of having achieved something meaningful, but I hope the true message of what is going on behind the scenes of globalisation will hit home for people. This is not about me. My work is to highlight *them*: those rare, beautiful cultures, their desire to live the way they choose to, and their role in helping humanity survive.'

Work kept pouring in, and his sights shifted to a photographic competition he'd wanted to enter but had not yet: the Hasselblad Masters Contest. Admissions opened in April, and he submitted his entry for two out of the twelve categories: Landscape/Nature and Wildlife. The timing was perfect since the competition was biennial. It was sort of a hurry-up-and-wait business. Once he entered, there was no point hanging around until he received an answer. He had enough to keep himself busy and was seldom home for months.

He and Laia were friends again. Friends: it sounded odd in his ears, but then he supposed that's what they've always been, now with a deeper bond forged out of hardship. Was it even possible to love her more than he did before? It felt that way.

She was still married, though it was obvious that she was unhappy. How did you tell your best friend not to be so unhappy? He didn't know what to say to her.

'I know you're wondering why I'm staying with him. I've been asking myself about this indecision; it's banal.' She turned her head, avoiding looking at Lejf and he studied her lovely profile. 'I used to resent my parents for staying in an unhappy marriage; now I understand why they do. It's better to be unhappy with someone than unhappy with yourself. And it isn't always miserable. He can be so sweet, and I don't know...'

'Do you think you could be justifying your inertness?'

'Perhaps I am.' She stared at him and he wished he knew what her exact thought was at that moment. She said, 'Marriage seemed easier than loneliness. Now it feels the other way around. I wish there was an easy way out.'

Leave him and come live with me! He wanted to shout, but God, he lived with his parents in Otjiwarongo. That would be a double blow to Laia's independence.

'Are you worried what people might think? Because you shouldn't be.'

'Two years isn't exactly something to be proud of.'

'Anything in life is a gamble. Trying isn't failing. You can start over.'

'Hmm ... Walking away would have been easier to conceive if I hadn't given up my old flat, my things,' she said.

She was clinging to the last shreds. Lejf missed those things too. Not the stuff per se, but that they had Laia's special touch. The two of them communicated best with each other through visuals. He through his lens, and Laia through the abstract colours and objects she liked to surround herself with. All those happy short bursts somewhere in time, where they lived disconnected from the world outside in that cosy space with their synchronised thoughts and anti-social sentiments. Their make-believe world. Yet that had been the problem: it was an artificial reality; they didn't speak about what they needed from each other. They both became the thing they feared. They were a self-fulfilling prophecy.

How he missed her company.

'You've kept some of your things, didn't you? You can buy new furniture.'

'Stop being so damn practical. I thought you were on my side.'

'Of course I'm on your side.' He smiled at her little girl's pout.

'I know, I know; I sound ridiculous in my own ears. I want to move forward Lejf, and stop making preposterous excuses. Iben's told me countless times how boring I've become and I do long to embrace independence again.' She looked at him, and again there was an unexpressed thought in her gaze.

Perhaps Laia was afraid of elaborating on that statement because she didn't know if he needed more time to recover. To an extent, he was worried about the same thing. Letting go and moving forward was what he needed to do – what they both needed to do. But he and

Laia struggled to wriggle out of fear's grip.

***

A few months after entering the competition, Lejf received a letter from Hasselblad stating he'd been nominated for an award in the Landscape/Nature category. Signe, who took the liberty of opening the letter because she was too impatient to wait until she got home from getting the mail in town, was ecstatic.

'I'll forgive the violation of my privacy this time,' he said with a slight lift of his brow. His mother had wanted him to enter the contest for the longest time; he thought it had more to do with it being Swedish than its prestige.

'You are going to win. I know you are,' she said, unapologetic, and her face beaming like the sun.

'You don't know that,' said Lejf as Signe walked around holding the letter as if it came from the personal office of Carl XVI Gustaf, the King of Sweden. 'Let's not get our hopes up, shall we?' he cautioned. Would he admit to her how much he hoped to win? It surprised him how much he did.

By the end of November, the winners were announced in a press release. Lejf had won in his category and was now a Hasselblad Master. It was an immense honour as a photographer to receive this title, and a busy year awaited him and his fellow winners. They were required to do a collaborative project – themed 'Transformation' – that would later be published in the *Hasselblad Masters* book. It would contain a special feature on each winning photographer and a selection of images in their category. They received a medium mirrorless Hasselblad camera in addition to their prize money and were only allowed to use this camera for the project.

Having artistic freedom, Lejf felt a surge of excitement. He had a clear vision of what he wanted to do.

***

In the Namib Desert, near the southern end of the Naukluft Mountains in the Namib-Naukluft National Park, lay a small settlement called Sesriem. It was nothing more than a filling station with basic food and water supplies and public telephones. A few kilometres outside this little speck on the map lay Sesriem Canyon, a kilometre-long, 30-metre-deep gorge carved by the Tsauchab River. Although not big by canyon standards, the rock formations were stunning, and it was also one of the few places in the area that held water all year. In a harsh, dry world, this meant the difference between life and death for many animal species.

Sesriem was the gateway to one of the most mesmerising places on earth: Sossusvlei, a dead-end drainage basin for the Tsauchab River. In its broader definition, Sossusvlei referred to the whole area rather than the name of the salt and clay pan. Ancient terracotta dunes, like giant waves suspended in the air, shaped the landscape, as the skeletons of dead camel thorn trees stood watch, guards over their desert kingdom, their silhouettes etched against the breathtaking contrast of blue sky and the sea of sand below.

Lejf's strategy was to capture a sequence of occurrences from different locations, starting at the research centre at Gobadeb, about 50km south of Walvis Bay, and moving down to Sossusvlei, 325km further south.

The fog of the Namib Desert was something spectacular to behold. It had been photographed and covered in research more than any other desert. Capturing the rolling mass of water vapour across the sand sea, something he had done many times over, was a new thrill every time. With nature, there was the endless element of surprise.

You could return to the same spot for a week or a month, and a new scene would await you there each day.

If the American hurricane belt had its storm chasers, this was the opposite, non-violent version: the fog was the silent thing chasing you. To the Namib Desert, dawn was the pivotal moment of transformation. The cold Benguela current collided with the warmer air from the south in the Atlantic Ocean, bringing heavy fog and a cold humidity that crept underneath your clothes and into your bones.

The world of a photographer was about living in the seconds, the minutes, the hours, and days of nothing happening, and then everything happening all at once. Timing was of the essence: the difference between a good shot and an award-winning shot. Lejf couldn't have asked for better timing to do the project, either. There were more foggy days in summer.

The fog moved at a rapid pace, and he felt as if he was swept along in a wild adrenaline rush that propelled him to keep up. It was like holding his breath underwater during those slow-ticking moments before sunrise. And in the half-light before the horizon turned into navy blue, then pink, there was palpable magic in the muted grey colours. At times the fog was so dense that he couldn't see his hand in front of him. He stuck out his tongue and could feel the droplets from the thick air resting there – a taste of the clouds kissing the Earth.

Lejf rode that exhilarating wave as the swirling fog moved with force: from the sea to as far as 60km inland, transforming the landscape into wet crested dunes and grassy interdune plains glistening with moisture. Wherever the fog deposited, he witnessed the desert exploding into an outbreak of animal activity. It was like a gigantic movie playing on a 3-D screen.

The fog was the Namib Desert's lifeline. The interval between fogs was hypothetical, animals couldn't predict when the next fog cycle would occur. Global warming was also causing a significant decline in the fog that reached the interior Namib Desert.

As he stood there on the highest dune, overlooking Sossusvlei and the surrounding sand mountains, Lejf couldn't help but wonder what would happen to this place that had not only shaped history and the people who'd moved through it over time's passage but had transformed the soul contained in this man. Here, he'd stood between reality and illusion; he'd moulted off many layers of skin – enveloped by the fog in a moment of obscurity before the sun broke through. He'd wrestled with his father's voice in his head, heard great truths from his mother's lips, spent late nights around the fire with his brothers, and he'd made love with Laia underneath the stars.

'I am becoming!' he shouted, and his voice echoed for a moment before it was gobbled up by the greedy warm breath of the sun, and the silence of the desert surrounded him.

What would he change into when his metamorphosis was complete? This was the desert's truth: those who depended on it took what it gave them to survive, but they had to come back to receive it again and again. The fog was the desert's lungs; without it, the dunes would be lifeless, dry sand blowing about in the wind. So, his soul would also be without this place.

He was a nomad of the Namib, a roamer of the old, red dunes. A wandering dreamer like Signe. But he was also a son of this desert earth like his dad. Lawrie couldn't leave even if he wanted to. Neither could Lejf.

Had he overcome the constraints of his paradigm of reality? Lejf knew his story wasn't that of a naïve, good-hearted Pip, who became a madman of the world and then returned to his former good-hearted self. Pip had many more disadvantages, not to mention virtues, than he did. That being said, his great expectations had been shattered at times, and that had caused him to reflect on his assumptions. How far you made it in life boiled down to how much you kept going, no matter what you'd known about the less-than-dignified side of your character all along.

He needed the space of the desert for his evolution. It was where he breathed deeper, where ideas came to him, and he could process thoughts and feelings. The desert was the place where he retreated into his misery at times and, at other times, emerged, reborn with a new perspective.

Yes, his dark mind had been tamed, but Lejf knew his inner battle was only half-won. He still had to face up to the other side of himself.

36

THE REASON AND THE REAL REASON

In the year following the awards presentation, which his parents and brothers attended, Lejf had to show a presence at a few Hasselblad-sponsored events in cities around the world. These events weren't too invasive to his schedule; they were, in fact, quite helpful, considering an artist's constant need for exposure. The flashy crowds and put-on-a-smile scenes weren't his thing, in any case. He preferred to be on the other side of the camera lens.

He'd also received five copies of the commemorative *Hasselblad Masters* book, featuring the project he did on the fog in the Namib – a stunning ensemble of a group of artists he was proud to be featured with. He gave a copy each to his parents, Ingve (who had been moved to near tears by the gesture), his longtime sponsor, Laia and the last copy he kept for himself.

'Why can't I have a copy?' Erik asked him with a skew smile. He fiddled with his laptop's screen to adjust his position from where he sat at a restaurant table on an outdoor patio. Lejf recognised it to be somewhere in Camps Bay. Erik was back in Cape Town, and he and Iben were going strong.

'You're not sophisticated enough. Besides, it would end up dog-eared and lying in a dusty corner somewhere.'

'I appreciate beauty, brother. I'm a lover of all fine things,' Erik said, giving someone Lejf couldn't see behind his laptop a devastating smile.

That someone was Iben. They greeted each other with a kiss, and she turned to Lejf and said with a beaming face, 'Hi, Lejf. Howzit going?' Her eyes were hidden behind big sunglasses, yet he could almost see the mischief through the dark lenses.

Iben and Erik were a perfect match because neither was too serious about anything. With some couples, it balanced the relationship out for one to be more staid than the other, but not with them.

Lejf had asked Ingve what he thought of his ex dating his youngest brother (he and Iben had dated briefly in high school). 'For amusement's sake, I shall have to say that Erik the Viking had met his Helen of Troy. They are an unlikely pair, yet, they're a good duo. Erik might be the best solution after all for the restless temperament of beautiful Helen, and she is just what his profuse animal magnetism needs to stay in check,' Ingve had said after some rumination.

'It's going great, thanks, Iben. How are you?' Lejf said.

'Same old. Now that I have this one in my hook, I'm keeping him in line,' she answered tongue-in-cheek, and Erik sniggered.

'That's good to hear; he needs that. Yes, Erik, you may love fine things, but I doubt you'd become invested in a copy of the *Hasselblad Masters* book,' Lejf continued their conversation. 'You and Iben can visit the Göteborg Museum of Art and view the full exhibition to your heart's content. Iben is at least cultured enough for the both of you.'

'Damn right, I am,' she said, giving Erik a long, hard kiss.

Erik wasn't interested in owning a copy of the *Hasselblad Masters* book, and he knew his brother knew. Lejf also knew Erik didn't place much value on things in print. His philosophy was to enjoy real-time. Throughout their childhood, Lejf had wondered how Erik managed to do well enough in school to get accepted into university since he seemed to ride the edge of the cut-off mark to absolute perfection. Not for lack of ability, but because he didn't see the point of doing more than he needed to – this pertained to reading academic books since he excelled in the areas of his love life, first and foremost and then his job performance.

Erik told him one day, midway through his BEng, when Lejf questioned him about that, 'Tolerance should override your sense of displeasure if you must get something done to achieve a greater goal.' This made Lejf wonder even more whether Erik thought he should have given in to their father's desire for him to get a degree. He believed Erik thinks that's implied.

Erik had Signe's remarkable resilience. Lejf doubted he achieved academic success because he feared their father's opinion of him. Then again, with Erik, there was always the possibility of using eccentric tactics to achieve some goal that may not have been ambiguous but wasn't 100 per cent explicit either. What perplexed him was how Erik had their father's unconditional support through it all. It could be because he was so damn likeable.

'Why don't you take Laia to see the exhibition?' Erik asked.

'I will, but Laia has to go through the motions of her divorce right now.' Pausing, Lejf said, 'I want to give her time to collect herself.'

'You are being furtive. May I be frank without you jumping down my throat?'

'When haven't you been frank? And when have I ever jumped down your throat?'

Erik and Iben both laughed at his indignant response. 'Your definition of giving her time may not be what Laia's looking for, brother,' Erik said with a grin that disguised his accurate observation. He knew Lejf, who didn't answer, far too well.

Iben added, 'Oh, for God's sake, you sloth, just go to her!'

THE REASON AND THE REAL REASON

***

That was all good and well for Erik and Iben to say, but Lejf possessed neither strategy nor chivalry to do good by Laia. He'd been cured (that was the hope) of one form of delusion, too many as it was. In re-evaluating things, what would a constructive plan be for them anyway? With plenty of notches carved on the stick for what they could or should have done and her starting to find her footing again, he wasn't sure. This was the crux of the matter: he didn't know if Laia would have the confidence in him that he lacked.

The internal reasoning exasperated him; he was going around in circles, avoiding the issue as Erik had pinpointed. The snag was that when you walked around avoiding one difficulty, it was easy to transfer unresolved matters onto another. Dr Lang told him he was good at that. Since the incident with his dad, he's been going over a hundred ways about how to approach him to apologise. How did you say, I'm sorry, to your father for almost killing him? Instead of resolving that weighted controversy, he created a new one, which he supposed was connected to the main problem on a subconscious level. Dr Lang may well have agreed with his theory if he'd been man enough to tell him.

After walking around all morning, arguing with himself and feeling the tension mounting, Lejf went in search of a vent and found his parents in his dad's study. Signe was doing admin, and Lawrie was dusting off and reorganising his wall-to-wall bookshelf. His parents had an enviable relationship. His father had his quirks – many of them – but he respected his mother more than any other woman. Was Lejf sour at that moment because they were having a great time in each other's company, whereas he was having a rotten time with his moot thoughts? Boy, he sure knew how to kill a relaxed mood.

'That would go better with Mom's books, don't you think?' he said, indicating with his head the *Hasselblad Masters* book his dad was holding. Both Lawrie and Signe looked up from their tasks, surprised at the comment.

Lawrie put the book on the shelf with other travel and nature-related books. In fairness, his father had an impressive collection of literature and illustrated books. When they were children, Lejf and his brothers were allowed to borrow them with the arrangement that they be returned in the same condition and put back in the same place they found them. His dad was fond of his beautiful library stocked with high-quality reading material.

Lawrie turned to face him and asked, 'You don't think it ought to come here?' Lejf thought his dad's composure was commendable; then again, if he'd behaved like a mature adult, he wouldn't be standing in his father's study, looking for an excuse to argue with him.

'I'm just saying, Dad. You've never been a fan of my work.' Any person would have interpreted the comment as loaded with innuendo, and from his dad's increasing agitation and defensive body language, Lejf could see it hadn't gone over his head. It was an outright hostile attack on him, and this was out of nowhere.

Lawrie frowned. 'And when did you arrive at that conclusion?'

Such sensitive triggers: the tone, the language and in a blink, Lejf's childhood filled with endless battles with his father flashed before his eyes, and all rationale flew out the door. He should have been kinder, more diplomatic. His ornery behaviour was the consequence of him not confronting Laia and not knowing how to apologise to his father. Lejf turned his dad into a scapegoat for his lousy convenience and drew his mother into it too.

'Why would you keep it in your library when Morsa's the one who has supported my work? You haven't been interested in it before. Why now, all of a sudden?'

His dad didn't suffer this fool gladly. 'Well, if it bothers you so much to see it here, I'll give it to your mother.' He took it off the shelf, holding it out to Signe.

'Put that back, Lawrie.' Lejf knew when he'd said something to perturb his mother: her displeasure with him was written all over her face. 'Lejf, that was unnecessary.'

'No, no, Signe. Lejf feels I am an unworthy custodian of this precious book of his, and it should go with yours. He's entitled to feel the way he does, misconstrued as it may be.'

'I'm not misconstruing anything.'

Signe got up, took the book from Lawrie and put it back on the shelf. 'What are you trying to prove, Lejf? Did you come in here because you wanted to pick a quarrel with your father, hm?' Although her diplomacy (and only Torsten could match it) was legendary in their house, she wasn't known for beating about the bush. Lejf supposed years of practice with him and his dad had sharpened the saw.

'Of course, he did,' Lawrie said.

Petulant child that he was, Lejf said to him. 'You didn't congratulate me on winning that award; now you want to put the book on your shelf to show it off.'

'So, *that's* what this is about. I did congratulate you.'

'No, you didn't.'

'Yes, I did. When you came off the stage, I congratulated you.'

'You patted me on the back, but you didn't say the words, "congratulations, Lejf", or "I'm proud of you". Fact is, you've never been proud of me.'

Lawrie looked like he wanted to say something, then thought better of it. He removed the book from the shelf and, shoving it in Lejf's hand, said in a gruff voice, 'You like to put words in my mouth don't you? Here, take the blasted book.' He stormed out.

Signe took the book from him and put it back on the shelf. 'There, you've interrupted a perfect morning for us, and now your father's gone on a rant. Are you happy now?' She sat down on the edge of the desk with an emphatic tut and her arms folded across her chest, eyeing him. 'I wish you would speak about the real things bothering you. It's not healthy to keep them inside. I'm worried –' She cut herself off.

'You're worried that it could trigger another episode.' Lejf finished her sentence and thought he might just bring it upon himself if he continued his diatribe. 'He didn't congratulate me,' he said, still with too much self-pity.

'Not in so many words, but then, you and your father are so alike – neither of you speaks to each other in words locked inside your hearts. They originate from your stubborn heads.' She shook her head. They were quiet for a while, and he wished the silence didn't sound so accusing. 'I want to show you something,' she said, reaching behind a large book and producing a key. 'Don't worry; he knows I know where he hides it.' She took a thick brown folder from the bottom drawer and put it on the desk. 'Have a good, long look, älskling. Things aren't how they may appear on the surface. You'd therefore be wise to reconsider your words to your father,' she said and left the room.

Opening the folder, Lejf's mind didn't understand what his eyes saw. Gradually he registered. All the clippings – from that first story he did on his dad for *Africa Geographic* magazine when he was sixteen – every article, every mention and award. It was all there. In an instant, the knowledge and relief. Lejf held the unmistakable evidence of his dad's pride in his accomplishments in his hands. The urge to hug his father was overpowering; he needed to find and tell him.

Lawrie kept out of sight, the cunning old jackal, and Lejf discovered his hiding place behind the garage, fidgeting with a water hose.

It wasn't as easy to walk up to him and apologise as Lejf had thought a moment ago. 'Looks like it would be better to get a new one,' he said. His dad shrugged, with no intention of letting him off the hook; that would be far too easy. After an uncomfortable silence, Lejf swallowed his pride. 'I wasn't being fair to you earlier. I'm sorry, Dad.'

His father looked at him then. 'If it doesn't want to cooperate, you need to chuck the old, useless thing and get a new one,' he said, throwing down the hosepipe.

For a brief second, Lejf wasn't sure if his dad meant himself or the hose. He wouldn't put it beyond him to make such a joke. 'Do you think we can talk?' Lejf asked.

Lawrie nodded. 'I was planning on driving out to the *koppie* with your mother. You could come with me instead.'

Signe made sandwiches and filled one flask with cold water and another with tea. There was a high likelihood she'd suggested that he go with his father. The koppie his dad was referring to was the Waterberg Plateau Park, where Laia had had her twenty-first birthday party at one of the lodges. They walked a loop trail of about 4km which wasn't far, but was challenging. His dad kept up without showing signs of discomfort, and at the top, they sat down to have their lunch and drinks as they looked out over the green Kalahari plains below, with navy blue storm clouds hovering in the distance. The spot was a favourite with Lejf's parents.

'Those look like hail clouds to me. We'll have to keep an eye out, but they're dramatic to film. You should have brought your camera,' his dad remarked.

'Yup, here it is.' Lejf reached for it in his backpack and captured a few expansive landscapes and a couple of close-ups of his father, then showed him what they looked like.

Lawrie stared at his image. 'Almost better than the real thing.'

'But not quite as good.'

'Hmm, they're pretty good,' he said with a flick of his brow.

Lejf watched him out of the corner of his eye. His father was in his late seventies and still in great shape. It would take a lot to break him. He came close.

'Morsa showed me your folder,' Lejf started cautiously.

'I know, she told me.'

He couldn't help smiling. 'She's unable to keep secrets. Not from you anyway.'

'That's part of what love is: keeping secrets with each other, not from each other. And it isn't so much that, as trust.'

'Why do you think you and I have such a hard time with that, Dad?'

Lawrie turned his head to look at Lejf, scanning his face. 'It's hard to face yourself in the mirror. More often than not, our expectations of ourselves are unrealistic, and unfortunately, they become our expectations of others. The bizarre thing is that we know we are doing it, but we continue in the same patterns. Futile habits nobody benefits from, least of all yourself.' He looked out over the plains, wringing his hands as he did when he was in deep thought. Then he said, 'Most children have a trainable will. I'm not speaking about conforming them to the point of breaking their spirits, but they go with the flow and test boundaries without venturing too far. You weren't like that. From the first day we brought you home from the hospital, you wanted to do things your way.' He smiled.

'The older you grew, the more I worried for your sake because you had too much of my stubbornness, yet you had something that wasn't from me: that wild, curious heart of yours had your mother's kindness and enormous compassion. It was difficult to see how you were taking on other people's struggles and what it was doing to you. Trying to change a world where there is little benevolence around ...' He shook his head. 'And you kept doing it until you broke down. I tried to stop you from getting hurt, and all I achieved was that I became a stumbling block, a big obstacle in your path you had to bump into and navigate around. Our best intentions are sometimes our worst mistakes. That's a lesson I've had to learn many times over.'

Lejf swallowed, looking at his father for a moment. 'Dad, I'm sorry for what I did to you. I wish I could undo –'

Still not looking at him, Lawrie interrupted, grabbing Lejf's thigh and shaking it a bit. 'I know, I know, son. You were under unbearable strain. It's hard for a parent to watch their child suffer, but Lord knows, I could have handled it much better. I could have been more understanding.' He looked into Lejf's eyes. 'You came through. I'm proud of you, Lejf, for all your accomplishments. You should know that I'm as proud as a parent can hope to be.'

'I know that now. Thanks, Dad.' He got up and took a few more pictures. Turning to his dad again, he said, 'When I was in Sinai, I met a remarkable man. You may have heard me speak about him to Mom. His name is Dr Ibrahim.'

'I remember the name.'

'It's unnerving when a stranger identifies things about you. He asked about the conflict in my heart, and I told him about you and me.' Lightning flashed in the distance and they both waited for the rumble; it followed a few seconds later, crackling across the sky. Lejf continued. 'He said I should find out what you need from me because maybe what I gave you wasn't what you needed.'

Lawrie lifted his brow. 'Interesting,' he said, neither confirming nor rejecting what Lejf had said.

There was no easy way for the two of them. It was like walking around yourself, trying to figure out how to change the most complex part about you when it was rooted deep inside where it was hard to reach. The love was there, but articulating it was hard. Laia once told Lejf that love doesn't have to be about perfect synergy and that expressing your differences was a form of love's language.

The problem was that their similarities were superlative – like poles repelling each other. It was a constant battle to balance the forces in them to stay in harmony. His dad was like the shadow of his conscience: keeping him aware of the side of himself he couldn't change but had to live with.

Could he have been looking at the similitude between them the wrong way? Or did it cloud his ability to see his dad? He'd resisted his father's stubbornness, but in doing so, he'd fought himself. Was that what Dr Ibrahim had perceived?

His father had admitted that he could have been more understanding. Lejf knew that he could have dealt with things much better too. He could have afforded his dad more opportunities to tell him the things in his heart. He could have listened better. He wasn't a good listener, not where the people in his life were concerned. Look where it had got him and Laia.

There was no way he was going to make promises to his father he couldn't keep – neither his mother nor his father deserved that – and as much as he didn't want his dad to worry, his father had a right to. Wasn't that the right of any parent?

'You know the stories are what it's always been about for me; capturing them and sharing them,' Lejf held up his camera. Lawrie nodded. 'It was never about disregarding your feelings, but if it felt like I did, I'm sorry, Dad. I want you to know that I understand why it's hard for you to accept everything that comes with this job. That's okay; you're my dad; you may feel like that.' He sat beside his father again, hesitated and placed his arm around his shoulders.

They stared at the scene in the distance.

'See, the storm clouds are dissolving,' Lawrie said. 'The sun will break through, but the threat of the storms will be back. The pressure builds and the hail clouds come in with a big show. Most of the time, they blow over without causing any damage. Sometimes they even give us much-needed rain, too. That's the unpredictable nature of life, my boy.' He patted Lejf's leg.

Change was a never-ending cycle. Lejf thought about the times he'd camped with his mother, and they talked about how the waxing and waning moon symbolised inconstancy and all the instability and fickleness we carry around.

'There comes a time we must let go of things to revivify the balance. We have to take steps to go where we need to be in life,' his mother had said on one such moonlit desert night.

Signe was like the acacia tree: a symbol of regeneration, integrity and endurance. It took her kind of resolve to love men like him and his dad.

37

WHERE HE WISHES TO BE

Lejf was in Karlsruhe with Laia for a quick two-day stopover on his way to an assignment. They would see each other again in a few weeks in Cape Town for Erik and Iben's big event.

'What in the world is a "not-getting married ceremony?"' Lejf asked, holding up the invitation and sniffing it again. It smelled of vanilla, rather pleasant.

'It's the same as getting married, but without legal marriage vows. They are declaring in public their commitment to each other to be partners for life,' was Laia's response.

'Interesting.'

'Iben won't get married. That was a vow she'd made with me when she was twelve and I was fifteen. She had the whole ritual worked out: I was a witness and her *Blutsschwester*.' She quoted the last part with her fingers. 'She'd timed it until the day her first period started so that she could make a serious commitment as a woman. Then she cut our palms with our mother's favourite paring knife, pressed them together and sealed her written promise to herself with our blood. She meant business; I still have the scar. See here.' She showed him the thin, pale line on her palm, and he kissed it. 'It was a big gothic drama. Our father was on the brink of a heart attack, not when he saw our gaping wounds but when she told him why it had been necessary to inflict them. Our mother didn't use that paring knife again – said it traumatised her too much to think about it.'

'No kidding. Why haven't you told me this *makabere kleine Geschichte* before? Many things about Iben would have made sense much sooner.' Lejf put the card on a stool Laia kept in her bedroom. It served as a place to sit, say, when you needed to put on socks, or, a more popular purpose, to leave the day's mail she hadn't had time to sort through. Laia was organised, and everything had its place, but she wasn't rigid.

Lejf noticed a letter from Ravi, and she shrugged. 'I have a few small things to pick up at the house. He's let me know when I may come by.'

'Rather formal about it, isn't he?' Lejf said. She shrugged again.

She'd found a flat close to her old spot, equal in size but not with the same character. He could tell she didn't have an emotional connection to it yet. In time, she'd acquire good furniture pieces – she needed a few things, not much – to create a personalised space again. Laia was sentimental. She'd told him that when she was married to Ravi, she'd often driven to her old place after work out of habit, then sat there in her car, staring at the building, remembering how she'd gone through her routines when she got home from work, missing her space and her independence.

No matter how much we wanted to, we couldn't go back and undo things. And when we tried to replicate times and events, they didn't fit into the vacancy of the moment that was gone.

She laughed, shifting position on the bed to be more comfortable. Her silk robe parted in the front when she crossed her legs, and Lejf couldn't resist running his hand up their smooth, long length. Her hair was spread against the pillow, and those dark pools were so inviting. He wanted to dive into them.

'*Über Ibens leiche*! I wasn't allowed to,' she answered his question.

'She'd made me swear that I wouldn't reveal the secret until she found someone she could *not* marry.'

'Who, unbeknownst to you both at the sealing of the blood pact, turned out to be Erik.'

'*Exakt*. Weird mystery solved.'

'And yet, she told your parents.'

'They don't count. I don't think they believed she would go through with it, which proves how little they knew their child. Iben doesn't make feeble commitments. She's either in or out.'

'What about kids? Do you think she'll want any?'

'Sure. Iben doesn't have a problem with children. It's adults' rules that have been the contentious issue throughout her life, and I have to concur.'

'Well, if she and Erik do have children, they'd at least have one *mormor* who'll be in full support of their mother's bohemian ways.' He plopped down next to her, pressing his face into her neck.

'Signe will make a fabulous grandmother.' She turned and wrapped her arm around his waist. 'Do you think the fates sometimes give us the wrong parents?'

'That's a question that's haunted me throughout my childhood,' Lejf mumbled with his lips against her soft skin.

He heard her words, felt their warm vibration through his hair, and gave in as she pulled him toward her eternity. 'I hate that you're leaving tomorrow. Let's stop the clocks and stay in this moment for as long as we want to. Let's exist like this forever.'

Where was her forever? With him, or in the physical space they occupied?

***

Things had been better between Lejf and his dad since they worked out their idiosyncrasies, but heaven knows, it wasn't perfect. Two stubborn minds, set in their ways – the only way to vent the frustration was to smash it against something harder than their wills. Travelling alleviated the peevishness. Although Lejf wasn't home much, it didn't take much to bring it on. But there was unspoken respect. A boundary had been drawn: they knew and understood, and that was enough.

Life was filled with mystery. It was at the least expected moment that the truth about the things Lejf was battling to come to terms with was brought to light by no more unlikely a person than Lawrie. Were it Signe, he wouldn't have blinked. It was his father sharing his soulful wisdom, which was a new experience for him. Something like that could make you wonder if the person sitting in front of you had always been that way and you simply hadn't noticed, and this caused Lejf to reappraise his opinion of this strange yet familiar man.

'Torsten now married, Erik in a life partnership, and Søren and Ingve, neither fearful of commitment but not too eager to relinquish their bachelorhood,' Lawrie commented, an unanticipated philosophical aside to his morning paper and coffee.

Not much news was happening in Namibia, so one might suppose the instinct for a parent to dwell on the lives of their offspring brought its share of amusement.

'And me?' Lejf dared to venture on that ruminative train of thought.

'I was going to ask you the same question.' Lawrie looked up from his paper. 'You are here, although it seems your thoughts are straining against a cage barring them from freedom.'

Ah, yes. The cion didn't know to which soil he belonged. His heart had been stretched in all directions for most of his life so far. Wherever his work took him, however near or far from Laia, his heart reached out to the other side of that point to touch hers. And if he was anywhere but home – which meant Namibia, not his parent's home – the tentacles reached out to that point on the other end where he could feel his land of big open spaces. It required an elastic heart, but its elasticity was starting to wear thin.

'I am not there where I wish to be, and when I am there, then I will not be there where I wish to be,' Lejf said.

Signe looked up from the portion of the newspaper she'd taken after Lawrie had finished with it.

'Would you care to hear my opinion?' Lawrie asked.

'Sure, why not?' Lejf took a sip of his coffee.

'Wishing is nothing more than a nice to have. It requires no commitment and seldom comes to pass, leaving you going down the same rabbit hole without end. I think it's time to find a way to where your heart longs to be. Life is knowing what you want as much as what you don't want. It will require a decision from you: perhaps the most difficult decision you will have to make, so you must prepare yourself to live with the consequences of that decision. Once you do that, you will find the peace you seek. Who knows? It may be painless, and you may wonder why you haven't done it sooner. And then it may not be easy to accept. Either way, you won't know until you make that choice, but it will give you closure and help move you forward.'

'I agree with your father, min älskling,' said Signe.

'You sound like Dr Lang,' Lejf said to his dad.

'It may not appear that way, but I pay attention. Why don't you tell Laia what you want, Lejf? Then ask her if it is what she wants too.'

Lejf walked around for weeks, contemplating what Lawrie had said. His dad was right: his heart was tied to the truth.

* * *

'When I was pregnant with Torstie, your father and I used to drive to Swakopmund, and I'd stand right there on the end of the pier, where the waves crash high.' Signe pointed as they drove by. 'The ocean is incredibly temperamental here; it's like a pregnant woman. The feeling of the wind on my face, the salty smell and taste of the sea – how I loved that bizarre craving. Your father didn't share my enthusiasm; he was worried the wind would blow me over the rail, but it relieved the morning sickness. I don't know why the sea breeze did that. I should have stayed in Swakop for my whole pregnancy, come to think of it.

'We had a plan mapped out to accommodate my changing mood. Your dad was so sweet about it.' She smiled. 'From Swakopmund, we drove to Walvis Bay Lagoon to watch the flamingos because seeing all those dancing sticks with pink pom-poms stuck on top of them calmed my raging hormones and made me happy. Mind you, I had to sit and watch them from the car since the smell was too revolting to bear. Did I tell you this story?' Signe asked.

'You did, but I don't mind hearing it again,' Lejf said with a big grin.

She patted his arm. 'Oh, I love telling it too, because then I'm transported to that wonderful moment. There were a few developments on the side of the road then; all you could see was the sea to the right, the dunes to the left, and a narrow straight road ahead.' She looked around. 'That was forty-four years ago. Where does the time go? And now all my babies have become grown men.'

'We've been semi-grown up for a while now.'

'Hmm.' She smiled as she looked out the window, lost in her memories.

Now and then, he watched the kilometres click over on the speedometer of his Land Cruiser: 100, 200, 300, 400, 500 – keeping the beat in a slow, noiseless rhythm to the smooth jazzy sound of his mother's voice. She had that peculiar and charming pronunciation of long 'a's and 'o's and emphasised 't's and 's's, the way Swedes spoke English. He was thrilled that she'd never lost it.

'You know, älskling, we can look back on our lives and see whatever we choose: the difficulties, the uncertainties, the mistakes, the misunderstandings and petty feelings. Or, we can remember those unforgettable moments which fill our hearts with joy, like when the acacia trees break out in bright yellow flowers at the first whiff of the rain that comes over the Namib. Isn't that a glorious image?' she asked, and her eyes sparkled.

The picture that sprung to Lejf's mind was an iconic scene he had captured in the Naukluft Mountains of a gold-puffed acacia tree with the long neck of a giraffe sticking out behind it, yellow pollen smeared across its mouth and the most satisfied grin on its face. Signe had had a poster-sized print made and framed. She named it 'Eating Sunshine'. She'd put it up in her special corner. It was a small nook where she liked having a quiet time with a cup of tea and gentle music while she stared at the photograph as if she were in the desert in real time. His mother could enjoy a moment like few people he knew; it was a thrill to watch her.

'I think we have many more chances than we deserve. The reality is that they aren't limitless. We would live with much less remorse if we didn't squander our opportunities.' She thought about something and shook her head as she continued, 'Of course, I have regrets – there are things I could have approached in a different way or better. When you look at your life from the vantage point I have now, you understand that if you had known more at that moment, there would have been something else you wouldn't have been able to foresee. That's life. To forgive oneself is as important as forgiving others. It allows you to become kinder to yourself in the areas where you are most self-critical.

'Nobody's perfect; I know you boys think I am, but I am far from it!' She slapped his leg and chortled. 'Still, I know that I have loved those whom I love, well. Love is the ultimate verb because its whole purpose is to give. It's our most noble form of expression as human beings. It endures and forgives so much; its sheer capacity astounds me.'

They didn't speak for a while, each processing the thoughts running through their minds.

'You are the sunbeam in our dreary lives, Morsa. I hope you know how much your men love you, this one in particular.' Lejf took her hand in his and squeezed it, then, gazing around, registered the changing landscape; the shape of the old dunes, signalling they were not far from their destination.

They went through the familiar ritual of setting up their tent and camping gear. They had camped together many times; they were like a well-oiled machine. She and his father camped together also. Signe didn't neglect Lawrie, which was perhaps why he didn't even blink when she and Lejf headed off now and then. With his parents, he realised that the happiest couples need their space from each other.

He and Laia were on the opposite side of that ideal world: they loved each other's company, yet they hadn't had enough of it. Wasn't that ironic? When they did manage to make their getaway, it was a race against time before they had to repeat goodbye.

Sitting by their campfire, every shape swallowed up by the black new moon night around them, except the stars above, Lejf said, 'The speed of life is blinding, isn't it? I wish I could slow it down and hold on to it a while longer. Every time I tell myself: this instant right here, I will appreciate more, love deeper. Then, when I look, I see how the opportunity has slipped like sand through my fingers.'

Signe gazed at the stars for a while, then said, 'That's the thing about life, min älskling: it can open up the window of chances, but it can't give us more time to take them.'

38

THROWN TO THE STARS

The joy for Laia had always been there. He wanted to exist and breathe with her, but on what terms? Was it anything more than hypothetical? Laia had longings just as he did, and their love was somewhere in the middle of that. She didn't have to tell him; he could see how she was flourishing on her own despite the let-down of her failed marriage. Would her regained independence be enough of a motivation for her to face the loneliness that came with it? The risk was the choice she'd made. And he'd made his choice too.

Lejf turned his head to look at the darkness on the other side of the window, but all he could see was his reflection staring back at him, constantly confronting him with the truth. He shifted his gaze back to his laptop, illuminated by the desk light, an impersonal thing that would capture and, if he dared press send, transport the words so difficult for him to express.

* * *

I wouldn't assume what I saw in your eyes, the last time I went to see you, was unhappiness because of where you were. You have had many fulfilling years in Karlsruhe – it is the place where you developed into the courageous woman you are.

Was your unhappiness the result of your divorce, and the reason you're feeling like a failure the mere consequence of that? You shouldn't feel that you have failed. The idea that you might entertain such a notion pains me. All I can see are your successful attempts to bring yourself back to where you have control over your life again, which is a testament to your strong character.

Our choices and circumstances have indeed had their share in keeping us apart. If I know one thing for certain, it is that we love each other, regardless of where our love will come to rest.

I didn't want to lay the choice before you, Laia. I thought it would be too selfish of me to ask you to reduce yourself to having to choose between the city and the life you love, and me. It seems such a cruel demand. Believe me; I have agonised over this for as long as we've been lovers. My ultimate conclusion is that no matter how many times I've twisted the thought around, no amount of reasoning has resolved anything. We both bear the scars as proof, and our absence from each other speaks louder than anything else.

The old man and I have at last reached a place where we talk about heart matters, and that is a wonder. He was the one who pushed me from lethargy into an awakening, if you will. In the end, no one else can give us the answers we seek; we are the ones who must live with our decisions. What complications we've brought upon ourselves, Laia, my love.

If a choice is what you desire of me and I of you, let us throw our needs up to the stars and wait for the answers to rain down on us. Would it be that simple, do you think? I shall set out my case, and then I will give you an opportunity to weigh the cost of my appeal. I resolve to accept what will be, will be.

I am working daily to ease my mind, to relieve it of these anxious thoughts and feelings. They have become a familiar burden that I'm learning to cope with. It seems the only place I can be free is at my Walden; a needless thing to mention to you, I know. So, that is where I went in search of the most relevant, albeit most relative of all things: truth. I cannot say I've ever left that place without gaining some surprising insight about myself or life. My mother calls such revelations the desert's pearls.

What I have discovered in my quest for direction are not the meditations of a man plagued by sickness in his psyche but the utterances of a soul who, for too long, had withheld its lament. They are the mysteries of the universe and the enigmas about you and me.

We two are like the ephemeral rivers that form from summer rainstorms in the mountains – we come and go from each other's sight. Yet, we are much more than that: our love is high above the Earth, but it also exists like the underground streams that branch out and connect at some point deep in the heart of the Namib, where we become transformed.

I mutate into your beloved desert creature, the little shovel-snouted lizard, dancing on the dunes, anticipating the arrival of your life-giving fog. When it becomes unbearable, I dive deep underneath the sand where my heartbeat slows down, and there I wait long days for you.

My ability to endure depends on the desert's whim. It's a hard existence, yearning for you in that dry place, but it is there I am able to survive, nowhere else. And there, I beg, is where you must rescue me from my thirst for you.

Dare I be bold enough to say even you do not become alive until you are formed at the threshold where the sea and the wind meet, and you rush to my aid with force. And I drink you in, and you permeate me. Melting into the sand, you become a gypsum rose, and I keep guard over you, my jewel, as we exist in those cool depths until the sun and the wind expose us.

My death had been my own doing. I had to go back there, so I could witness my lizard self in rigour mortis, and only then was I able to experience the new man rising from that lifeless pit. The epiphany: our rebirth is endless; we can become anything and everything. I want to grow and vanish with you again and again, Laia.

I have dug up my buried words, gone deep to find them all, and thrown them to the stars. They are scattered prayers to shine over your darkest night.

Now I will watch out; stand guard like the camel thorns in Sossusvlei – a hundred years, a thousand years – for a sign that will tell me if the fates have heard my plea and if you will come to me or not.

I am yours forever.

He hesitated for a moment, with his finger hovering over the mouse. Then he clicked and heard the sound of the sending swoosh.

About the Author

Leonora Ross is an artist and novelist from Western Canada. She enjoys painting and writing whimsical poetry and prose when not writing novels. She is also an avid mountain hiker and amateur photographer. Her writing and photography regularly appear in literary journals. *A Life in Frames* is her third novel.

Thank you for taking the time to read *A Life in Frames*! Your feedback is incredibly valuable to me. If you enjoyed the book, please consider leaving a review on Amazon, Goodreads, or wherever you are able to. Your thoughts help other readers discover my work and support my journey as an author.

Best regards, Leonora

You can connect with me on:
- https://www.leonoraross.com
- https://x.com/LeonoraAuthor
- https://www.facebook.com/leonorarossauthor
- https://www.instagram.com/leonorarossauthor
- https://www.goodreads.com/author/show/22629239.Leonora_Ross

Subscribe to my newsletter:
- https://www.leonoraross.com/#contact-1

Also by Leonora Ross

Leonora writes about the complexities of family and relationships in expansive, culturally diverse settings.

Tess Has a Broken Heart and Other Comedies Full of Errors
Tess, her best friend Zara and Zara's daughter, move from LA to Calgary and rent a big house with subtenants. Unexpected friendships form. Tess is afraid of letting love in, and her girlfriends worry that she'll miss out on something amazing.

The Suncatchers
Luka Bakker meets the charismatic Espen De Cleene at a market in Amsterdam, then he vanishes. An unexpected chance encounter reunites them. Her carefully mapped out world is shaken, and her faith in her inner compass put to the test.

www.ingramcontent.com/pod-product-compliance
Lightning Source LLC
LaVergne TN
LVHW031615060526
838200LV00007B/216